Delayed Justice

A Marc Kadella Legal Mystery

by

Dennis L. Carstens

Previous Marc Kadella Legal Mysteries

The Key to Justice

Desperate Justice

Media Justice

Certain Justice

Personal Justi~~

JUSTICE DELAYED IS JUSTICE DENIED

British Prime Minister William Gladstone 1868

ONE

"Would either of you care for champagne?"

The question was asked of the two casually dressed businessmen seated together in first class. The flight attendant, an attractive woman in her mid-forties smiled down at the one in the aisle seat waiting for a reply. His companion, the younger of the two, ignored her while glumly staring out of the window.

"Sure," the older man answered her. He lightly poked his partner with an elbow who turned and looked at the woman.

"Champagne?" she politely asked again.

"Um, yeah, why not? Wait, make it half orange juice, please. It's a little early."

They were barely twenty minutes out of George Bush Intercontinental Airport in Houston on a four-hour flight to Panama City, Panama. Both men had reclined their chairs taking advantage of the ample legroom available in first-class. The younger man was again staring out the window while the attendant went for their drinks.

"I hate this shit," the younger one whispered loud enough for his companion to hear.

"I know you've told me at least a dozen times. Relax, life's too short to worry about every little thing."

The younger man turned his head to his right to speak to his companion and said, "Life's too short is exactly it. I've been up and on the go since three A.M. to fly to a meeting with a sociopath who would think nothing of slitting my throat just to watch the blood drain out."

His traveling companion, Victor Espinosa, heartily laughed at the nervous man, Walter Pascal. At that moment the attendant brought their drinks and departed.

"Relax, Wally. Trust me, if Javier had anything like that in mind, he'd send some guys to Minnesota. He wouldn't bother having us fly to Panama. Besides, he has nothing to be upset about."

2

"I know," Walter said relaxing a bit. "He just makes me nervous. He's the scariest guy on the damn planet."

"He is that," Victor agreed. "But he's been damn good for business. At least we're not shoehorned into a sardine seat in back," Victor continued referring to the seats in coach.

A short while later the flight attendant reappeared and asked about refills. Walter handed her his glass and told her to wake him when they served the meal. Victor accepted a refill.

"Don't drink too much," Walter said as he turned his head, closed the window blind and relaxed to get some sleep.

A little more than three-and-a-half-hours later they felt the bump and heard the whine of the landing gear being extended. The aircraft was on its final approach into Tocumen International Airport and was right on schedule.

"Why is it these flights are always on time when you're in no hurry to get there?" Walter asked.

Victor laughed then said, "Relax. We'll be home by midnight. This is no big deal."

"Oh, I know. I'm just being…"

"A total pussy," Victor said.

As promised, a limousine was waiting for them as they exited the airport. Even though it was late May in Minnesota and a warm spring and they were dressed in light, casual clothes, the Panamanian heat and humidity hit them like a blast furnace when they stepped through the sliding glass doors.

"I wasn't ready for that," Victor said as they walked toward their ride.

There was a driver at the wheel and a serious looking Latino standing by the doors. A third man, one the Minnesotans both knew, exited the car as they approached. He looked at the two men, flashed a bright, warm smile and held out his right hand to greet them.

"Carlos, my friend," Victor said. "Thanks for picking us up."

As the two of them shook hands, Victor reminded the vicious cartel member who Walter was.

Carlos Rodriguez was one of the top lieutenants in the Del Sur — The Southern Cartel. It was one of the smallest of the major Mexican drug gangs but also one of the most successful. Most of their business came from acting as a go-between, almost a wholesaler, for the larger cartels in the northern area of Mexico.

The leader was a man named Javier Ruiz-Torres. Fifty-two years old, he was known as El Callado — The Quiet One. In meetings, he rarely spoke and when he did, it was normally to his top aide, Pablo 'Paul' Quinones.

Quinones was what the Italians called his consigliore or, in Spanish, consejero. Born into an upper-class family, Quinones was educated at Stanford and the Sorbonne in Paris. He spoke several languages fluently and was drawn to the wild side of business rising rapidly alongside El Callado.

It was these two men that the Minnesotans were being chauffeured to meet.

"Good to see you too, Victor. Come," Carlos said as he held the door for them. "He's anxious to see you. No luggage?" he asked.

"No, we have to return tonight," Victor answered as he and Walter slid across the tan leather seats.

The ride from the airport to the hotel normally took ninety minutes. With the two motorcycle cops guiding them through traffic, they were entering the Marriott Villa in less than an hour.

The limo pulled up to the walkway in front of the villa, stopped and the thug in the passenger seat jumped out to open the door. Again the heat hit the two Americans in the face and Carlos led them to the villa's front door. As he did, both guests walked a bit slowly looking over the grounds. There was a beautiful pool with a view of the Pacific Ocean and to their left was the fifteenth fairway of a championship caliber golf course.

"Nice digs," Walter said.

"Sure is," Victor agreed as he finished counting the guards that he could see. An even dozen not counting Carlos.

In the foyer, another serious-looking Latino man wearing a holster with a small, fully-automatic machine pistol in it, awaited them. He quickly, but politely and thoroughly frisked them both for weapons. Satisfied, the guard led them into the living room while Carlos stayed at the door.

They entered the living room where the two men they were meeting were waiting for them. Seated by himself on a plush, off white, suede couch was the old man himself, Javier Ruiz Torres — El Callado.

To look at him you would never guess he was the ruthless head of a drug cartel. An attractive man with a well-tanned look, he could easily pass for a banker or any legitimate businessman, except for the way he was dressed. He wore expensive, soft-leather, brown loafers, tan slacks and a silk shirt. The only jewelry he wore was a simple gold wedding ring and a modest gold chain with a crucifix around his neck.

"Welcome to Panama," the second man said as he shook hands with each of them. This was Paul Quinones, the man to whom they would actually converse. "Please, have a seat," he pleasantly gestured toward two of several matching chairs in the room.

Quinones took one of the same chairs next to his boss — no one sat on the couch with El Callado — and asked, "Something to drink? It's a warm day today even for Panama."

"That Evian looks good," Victor said referring to the bottle on the glass-topped table between them.

Quinones made a gesture toward a doorway, said something in Spanish and a minute later a young Latina girl set a tray with four bottles, glasses and ice on the table. Quinones dismissed her, then filled the glasses with ice and water for all of them.

"You're undoubtedly wondering why you're here," Quinones began the discussion by saying. "First of all, let me assure you we are quite satisfied with your services."

5

This statement caused Walter Pascal to almost faint with relief. He had been doing his best not to stare at the sociopath on the couch. He was also struggling with his breathing in an attempt to appear calm.

"In fact, we're interested in increasing our deposits each month," Quinones said.

The three of them, with El Callado listening to his counselor's translations, discussed rates of return, investment strategies and finally fees.

"Since we are doubling our investment with your firm, a twenty-five percent reduction in your fees is acceptable to us," Quinones told them. Noting that Quinones did not put that statement in the form of a suggestion, let alone a request, Victor Espinosa quickly agreed.

The three of them toasted the new arrangement, smiles all around even from Quinones' boss. Then Ruiz Torres gestured to Quinones who leaned over so his boss could whisper in his ear.

"Get rid of them. I hate talking to bankers. They bore me," he said.

"Si, jefe," Quinones replied. He looked at his two guests and said. "Senior Torres asked me to express his gratitude to you for coming today. Unless you have anything else...?" he said with an inquisitive look.

"No, I don't think so," Espinosa answered.

"Good," Quinones said as he stood. "Carlos will have you back in plenty of time to make your flight."

The limo taking their guests back to the airport had barely pulled away from the curb when El Callado and his counselor were conferring.

"He is here?" Torres asked as Quinones held the lighter for his boss to light his eighty dollar Cohina.

"Yes, Javier," Quinones answered him using his first name as he was allowed to do in private.

"I want that taken care of today."

6

"Yes, Javier. It will be," Quinones said retaking the chair he had used. "What did you think of the gringos?"

Torres blew a cloud of sweet cigar smoke than said, "They are bankers. What do I care," he shrugged. "You are satisfied they do a good job with our money?"

"Sí, Javier. It comes out clean with a fourteen percent return."

"Good. When Carlos returns…"

"He is here. He didn't go to the airport."

"Good. Have him take care of the problem."

The six-seat Beechcraft was an hour out of Panama City when the pilot dropped to a thousand feet. Besides the pilot, there were three men in the plane. Carlos, who was in charge of the mission, a young man name Juan and the object of their attention, Rafael Ortiz.

The small plane began to bank slightly to the right while Rafael stared out the back seat passenger window.

He had been told they were searching for a place for a new landing strip.

"It is all jungle," Rafael said to Carlos who was in the copilot's seat. "There's no good place for a landing strip."

Carlos turned around, nodded at Juan who jammed a hypodermic needle into Carlo's neck and emptied the syringe.

Rafael yelped, grabbed his neck and tuned to Juan who stared impassively back. Within seconds Rafael was completely immobile although still very conscious. Juan unbuckled his seatbelt, opened the plane's door and began to push Rafael out.

Rafael tried to speak, tried to beg or scream but nothing came out. All he could do was stare at the younger man with his eyes wide open while trying to understand why this was happening.

Juan managed to get the man positioned in the doorway. Juan looked at those terrified eyes, muttered the word traitor, spit in Rafael's face then pushed him out.

Crashing through the trees broke Rafael's neck and mercifully killed him before he hit the jungle floor. Within a few days the indigenous wildlife would leave only strips of clothing and bones. In barely three or four weeks the jungle growth would be grown back and if you walked within a foot of him, you would not have found Rafael's remains.

The unfortunate part of the poor man's demise was that he was not the traitor. That man was still very much alive and well.

About the same time Rafael was making his free fall into the Panamanian jungle, a meeting was taking place in downtown Minneapolis. It was being held on the twentieth floor of the LaSalle Plaza, a thirty story glass and chrome beauty on the south edge of downtown. Suite 2010 held the office of CAR Securities Management, LLC. The three hundred square foot corner office, with windows overlooking downtown and the western suburbs, was where the meeting was being held. There were two men present. The forty-two-year-old founder and CEO, Corbin Andrew Reed, whose initials, CAR formed the acronym for CAR investments and the firm's CIO, Chief Investment Officer, Jordan Kemp.

Corbin Reed and Jordan Kemp gave meaning to the phrase 'opposites attract.' The two of them had met in college at the University of Minnesota twenty plus years ago and hit it off right away.

Corbin was six feet two and sported a slender waist and full head of hair. Never married, his numerous relationships with women rarely lasted longer than a weekend. Jordan was barely five-feet-six-inches and was almost as round as he was tall. He was also still married to the only girl he ever dated and she had initiated that. The two men complimented each other perfectly. Corbin could sell ice to Eskimos and Jordan was a statistical genius. Despite being a small firm with barely twenty employees, including themselves, they had made each other into millionaires many times over.

For a man running a company making the millions this one did, you would never know it by the decorations of his office. Other than the office's size and plush carpeting, it was hardly the lavish office of a rich CEO.

"Did you hear from our guys?" Kemp asked Reed after taking a seat in front of his desk.

"Yeah, I did," Reed replied.

"And they made it out of there without getting their throats cut?"

"Yeah and with an assurance that all is well and we're going to see more money coming in."

"How much?" Kemp asked.

"Another ten mil each month," Reed said. "We'll put that to good use."

"Where are you with the Corwin guy? What's his name?"

"David. He's on the verge of practically begging me," Reed said.

Kemp looked out the window facing north of the fifty-story Corwin building and said, "How cool would it be to get our hands on that money?"

"Patience. Besides, it's his aunt we need to snare. David is small potatoes compared to what she controls."

While they waited in the passenger loading area, Walter said, "So that's it. We get out of bed at three A.M., fly to Panama, damn near melt from the heat for a fifteen-minute meeting?"

"They're increasing their deposits by ten million a month. For that kind of money, yeah, we go to a fifteen-minute meeting in Panama. By the way, I forgot to mention, the old man speaks English as good as you."

"I don't understand something. Ten million per month is nothing to these guys. What do they want?" Walter asked.

"They're checking us out. We are getting him the best return for his money," Victor said. "They have a lot of others to do this kind of business with, not just us. We're being tested."

TWO

In a continuing effort, albeit a losing one, to get some exercise, Marc Kadella took the stairs two at a time up to the second floor. The stairway had a steep angle and ran straight up. When he reached the top he stopped for a moment to check his breathing, mildly pleased to find it had not increased.

"Making progress," he quietly sad. He then poked himself in the midsection and said, "Could do better."

Marc was a lawyer in private practice and as a sole-practitioner rented space in a suite of offices shared by other lawyers. His landlord, Connie Mickelson, a crusty, older woman working on her sixth marriage, did mostly family law and personal injury work. Also, there was Barry Cline, a man about Marc's age, who was becoming modestly successful at criminal and business litigation. The fourth and final lawyer was Chris Grafton, a small business, corporate lawyer with a thriving practice who was a few years older than Marc and Barry.

Marc was sandy-haired, blue-eyed of Scandinavian and Welsh ancestry. He was a little over six-feet tall, in his mid-forties and the recently divorced father of two mostly grown children; his son Eric, age nineteen and a daughter, Jessica, age eighteen.

He was returning from court where he made a deal for his client, a low-level drug dealer, to receive probation. The client was the son of a business client of Chris Grafton. Marc tried to steer clear of drug cases. He did not want to become known as a drug lawyer. With the pervasiveness of drug involvement in practically all criminal behavior, his attempts to stay away from it were becoming more and more difficult.

Marc's client, a sometime, sort of, college student, was busted for the fourth time holding enough cocaine and pot to prosecute for possession with intent to sell. And for the fourth time he was given probation, rehab and a stern lecture. Marc always marveled at how quickly drug dealers got turned loose with a promise to be good and not do it again. Despite what liberal politicians believe, it was becoming harder and harder to get these people sent to prison.

Marc entered the suite of offices and heard Sandy Compton, one of the secretaries, say into the phone, "Let me check. I'll see if he's available," and she put the caller on hold.

"You available?" Sandy asked looking at Marc.

"Who is it?"

"Mary Cunningham. Before you say anything," Sandy quickly continued cutting off the protest she knew was coming, "She's called three times. She says it's important."

"It's always important with her," Marc said heading toward his office.

While Marc was on the phone listening to the woman, one of his divorce clients, Chris Grafton appeared in his doorway. Chris listened while Marc repeatedly said, "uh huh, I see, you're right, I don't blame you."

Finally, Marc ended the call by saying, "Don't worry, Mary. We'll get it all straightened out in the end."

Marc hung up and Chris said, "What was that all about?"

"I don't have any idea. I didn't listen to a word she said. A woman scorned. She cheats on him, multiple times, he finally gets fed up and wants a divorce and she's mad at him. She should be thankful he doesn't own a gun. I don't know how he put up with her as long as he did."

"Why do you do divorce work?"

"It pays the bills. Plus, it reminds me how glamorous the practice of law is. What's up?"

"How did this morning go?"

"Great actually. I thought he'd at least get six months on the county. No jail time. Probation and another promise of going through drug rehab. Probation services gave him a good report," Marc told him.

"He knows how to play their game and con them," Chris said referring to probation services.

"Sooner or later, he'll end up with a tag on his toe, lying on a slab covered with a sheet. Does his dad know he's moving into heroin?" Marc asked.

"Are you serious? How do you know?"

"I'm not positive, but I think so. You may want to pass it along to Bert," Marc said referring to the father.

"Did the kid tell you that?"

"No."

"So it's not privileged?"

"Nope."

Connie Mickelson appeared in the doorway next to Chris. Connie was their landlord who shared office space with these two men and one other lawyer.

"Hey," Marc said to her. "Where have you been?"

"Ramsey County," she replied. "Listen, I heard a lawyer joke I haven't heard before."

"Okay," Marc said eagerly listening.

"Terrorists break into a conference room where the American Bar Association is holding its annual convention. They take a hundred lawyers hostage.

"The FBI arrives and the terrorist leader tells them if their demands aren't met, they threatened to release one lawyer every hour."

"Not bad," Chris said, "but I heard a better one the other day.

"An anxious fifteen-year-old-girl comes home from school and asks her mother if you can get pregnant from anal sex. The mother says, of course. Where do you think lawyers come from?"

The three of them laughed, and then a voice behind them said, "I like that one."

"You looking to get fired?" Connie said to Carolyn.

"Right," Carolyn said. "I know where all the bodies are buried, remember?"

"She's got a point," Marc said.

Shortly before noon Carolyn buzzed Marc to tell him Tony Carvelli was on the phone. Carvelli was a private investigator Marc occasionally used and was also a good friend.

Carvelli was in his early fifties and, due to his years on the streets of Minneapolis looked it, but could still make most women check him out. He had a touch of the bad boy image they couldn't resist plus a flat stomach and a full head of thick black hair touched with gray highlights; a genetic bequest from his Italian father.

Carvelli was an ex-Minneapolis detective and had the reputation of being a bit of a street predator, which was well deserved. He looked and acted the part as well. Dressed as he normally was today, he could easily pass for a Mafia wise guy. Growing up in Chicago, he knew a few of them and could have become one himself and very likely a successful one. Instead, after his family moved to Minnesota he became a cop.

He was retired from the Minneapolis P.D. with a full pension then became a private investigator. Over the years he was able to build a nice, successful business doing mostly corporate security and investigations.

"What's up?" Marc asked when he answered.

"I thought I'd call and offer to let you buy me lunch," Carvelli said.

"That's awfully considerate of you. What's the occasion?"

"I just got a call from a guy I know who works for 3M, a high up the food chain executive type. He's got a kid in a jam and needs a defense lawyer. I told him I knew you and he recognized your name."

"What did he do?"

"I don't know the details. Drug bust. I didn't ask what or how or anything," Carvelli told him.

"I hate doing drug cases," Marc said.

"I know. Look, this guy, the dad, gets me a lot of business. Not just 3M but other corporate guys he knows. I would appreciate the favor," Tony pleaded.

Marc hesitated for a brief moment then said, "Okay. I may owe you one anyway. The dad has money?"

"Oh yeah. He can pay. Try not to gouge him too much."

"I won't," Marc replied. "I'm meeting the girls for lunch. Want to join us?"

"Maddy and Gabriella?"

"Yeah," Marc said.

"I need to talk to Maddy anyway. Where and when?"

"Axel's and I'm already late," Marc replied.

"See you there."

By the time Marc arrived at the restaurant, his three lunch companions were already there. He joined them at a booth and sat next to Gabriella Shriqui, across from Tony and Maddy Rivers.

Gabriella was a minor local celebrity. She started her career in TV news as a reporter for local Channel 8 covering local courts and criminal activity. This is how she first came in contact with Marc and Maddy.

She was excellent at her job and looked great in front of the camera. Gabriella was stop traffic gorgeous. The product of Moroccan Christian parents who immigrated to America when her mother was pregnant with her older brother. Gabriella had silky black hair six inches below her shoulders, light caramel colored skin that looked like a perpetual tan and dark, almost black, slightly almond shaped eyes.

A job hosting a half-hour show entitled *The Court Reporter* had opened up when the previous host was murdered. Gabriella had done a bit of work for the show and was given the job. The show was, as the title implied, about what was going on in the courts both locally and nationally.

Madeline Rivers was an ex-cop with the Chicago Police Department in her early-thirties. In her three-inch heeled, suede half-boots she liked to wear, she was over six-feet tall. She had a full-head of thick dark hair with natural auburn highlights that fell down over her shoulders, a model gorgeous face and a body worthy of Playboy. In fact, foolishly posing for that magazine was what led her to quit the Chicago P.D.

Maddy, as she was called by her friends, had moved to Minneapolis after quitting the Chicago cops following her Playboy pose. At the same time, she went through an ugly breakup when she found out the doctor she had fallen for was married. After arriving in Minnesota she got a private investigator's license. Maddy was befriended by Tony Carvelli and she was now doing quite well for herself. It was through Tony that she had met Marc. They had done several criminal cases together and had become great friends.

Marc's appearance interrupted a conversation taking place between Tony and Maddy. Maddy was not as successful as Tony, although she was making a good living. A lot of her work came from advertising for investigating prospective boyfriends and on occasion, girlfriends.

With the advent of online dating services came a growing market for quietly investigating people who were beginning to date. Maddy had saved quite a few women from involvement with men of questionable character. Even so, it surprised her how many women did not heed Maddy's warnings and refused to dump a guy whom Maddy found out was a total sleaze.

Madeline also did some criminal work for a few defense lawyers, mostly Marc and his officemate Barry Cline. This was her favorite work. To help supplement her income, she handled the occasional wayward wife or husband in a divorce, which she hated.

"So, when I get some overflow stuff from my corporate security clients, you want in?" Tony asked Maddy.

"God, yes! Please tell me I can stop doing divorce work," Maddy said.

"Yeah, I can probably get you enough so you can drop that," Tony assured her. "But don't be stealing my clients. Some of the guys I work for will like you, maybe a little too much."

"Hey, maybe I'll meet a rich executive type."

"Find one for me too," Gabriella laughed

While they ate lunch, the four of them chatted amiably. Marc told his lawyer jokes and Tony added two that he had recently heard. After the table was cleared, Tony told Marc about the drug

15

case he had called him about. Tony gave Marc the father's name, information and, of course, the son's name and information also.

It had been long established that anything said at these informal get-togethers was not to be used by Gabriella as a newsperson unless agreed upon.

"He's out on bail?" Marc asked.

"Yeah, Ramsey County," Tony replied.

"We need a good, juicy murder case," Maddy interjected.

"Yeah," Gabriella quickly agreed. "My show could use something spicy." She looked at Marc and continued, "How about a sex scandal murder involving some rich people or politicians?"

Marc looked at her and said, "You want me to see what I can do to create one?"

"Would you?" Maddy asked smiling.

He frowned at her across the table and said, "I'll do my best."

Changing the subject, Gabriella asked Maddy, "How's the new boyfriend?"

"Good, we get to listen to the girl-talk part of the conversation," Carvelli sarcastically said.

Maddy turned to look at Tony with a steely-eyed, stern expression.

Uh-oh, Marc thought, and then quickly said, "I always enjoy hearing about these things."

Maddy turned her head to Marc and gave him the same look. After a few seconds she looked at Gabriella and said, "He's great."

"Really? Wow! He is a bit of a hunk," she added. "Great, huh?"

"Well, he's you know, good. I mean he's okay… we're doing all right."

Tony looked at Marc and said while ticking off each item on his fingers, "She went from, he's great to, he's good to, he's okay to, we're doing all right all in one breath."

"He's history," Marc said.

"Probably tonight," Tony agreed.

16

Maddy scratched her nose with the middle finger of her left hand while looking back and forth at the two men. Gabriella had a hand over her mouth trying not to laugh.

"What's his name and what does he do?" Tony asked.

"His name is Rob Judd and he works for a small, local investment firm in their bond department. He makes a good living; he's good looking and not an asshole."

"Everything your dad told you to look for. Maybe you could murder him. That could make a great local story," Marc said.

"Why are you being so mean?" Maddy seriously asked.

"I'm sorry," Marc and Tony both said.

"We're just teasing you a bit," Marc added.

"Well, stop it," Gabriella said. "You guys have no idea how hard it is to find a nice guy."

"With a job," Maddy interjected.

"It's no easier for us," Marc said.

"How's Margaret?" Maddy asked.

"I don't know," Marc said and sighed. "I think she wants marriage and I'm in no hurry. In fact, the longer I live alone the more comfortable I get with it.

"I need to get back to the office," Marc said wrapping up the discussion.

THREE

The two visitors returning to the states from Panama City had barely made their 6:16 P.M. connection in Houston. Victor checked his watch as the American Airlines 737 smoothly cruised across the American heartland. They were due into Minneapolis/St. Paul at 10:59 which would get them home by midnight.

Victor looked past the softly snoring Walter Pascal and through the window into the starlit sky. The flight down to Panama had been very stressful on Walter because of his fear of the Torres. The moods of the two men were reversed for the return flight. Victor had his misgivings about how they would handle the drug money and the firm's ability to provide a fourteen percent return. The cash flow was nice, but to make an interest payment plus a laundered five million dollars pressed and cleaned each month could cause problems. And Victor was well aware of how these particular clients solved problems. His friendship with El Callado's counselor, Pablo Quinones, was helpful but certainly no guarantee.

Like Corbin Reed and Jordan Kemp, Victor and Pablo had met in college twenty plus years ago at Stanford. They remained very close over the years then a year or so after Victor had joined CAR Securities, Pablo paid him a visit. Victor had mentioned to him how the firm could really take off with a steady cash flow from just one or two customers. By the end of their first meeting, CAR Securities had a five million dollar a month commitment. Ironically, it was Victor who was the lone hold out to turn it down. No one on the decision making team was a virgin. Everybody knew exactly where this money was coming from and exactly what was being done with it.

Corbin Reed was the smoothest salesman Victor had ever met. Having spent ten years in a New York investment firm as a sales manager, Victor Espinosa had met more than his share of smooth talking sales people, both men and women. None of them could hold a candle to Corbin Reed. In fact, Corbin was becoming so good at it, so sophisticated, he did not have to sell at all. His reputation in the Twin Cities and Upper Midwest was such that investors were beginning to ask him to take their money.

Typically, the way this worked, a current client would brag to a friend or fund manager that he knew about Corbin's solid returns in the eleven to fourteen percent range through good times and bad. The friend would end up begging Corbin's client to set up a meeting. During the course of the meeting, in fact it usually took two or three meetings, Corbin would almost reluctantly agree to take the friend's money.

Corbin would say something along the lines of, "Well, I don't know. We're trying to stay small so we can give our customers personal service. I'm just not sure we want to grow much faster."

Of course, by this time, the would-be new client was practically barking like a seal begging Corbin to take his money.

The best ones were the fund managers. Corbin had managed to net a dozen local funds, mostly 401k's set up for small and mid-size business employees and several local school district pension plans and even a couple of churches. The steady returns his current clients always bragged about made the eyes of the fund managers light up. The fund managers' bonuses were tied directly to returns they generated. And, of course, the cash flow from these clients was always put to good use.

Walter Pascal woke up, yawned, sat up and stretched then asked Victor, "How much longer?"

"About a half-hour."

"We on schedule?" Walter asked while taking a peak down below at the darkness of southern Minnesota.

"A far as I know, they haven't said anything."

"Been a long day. Too much time spent on airplanes."

The next morning the two travelers, along with three others, all men, were in a meeting in Corbin Reed's office. Victor Espinosa related the trip, the meeting in Panama and the results. He also expressed his reservations.

19

"Do we really want to guarantee that kind of return on this money? Will we continue to have the cash flow long enough to do so and meet our goals?" Victor asked.

The five of them were seated around an inexpensive, round, wooden table that had six chairs around it. There was coffee, water, pastry and fruit in the center of the table and the pastry was rapidly disappearing.

"Yes, Victor," Corbin answered him. "Everything is going better than I had hoped."

"As long as the market stays stable," interjected the small firm's numbers wizard and CIO, Jordan Kemp. "They need to have a big uptick just to avoid a large collapse."

"Unless we see it coming and short sell," Walter Pascal said.

"I'm not worried. We have the cash flow and more investors circling the bait," Corbin said, proud of his metaphor. "The politicians in Washington can't afford to let another meltdown happen again."

"We may have another problem I need to show you," Ethan Rask said. Rask was technically listed as the firm's compliance officer. His job was to make sure that the firm's trades and business practices were in compliance with the state and federal laws and regulations. That was his title but it wasn't his job. In fact, the only thing he knew about securities and investment was what little he was able to grasp in these meetings. But it helped that he had his hooks into the chief investigator for Minnesota of the Securities and Exchange Commission. Rask was both blackmailing and bribing the man.

"Listen to this," Rask said as he opened a laptop, set it on the table and played an audio recording.

What they heard was a recorded conversation between a man, whose voice they recognized, and a woman. The man was an employee in the bond department and he was sharing his concerns about things he believed did not add up at work.

"They are getting their customers good rates of return and you think this might be a problem? I don't understand why that would be a problem. Isn't that what they are supposed to do?" the men at the table heard the female voice say.

"I think they're getting a little too good," the man in the recording said. "I tried to ask my boss about it and he just laughed it off. I don't know, maybe he's right. There are probably things going on there I don't know about. They're pretty compartmentalized that way."

"You work in the bond department and not in the brokerage or new customer sales, right?" the woman asked.

"Yeah," he answered.

"Then I'm sure there are a lot of things going on that you don't know about," she said.

"There's another office across the hall from the main office. It's room 2007. I see some of the higher ups go in and out sometimes when I'm in the hall. But no one ever talks about what goes on in there. I asked Walter about it and he just smiled and said, 'That's the magic room' or some bullshit. I asked one of the other guys who works with me, Rob Judd, and he didn't know anything about it. Said, it was none of his business and blew me off."

"You need to stop worrying about it and leave it alone. It could get you fired," the girl said.

"I'm a little worried they might be doing something illegal. I don't want to get caught up in it," he said.

"Like what?"

"I don't know, that's what I'm afraid of."

"Well, be careful. You don't want to get fired, either."

"I will, don't worry."

There was a long pause of almost forty seconds during which it was obvious the couple were kissing.

"So, am I coming up?" they heard the man ask.

"Not tonight. It's already late and I have to get up early. Let's go somewhere this weekend," she said.

"How about we go camping? We could go up North. Spend the day hiking Gunflint..."

At that point Rask shut off the recording and said, "The rest is just them fooling around a little more, then she gets out and he takes off."

Corbin looked at Walter Pascal, the man's boss and clearly annoyed said, "You knew about this and…"

"How do you think Ethan found out? I went right to him," Pascal said.

"Sorry. I'm sorry, Walter. I didn't mean …"

"It's okay, Boss," Pascal said, "You got a bug in his car?"

"Last night," Rask said. "We've got his phones, car, apartment and pretty much everything wired."

"What about this guy? Will he let it go or will he keep digging?" Victor Espinosa asked Walter.

Walter hesitated for a moment knowing his answer was crucial to his subordinate's future and possibly his life. He finally said, "I'm not sure. We could keep an eye on him."

"What about the other guy he talked to, this Rob Judd?" Rask asked.

"He's exceptional," Corbin Reed interjected. "He consistently gets the highest yields in the department and has a sharp eye for convertible bonds that he turns into very profitable equities. He's been terrific for the cash flow we need."

"I can keep an eye on him too," Rask said, "but it didn't sound like he was interested in what McGarry, the guy on the tape, asked him about."

"Okay," Corbin said. "That'll do for now. Anything else? Good. Let's get at it. The clock keeps ticking and we're still on schedule."

Two days later, Friday morning, the five of them met again only this time across the hall in 2007 in a windowless, secure conference room. When they finished discussing the business of the firm, Rask pulled open the same laptop they had listened to the illegal recording on and he again placed it on the table. Rask hit the play button and a video appeared on screen.

The five of them watched and listened for twenty minutes to a conversation between two of their employees in a semi-crowded downtown bar. They were in the patio area seated opposite each other on the end of a long picnic table. The camera and microphone were in a woman's purse on the next table barely five feet away with an excellent view of the two men.

The man on the left was Patrick McGarry, the same man recorded in his car with his girlfriend three nights ago. The second man, his white shirtsleeves rolled up and his tie loosened, was McGarry's co-worker, Rob Judd.

Rask stopped the film and said, "I've fast forwarded to get to the relevant part. Most of the stuff before this is just what you'd expect from a couple of guys having a beer or two after work."

"Who filmed this?" Walter Pascal asked.

"That's not important," Corbin answered him.

Rask started the film again and McGarry asked Rob, "You don't think the returns they're getting are a little too good to be true? The market's been on a roller coaster for months."

Judd set his empty beer glass down, looked at McGarry and asked, "How do you know what they've been paying for returns?"

"I've heard some things on the street from competitors. People saying CAR Securities is getting a steady fourteen to fifteen percent ROI. I have friends at other firms who have told me their customers want to know how we can do it and they can't. Their customers would move their money to us if they could, but Corbin won't let them.

"I'll tell you something else," McGarry continued, "I've checked into some of our securities, the mortgage backed securities, and they're bullshit."

"What do you mean, bullshit?" Judd asked.

"I mean they aren't what they're supposed to be. They are all supposed to be triple and double A only and they're not. All of them have B level ratings in them."

"Are you sure?" Judd asked. "That's a serious charge and…"

"I know it is and I can prove it. I'm going to Walter with it and ask him about it. I'm telling you, something's very wrong."

"Well, let me know what Walter says. There's got to be a mistake somewhere. These guys aren't stupid."

"I will," McGarry agreed.

The waitress brought Judd another beer and made a little too much of a show telling him that whatever he wants he should just ask.

"I hate that," McGarry said. "Women just fall all over you. It's disgusting."

"Animal magnetism," Judd smiled. "Look," he continued, "I like my job, I like where I work. I like the people and the small firm atmosphere. I don't know what kind of returns they pay and I don't care. Besides, your friends are probably blowing smoke up your ass or their clients are. As for me, I make a damn good living, I have a nice home, a beautiful girlfriend and I'm not going to make waves again. I did that once and it was a nightmare."

"You did? When and where?"

"Forget I said that," Judd continued clearly regretting what he said. "Besides I'll tell you something, I'm a really smart guy. I know that. But when I talk to Jordan about business stuff, he makes me feel like an idiot. He's off the charts smart. He doesn't try to make you feel like a moron — you know him, he's too nice for that — you just can't help it. If anybody can beat the market and get steady, top returns, it's him."

McGarry paused for a moment, took a swallow of his beer then said, "Maybe, but I'm not gonna get caught in the switches. I'll keep my eyes and ears open to make sure I keep my own ass covered."

"There's nothing going on. I'm taking off," Judd said as he finished his beer. "I'll see you tomorrow."

Rask shut off the recording and Pascal said, "I'll fire him, today."

"Let me think about it," Corbin said. "Keep your friends close but your enemies closer."

24

"Maybe we try to convince him there's nothing going on," Victor Espinosa said.

"Let's take the weekend to think about it. Think of a way to calm him down," Corbin said. "I need to talk to Ethan for a minute, guys. Give us the room will you please?"

When the other three had left and closed the door to the soundproofed room, Corbin said to Rask, "I want that little asshole taken care of this weekend."

"Yeah, I figured that. It's all set. I can do this myself. I'll get him up North. Don't worry."

On page four of the Sunday Minneapolis Star Tribune, there was a short, three paragraph article about a young couple being killed in a hiking accident. It looked to investigators that the woman, whose name and her companion's was withheld until notification could be made, probably tripped and went over a ledge. The man likely tried to grab her and she dragged him over with her. The pair fell a hundred feet to a rocky stream bed they were hiking above.

FOUR

"Mr. Grant," the executive assistant for Executive Vice President Blake Grant of 3M Company said through the phone's intercom, "There's a Marc Kadella on the phone for you. Says it's personal but you would know what it's about."

"I do, Jen, and thank you. Put him through, please," he said.

A moment later Marc's voice came through the phone, "Blake Grant, please."

"Mr. Kadella? This is Blake Grant."

"Please, call me Marc. Tony Carvelli gave me your number and asked me to give you a call. Tony told me your son has a problem. Tell me a bit about it."

Grant took a few minutes to give Marc a brief rundown of the arrest and his son's history. When he finished there was silence between them.

"Are you still there?" Grant asked.

"Oh, yeah, sorry. I was making some notes," Marc apologized. "How much was bail?"

"Half a million dollars," Grant said.

"I'm a little surprised they set bail that high."

"I was in the courtroom. He didn't have a lawyer, he had a public defender."

"Public defenders are lawyers and are mostly very good ones," Marc softly said.

"Of course. Sorry. I was there and the prosecutor convinced the judge that Kenny is a flight risk."

"Is he?" Marc asked.

"No, of course not. He did have a couple of missed court appearances in the past."

"That explains it. Is he wearing a bracelet on his ankle? A monitor," Marc asked.

"Yes. Tony told me you don't like to take drug cases. Is that true?"

"In general, yeah. But it's getting harder and harder because drugs are so prevalent in almost all criminal activity these days," Marc said.

"Will you take his case? I certainly know of your reputation from cases you've done that the media has covered."

"Don't believe everything you read in the papers. The first thing I need to do is meet him and you. Tony told me you would be responsible for the fees."

"If that's all right," Grant said.

"Sure, but I'll need to meet with you and Kenny to discuss it." Marc pulled his calendar up on his computer screen and said, "How about tomorrow at 2:00? Can you make it?"

"We'll be there," Grant said.

Marc gave him his office address then Grant said, "He's really not a bad kid. He's just well…"

"Has a drug problem. That's one of the things we'll talk about. I look forward to meeting you. See you tomorrow."

"Wait, wait a second. There is one other thing I meant to tell you," Grant quickly said before Marc could hang up.

"What's that?"

"Well, I don't know if this means anything, but Kenny swears he's innocent. He swears he was not holding any drugs and the cop planted them. I know you've heard that a thousand times but not once has Kenny tried to duck his responsibility. He's never claimed he was innocent before. I just thought you should know."

"I'll keep it in mind," Marc replied while thinking, *first time for everything*. "Bring any paperwork you have."

"Will do."

"And make sure Kenny calls the probation people who are monitoring his movements and gets permission to come here."

Marc took a moment to enter the appointment onto his computer which would also be put on the computer of everyone else in the office. The office sharing was such a casual arrangement that everyone answered phones and made appointments for each other. They all needed access to each other's calendars when this happened.

27

The Grants arrived the next morning twenty minutes early. The father looked exactly the part of a mid-fifties corporate exec; a dull blue suit, striped tie, black loafers. Kenny was an obviously twenty-something slacker who could use a 2x4 across the forehead once a day just to make sure he was paying attention. Not a bad young man, simply more interested in a good time than hard work.

Marc brought them into his office and they all took their respective chairs. Blake sat to Marc's left, Kenny to his right.

"I didn't do this one…" Kenny started to say.

Marc held up his right hand and Blake gently placed his left hand on his son's right arm.

"Allow me to be brutally honest," Marc said. "The simple truth is: I don't care whether you did it or not. It doesn't matter what I believe, it only matters what they can prove and if I can create reasonable doubt."

"Let's go," Kenny said to his dad visibly annoyed.

"No," Blake said.

"Kenny," Marc began again, "Your dad told me that you believe the cop planted the drugs. We'll definitely hire an investigator and look into it. Now, tell me what happened."

Kenny quickly and concisely went through the stop and search by the two St. Paul cops. He had failed to signal a turn from Rice Street onto Pennsylvania Avenue a few blocks north of the Capitol. The cop pulled him over, searched his car and found the drugs underneath the front passenger seat.

Kenny had given Marc what little paperwork he had. Marc looked it over and said, mostly to himself, "No police report or arrest record. Did they tell you why they were searching the car?"

"No," Kenny said shaking his head. "I sat in the cop car with the young guy while the older one searched the car. The older guy's name is Kubik…."

"You know him?" Marc asked.

"Yeah, I know him. He's an asshole. He busted me once before and tried to turn me into a snitch. I wouldn't do it."

"Is he a uniform cop or…" Marc started to ask.

"No, no," Kenny said. "He's a detective. So's the other guy."

"The other guy," Marc said, "the other detective could see into your car to see what this Kubik was doing?"

"No, no way. We were in their car parked too far back. Kubik planted the drugs. I wouldn't snitch for him and he was pissed about it. Sorry, Dad," he said to Blake.

"It's okay, son," Blake said. "What do you think?" he asked Marc.

Marc shrugged his shoulders but before he could say anything, Kenny blurted out, "I'm telling the truth. Dad, I want a lawyer that believes me!"

"Kenny, relax," Marc said. "Your story sounds credible. Let me look into it. I'll get the police reports and arrest records. I'll set up what's called an Omnibus hearing for about three weeks from now."

"What happens then?" Blake asked.

"We'll find out what evidence they have and put the cops on the stand to testify about why they stopped him and the search," Marc said then looked at Kenny. "It does smell a little fishy. Why are two detectives stopping anyone for a traffic infraction then do a search and conveniently find drugs; sale weight amounts?"

"What about money? Your fees," Blake asked.

Marc smiled then said, "I'll give you the Tony Carvelli retainer discount since he assures me you're good for it. I'll take five thousand to bill against at three hundred per hour. I'm also going to hire an investigator..."

"Tony?" Blake asked.

"No, a woman I've worked with. Don't worry, she's good. If anybody can get cops to talk and find out what this Kubik guy is up to, she can. Tony's always available if I need something from him. He's a busy guy but he will help on anything I ask him for.

"There's something else I need to get clear with you, Blake. Please don't be insulted, but paying the fees doesn't give you the right to call the shots," Marc said then held up his hand to cut off the father's protest. He softly continued by saying, "Please hear me out. I don't mean to imply you would and from what Tony told me I don't think it will be a problem. But it happens. Especially in divorce cases where mom or dad is paying the fees for a young woman. Kenny is my client and he is the decision maker."

"I get that absolutely. Don't worry. Is it okay for him to tell me what is going on? To keep me informed?" Blake asked.

Marc thought for a moment then said, "Probably not. He's my client and what is said between us is absolutely confidential. But that does not cover you. If he were to admit something to you, you could be forced to testify. Tell you what, if you want to come to these meetings and court hearings, feel free to do so. If I think we may discuss something I don't want you to hear, I'll simply ask you to leave the room. Will that be okay?"

"That will be fine," Blake said.

"Good," Marc replied.

While he wrote a check, Marc filled out a retainer agreement for Kenny to sign. He also had Blake sign a document guaranteeing the fees.

Marc also gave Kenny a list of drug rehab centers and clinics and told him to get evaluated and to enroll if they recommended it.

"What do you think, Mr. Kadella?" Kenny asked.

Marc paused for a moment before saying, "Kenny, don't take this personally, okay? Right now I've heard your story. Let me find out what the cops have to say. I'll say this, without seeing a list of all of the charges, if this Kubik guy has it in for you, you're looking at a lot of jail time."

"How long?" Kenny quietly asked.

"Relax, you haven't done anything yet. We'll cross that bridge when we come to it.

"Do you have anything else?" Marc asked both men. "I'll be in touch," he added when both shook their heads. "Okay, let me get started."

When the two men left Marc got right to it. He called the Ramsey County Attorney's office and spoke with the lawyer handling the case, a woman by the name of Gloria Fenton. Marc didn't know her and while talking to her made a note to have Maddy check her out.

Fenton agreed to fax the discovery to him after Marc emailed a Notice of Appearance to let her and the court know he represented Kenny Blake.

Later, while he was reading through the police report, Maddy arrived.

"We have a juicy murder case?" she asked as she sat down.

"No, sorry, Tony's drug case. The one he told us about at lunch."

Marc quickly brought her up to speed on the case then told her what he wanted.

"I want you to check out these two cops and find out what you can on the prosecutor," he said as he handed her a sheet of paper with their names on it.

"Dale Kubik," she quietly said while looking at the name. "Why does that sound familiar?"

"He was one of the original investigating cops on the Bob Sutherland homicide," Marc reminded her. "When Mackenzie shot him in her living room."

"Who's this Richie Newsom? His partner?"

"Guess so. The woman on there," Marc said referring to the sheet of paper she held, "is Kubik's former partner, Anna Finney. She was also at Mackenzie Sutherland's."

"Yeah, her I remember. And Max Coolidge. Okay, I'll get going," she said.

"You need some money?" Marc asked.

"No, I'm okay for now. I'll see you later."

FIVE

The first thing Maddy did after leaving Marc's office was to place a call to Tony Carvelli. Maddy had not been in Minnesota as long as Carvelli and had nowhere near the number of connections he did, especially in St. Paul. Maddy lived and worked out of Minneapolis. Despite their close proximity, the two cities were distinctly different and almost different worlds.

"You could start with John Lucas, Carolyn's husband," Tony told her after she explained what she was looking for. He was referring to one of the two assistants in Marc's office. Carolyn's husband was a detective with over twenty years in St. Paul.

"Damn," Maddy said. She was in her Audi and had just pulled out of the Reardon Building parking lot. "I forgot about her. I'll call her back. Anyone else?"

"Sure, I know a few guys who would know this Kubik and his partner, Newsom. The first one I'd call is Max Coolidge. He knows everybody."

"Um, that could be a problem," Maddy said.

"Because of the Sutherland case? I don't think Max would hold that against you," Tony said. "Tell you what, I'll give him a call and see if he'll talk to you. Where are you?"

"I'm on Lake Street heading east toward St. Paul," Maddy replied.

"Okay, call Carolyn and get John's number. Wouldn't hurt just to see if she'll call him and set it up," Tony said.

"I hate to impose," Maddy said.

"I know Carolyn and John. She'll probably volunteer. Don't worry about it. I'll call you after I talk to Coolidge."

Maddy had the office number on speed dial and Carolyn answered right away. Maddy quickly explained what she needed and Tony was right, Carolyn volunteered to call her husband.

Carolyn dialed her husband's personal phone and he answered on the third ring.

"Hey babe," he said to the only woman he had ever been with and was still totally in love with after three kids and twenty plus years.

"Hi Johnny. Listen. Maddy Rivers needs some information…"

"Who's she?"

"Yeah, right" Carolyn drolly replied. "Like you don't have her in your tiny little imagination right now wearing a thong bikini. Give me a break."

"Oh, oh, that Maddy Rivers. I remember meeting her but can't recall what she looks like."

"Shut up," Carolyn dryly said. "She's going to call you."

"What does she need?" John asked turning serious.

"Information on a St. Paul cop…"

"I can't do that," John protested.

"…by the name of Dale Kubik."

"Kubik?"

"Yeah, that's what she said," Carolyn said.

John paused for a moment then said, "Okay. Have her call me and I'll set up a meeting."

"You know this guy?" Carolyn asked.

"Sure. Just tell Maddy to give me a call."

Madeline took Carolyn's call, thanked her profusely and called John back right away. They agreed to meet at a bench at Merriam Park, a small park and community center in the Midway District of St. Paul. John was in his car and would be there in five minutes. Maddy was almost on the Lake Street bridge crossing the Mississippi into St. Paul. She would be there a minute or two behind John.

Maddy crossed the bridge and was headed uphill on Marshall when her phone went off.

"Hi, sweetheart," Tony said. "I got a hold of Coolidge for you."

"Okay," Maddy cautiously said.

33

"At first, he wasn't real crazy about talking out of school about another cop. Then I mentioned it was Kubik and he said okay. I was a little surprised he was willing to do it."

"Thanks, Tony."

"He said to give him a call..." Tony added then read his number to her. "Oh, ah, one other thing. I, ah, sort of told him you'd be wearing a black, leather miniskirt, knee-high black leather boots, a see-through blouse and black bra."

"You're lucky I like you, Carvelli," she said.

"Hey, if I didn't tease you a little bit you'd think I was mad at you," Tony added defensively.

"That's true," Maddy agreed.

"Give me a call later. Let me know what they said."

"Will do. Bye."

Madeline parked in the small lot of the community center and took the path up the short hill. John Lucas saw her coming and waved to her. A moment later she arrived and they shook hands and sat down on the bench.

It was a beautiful, sunny day, one of those days native Minnesotans did not want people on the coast to know about. Being referred to as fly-over country was not taken as an insult even if it was meant to be.

For the next fifteen to twenty minutes, while Maddy took notes and asked an occasional question, John told her what he knew about Dale Kubik. None of it was positive.

"So, he won't make the centerfold of detective of the month magazine," Maddy said. She looked at her notes and continued, "This is the official stuff. Now tell me the rumors."

"He was a good detective when he got his shield. A little cocky and maybe a bit full of himself, but willing to learn. The past two years he's gone through three partners and is on his fourth. You want the rumor, drugs, drinking, women and maybe gambling."

"Is he married?"

"Not anymore. That's hardly unusual. It's tough being a cop's wife. I got lucky with Carolyn," John said.

"Yes, you did," Maddy said and playfully poked him in the chest. "And don't forget it. What about his partner, Richard Newsom?" Maddy asked.

John paused before saying, "I don't know anything about him. He just showed up one day, a new shield and was assigned to partner up with Kubik. Young guy. Probably late twenties but looks even younger. Quiet, doesn't say much or socialize."

"What do you think, John? Just between us, would Kubik plant drugs?" Maddy asked.

John smiled and said, "Tell Marc I'll deny it but the answer is, hell yes, if he had the right motivation. Find that and you'll have your answer."

"Any history of violence?"

"Yeah, he's been reprimanded two or three times and has complaints about excessive use of force. I don't know the details. You should talk to Max Coolidge. He'll know more. He's been around him more than I have.

"You could also check with Anna Finney. She's Max's partner now. Used to be Kubik's."

"Anything else you think I should know?"

"No, not really. Say hi to Marc for me. We need to have him over for dinner sometime. It's been a while. I'll tell Carolyn to have him bring you, too."

Maddy smiled and said, "I accept. Carolyn has to be a better cook than me."

Maddy saw the forty-something bald, black man seated in a booth and slightly waved to him. She indicated with her right hand she was getting herself something to drink then pointed at his coffee inquiring if he wanted a refill. Max shook his head to indicate he did not.

Maddy went to the counter of the McDonald's where they were meeting and ordered a Diet Coke. A minute later, after sliding onto the booth's bench seat, they shook hands.

"I appreciate you meeting with me," Maddy started. "Especially after the, well, you know, Sutherland case."

"No problem," Max said flashing a brilliant smile. "You and the lawyer were doing your jobs. I was the one that got caught up in it emotionally."

"It's hard not to, sometimes," Maddy said.

"I heard she left town, Mackenzie I mean," Max said.

"She did. I don't know where she went," Maddy replied sensing Max was digging for information. "I liked her, I liked her a lot."

"Sorry," Max said holding up both hands. "I was prying and I didn't really mean to. And, I don't want to rehash the Sutherlands. Tony told me you're looking for some information on Dale Kubik. What's up?"

"Marc Kadella, the lawyer for Mackenzie Sutherland..."

"Oh, yeah. Trust me, him I remember," Max smiled.

"Marc has a drug bust case, he doesn't usually do them. It's a favor for a friend of Carvelli, Kubik is the arresting detective and his client swears Kubik planted the drugs. Marc told me I could tell you, the kid's been busted before a few times and always took responsibility for it. This time he swears he's innocent."

"They all do, Maddy," Max smiled.

"I know that Max. The drugs always belong to a cousin or a friend. I get that," Maddy agreed. "I just want to get a sense of whether or not Kubik would do something like this."

"You're asking me to step on another cop's toes," Max said.

"I don't want you to do anything you're not comfortable with," Maddy protested.

Max thought it over for a moment then said. "Normally, right about now I'd tell you to go to hell and walk off. But this Kubik guy is a first class asshole so, yeah, I can see him doing that. Hang on a minute."

Max pulled out his phone, dialed a number and a moment later said, "Hey, where are you?"

He listened then said, "Good, No, no, I just wanted to be sure you weren't at the department. Are you alone?" he asked.

"You are, good? I have a question for you. You know Kubik pretty well," a statement, not a question. "Do you think he'd plant evidence?"

Max listened then said, "Sale weight cocaine and meth."

He listened some more then said, "You remember Maddy Rivers, the P.I. from the Sutherland case? She's here with me. The Sutherland lawyer, Kadella, has a case where the guy insists Kubik planted the drugs."

Max listened some more while Maddy continued to patiently wait.

"Okay, thanks. I'll tell her. Talk to you later," Max said then ended the call.

"That was Kubik's ex-partner, or, one of them. Anna Finney. She agreed he could do something like that.

"Let me tell you something, Maddy. I know you were on patrol in Chicago and I've heard stories about Chicago cops being willing to do something like this…"

Maddy instinctively started to protest to defend her Chicago brethren then realized Max was right.

"It's okay," Max said. "They have their ways. But believe it or not, cops here are pretty straight. They'll stretch the truth in court quick enough to convict a guy they know is guilty. Planting sale weight drugs on an innocent guy, even one with a history, not too many guys will go that far. If Kubik believed he had a reason, he'd do it."

"What would be reason enough for him to do it?" Maddy asked.

"I don't know," Max said. "Get even for something maybe."

"What can you tell me about Kubik's partner?" Maddy asked as she checked her notes for his name. "Richard Newsom."

"Not much, actually. He just all of a sudden appeared. After a couple of days he was partnered up with Kubik. Young guy. Seems nice enough, keeps his mouth shut to listen and learn. Where was he when Kubik allegedly planted the drugs?"

"In the department's car with our client. He couldn't have seen what Kubik was doing while he searched the kid's car and supposedly found the drugs," Maddy told him.

"So, he didn't see anything?"

"Nope."

"Figures. Unlikely he'd be in on it as new as he is," Max said.

Max pulled a small notebook from his inside coat pocket and took a minute to write something in it. He tore off a single sheet of paper and handed it to her.

"That's my cell number and the woman I talked to, Anna Finney. I wouldn't normally do this and there's no way either of us will testify, but Kubik's a bad cop. He shouldn't be carrying a badge and gun. And Anna thinks he has some other problems. Booze and drugs. I'll deny this meeting ever happened."

"We won't put you in a spot to hurt yourself on the job with other cops. Right now I'm just looking for a little background to see if what our client says is possible," Maddy said.

"One more thing," Max said. "Anna told me you need to get Kubik's personnel file from the Records Department. She didn't tell me what's in it, just you need to get it."

"Any suggestions how I get his file without a subpoena?" Maddy asked.

"Check with Carvelli. I'm sure he knows someone," Max smiled.

"One last thing," Maddy continued. "Why meet at a McDonald's?"

Max smiled and said, "I like their coffee, as long as you don't spill on yourself."

"Oh, yes," Maddy said. "The infamous McDonald's coffee case. I remember it. In fact, I was too young at the time, but years later I briefly dated a lawyer, quite a bit older than me, who worked on that case for McDonald's. I remember him telling me that whatever you heard about it, whatever you believe you think you know, whatever was reported, is absolutely not true."

"Really?" Max said.

"Now, this is one of the lawyers for McDonald's. One of at least a dozen. He told me McDonald's was dead wrong and totally to blame. He said they had hundreds of suits pending from people being severely burned and they tried to keep it quiet and make it go away. He said McDonald's knew their coffee was way too hot for years and seriously injuring people and they decided it was cheaper to pay the claims than to fix the problem."

"Coffee burns?" Max said obviously skeptical.

"Yeah, coffee burns," Maddy said. "In fact, he showed me pictures of that woman's injuries. It was sickening. Second and third degree burns all over her upper, inside thighs and vagina. Trust me, you would not want to have happen to you what happened to her. He said McDonald's got off cheaper than they should have."

"Well, that's interesting. I still like their coffee," Max said.

"Be thankful they fixed the problem, or Mr. Johnson might be Tiny Johnson if you spilled the stuff on him," Maddy said which made Max heartily laugh.

SIX

Maddy patiently waited in her car for the text message she was expecting. She was in the parking lot of a popular Twin Cities sports bar, Senser's in Roseville, a St. Paul suburb. Joe Senser, the owner, was a retired Viking football player who had done very well for himself in the restaurant business. While Maddy waited, she mentally reviewed her day.

After the meeting with Max Cool, a name that made her smile every time she thought of it, she called Marc to check in and give him a quick update. She then called Tony Carvelli to get a little help from him. Initially she had only wanted the name of someone with the St. Paul cops who could get her the files for Kubik and his new partner, Richie Newsom. Not having the contacts Tony did, she needed a little help.

An hour later a copy of Kubik's file was on her phone, forwarded from Carvelli. A minute later he called her with some interesting news. The file for Kubik's partner, Newsom, was flagged as classified. Carvelli's contact, who had gotten him Kubik's file, was in his boss's office within minutes trying to explain why he even tried to access it. The poor guy stammered a couple of bad lies about pulling it up inadvertently and left with a decent chunk of his ass missing.

"What do you think?" Maddy asked Tony when he told her this.

"I promised him two c-notes for the files so we better get him an extra one for the ass chewing he got," Tony told her.

"That's not what I meant, but you're right, we'll expense it to Marc's case. I meant what do you think is the reason for Newsom's file being flagged like that?"

"Could be any number of things," Tony replied.

"Bull," Maddy said. "It's Internal Affairs."

"I don't think so," Tony answered her. "I know a guy and I called him. He has no idea who Newsom is."

"He's Internal Affairs?"

"Yeah, a lieutenant. He could be lying to protect something but he sounded sincere. Tell you what," Tony continued, "get me a good, clean, quality photo of Newsom and I'll see what I can find out."

"Your computer guy won't tell *me* about it?" Maddy asked, teasing her friend a bit.

"Trust me, you don't want to deal with this guy. Most of these tech geeks don't deal well with humans and this guy is worse than most."

When she finished replaying this conversation in her head, she felt the vibration of the phone she was holding. Maddy checked the screen and read the message she had been waiting for. 'All set,' was the entire message.

For one hundred dollars Maddy had hired an off-duty Minneapolis patrol cop she knew to do her a favor. He was to sit down at the bar next to Maddy's target and hold the seat for her.

She replied to his message, waited ten minutes then went into the restaurant. Maddy removed her sunglasses, placed them on her head then searched the bar and found what she wanted in a few seconds. She walked through the sparse crowd, ignored a few turned heads and when she was two stools away, her cop friend quickly swallowed the remainder of his beer, stood up and headed toward the exit. As he passed Maddy they lightly fist bumped in a way that no one noticed.

"Excuse me," Maddy said to the man sitting next to the empty barstool. "Is your name Bob?" This is a ploy she has used numerous times to get an unsuspecting man, usually a target, to end up barking like a seal for her.

Her target turned his head away from his glass on the bar to the voice he just heard.

"Uh, um, I'm sorry," Dale Kubik started to say.

Maddy flashed him a smile and asked, "Is your name Bob? A friend set me up with a blind date and you fit his description. I'm a little late and I was hoping you were him."

The message that flashed through Kubik's head was that this gorgeous creature smiling at him was going on a date with someone who looked like him. In fact, she was hoping he was this mysterious Bob she was looking for.

With the help of the booze he had been drinking Kubik gathered himself and managed to say, "I certainly wish I was, but sorry, I'm not."

"Oh, darn," Maddy said sounding disappointed. She quickly looked over the people in the bar, sighed and said, "I don't see anyone else who could be him. I bet he left already." She looked at the still staring detective then asked, "Do you mind if I sit here? He may show up yet."

"Ah, sure, ah, no, please," Kubik stammered. "In fact, let me buy you a drink."

"Okay, thanks," Maddy smiled as she took the seat. She ordered a glass of house chardonnay and Kubik ordered another scotch and soda.

For the next two hours while Madeline made sure his glass was full, she listened to the life story of Dale Kubik. Within two minutes she pegged him as being quite narcissistic and getting him to talk about himself, his job and what a super-detective he believed he was, was not a problem. In fact, getting him to stop was the difficult part. That and after he was well passed the legal alcohol limit, fending off his roving hands.

When she gleaned about all there was from him, plus all she could stand, she called it a night. Of course, he tried to get her to leave with him but the 'early to work in the morning' excuse worked to get away from him. That and she mollified him by writing down her name and number on a napkin. Of course it was a fake name and the phone number was to an A.A. group she kept handy exactly for these occasions.

As she walked across the parking lot, she quietly said to herself, "Wonder if he'll get the message?"

The next day, a few minutes before noon, Maddy pulled her Audi into the lot behind Marc's office and parked. As she walked toward the building's back door she marveled at what a beautiful, sunny day it was again. *Minnesota summers are the native's best kept secret*, she thought.

Being in much better shape than Marc and more casually dressed, she went up the straight flight of stairs to the second floor taking them two and three at a time. She was carrying a leather satchel briefcase filled with documents that didn't slow her down at all.

At the top of the stairs, she checked her Fitbit and saw that her heart rate had skipped up a bit. *Need to find more exercise time*, she thought.

"Hello, everyone," she said as she burst through the office door. When Maddy made an appearance she never failed to light the place up.

After greetings all around, including Connie who came out of her office, Maddy shifted her eyes toward Marc's door while Carolyn watched her.

"He's on the phone," Carolyn said.

For the next ten minutes, while waiting for Marc, the women gabbed and laughed while catching up with each other.

"Hey," Marc said while exiting his office, "you ready?"

"Let's go down the street to that Mexican place with the patio. It's beautiful and…"

"I already made reservations," Marc interrupted her.

The hostess seated them on the patio corner table, as much privacy as they could get from the noisy lunch crowd. They ordered and when the waiter left, Maddy started.

"Okay, here's what I have," she said while reading her notes. "Dale Kubik. Forty-one-years-old, with the St. Paul P.D. sixteen years. Went to night school to earn a degree in criminal justice, divorced, two kids.

"Did four years in the Army before joining the cops. I don't have his military record, but according to his St. Paul file, he was an M.P. with a tour in Iraq and Germany and honorably discharged.

"He was a patrolman for six years. Very good to excellent performance reviews right down the line. During year seven he got his detective shield. For the next two years, good, not great reviews. Decent case closure rate. Not spectacular but solid. Oh, I went over this with Tony last night so this is his opinion also."

"Okay," Marc said then paused while the waitress brought their salads. "Decent cop. Won't make chief but is doing fine."

"Exactly," Maddy agreed. "Then during his third year as a detective he gets an official reprimand for excessive use of force. Tony checked into it and called me this morning. A pimp slash drug dealer took a swing at him and he pounded the hell out of the guy. Put him in the hospital. Because it was a first offense and the pimp slash drug dealer agreed not to push it, he was only given a reprimand."

"How does Carvelli come up with this stuff?" Marc asked.

"You know Tony," Maddy smiled. "He knows everybody."

"I'll call him and make sure he bills me," Marc said, mostly to himself.

"Over the next couple years, no more problems, good reviews. Then he gets another excessive force complaint. This one goes nowhere. About this time, he gets divorced. According to Tony, his wife packs up the kids and moves in with another man."

"Ouch," Marc said.

"Yeah, that might have been the trigger. Ever since then he's been sliding downhill. His closure rate has fallen, he's got an obvious drinking problem and over time he gets three more excessive force complaints, none of which goes anywhere but there's a pattern."

"And for every complaint filed, how many has he done without drawing a complaint?" Marc wondered.

"Hard to say, but probably a few," Maddy agreed. "It's gotten to the point where no one wants to work with him. I can see why."

"That reminds me, how was your date last night?" Marc asked with a smile.

"I should charge you double for that," Maddy snarled. "I spent two hours with him and wanted to slap the shit out of him. Narcissistic, whiney, and thin-skinned braggart."

"He was trying to impress you," Marc said.

"Why do guys think they need to act that way?"

"It's all a very primal, mating-ritual kind of thing. Ask a shrink. That and he'd like to get in your pants," Marc said.

"That doesn't work," Maddy said clearly annoyed.

"Let me tell you something, I'll bet it works a lot more than you think."

"That's depressing," Maddy said.

"Anything to indicate he would plant sale weight drugs on somebody?"

"Other than he's a bad cop with an alcohol problem and likely a drug problem? Plus, he has a bad closure rate and his career is in a steady, downhill slide?"

"What about the ex-wife? You want to take a shot at her?" Marc asked.

"They moved to California. He hasn't seen her or his kids for at least a couple years. I can fly out and find her," Maddy said angling for a little California vacation time on someone else's dime.

"So could I," Marc replied. "No, not unless it becomes necessary. We've got enough to go after his credibility. What about his partner, what's-his-name?"

"Richard Newsom," Maddy said.

"What's the deal with the classified personnel file?"

"Usually that's for someone who's undercover. It seems odd. He's too young and too new. Tony thinks he can find out who he is, if there's something going on, when we get him a good picture."

"His computer guy that he won't tell anyone about," Marc said, "must have facial recognition software…"

"Or can tap into the Feds," Maddy said.

"That, I don't want to know about," Marc said.

Later that afternoon, a frumpy, mostly bald man in an inexpensive suit and tie sat in his car on Selby and Snelling Avenues. He was across from O'Gara's, a bar and St. Paul institution, waiting for Kubik and his young partner. The man's name was Zach Scott and he was a professional and very discreet photographer.

Zach had gone into O'Gara's after the two detectives and casually watched them. Newsom was drinking a Coke while Kubik knocked off a couple of whiskeys and beer chasers. That was twenty minutes ago and since they were still on the clock, he expected them any minute.

Patience was certainly a virtue in his chosen field. It finally paid off when the two men emerged. He put his Nikon DSLR to his face and hit the auto button. He continued to shoot as Newsom practically ripped the car keys out of his partner's hand. Zach took at least thirty shots and knew there had to be at least one good one for Tony's use.

SEVEN

"I thought you had a date tonight. You must have brass balls to keep a woman like that waiting," Turner Smith, Rob Judd's workplace cubemate said referring to Maddy Rivers.

At first Rob acted as if he had not heard him. He continued to alternate between staring at one of his screens and making notes on a tablet.

"Hey!" Turner almost yelled to get Rob's attention.

"What? Oh, sorry. Um, she called. She's running late. You're right though, I should get going," Rob said when he read the clock and saw it was after six P.M.

Turner pushed his chair across the fourteen-foot cubicle space without getting up and asked, "So, how do I meet a girl like Maddy?"

Rob put the material he was working on in a desk drawer, locked it then said, "Well, in your case, I'd suggest you get one of those old-style sandwich boards to wear. You know, like they had during the Depression. Then put it on and walk around the street downtown on sunny days when the girls are out. On the board write 'multi-millionaire with terminal cancer seeks soulmate' on it. That should help."

"Hey, thanks for the advice, Mr. Smartass. Has Maddy figured out that you're gay?"

"Didn't I tell you?" Rob asked as he put on his sport coat. "She's converted me. I'm on your team now."

The two men started toward the front door of CAR Securities and Turner said, "You know, I think she *could* convert a gay guy."

Maddy was able to find a parking spot right next to Rob's Toyota 4-Runner. On the drive over she had, once again, gone over her thoughts and feelings about Rob. He was six-foot-three, which made him tall enough for the five-eleven Madeline, good looking and at thirty-seven, the right age. Never married, no kids. All good qualities. There was something missing and Maddy knew what it was. There wasn't a hot enough flame.

Maddy had talked to her best friend Gabriella Shriqui about it and they came to the conclusion Rob was a bit boring. He was certainly nice enough, considerate, kind and occasionally affectionate but a bit of a bore. Plus, he liked his alone time. An avid kayaker, almost every weekend and two or three evenings per week he would be on one of lakes, always by himself.

Maddy turned off her car's engine and stared through the windshield for a minute. Once again, she thought to herself, she would make a decision after the upcoming Fourth of July party his office threw each year. Until then, she would go along with the relationship as is. She knew why she was putting it off. Outside the bedroom he was a bit dull but she had to admit the sex was great. The man knew his business.

They greeted each other with a brief hug and kiss then Rob held Maddy's chair for her. They made the usual "how was your day" chit chat for a while. The waitress came, took their orders then the conversation turned to current events. Maddy loved talking politics and major events in the news, even sports. Rob's interest was mostly economics and the market. Maddy did her best to sound interested in the minutiae of the bond market but was thankful when their meal came.

They ate mostly in silence for a few minutes, Rob staring off into space with a distracted faraway look.

"You're pretty distracted tonight," Maddy finally said. "What's up?"

Rob took another bite of his chicken, chewed for a moment while thinking, then said, "Your friend, the lawyer, what's-his-name?"

"Marc Kadella," Maddy answered.

"Right. You say he's a good criminal defense lawyer," Rob said.

"Very good. Why, what's going on?" Maddy asked, her investigator's antennae turning on.

"Oh, ah, nothing," Rob answered a little too quickly and with a nervous note in his voice.

He went back to his meal and ignored Maddy while she repeated herself trying to get him to open up.

"Then I decided to strip down naked and walk around Lake Calhoun and get some sun," Maddy finally said looking for a reaction from him.

It took a few seconds for Rob to realize she had stopped talking to him. He finally looked up at her, saw her staring at him, then said, "What? I'm sorry you went to Lake Calhoun. That's nice."

With a disgusted look, Maddy pushed her chair back, tossed her linen napkin on the table and stood up.

"You're obviously not here tonight..." she began to say as she put the strap of her purse on her shoulder.

"Maddy wait. I'm sorry, it's just work stuff. Please, sit down," Rob stood and said.

Maddy looked at him, shook her head and said, "No, it's not the first time. Call me. Maybe we'll do something this weekend."

"Madeline, please," he whined to her back as she walked away. He stood watching her go then quietly said, "Oh boy, you did it this time."

And instead of going after her, which is what she really wanted, Rob calmly sat down and finished his meal. Sometimes men are just too stupid for words to describe.

The next morning Walter Pascal, the head of the bond department at CAR Securities heard a knock on his office door. He was busy reviewing a document he and the other partners were given. It was a report regarding the firm's activities across the hall in 2007. Before Walter could respond to the knocking, Rob Judd opened the door and entered. Walter held up his right hand to stop him before Rob got too close to his desk.

"Let me put this away," Walter said. "Confidential partnership stuff."

"Oh, jeez. Sorry, Walter. I didn't mean to barge in…"

"It's okay," Walter said with a smile. The smile was not for Rob but was caused by what Walter had been reading. "What's up?"

"I need to see you about something," Rob said as he closed the office's door. Carrying an inch-thick stack of paper, Rob took a seat in front of the desk.

"It's our mortgage backed securities," Rob began. "I'm a little concerned about them."

"How so?"

"Well, as you know they are supposed to be backed by nothing but triple A and double A mortgages, mortgages that have virtually no risk."

"Okay," Walter said feeling a touch of trepidation believing he knew where Rob was headed.

"I've been reviewing a random sample of ours…"

"Well, that's not really your job," Walter pleasantly said.

"I know and if I'm stepping on somebody's toes, I apologize. But I thought you should see this."

Rob pulled his chair up to Walter's desk placed the stack of papers on a corner to his right. He took the top page from the stack and placed it on the desk upside down so his boss could read it.

"As you know, we're holding over three hundred forty million worth of these securities," Rob said pointing at a figure on the paper.

"Yeah."

"Correct me if I'm wrong, but that seems to be a little high for a firm of this size."

"Well, I don't mean to be a prick about it, Rob," Walter said with a nice smile. "But that's not really your concern."

"I understand that, sir," Rob quickly said. "And ordinarily I would never have stuck my nose into something that didn't concern me. It's just, well, sir," he continued sliding his finger down a row of figures on the right side of the paper. "I've been noticing a higher default rate than what we should be seeing."

"How high?" Walter asked a little concern in his voice.

50

"It's pushing five per cent. A couple of months ago it was less than two percent, which is okay. For triple A and double AA tranche mortgage backed securities, five percent is getting a little high. It's even a little worse if you just look at the triple A tranche."

"How bad?"

"My sample came up with a four point nine percent default for the mortgages in the triple A tranche. Those should be almost risk free. The firm's revenues are going to take a dip at the end of this month," Rob said. "That's only three days and if this continues next month, July, will be worse."

"How big was the sample you used?" Walter asked.

"A little over twelve million. I wanted some from every source we use to purchase these securities. Some were better than others," Rob answered.

"Twelve million out of three hundred forty million. Is that a big enough sample size?"

"I think so," Rob said. "I thought I should bring it to your attention right away. These defaults were the primary cause of the '07, '08 financial meltdown."

"Yes, I know that. Okay," Walter said. "Let me look at this," he continued as he picked up the documents Rob had brought in, "and I'll get back to you next week."

"What should we do about this guy?" Corbin Reed asked the group gathered an hour later in the conference room of Suite 2007.

"Wait a minute," Ethan Rask said. "I don't know what this means. What are mortgage backed securities and triple A and double A, what was the word you called them?" Rask asked looking at Walter Pascal.

"You're the compliance officer," Jordan Kemp the CIO said with a smile. "You're supposed to know this shit."

"Tell me anyway," Rask said to Pascal.

"A mortgage backed security is just what it sounds like. It's basically a bond backed by mortgages. It can have a very large number of mortgages backing them or just a few. Depends on what

51

you want. You're buying stacks of mortgages and in return you get the interest payments as they come in."

"We basically use them for cash flow and they look good on the books," Corbin Reed said. "Very conservative, almost risk free. Or, at least, they are supposed to be. The gambling that went on during the 90's and up to '08 with these was the primary cause of the meltdown. Too many risky mortgages being given out and not enough honesty by the bond rating companies."

"A tranche is what the financial world calls a group of mortgages with the same rating. Either triple A, which are supposed to be almost risk free or double A which are also good but not quite as good as triple A. Mortgage backed securities are not supposed to have any single A, triple B, double B or lower rated mortgages in them. Okay?"

"I get it but I'm guessing they do have lower rated mortgages in them even though they're not supposed to. Am I right?" Rask said.

Everyone in the room went silent for a moment then Walter Pascal said, "Yep, you're right."

"How does this happen?" Rask asked.

"The big financial outfits, the too-big-to-fail guys who package the securities for sale, well, let's just say they have a cozy and mutually beneficial arrangement with the companies that do the ratings," Jordan Kemp said.

"Back to my original question," said Reed. "What do we do with this guy? Our snoopy bond trader."

Reed looked around the table at each man then stopped when he got to Ethan Rask.

"Nothing right now," Rask said. "It's too soon since McGarry fell down the cliff. Let me think about it."

"How much will this affect our cash flow?" Reed asked Walter Pascal.

"A little, not bad. With the new investors you've brought in, it won't make a blip in our plans."

"Okay but keep an eye on him," Reed told Rask then looked at Walter.

Both nodded their heads in agreement.

As the meeting was breaking up, Ethan Rask motioned to their boss to follow him into his office. When the two men were seated in the windowless, soundproofed room, Rask lit a cigarette and Corbin Reed decided to take one also.

"I know a guy who can take care of this for us. He's among the very best. He never fails and will do it in a way that no one will ever trace it back to us," said Rask.

"How do you know him?" Reed asked.

"From my days working for the missing, presumed dearly departed, Leo Balkus," Rask answered.

While he enjoyed the rare cigarette he was sucking on, Corbin sat silently thinking about it for a minute.

"Go ahead," he finally said. "We're too close. Only six or eight more months and I don't think Judd is going to let it alone."

"I agree," Rask said. "The way this guy works is, he sets the price, you wire half upfront. Once he receives that payment, you won't hear from him again. If you change your mind, too bad, you won't be able to get a hold of him to call it off.

"He also makes it clear that if the target dies from a heart attack, gets hit by lightning or trampled by an elephant or any other unfortunate circumstance, you still pay the second half of the contract. Just so you know that. You want to think about it?"

"No, let's do it. But we have the Fourth of July party coming up. Make sure he waits until after that. I don't want this hanging over everybody at the party."

"If you stiff this guy, you're next and there are a couple stories floating around about what he did when guys tried that. I heard Leo tried and a good friend of his got sent to him stuffed in a box. Almost every bone in his body was broken before he died."

"Jesus Christ. Is that true?"

"Yeah, I heard it from a guy who saw it."

"Okay, don't worry, we won't stiff him. How do you get a hold of him?"

"I know a guy in Chicago I can work through. I'll have an answer maybe even by this afternoon. How soon do you want it done?"

"Like I said, just not before the weekend of the Fourth."

"Okay, I'll get the ball rolling."

"What's the guy's name?" Reed asked.

"Charlie Dudek and I don't know if that's his real name. He works out of somewhere in the Midwest or, so I hear," Rask answered.

Ten minutes after he left the meeting in Suite 2007, Victor Espinosa was walking down LaSalle toward downtown Minneapolis. When he was two blocks from the office and certain no one had followed him, he pulled out a flip phone and speed dialed the only number in the phone's directory. It rang once and a familiar voice answered. Without even saying hello, the man said in Spanish, "I'll call you back in two minutes."

In precisely two minutes Espinosa's phone rang and he answered it before the first ring finished.

"What's wrong my friend?" Pablo Quinones, the consejero to El Callado asked still speaking Spanish

"We have a problem," Espinosa calmly told him. He then spent two minutes explaining the meeting he had recently been in and what it was all about.

"I see," Quinones said. "Do you believe it is serious enough that we should take care of it?"

"Yes," Espinosa said while still walking around downtown. "We're too close. Only seven or eight more months. We can't let anything interrupt our plans. But the firm has the Fourth of July party coming up. Don't do anything before that. We don't want this hanging over everybody at the party."

Quinones paused for a moment and then said, "I agree. I'll take care of it. You continue to act as if nothing is happening. Keep me updated."

"Of course, my friend," Espinosa said.

At 4:15 that afternoon, Rask went into Corbin Reed's office and said, "We're all set."

Reed asked, "How much?"

"One fifty," Rask replied.

"He's not cheap, is he?"

"Nope, but he's worth it. You'll see."

"Did you pay the first half?" Reed asked.

"Yeah. It's all set. He acknowledged receipt and we won't hear from him again."

"Okay," Reed sighed.

"What?" Rask asked him.

"Nothing. I didn't want this and I just hope this is it."

"Yeah, me too."

EIGHT

Corbin Reed was at his desk reviewing the website of the Minneapolis Club in downtown Minneapolis. He had a lunch meeting with David Corwin, a sucker he was reeling in, and he wanted to learn as much as he could about the place they were meeting. Founded in 1883, it was a private club for the movers and shakers in the business, civic and social leaders of the Upper Midwest; the place where old and new money came together. The club featured a pool, large exercise facility, private dining and facilities to accommodate their members every need.

"Delivering on that promise has placed the Minneapolis Club amongst the Five Star Platinum Clubs of the world," Corbin quietly read out loud, a snippet from the Club's home page.

"Wow," he continued, "they even let in people of color and women. How progressive of them."

"Who does?" Jordan Kemp asked.

Jordan had entered Corbin's office without knocking, as he always did, just in time to hear Corbin's last remark.

"The Minneapolis Club," Corbin said. "Says so right here on their website."

"Through the front door or the back? Are you thinking about joining?" Jordan asked as he sat down in front of his friend's desk.

"By invitation only. I have a lunch meeting there with David Corwin and Alan Phelps, remember? Alan has been singing our praises and it's time to reel in Corwin. I'd love to get a meeting with the old gal that runs the bulk of the Corwin money, Vivian Donohue. That would be a score…"

"What did we decide about getting too greedy? Stay under the radar. Don't attract too much attention," Jordan reminded him.

"Yeah, yeah, you're right. But you know it isn't only about the money. We'll live extremely well. Sometimes it's the hunt. It's like Marlin fishing. Bringing in a thirteen or fourteen-hundred-pound Blue Marlin. You don't do it to eat the thing. You do it for the sport, for the excitement."

"Okay, go fishing or go grizzly bear hunting with nothing but a knife, macho man, if you need the adrenaline rush. But keep your head when it comes to customers and stay the hell away from Vivian Donahue."

Corbin laughed and said, "Yeah, you're right."

"What time's your meeting?"

"Noon," Corbin replied.

"Where's Rask?"

"Playing compliance officer and finishing up our SEC report with Woody Symanski."

While this conversation was taking place, the compliance officer, or at least the man with the title, Ethan Rask, was in a meeting. Woody Symanski was an agent of the Securities and Exchange Commission. His office was in Chicago at the SEC Regional office which had jurisdiction over Minnesota, among several other states. Rask and Symanski were meeting in a room at the Airport Hilton in Bloomington to wrap up the SEC audit of CAR Securities. Symanski, a lawyer and an accountant, was sitting at a table in the room rechecking the final document for the third time. When he finished, he placed it with the others on the table. Rask was patiently waiting, lying on the room's bed with his coat off and shoes on the floor. He had been watching a tabloid talk show while Symanski finished up.

"Everything look okay?" Rask asked.

"Yep, you're good to go," Symanski said.

"Great," Rask said. He bounced off the bed, clicked off the TV and said, "How do people watch this shit?"

Rask slid his feet into his loafers, stood and in one fluid motion, swung his suit coat over his head and slipped it on. He stepped over to Symanski who rose to meet him. Rask handed him the envelope with one hundred crisp, one hundred dollar bills in it and said, "Sure you don't want a ride to the airport?"

"No, I'll stick around for a while, have lunch and catch a flight around 3:15," Symanski replied. "No reason to hurry back to the office."

"Okay. Stay in touch if anything comes up."

"You'll be fine," Symanski said. "You're too small for anyone to get too excited about."

Corbin Reed had parked his car in a ramp, a block from his destination. The weather was nice and a short walk never bothered him. The Minneapolis Club is located on Second Avenue between Seventh and Eighth Streets. A beautiful, vine covered brick building, the exterior to which looked like it should be located on an Ivy League campus, not a city street in the Midwest.

Reed walked through the brick-columned entryway passed the spike-topped, wrought iron fence. He went inside, introduced himself to the concierge who smiled politely and led him through the walnut paneled interior and expensive furnishings to a small, intimate meeting room. Waiting for him were the two men he was meeting, Alan Phelps and David Corwin.

Phelps was the CFO of a mid-size local internet retailer owned by an investment group in New York. One of his functions was to administer the company's 401(k) plan. Phelps had known Corbin Reed for over two years, had invested the entire 401(k) plan with CAR Securities and never regretted it. In fact, it was a headache that Phelps was delighted Corbin Reed had taken off of his desk. Both the employee's and the employer's 401(k) contribution flowed directly to CAR Securities and the returns, month after month, were solid. It never occurred to Phelps that maybe the returns were a little too solid.

Phelps had met David Corwin by being teamed up with him for a charity golf tournament Phelps' employer sent him to. Both were about the same age and found out they were at Yale at the same time. A friendship ensued and eventually the subject of investing naturally occurred. Phelps could not have been more enthusiastic singing the praises of CAR Securities and his good friend, Corbin Reed. Approximately four months ago, after stalling for several months, Reed agreed to meet this member of the very wealthy Corwin family.

Reed had perfected his sales pitch almost to an art form. In fact, it wasn't a sales pitch at all. What he did was appear very reluctant to accept a new investor. He would make the mark believe that giving money to CAR Securities wasn't just a good investment idea, he would be buying into an exclusive club, very much like the one they were sitting in now.

The two men rose from the comfortable, leather-covered chairs as Reed was shown in. Pleasant greetings took place and before they could retake their seats at the table, a Latino waiter magically appeared.

"Would you like something to drink?" Phelps asked Reed.

"An iced tea will be fine," Reed said to the young man.

For the first half-hour, the three men talked about everything but money. Reed would never be the first to bring up that subject in any form. They talked about the NBA and Stanley Cup finals, the upcoming U.S. Open and even got into sport fishing.

During this time their lunch order was taken and after it was served, sirloins and salads all around, David Corwin broke the ice.

"The last time we met, we talked about me moving money to your firm," he said to Reed.

"I know, I know," Reed said with a sigh, sounding reluctant and disappointed that the subject even came up. He cut a piece of his steak, placed it in his mouth and while chewing the tender meat, dabbed his lips with the linen napkin.

"I still have the same reservations. I'd hate to disappoint someone of your stature…"

Corwin started to speak but was cut off by Phelps who said, "Oh, don't be modest, David. Don't be ashamed of the fact you have money. That's what politicians do: try to make you feel guilty and people who don't have much money envious. They do it to play class-warfare and sucker people into voting for them. It's shameful and most of these politicians that do it have as much money as anyone. They are in the same one percent class they try to denigrate. The whole thing drips hypocrisy."

"I'll tell you what," Reed said placing the napkin back in his lap, folding his hands on top of the napkin and looking into Corwin's eyes. "Like I told you, we're intentionally staying small to give the best customer service. If you really want to do this, we'll take the twenty million and set up an account that I will personally oversee."

Corwin looked at Alan Phelps who raised his eyebrows, nodded his head and smiled back at him. "You won't regret it," Phelps said.

"Thank you," an obviously relieved David Corwin said to Reed.

Reed removed an envelope from his inside coat pocket and said, "I brought along the paperwork necessary to set up your account and an extra copy for you. After we finish lunch, we'll go over everything. I'll get it set up this afternoon and you can have the money wired in at your convenience."

"How soon?" Corwin anxiously asked.

Reed slightly shrugged his shoulders and said, "Tomorrow, for sure. Maybe not today anymore, but we'll be all set for you for a transfer tomorrow. I'll see to it myself."

When Reed arrived back at his office he found Jordan Kemp and Ethan Rask in Rask's office in Suite 2007.

"How'd it go?" Rask asked when Reed walked.

"No problem," he replied. He handed the paperwork to Kemp then said, "Twenty million tomorrow."

"Just stay away from his aunt," Kemp reminded him.

"Relax. What do you think, I'm gonna go out and hit on the old girl? What is she, seventy, seventy-five?" Reed said, keeping it to himself that he had accepted an invitation to the mansion on Lake Minnetonka for this coming Saturday.

NINE

Tony Carvelli expertly slid his sleek, black Camaro into a parking spot in front of his destination. He was on the street in front of an eighty-year-old, two story brick house in South Minneapolis. The house's owner was a computer whiz Carvelli had caught hacking one of Tony's business clients. Instead of turning him into the cops or FBI, Tony scared ten years off of his life and kept him in his pocket. It was fairly often that Tony needed a little off-the-books computer research and the guy he was seeing was great at it. Of course, Tony paid him well and in cash.

Carvelli wasn't much of a morning person. Even though it was 9:30, for Tony, that was early. Despite the time, he was actually running a little late. He had called ahead barely five minutes ago to let the man know he was coming.

Paul Baker, christened Pavel Bykowski by his devout Roman Catholic mother, was a world class hacker. Whatever there was to know about someone, Paul could dig it out of the Internet. Baker's office was the entire second floor of his mortgage-free home. It was mortgage free because Paul had hacked the lender and wiped the debt clean. There had been two bedrooms upstairs and the wall separating them was gone, creating sufficient space for his setup. Unknown, but certainly suspected by Tony Carvelli, Baker had at least a dozen more cash clients, including two FBI agents. It was enough to keep Paul Baker supplied with the latest equipment and all the best weed he desired.

Tony reached the door and before he could knock, Baker shocked him by opening the door first.

"Wow," Carvelli said. "That's a first. Usually I have to break in to find you."

"Ah, kiss my ass, Carvelli. You never had to break-in. Maybe pound on the door a few times," the hacker said as he stepped aside to let Carvelli in.

"What do you have?" Carvelli asked.

Baker picked up a stapled, small stack of papers off of the living room coffee table and handed them to Carvelli. Tony walked into the living room and sat down on the couch. Over the next ten minutes Tony silently paged through the document.

"Interesting and it makes sense," Carvelli said. He held out the document and said, "Make two more copies of this for me, will you Paul?"

"Sure, Tony. And I have extra copies of each of the pictures I pulled offline. They're in the envelope on the table," Baker said.

A few minutes later Baker returned to the living room to find Carvelli on the phone.

"I talked to Marc and he's waiting. I'll be there in ten to fifteen minutes," he heard Tony say after which he ended the call.

"Okay, here you are," Baker said handing him the copies.

Tony stood up, took the documents and said, "Thanks, Paul, see you next time," and started toward the front door.

"Hey dude, you're forgetting something," Baker said.

Tony stopped, raised his head, pointed his nose upward and sniffed the air several times while swiveling his head back and forth.

"Hey, it doesn't smell like cannabis extremis in here. Did you quit or did you figure out how to open a window?"

"Ha, ha very funny. Do you write this stuff yourself? Money?"

"Oh! Yeah, sure," Carvelli said acting as if he forgot. "Here," he continued as he pulled a plain, white envelope from the inside of his baby blue, suede jacket. Inside the envelope were ten fresh, crisp, one hundred dollar bills. "Thanks, Paul. You did good. See ya," and he turned and went out the door.

Twenty minutes later, Tony was seated on one of the client chairs in front of Marc Kadella's desk. Marc was in his executive chair and Maddy Rivers was next to Tony. There was total silence in the room as each of them read a copy of the report Tony brought with him. Being a lawyer and a more careful reader, or just slow, Marc finished last.

Marc sat back, put his hands laced together behind his head, looked first at Tony, then Maddy and said, "Well, isn't that interesting?"

"Yes, indeed," Tony said. "Answers some questions…"

"…and fills in some holes," Maddy added.

"Your guy is very good," Marc told Tony. "When do I get to meet him, this phantom hacker of yours?"

"He's not a people person," Tony said shaking his head. "He's like a one-family dog."

"What are you going to do with this?" Maddy asked Marc.

"Sandbag them. I've scheduled an Omnibus hearing for the 20th, next Monday morning. My forty-eight days are almost up and I hate to continue these things. Since there aren't any witnesses except the two cops, their memories won't fade and they won't change their minds about testifying. No reason to drag it out."

"What about the drugs? Did you get your lab report back?" Maddy asked. Marc had been given a sample of the drugs to test to verify they were cocaine and meth.

"Yeah, got the report yesterday. No surprise there. Unlikely Kubik would have made that mistake. The coke was even cut to street level for sale," Marc answered.

"As much as I love you two and would like to hang out all day, I do have other things to do," Tony said as he stood to leave. He bent down and kissed Maddy on her cheek and stepped to the door.

"You want some money?" Marc asked Tony.

"I'll bill you," he answered.

"What did this report cost?"

"A grand," Tony replied. "Worth it."

"Yeah. I'll need to get more money from the old man. What about you?" Marc asked Maddy.

"See you, later," Tony said as he left.

"Well, yeah, I have an itemized statement," she said. Maddy handed him a two-page document and Marc looked at the bottom line.

"Can I give you two grand today and more when I get more? I have to pay the lab too," Marc said.

"Sure, that will be fine. No problem," she said.

"Okay. Now the retainer is gone, I still owe you and Tony, and I haven't been paid a dime," Marc said while opening the check writing program on his computer.

"You don't need to give me that much right now," Maddy said.

"It's all right. Blake Grant is good for it. I'll send him a statement today."

While Maddy's check was printing off on Marc's small printer, he said, "I want both Newsom and Kubik subpoenaed for 9:00 Monday morning,"

"I'll get them. He's going to be pissed when he sees me after the other night in the bar," Maddy said, smiling.

"You want me to have someone else do it?"

Maddy thought about it then said, "No, maybe, I don't know. It might not be a bad idea. I don't need the hassle over a subpoena."

"Tell you what," Marc said, "I'll call the prosecutor and make sure she's going to call him. If she is, then we don't have to worry about it," Marc said.

"What about his partner?"

Marc thought about it a moment then said, "Let's plan on serving him late Sunday afternoon or early Sunday evening. What about the prosecutor, Gloria Fenton?"

Maddy retrieved her notebook and opened it to the right page.

"Nothing unusual. Graduated from Mitchell five years ago. She spent two years with the State A.G.'s office doing consumer complaints…"

"I'd put a gun in my mouth if I had to listen to that all day," Marc interjected.

"Totally," Maddy laughed. "She's been with Ramsey County ever since. I had lunch with a colleague of hers that I know who said she was thorough, solid, competent and sensible."

"Okay. I'll call her and make sure she'll have Kubik on the stand."

Marc turned his Buick SUV onto the tree-lined driveway of the Corwin Mansion on Lake Minnetonka. Seated in the passenger seat with her left hand lightly placed over Marc's right hand, which rested on the car's gear shift, was Marc's only real relationship since his divorce, Margaret Tennant.

Margaret was a Hennepin County District Court judge. Her chambers and courtroom were located on the seventeenth floor of the giant, granite, glass and chrome Hennepin County Government Center in downtown Minneapolis.

The two of them had been a couple for several years. They recently went through a separation of several months mostly because Margaret had finally asked the big question most divorced or single men dreaded: Where is this relationship going?

Marc had been in a basically loveless marriage, was now divorced and in no hurry to do that again.

Margaret, a still very attractive woman in her early forties, was looking at the calendar and watching birthdays slip away. For her, the vision of old age and loneliness had no appeal whatsoever. If not Marc, then maybe it was time to go fishing elsewhere.

They had recently started dating again, Marc with anxiety about the unresolved *'where is this relationship going'* question still hanging over their heads. But Margaret had missed him and decided, for now, life was better with him as is than without him. She had also been reminded during their separation that the dating pool could use a good dose of chlorine to get rid of the bacteria.

Vivian Donahue, a woman who had become a close acquaintance of theirs was throwing a party for a couple hundred of her friends and family. It was being held at the Corwin Mansion on Lake Minnetonka and an invitation wasn't really an invitation. Vivian Donahue, known to Marc and Margaret as a truly down-to-earth, extremely pleasant woman, expected attendance if she asked you to her home for a social event.

Vivian Corwin Donahue was the current matriarch of a very well known family that was one of the most socially prominent, politically connected and old-money wealthy in Minnesota. The lineage could be traced directly back to the 1840's when the family patriarch, Edward Corwin, immigrated to the mostly empty prairie that was Minnesota at that time, started farming and began building an agricultural empire that was worth billions today. The family itself was no longer involved in Corwin Agricultural but Vivian, as the current head of the family, could still move political mountains and when she called a governor, senator, congressman or mayor, that person had better sit up and pay attention.

The Kadella party of two approached the short line at the door waiting to be admitted. There were two beefy looking security guards checking names off a list of invitees. When they reached the door, Marc showed one of the men his invitation and with a pleasant, 'enjoy your evening' they were allowed in.

A hostess employed by the caterers led them across the marble-covered foyer, through the house and into the back yard. Both Marc and Margaret had been here several times but the place still amazed them. They walked down toward the pool where they saw Vivian greeting guests. When she saw them she immediately almost ran to greet them.

Vivian was in her late sixties, widowed and unmarried. At her age she was what people called a very handsome woman meaning she looked a good twenty years younger and still an attractive woman.

"Wow, you look fabulous, Vivian," Marc said as she took both of his hands and kissed him, to Marc's surprise, lightly on the lips. Vivian turned her attention to Margaret and gave her an affectionate hug while they blew air kisses at each other.

Vivian stood back, looked them over as if examining them then said, "Two of my very favorite people. It's nice to see you together again."

She looped her right arm in Marc's left, Margaret took his right arm and the three of them made their way around the pool to where the tables were set up. At least fifty of the guests turned their heads wondering who the couple were that so obviously attracted the Grand Dame herself.

Marc looked ahead to where they were going and saw Tony Carvelli dressed similarly as Marc in slacks and a light shirt. At the same table were Maddy Rivers with her date and Gabriella Shriqui with her date. Margaret also saw them and waved.

When they were still thirty feet from their friends' table, two men and a model beautiful, very bored looking young woman approached them.

"Aunt Vivian," one of the men said.

"Yes, David?" Vivian asked.

"I want you to meet someone," he continued as Marc and Margaret separated from their host.

"We'll go to the table," Marc told Vivian.

"I'll be there in a minute," she replied.

"Vivian, this is Corbin Reed, the investment guy I told you about with CAR Securities."

"Hello, David has been bragging about you," Vivian said shaking Reed's hand.

"Mrs. Donahue," Reed said hoping she would correct him and tell him to call her Vivian which she deliberately did not do, "I am, well, awestruck, by your home. It is truly fabulous."

This went on for almost two more minutes, Reed gushing over Vivian to the point of nausea. All the while Vivian kept a practiced smile on her face. Finally, Vivian broke it off by politely excusing herself to attend to other guests.

Vivian made her way through the small crowd to Tony's table and sat down between Tony and Maddy and across from Marc and Margaret.

"What is this?" she asked Tony as she picked up his highball. Before he could answer her she drained the almost full glass.

"Vodka tonic," Tony said.

"I needed that," she said as she set the glass on the table. "Be a dear and get me another, please, Anthony."

"Sure," Tony said as he started to rise then stopped. "Never mind, here's an angel, now," He said to the waitress who stopped at their table.

When she left, Vivian asked Tony, "Do you know a man named Corbin Reed?"

"Never heard of him," Tony replied.

Vivian looked over the others and asked the same question. Blank looks and shaking heads were the only response she received. Maddy's date, of course, was Rob Judd. Maddy did not know that CAR Securities, where he worked, stood for Corbin Reed. Rob, his antenna going off, decided to keep quiet about knowing his boss. He could see nothing to be gained by opening his mouth in acknowledgment then being grilled for five minutes. Instead, he looked puzzled and shook his head.

"I may have a job for you, Anthony," she said to her part-time lover. "I just shook his hand and I felt as if I should wash afterwards."

TEN

Rarely, except on TV and in the movies, during the course of a hearing, motion or trial does a lawyer have an opportunity to drive a stake through his opponent's case. If both sides do their job, there should not be any big surprises.

Marc stepped off the elevator on the fourteenth floor of the art deco Ramsey County Courthouse in downtown St. Paul. He was feeling smug, a little too smug he realized. He had an ace to play in his back pocket and he didn't believe the prosecution was aware of it. He also realized that just because it appeared to be an ace, did not mean it would win his client's case. *Keep your head in the game*, he thought to himself as he walked toward the courtroom.

"Morning," Marc said to his client, Kenny and Blake Grant. Marc realized at that moment he had not told them what he was up to and decided not to.

"I'm pretty nervous and I'm not involved at all," Blake Grant confessed. "I don't know how you people do this all the time."

Marc shrugged, smiled and said, "I'm not the one going to jail," looked at Kenny and quickly said, "A little joke. Relax. No one's going to jail today.

"Like I said, this is basically a hearing to decide if the arrest and discovery of the evidence was okay. To satisfy the judge that the cops did not violate the Constitution. I talked to the prosecutor on Friday, Gloria Fenton. She's only going to call Dale Kubik, which is what I was hoping for. He'll get on the stand and testify about why he stopped you and then lie about the grounds he had to search the car."

"What will he say?" Kenny asked.

"He'll claim you are a known drug dealer and he was looking for any drugs that might be in the car," Marc said.

"Doesn't he have to have probable cause more than that?" Blake asked.

"Not really. Probable cause isn't that big a deal to come up with. A very liberal judge might rule he didn't have probable cause but they can get around that too."

"How?"

"They can say they were going to arrest him and impound the car. The car would have been subjected to an inventory search and the drugs would have inevitably been discovered then. All they really needed was grounds for the initial stop. After that, they gotcha. Let's go in."

The three of them entered the courtroom to find the prosecutor, Gloria Fenton and Dale Kubik already seated at a table.

Marc led Kenny through the gate while Blake took a seat in the otherwise empty courtroom. Marc introduced himself to Fenton and Kubik then sat down at the defense table next to Kenny Grant. A minute later he felt his phone vibrate. A text came in from Maddy informing him she and their surprise witness would be there on time.

Judge Helen O'Donnell came out a few minutes after nine. She read the case name and number into the record, noted the defendant's presence and let Fenton and Marc announce their appearances.

"Okay," O'Donnell began. "I understand we're here on an evidentiary matter. You may proceed, Ms. Fenton."

Fenton stood and quickly explained the prosecution's case. Since there was no jury present and O'Donnell knew what she had to say, Fenton kept it brief and to the point.

"Do you wish to add or comment to that, Mr. Kadella?" O'Donnell asked.

Marc stood and said, "Not at this time, your Honor. That's pretty much why we're here."

"How many witnesses do you plan on calling, Ms. Fenton?"

"Two, your Honor. The arresting detective and the lab tech who tested the drugs," she replied.

"What about that, Mr. Kadella? Are you disputing the contents of the two packages allegedly found in the defendant's car?

70

Have you had opportunity to conduct your own, independent lab test?"

"Yes, I have, your Honor and the defense is willing to stipulate that the items are street-level cocaine and methamphetamines," Marc said.

"Good," O'Donnell said turning back to Fenton. "Now the tech doesn't have to testify. That will save a little time."

Blake Grant, seated in the front row behind Marc, leaned over the rail. Marc saw him and swiveled his chair around.

"Who are you, sir?" O'Donnell asked obviously referring to Blake.

Grant stood and politely said, "My name is Blake Grant…"

"The defendant's father?"

"Yes, your Honor."

"You're welcome to be here, Mr. Grant but no interruptions. Is that understood?" O'Donnell firmly said.

An executive vice president of a company the size of 3M is not used to being slapped down. Grant, a little embarrassed, took it well, apologized and sat down.

"Mr. Kadella, take a minute to confer," O'Donnell told Marc meaning tell your client and his dad to keep their mouths shut.

Marc wheeled back to the rail, as did Kenny and Blake asked in a very low whisper, "Why did you let the drugs in?"

"Because we had no way to keep them out. We tested them and they are what the prosecution says. Sometimes giving a little helps with the judge.

"Now," Marc continued looking at Blake, "I'll be polite this time but don't ever question me in court again or get a new lawyer."

"I'm sorry," Blake pleaded. "I'm really, very sorry. It won't happen again, I swear."

Marc and Kenny returned to the table, Kenny silently delighted having witnessed his strong, sometimes domineering father, get his ass handed to him, twice.

Fenton called Dale Kubik to the stand who was sworn in and took the witness chair.

Having thoroughly prepared his testimony by practicing it for over an hour on Friday afternoon, Fenton talked Kubik through the stop, search and arrest in barely half an hour. Most of his testimony was contained in the police report that Marc had almost memorized so there were no surprises. Kubik, having testified many times, made the entire thing sound very routine, almost mundane.

When Fenton was finished, she turned the witness over to Marc.

"How did you know Mr. Grant was a known drug dealer?" This question appears to break the cardinal rule of never asking a question you don't know the answer to. Marc didn't really care what his answer was. He would handle whatever Kubik said.

"Well, just, you know, being a cop on the streets for over sixteen years. We pretty much know all of the bad guys."

"So, detective, what you're saying is the police know who the bad guys are and any time you need to make an arrest you simply go find one, find a reason to pull him over then search for evidence?"

"Objection. Argumentative. The detective said no such thing," Fenton said.

"Actually, he came pretty close to it but I'll sustain the objection," O'Donnell ruled.

"Isn't it true, Detective Kubik, you knew Mr. Grant because you had arrested him three times before. Twice for drug possession and once at a known drug house, yes or no, detective," Marc asked getting serious.

Kubik squirmed a bit and said nothing for several seconds.

"Your honor…" Marc said.

"Answer the question, detective," O'Donnell told him.

"Yes, that's true," he reluctantly agreed.

"You obviously hesitated, detective. Did you think my client would not tell me this?"

"Objection," Fenton said.

"Overruled," O'Donnell quickly told her.

"I, ah, I um didn't, ah, really remember, um, him, at first," Kubik said.

"Nice try," Marc replied.

"Mr. Kadella!" O'Donnell politely scolded him even though silently agreeing with what Marc had said.

"Let's get to the stop, detective. You testified you pulled him over for failing to signal a turn isn't that true?"

"Yes, that's correct."

"Did you give him a ticket?"

"What?" Kubik asked, a little confused.

"A traffic citation, you know, a ticket."

"Oh, no," Kubik answered. "I'm a detective," he added somewhat pleased with himself.

"Did you have your ticket book with you?"

"What? No, I don't have a ticket book, I'm a detective," Kubik repeated.

"How about your partner, Richard Newsom, did he have a ticket book?"

"I don't think so, no. He's a detective. We don't issue traffic citations."

"Over the course of the last month, detective, how many traffic stops have you made?" Marc asked.

"Um," Kubik began while squirming a little more, "I'm not really sure."

"Over the past two years, you've had three different partners, have you not, yes or no, detective?"

"Yes."

"If we bring them in how many traffic stops would they say you made in the past two years?"

"I, ah, don't know," Kubik said.

"Wouldn't it be a grand total of none, Detective Kubik?"

"Oh, I don't know, I don't think it's that," Kubik started to protest.

"Your Honor," Marc said as he stood up, "Would you remind the witness that he's under oath please?"

"You're sworn and under oath, detective," O'Donnell sternly reminded him.

"Okay, none," a relieved Dale Kubik finally admitted.

"Isn't it true that the last time you arrested Mr. Grant, you tried to get him to become an informant for you? That you told him you would make the charges go away if he agreed to become an informant, a snitch for you?"

"I may have, I talk to a lot of guys I arrest and try to turn them. We all do," Kubik answered.

"Really? Isn't it true you worked on him all day, eight hours and he refused, didn't he?"

"I don't remember working on him for eight hours. That's not true. Maybe an hour or two."

"And he turned you down, didn't he?"

"Yes, some do," Kubik shrugged.

"In fact, he told you the same thing over and over, didn't he? What did he say to you?"

"I don't recall," Kubik said squirming again.

"Yes, you do, detective. What did he tell you to do to yourself?"

"Objection your Honor, the witness has answered the question," Fenton almost yelled at the judge.

"Goes to credibility, your Honor," Marc said.

"Overruled," O'Donnell said.

"I don't recall," Kubik said again.

"He told you, over and over, to go fuck yourself. That he'd rather do time than snitch for you, didn't he?"

"Could be, I don't recall."

"Then after eight hours of it, you grabbed him by his shirt, slammed him up against a wall and screamed in his face, 'You spoiled, rich little asshole. I'm gonna make you sorry you were ever born', didn't you, detective?"

"Never happened," Kubik said with a smartass smirk.

"Then two weeks later, after you found out he was given probation and doing rehab, you saw him on the street and saw your chance to get him, didn't you?"

"Objection! Argumentative," Fenton yelled again.

"Sustained. Tone it down Mr. Kadella," O'Donnell ruled.

If looks could kill Marc would be a dead man. Kubik was staring holes in Marc's forehead while thinking about how much fun it would be to get this shyster lawyer in a cell. Unfortunately, Judge O'Donnell saw it and it confirmed what she already believed. Kubik was lying.

"Since you had no intention or way to do so," Marc calmly continued, "you did not give him a ticket, correct?"

"Yes, that's correct," Kubik answered also more calmly.

"Then why did you put him in your car?"

"I told you to check for drugs. He was a known drug dealer. And maybe guns. Drug dealers usually carry guns."

"You were driving your car, not Detective Newsom?"

"That's correct."

"And you parked it, didn't you?"

"Yes, I drove, I parked it," Kubik said as if speaking to a child, a little cop arrogance returning.

"And it was you who told Newsom to put handcuffs on Mr. Grant and take him back to your car. Isn't that true?"

"Yeah, I guess."

"And that's when you planted the drugs in my client's car, while Newsom was too busy and couldn't see you?"

"No, counselor. I did not plant the drugs."

"Were the packages the drugs came in dusted for fingerprints?"

"Um, yes," Kubik reluctantly replied.

"And my client's fingerprints were not found on either package, were they, detective?"

"That doesn't mean …"

"Nonresponsive, your Honor," Marc said.

"Answer the question, detective," O'Donnell said.

"No, they were not," Kubik admitted.

"I have nothing further, your Honor," Marc said in his best dismissive tone.

"Would you like to redirect?" O'Donnell asked a clearly rattled Gloria Fenton.

"Um, yes, your Honor," she answered.

Fenton gathered herself well enough to spend fifteen minutes getting Kubik to restate his case that he was not on a vendetta when he did the stop and search.

While Fenton was trying to rehabilitate her star witness, Maddy Rivers came into the courtroom. When he saw her, Kubik, of course, immediately recognized her and remembered her from the bar. At first he could not process what she could possibly be doing here until she sat down next to Blake Grant behind Marc. Then a cold panic swept over him as he tried to remember what he might have said to her.

Fenton finished her redirect and Marc had no more questions. Kubik was excused and took his seat behind Fenton in front of the rail. O'Donnell asked Fenton if she had any more witnesses and Fenton replied she did not.

"Mr. Kadella, do you have any witnesses to call?"

"Yes, your Honor. The defense calls Alan Niemi."

By this time Maddy was back at the entryway door holding it open for Marc's witness. Unable to serve him the subpoena over the weekend, she was up early and caught him coming out of his apartment this morning.

When Kubik heard the name Alan Niemi, he wondered who this could possibly be. When he turned around to face the door, the blood drained from his face as he watched the man he knew as Richie Newsom, his partner, walk up the center aisle.

"Wait a minute," Kubik jumped up and yelled. "What the hell is this? This is Richie Newsom, my partner. Who the hell is this Alan guy?"

"Alan Niemi," Marc said after standing to address the court.

"What's going on?" Fenton asked. "Who is this man?"

"All right. Everybody sit down and shut up. Mr. Kadella, please explain," O'Donnell said taking control of her courtroom.

"Perhaps we should take a few minutes in chambers, your Honor," Marc said.

"Very well, lawyers in my chambers. Doug," she said to the court deputy, "you keep an eye on everybody. I want no one discussing anything with each other until I come back. Mr. Niemi, please sit up here," she said indicating the witness stand, "and we'll be out in ten minutes."

"All right," O'Donnell said settling into her chair while the lawyers still stood. "What is going on?"

"That man's name is not Richard Newsom, newly minted detective of the St. Paul police. His real name is Sergeant Alan Niemi of the Duluth P.D. your Honor," Marc replied.

"And?" O'Donnell said.

"Sergeant Alan Niemi of the Duluth P.D. Internal Affairs Unit. I'm not sure, but my guess is he's on loan as an undercover investigating your star witness," he said to Fenton who looked as if she needed to sit down, "who is up to his ass in corruption and trouble with the police department."

Marc looked down at a frowning Judge O'Donnell and said, "I've also been investigating Kubik, your Honor. We have a bad cop here."

"Why didn't you bring this to me?" Fenton asked, seriously steaming.

"And give your office a chance to try to fix things and still come after my client? Not likely. First, it's not my job. Second and more importantly, I wanted everybody under oath to expose him, let him perjure himself and force a dismissal."

O'Donnell punched a number on her desk phone, waited a moment then said, "Darlene, bring the guy in the witness chair back here please."

A minute later Alan Niemi joined them.

"Is it true," O'Donnell asked. "Is your name Alan Niemi and are you on loan from Duluth?"

Niemi looked back and forth at the lawyers, shrugged and said, "Yes, your Honor."

"Are you going to tell us on the witness stand that you're doing undercover on Kubik for St. Paul?" Marc asked.

"If asked," he reluctantly agreed. "I won't lie about it."

O'Donnell looked at Fenton and said, "I'm going out there and entertain Mr. Kadella's motion to dismiss with prejudice to refile. A motion I will grant. You can put your objections on the record for appeal but I will include that your detective, in my opinion, planted those drugs and committed perjury."

Ten minutes later, after O'Donnell dismissed the case, Dale Kubik, knowing his life as a cop was done, sat fuming. While Marc accepted congratulations from the Grants, Kubik sat staring at Maddy Rivers, who he blamed for exposing him, with a burning hatred in his heart.

ELEVEN

"Hello, David," Vivian Donahue said to her nephew. David Corwin was in the foyer of the Corwin Mansion and his aunt was approaching him with, as usual, a warm smile on her face and her arms extended. The two of them gave each other a very warm and genuinely affectionate embrace. Vivian then took her nephew's arm and the two of them walked together through the big house into the library.

Of all of the Corwins and Donahues of David's generation, David was secretly Vivian's favorite. Too many of his cousins were a little too self-indulgent and their progeny, Vivian's Grandnephews and nieces, the millennials, were proving to be totally self-absorbed slackers. But David and a few others were genuinely hard-working, solid citizens.

The two of them sat opposite each other on the matching sofas set perpendicular to the fireplace. But before she sat down, Vivian poured coffee from the silver antique pot on the coffee table between them. Vivian took her seat and straightened her skirt while David sipped his coffee and patiently waited.

"David," she began, "I had a very difficult time wrestling with the decision to ask you here to meet with me. To be blunt, of all of my nieces and nephews, I trust your judgment above all of them."

"Well, thank you, Vivian. I appreciate that," a slightly startled David responded at the compliment.

"And I am very reluctant to stick my nose into your business," Vivian added.

"You never have, Vivian. Out with it. What's on your mind?" David asked as he leaned forward, placed his cup in the saucer on the table and looked directly at his aunt.

"Very well," she said. "How well do you know this Corbin Reed person you introduced me to at the party?"

"Personally? Not well at all. He was introduced to me through a mutual friend, a man you know, Alan Phelps. Alan's been investing with him for a couple of years and he swears by him.

Exceptional returns. Alan told me CAR Securities has a couple of genius analysts that are gods at anticipating market fluctuations, which is how they stay ahead of the curve and are able to get steady, solid, twelve to thirteen percent returns. Alan told me he hasn't pulled a dime out of CAR Securities. In fact, he has transferred his entire portfolio into his account with them.

"Tell me about Corbin Reed," Vivian said.

David continued by explaining that Phelps had bragged about him for months. Then David finally gave in and asked to meet Reed and was impressed by the man. Over the next several months, the three of them met occasionally and not once did Reed ever bring up the subject of money, investing or CAR Securities.

"When I finally became convinced, after reviewing a year's worth of Alan's account statements, I practically had to beg Corbin to take my money. Why, what's wrong?"

Vivian sighed, set her cup down for David to refill then finally said, "At the party, when you introduced me to him, for lack of a better way of putting it, I got a really bad vibe from him. I know, that's my generation kind of statement," Vivian said with a smile when her nephew gave her a dubious look.

David thought for a moment before saying, "Aunt Vivian, I have the greatest respect for you and your instincts, you know that. Actually, I'm glad you told me this. And, because of that, I'm going to keep a close eye on this."

"You're not offended with your old aunt sticking her nose into your business?" Vivian smiled.

"Of course not," David replied. "I trust your judgment."

"May I ask how much you gave them?" This, of course, was not a request but a pleasant command.

"Twenty million," David replied.

"Twenty million dollars is still a lot of money, David."

"Yes, ma'am," he replied.

"Would you be terribly offended if I did a little snooping and checked this man and his company out myself?" Vivian asked.

"Of course not. In fact, with your 'bad vibe' I'd appreciate it if you did. You have resources I don't have. Please, go ahead," David sincerely replied.

Vivian smiled and said, "I didn't get a chance to talk to you the other night. How are Mitchell, Jennifer and Scott doing?"

"They're great," David replied. "You know, Mitchell starts high school this year," he added referring to his oldest son.

"Oh my god, really? Time passes too fast," Vivian said.

For another twenty minutes they chatted about family and other small talk before David finally excused himself.

Later that same day, Vivian received a phone call from Tony Carvelli. He told her he had some preliminary news to tell her from his investigation into Corbin Reed and CAR Securities Management. Vivian invited him over for dinner and Tony accepted agreeing to a 6:00 o'clock time.

Carvelli reached for the mansion's front doorbell and before he could push it, the door was flung open and a beautiful, twenty-year-old girl jumped on him. Adrienne Donahue, Vivian's favorite granddaughter, wrapped her arms around his neck and kissed his cheek while laughing at his shocked expression.

"Gotcha," she said, still laughing.

Holding his right hand over his heart feigning a heart attack, Tony said. "Will you stop that? One of these times I'm going to flop down on the ground with a real heart attack."

"No chance," Adrienne smiled. "You're too much of a stud."

"Too much of a what?" they heard Vivian icily ask from the doorway.

"Oh, oh," Adrienne smiled at her grandmother then looked back at Tony, winked and said, "She hates it when I try to steal her boyfriends."

Tony cringed at the precocious kid while Vivian said, "Go to your room, young lady."

"I'm actually heading out," Adrienne said as she started down the eight semicircular, granite steps to the parking area in front of the mansion. "Have a nice night you two. Don't wait up."

Vivian led Tony by the arm into the mansion toward a small, intimate dining room. As they walked along she said of Adrienne, "That child is incorrigible."

"And an absolute delight, you love her to death and enjoy having her around for the summer," Tony added.

"All true," Vivian laughed.

While they enjoyed their dinner, Vivian told Tony about her meeting and conversation with her nephew, David. When they finished eating and Vivian had completed her story, she suggested coffee on the patio by the pool. Having sent the household staff home, Vivian served the coffee herself.

The two of them were stretched out in patio lounge chairs facing Lake Minnetonka and quietly enjoying their coffee and the view of the lake. After several minutes, Vivian broke the silence.

"No matter how long I've been here I still love this site. A pleasant summer evening and that view of the lake. I'll tell you what," she continued, "I know this is very snobbish and elitist, but if I had my way I'd ban motorized boats from the lake after six P.M. Just sailboats. I love to watch them silently glide past."

"Especially ones like that one," Tony said referring to the two-masted boat directly in front of them.

"You mean the one with the four young girls in bikinis?" Vivian slyly asked.

"Oh, gosh, I didn't notice them," Tony poorly lied.

"Okay, time to stop watching the girls and tell me what you found out," Vivian smiled as she held out her cup for Tony to refill.

Tony poured the coffee then swiveled around to sit on the edge of the lounge chair facing her. He pulled a small notebook from his back pocket, flipped it open and began.

"Corbin Andrew Reed. Age 42, single, no kids, never married. CEO and founder of CAR Securities Management, LLC. It's his initials that make up the acronym, CAR. Graduate of Penn

State University with a BA in finance. Then he got an MBA from the Wharton School of Business."

Tony sipped his coffee and then placed the cup on the small, wrought iron table between them.

"He worked on Wall Street for almost ten years for four of the larger firms. His employment history with them is a little murky. Not sure why he moved around so much. Don't know if he moved on or got fired but we're still digging."

"Yes, do that," Vivian said. "There could be something worth knowing."

"Founded CAR Securities about four or five years ago after moving from New York to our fair city." Tony continued.

"Or, was run out of town," Vivian dryly said.

"Ah, let's not jump to conclusions," Tony said. "At this point, he may be perfectly legitimate."

"You're right, sorry. Please go on."

"Mostly personal stuff. Lives well. Probably makes a good living. Nothing to raise any flags yet. Single guy making a lot of money.

"Next up is the chief investment officer — I have information on all of the main principals of CAR Securities — is Jordan Kemp. Forty-seven years old, has a BA and MBA from Dartmouth. A BA in economics and an MBA in statistical analysis.

"He worked for five years teaching various mathematics courses at his alma-mater…"

"Probably while working on a PhD," Vivian said.

"Likely," Tony agreed. "Then he abruptly left academia for the greener pastures of Wall Street. Bear Stearns snatched him up. I don't have anything on him during those years yet."

"I know some people I can contact to find this out," Vivian said. "I'll see what I can find out about Corbin Reed also."

"Ah, okay," Tony replied. "The rest I have so far is personal stuff. Pretty mundane. Married, a couple of kids, one out of high school but not in college, one about to finish up at St. Thomas Academy.

"Next is a guy named Walter Pascal. He heads up the bond department. Same kind of academic pedigree, you want the detail?"

"Yes, please."

"Okay. BA from University of Virginia, MBA from Penn. Went to work on Wall Street right out of graduate school. Worked for a couple different firms. The last one was Bear Stearns."

"Where he likely met Jordan Kemp," Vivian said.

"Probably," Tony agreed. "Wait a minute," he said then flipped back several pages in his notes. He found what he was looking for then said, "God, I'm an idiot. Corbin Reed, last employment on Wall Street," he stopped and looked at Vivian.

"Bear Stearns," she said.

"You got it. I can't believe I didn't notice it before. Anyway, moving on, Pascal is forty, divorced, three kids. The ex has not remarried and Walter lives pretty modestly for a guy who heads up a department of a successful investment firm. Has a townhouse in south Minneapolis with a tax value of two-hundred-fifty grand and a maxed out mortgage."

"Alimony and child support," Vivian commented. "Where does she live?"

"Chicago," Tony answered.

"See what you can find out about the divorce."

"Vivian, other than they all worked on Wall Street, there's really nothing here to raise any red flags. Are you sure you want to keep digging?"

"Yes. I had lunch yesterday with an old friend, a man who heads up a medium size financial group in Minneapolis. He knew all about CAR Securities and is very leery of them. He believes their returns are a little too good to be true. Something's wrong here and I have a favorite nephew who has invested quite a bit of money with them. So, to answer your question, yes, we'll keep digging."

"Okay. There is something my guy found that raised my eyebrows a bit. Pascal and another one of the principals, a guy named Victor Espinosa, took a one-day trip to Panama at the end of May."

"Why would they go to Panama for one day?" Vivian said, mostly rhetorically to herself.

"The best guess would be for a meeting with someone," Tony replied.

"Who is Victor Espinosa?"

"Mexican citizen. Age forty-five. Listed as executive vice-president of CAR. No history on Wall Street but he did work for an investment outfit in Chicago that collapsed in '08. I could find no personal history other than school in California, UCLA and Stanford. I'll keep working on him."

"So, he's a Mexican citizen and he and Pascal went to Panama for a meeting. What do you think? In your gut."

"Money laundering," Tony replied. "It's an obvious connection."

"Do you think you should take a trip to Panama? Would it be worthwhile?"

"Let my guy do some things on his computer first," Tony said. "Maybe he can find out if there was someone in Panama at the time they might have been meeting."

"Yes, I'd rather. These drug cartel people are barbarians. I'd rather not have you down there poking around. Who is this hacker of yours and why can't I get him to come to work for me?"

"Trust me, Vivian. You don't want to be anywhere near this guy's world."

"You're being very selfish, Anthony," she said giving him a sly look.

Ignoring her, Tony continued, "Last but not least, is Ethan Rask. He is listed as the chief compliance officer and my guy came up with nothing on him. And I mean nothing. As far as we can tell, he dropped out of the sky and landed at CAR Securities and has been there since the beginning."

"How is that possible?" Vivian asked.

"It means Ethan Rask is not the man's name. We can't even find an address, phone number, car ownership or bank account for him."

"He's a criminal," Vivian said.

"Yes, that would be the obvious conclusion. He has no securities licenses and as far as we can find out, no background in the financial world, at all."

"Now what?" Vivian asked.

"Now I'll try to get a photo of him and have my guy run facial recognition programs to see if he can find out who he is."

"Your guy has facial recognition programs?" Vivian asked with a touch of sarcasm and skepticism. "You mean he's going to hack the FBI to use theirs."

"I don't ask questions I don't want to know the answer to," Tony smiled.

The next morning, while the two lovers were having a light breakfast, Tony asked Vivian, "Why did your nephew, what's his name, invest with CAR Securities? Tell me how this came about?"

Vivian told Tony what David had told her about meeting Corbin Reed through a friend and their subsequent conversations.

"That's exactly how a good con man would do it, Vivian," Tony said when she finished. "He strings you along making you believe he's not interested in your money until finally, you're practically begging him to take your money. You're right," he continued, "there is something a little fishy going on here."

TWELVE

Charlie Dudek was a professional killer who lived a quiet life in a suburb of Kansas City, Missouri. One of the things that made Charlie so effective was the fact that he was about as ordinary looking as any man could be. At five-feet-eleven inches, one-hundred sixty-five pounds, with his normal physique, he was the epitome of the average American male. His light brown hair was totally unnoticeable and if five people saw him and described him, there would be five different descriptions. And, if his neighbors knew what he did, they would be shocked down to their toes.

What did not show from his appearance was his background. Charlie had spent ten years in the Army, the last four with the super-secret Delta Force. He had been trained by the very best instructors to kill in so many different ways he could not remember all of them. Plus, Charlie was also absolutely fearless. During the battle for Tora Bora in Afghanistan, when the U.S. was hunting Osama bin Laden following the 9/11 attacks, it was Charlie who went into the caves and only Charlie who ever came out.

While serving in the army, he had been given several IQ, aptitude and psychological tests, including the Minnesota Multiphasic Personality Inventory. The IQ tests came back consistently around 130 and his aptitude testing placed him in the upper two percent for analytical reasoning. The MMPI came back showing Charlie as a borderline sociopath meaning he could function quite normally in society but had very little empathy.

The psychologist who interpreted his tests joked that Charlie would probably make a good lawyer. Unknown to Charlie, the psychologist was an employee of the CIA. A few days before Charlie was set to leave the army, two CIA recruiters paid him a visit. Unfortunately for the government, Charlie had made a friend, or at least as close to a friend as Charlie was capable of making, named Anthony Scarpino from Brooklyn, New York.

Scarpino had written a letter to his favorite uncle, Louis Scarpino, and told Uncle Lou about a special talent he should meet. Anthony set up an interview with Uncle Lou for Charlie and when

Charlie found out how much he could make as a freelance hitman, the CIA never saw him again.

Charlie was also very expensive. You had to know someone with certain connections to even contact Charlie. And you did not hire Charlie to knock off your spouse or a rival drug dealer. He was a true professional.

Over the years he had turned his profession into an art form. Charlie had learned disguises, makeup and little tricks to alter his appearance enough to fool any witness. When Charlie Dudek came to town, he was the rider on a pale horse and death would certainly come with him.

Charlie loaded his nondescript, two-year-old Camry with his luggage and a few moments later was pulling out of his garage. He stopped in the driveway, opened his window and waved to his neighbor. She turned from her gardening and the two of them amiably chatted for a minute, Charlie explaining he was going on a business trip. The neighbor assured him they would, as usual, keep an eye on his house. Several neighborhood kids were playing, running back and forth between Charlie's yard and the neighbor's. He leaned his head out of his window and, smiling and waving, yelled at the kids to watch out. They all stopped, waved goodbye and yelled "Bye, Charlie" back at him as he backed out of the driveway.

He started down the mid-American suburban street and waved to a couple more neighbors. As he did, he made a quick inventory check in his head. Behind and under the back seat were the tools of his trade. He had three handguns, all with sound suppressors, several knives and two rifles including his favorite, a Remington 700 SPS Tactical with scope and suppressor. Charlie could hit a man in the forehead at five hundred yards with it and be gone before anyone knew where the shot came from. In fact, he had done just that several times.

Charlie drove down the entrance to northbound I-35 and calculated his ETA. At a steady 60 mph he should be at his motel on the Bloomington Strip, a place he still remembered having stayed there before, around three P.M. With over a week to go before the job was to be done, he had plenty of time to prepare.

While Charlie Dudek was on the road heading north to Minnesota, Dale Kubik and his union lawyer were waiting in the hall after his review board hearing. The fiasco of the arrest and omnibus hearing of Kenny Grant had brought an immediate suspension for Kubik pending the Review Board hearing. His lawyer, an ex-cop with a lot of experience defending cops, had put on a good argument on his behalf. Kubik's fate with the St. Paul PD was now in the hands of the three Board members. They had several options open to them. They could suspend, fine, fire or none of the above and put him back on duty.

"What do you think?" Kubik asked the question everyone asks their lawyer while waiting for a verdict.

"I don't know, Dale," the man, Howard Klein, said even though he knew Kubik's fate was likely sealed.

"I'm gonna get the bitch," Kubik quietly muttered.

"What? I'm sorry, Dale, I didn't get that," Klein asked even though he had heard him quite clearly.

"Oh, ah, nothing, Howie," Kubik said a little too quickly.

For the next ten minutes the lawyer sat patiently on a hard, wooden bench while Kubik paced. They were alone in the hall, the lawyer sitting with his legs casually crossed while Kubik paced and worried.

Finally, the hearing room door was opened by a deputy and the two men went back inside. Barely five minutes later, a furious Dale Kubik crashed through the hallway door. Steaming, he jammed his thumb repeatedly into the down button of the elevator for three or four seconds then impatiently hurried off to the stairway.

Even though Howie Klein had warned him this was likely to happen, Kubik had been in denial right up to the reading of their decision. Without even waiting for the senior police official to finish speaking, Kubik stood up and stomped toward the door.

Dale Kubik's career as a police officer was finished. And, at least in his mind, he knew who was to blame.

Paul Quinones sipped his morning coffee while standing in front of the ten feet by twenty feet, hurricane proof, bay window overlooking the Gulf of Mexico. He was at one of the homes owned by El Callado, this one on a beach of the Yucatan twenty miles from Cancún. He was dressed in nothing except silk, black boxers, the better to admire himself in the window's reflection. At forty-four, his waist was still a size 32, his stomach flat and he made sure he spent several hours per week with his personal trainer.

Quinones had told his jefe he needed a few days to relax and recharge. El Callado not only agreed but flew him to the Yucatan and let him use his house.

The two young prostitutes who had serviced him well the previous evening were long gone and he had the house to himself. Having finished his coffee, Quinones went out to the patio, stripped out of his shorts and quickly dove into the pool. For the next twenty minutes he swam leisurely laps, then did ten minutes as fast as he could. When he was done, the problem that had been nagging him in the back of his mind was, unfortunately, still there unresolved.

After showering and dressing, he relaxed in front of the big window to read his newspapers; a half a dozen each day. When he started on the third one, the phone on the glass and chrome table to his right went off. Quinones checked the number and, quite relieved, quickly answered it.

Instead of going to El Callado with the problem in Minnesota, Quinones decided to resolve it himself. El Callado would have handled it in his usual crude manner. He would have sent a team of mindless thugs, four or five at least, who would have left a pile of bodies in their wake. The man's ignorance of America was astonishing and Quinones would not trust the fool to handle this. No, no need for a massacre when a surgical strike was the best option.

"How are you, my friend?" Quinones asked.

"I am well, Paul," the man answered. "What can I do for you?"

"I have a job for you. It needs to be handled quietly, with discretion. Are you available for the next two to three weeks?"

"For you, of course," the assassin replied.

"Good, this is what I need you to do…"

THIRTEEN

Marc Kadella was at his desk trying to finish up a divorce decree to submit to the court. The case had been one of those exceptionally acrimonious ones that he hated to handle. It should not have been. There were no minor children and the lawyers had exchanged a complete list of assets very early on. The only thing to do was equitably divide the money. The case was heated and dragged out longer than it should have because of Marc's client who was the wife, and the husband's lawyer.

The husband, Otis Carr, was a now retired judge from Ramsey County. His soon-to-be ex-wife, Claudia was the proverbial woman scorned. Otis had carried on an affair with a married woman going back almost twenty years. The woman was the recently disbarred former Ramsey County attorney, Shayla Parker. Ironically, it was Marc or, more precisely a client of his, who made the affair public at the end of a trial Marc had done. Judge Carr presided over the case and, for personal reasons, Marc's client sent proof of the affair to the St. Paul newspaper.

Claudia Carr wanted to drain every drop of blood from her philandering husband. Marc did all he could to calm her down to get the divorce finished as painlessly as possible. Unfortunately, Otis Carr's lawyer did all he could to keep things stirred up to bill more hours to it.

"Well, thank God it's over," Marc quietly said to himself as he signed the decree.

He swiveled around in his chair and opened the window behind his desk. Marc took a minute to look down on Charles Avenue, enjoy the fresh air and sunshine and watch the light, midday traffic go by.

"Is that the Carr decree?" he heard Connie Mickelson ask.

"Yeah," Marc acknowledged as he swiveled back around to look at her.

"How much did that snake, Torkelson, bill Otis?" she asked referring to Jared Torkelson, the husband's lawyer.

"Over twenty-five grand," Marc replied. "This thing should have been done for less than a third of that."

"I'm not surprised," Connie said. She sat down in one of Marc's client chairs and continued, "Maybe Otis will file a complaint on him."

"I doubt it," Marc shrugged. "They don't like getting involved in fee disputes."

"What are you up to this weekend?" Connie asked. It was the Thursday before the long Fourth of July weekend. The Fourth was on a Monday this year.

"I'm going up to Brainerd," Marc said referring to a popular resort area a couple of hours north of the Twin Cities, "with Margaret. There are several other couples, mostly friends of hers from the Hennepin County bench that will be there, too."

"Oh, oh," Connie said. "The long weekend relationship killer. You know these other people?"

"Most of them, yeah."

"You worried?"

"About what?" Marc asked.

"Things between you and Margaret."

"You know, I miss her when she's gone, but…" Marc said, letting the word 'but' hang in the air.

"But you haven't completely let go of Mackenzie," Connie said.

"Maybe," Marc somewhat agreed. "I'm mostly just getting very comfortable being single. There's something to be said about not having anyone to answer to all the time."

The intercom on Marc's phone buzzed and when he answered it, Sandy told him his ex-wife was calling. Marc thanked her, told Connie, who quietly slipped out and closed his office door. As she left Marc answered the call.

"Hello," he said.

"Hi, I was wondering what you are up to this weekend?" she asked.

"I have plans, Karen. Why? What's up?" Marc asked.

"Oh, nothing. We're having a little party Sunday. No big deal just a backyard barbeque kind of thing. I thought maybe, if you didn't have plans, you could come."

"Thanks, but I have plans, sorry," Marc politely replied.

"Okay, no problem. Maybe we could get together for lunch some time," she said.

"Ah, sure, we'll see. Listen, I have to get back to work. I'll talk to you later, okay?"

"Sure, bye. Oh, and Marc, have a nice weekend."

"Yeah, you too."

He hung up the phone and with a puzzled expression stared at it for almost thirty seconds.

"What the hell was that all about?" he whispered to himself. There was a soft knock on his door and before he could respond, Connie re-entered his office. She closed the door and sat down again in the same chair.

"How are you two getting along?" Connie asked.

Marc, still thinking about the phone call, stared at her without saying anything.

Connie passed her hand before his face and said, "Hey, are you here?"

"Oh, ah, yeah, sorry. We get along fine. That was a weird call, though. She invited me over on Sunday. They're having a picnic kind of thing."

"Why is that weird?"

"In all the years we were married, I don't remember her inviting me to anything."

"Maybe she's just being nice."

"Karen? No, she wants something. It will be interesting to find out what," Marc said.

Charlie Dudek took the elevator in the LaSalle Building up to the twentieth floor. He had been in the Twin Cities for a couple of days and was doing part of his pre-mission planning and scouting, running the risk of being seen, recognized and later identified. However minimal that risk was he had gone to the trouble of putting on a simple disguise. A mustache, glasses, a little nose putty and a black baseball cap without a logo. A logo on a hat could be something someone might notice and remember.

The target's place of work was not very likely to be the best venue for the job. On the other hand, Charlie was nothing if not thorough and professional. He could never be sure until he checked for himself. Besides, he still had several days to wait before completing the assignment.

When Charlie entered the elevator car on the ground floor, a half dozen people joined him. When he got off on twenty, he was relieved to be alone. The sign on the wall pointed him in the right direction toward Suite 2010. Instead of going into the office right away Charlie walked past and wandered around the entire floor as if looking for something. When he got back to CAR Securities, he opened the heavy glass door and walked right in.

"May I help you?" the receptionist smiled and asked him.

"Um, yeah, I hope so," Charlie replied acting a little uncertain. "I was looking for a law office," he continued giving her the name of a firm on twenty-one he had seen on the building's directory.

"I believe they're on twenty-one," the young woman politely said.

"Oh, I thought it was twenty," Charlie replied. He very deliberately looked around the open office space behind the receptionist's desk. "Nice place," he said. "What do you guys do here?" he asked.

"We're an investment firm," she answered.

Charlie looked around again in time to see Rob Judd walking by with a stack of papers in his hand. Charlie casually watched him but gave the impression he was not watching him at all.

"Well, if I ever get any money, maybe I'll come see you," Charlie told her as Rob passed from his view. "Well thanks," he smiled, backed up and walked out; mission accomplished.

While Charlie was waiting for the elevator to take him up to twenty-one, he thought about what he had seen. *Not a very good place for it and the guy was too young for a drug induced heart attack*, he thought. *No, the place you saw is still the best spot,* he continued thinking as he got on the elevator.

In case someone was watching him, Charlie rode up to twenty-one. Once there, he would take the stairs down and back to his car.

Rob had been waiting all morning for an opportunity to see his boss, Walter Pascal. He had seen him come in with Corbin and Jordan Kemp, probably from across the hall, a few minutes ago. Rob waited long enough for Walter to get in his office then picked up the documents he wanted to show him and headed across the floor to see him. As he passed behind the receptionist's desk, he paid no attention to the man in the black baseball cap who was talking to her.

Rob knocked on Walter's door, waited one second and then turned the knob as he heard Walter tell him to come in.

"Got a minute?" Rob asked.

"Sure, Rob," Walter said. "What's up?"

Rob sat down and set the paperwork on Walter's desk. "You remember I told you about the rising default rate on our mortgage backed securities?"

"Sure. It was almost five percent. A little high but not really cause for concern you said."

"Right. Well, I think there may be cause for concern. I went through all of them over the last few evenings and it is now over six percent."

"You went through all of what?" Walter asked a little puzzled.

"All of our mortgage backed securities…"

"All three hundred and forty million dollars worth? That must have been quite a task," Walter said.

"Yeah, I guess. Well, whatever," Rob said brushing off the comment. "Anyway, I know these are coming through you but maybe we should think about getting our customers and the firm out of these. Plus, you and the principals need to be aware of this. If ours are indicative of the market, there could be another real estate crash like in '07 and '08. If the default goes to eight or nine percent, it will happen. The interest payments on these are already barely covering the defaults."

"I know. I can see that for myself," Walter said while he reviewed Rob's spreadsheet. "Tell you what, leave these documents, I'll look them over and meet with Corbin and the others."

Slightly taken aback at Pascal's almost casual attitude about the coming crash, Rob simply agreed and quietly left.

Maddy silently worked on her shrimp and chicken salad while waiting to see if Rob was going to come back to Earth. He was seated opposite her, but once again seemed a thousand miles away. Maddy put her fork down, dabbed the napkin to her lips and picked up her wine glass. She sipped her wine and shifted her eyes between Rob and a man seated alone across the room. She believed the man had glanced over at them several times. Maddy was quite used to men looking at her, but this was different. He was not looking at her, she believed, but Rob.

"I've been poor company again, haven't I?" Rob finally said.

"Well, yes, to be honest, you have."

"I'm sorry. I've been very preoccupied. Something's wrong at work and I can't put my finger on it."

"Maybe it's time you told me about it," Maddy said.

Rob put his utensils down, folded his hands on the table, looked her in the eyes thinking it over then said, "You're right."

For the next hour, Rob spilled it all. Everything he could think of about the firm. The secret room across the hall, the troubling securities he had shown to Walter; Pascal's almost uninterested attitude and the concerns that Pat McGarry had expressed.

"And shortly after he told you about his misgivings both he and his girlfriend die in a hiking accident?" Maddy asked.

"The suspicious cop," Rob smiled and squeezed her hand.

"Seems a little too coincidental," she replied.

"Maybe," he agreed. "But the authorities checked it out and ruled it an accident."

"Do you think they're up to something illegal?" Maddy asked.

"Between you and me, probably, or at least they're pushing the envelope. But almost every investment firm does. The SEC's investigation department is a joke. If you think Congress and lobbyists have a revolving door going, it's nothing compared to Wall Street and the SEC. I believe the SEC is where people go to make employment contacts with the big boys to land big bucks jobs when they leave the SEC."

"What do you want to do about it?" Maddy asked.

"I think I'll keep my eyes and ears open and my mouth shut. That's all I can do for now," Rob replied.

"You see that man over there?" Maddy asked. "Don't turn around."

"How am I supposed to see him if I don't turn around?"

"There's a man eating by himself," Maddy continued ignoring the smart-ass question. "Oh, wait, he's leaving. Quick, turn around and take a look."

Rob did as she requested and got a good look at the man.

He turned back to Maddy and said, "Yeah, so?"

"Do you recognize him?"

"No, don't think so, why?"

"He's looked over here at us a few times…"

"No doubt checking you out," Rob smiled.

"No," Maddy shook her head. "I know *that* look all too well. I think he was looking at you."

"Really? Interesting," Rob said. "Well, I don't know who he is. Are you coming over tonight?" he asked trying to change the subject.

"And I'm certain I've seen him before, recently. I can't remember when or where but I'm pretty sure it was two or three times over the past week or two," Maddy said.

Rob turned toward the door just as the man was leaving. "Sorry, I don't know him," he lied again.

"Are you working tomorrow?"

"Yeah, but it's the Friday before a long weekend. Most of the hired hands will be in but the big dogs won't be around long."

"Okay, I'll come over," Maddy gave him a sly look and added, "and you better not be tired, bub."

FOURTEEN

Dale Kubik waited impatiently in his car in the restaurant's parking lot. He was following the woman he blamed for ruining his life. The police Review Board had ruled against him and recommended his termination from the job. Ever since then he had allowed his ego to fuel the flame against the conniving bitch who had caused his problems whom he blamed for being fired, Madeline Rivers. Of course, he was appealing the decision but his lawyer told him it was a long shot, at best.

Kubik was also convinced that certain people, cops envious of him, were also involved. How else would the Rivers woman know where to find him to ply him with liquor? These other cops pointed her at him but she was the one. And she was going to pay.

Rivers and her boyfriend had been in the restaurant almost an hour and a half. While Kubik waited, he sipped scotch from a leather encased, glass flask he carried with him. He had an excellent view of her car and the restaurant's door. Being a detective for many years, sitting on a stakeout was very familiar to him. He even still had a pee bottle in the car which he had used about a half hour ago.

Kubik's patience finally paid off. He watched the couple come through the doors holding hands. They parted at the curb, each going to their own cars.

Kubik was well aware of Maddy's background. He knew she was ex-Chicago PD and a licensed investigator. Tailing her was a job that required care and finesse. From what Kubik had learned, if she thought she was being followed, she would not be shy about stopping to find out why. Or, more likely, she could lose you without much effort.

It was barely two minutes after they left the restaurant that Kubik realized she was not headed home. Maddy was obviously following the boyfriend and knowing his address, Kubik was able to drop back in traffic so as not to be noticed. Fifteen minutes later, from almost two blocks behind them, Kubik saw them pull into the parking lot of Judd's condo a block west of Lake Calhoun in

Minneapolis. As he drove past he saw them go in the front door, Maddy carrying a small overnight bag. Kubik continued along the street without stopping, took another swallow from his flask and smiled to himself. An idea he had been working on in his alcohol-soaked imagination completed itself. He smiled with the realization that what he would do to her would hurt her far more than she hurt him.

Fortunately for Dale Kubik, Charlie Dudek did not notice him drive past Rob Judd's condo. Charlie was also watching the couple but was only interested in one of them so he had left the restaurant ahead of everyone. He was in the condo's parking lot two minutes before Rob and Maddy and watched them go in. If Charlie had known about Kubik, it's likely Dale Kubik would not have seen another sunrise.

Early the next morning, Friday, shortly after 6:00, all five principals of CAR Securities met in the soundproof conference room in Suite 2007. The topic of the meeting was the default rate discovered by Rob Judd that he presented to Walter Pascal the previous afternoon.

Walter had tried to get everyone together the day before but was unsuccessful. Since it was his news, his department and his employee, Corbin Reed let him lead the discussion. He quickly filled everyone in on what Judd found.

"If these are triple A and double A mortgages backing these securities," Victor Espinosa began, "why is the default rate so high? The housing and real estate markets have been stable for years. I don't understand."

"I don't either," Ethan Rask said.

Corbin, Walter and Jordan Kemp knew the answer and the three of them silently looked back and forth at each other.

"What the hell is going on?" Espinosa asked, seeing the looks the three men gave each other.

"Look, don't take this personally, we decided the fewer people that knew, the better," Corbin said.

"You've been keeping something from us?" Rask asked, a trace of anger in his voice.

"Tell them, Walter," Corbin said.

"These are not Triple A and Double A mortgages. They're packaged and sold that way to get past the Feds. They is a significant amount of Double B and B rated tranches in them. Some double and triple A but mostly B rated mortgages."

"Seriously?" an incredulous Espinosa said. "How is that possible? I thought that was no longer allowed. That they were not even available on the market."

"Oh, they're available," Pascal shrugged.

"At a very nice discount and they pay four to five points higher than triple A backed securities. We've been using the returns to cover cash flow," Corbin added.

"Do the rating companies know about this? Are they in on it?" Espinosa asked.

"We've never tried to find out," Pascal answered.

"Don't ask, don't tell," Jordan Kemp added.

"How can this still be going on?" Ethan Rask asked. "I thought the big boys were done with this."

Jordan Kemp smugly looked at Espinosa and said, "Let me put it this way, Victor. If you had a serious gambling problem and you could go to Vegas with an unlimited bankroll, would you go?"

"Sure," Espinosa said.

"And, on top of that, you could go knowing the government would make good on your losses, you'd have a great time doing it," Corbin said.

"Too big to fail," Rask quietly said.

"Exactly," Jordan replied. "The big firms that survived the crash of '07 and '08, they learned their lesson very well. They can keep gambling...."

"And rigging the game," Corbin added.

"...all they want," Kemp continued. "Even the most liberal politician is in their pocket."

"Where does that leave us?" Rask asked.

"Well, we can't just dump three hundred forty million in weak securities on the market at once. Someone would notice even as small as we are," Kemp said. "Besides, we need to hold them for a while yet."

"What about Rob Judd?" Espinosa asked.

"I can make sure he keeps his nose out of it," Walter Pascal said.

"So, we're still good? We're still on schedule?" Espinosa asked.

"Yep," Corbin answered. "Everything is fine."

"Corbin, I have to tell you, I'm not happy about being kept in the dark about this," Espinosa said. "Is there anything else?"

"No," Corbin emphatically answered him. "Victor, to tell you the truth, we didn't think it was that big a deal. Sorry. There's nothing else."

With that, the meeting broke up and the men left to start their long weekend early except for Corbin Reed and Ethan Rask. They went into Rask's office where Rask played an audiotape of Rob Judd and Maddy Rivers' dinner conversation of the previous evening.

"This is getting out of hand," Reed said. "What do you think we should do about the girl?"

"We may now have to remove her as a problem," Rask shrugged. "Or, move up the timeline. We might have to take less but…"

"Let me think about it over the weekend. We'll talk it over on Tuesday. You're right, moving up the timing might be best," Corbin agreed.

"Too many bodies can become too many coincidences," Rask said.

"Let's find out what we can about the girl first," Corbin suggested.

"I'll get right on it. I'll try to have at least a preliminary report by the time of the party."

"Good. We'll leave it at that for now."

The Fourth of July party was the brainchild and love of CAR Securities' chief investment officer, Jordan Kemp. Ever since he was a young child he had loved the Fourth as much as Christmas. Jordan believed himself to be a true patriot. He loved America and loved being an American. Each year on the Fourth he thought it was important to take a day and reflect on the one country where anyone truly could aspire to greatness. The one country where anyone could still go as far as your ability and ambition could take you. Jordan loved America; it was his wife and two worthless children who wouldn't get off the couch if the house was on fire that he was starting to loathe.

Jordan had a million-dollar home, mortgaged to the max, in an upscale Minneapolis suburb. It had a huge backyard with a swimming pool and a patio large enough for fifty. His yard abutted an undeveloped lot which would be used for a ten thousand dollar fireworks display at 10:00 o'clock that night. Right after a reading of the Declaration of Independence. Jordan Kemp loved the Fourth of July.

The party had been going for over two hours by the time Rob and Maddy arrived at 4:30. There were already over forty adults standing around chatting or seated at the rented tables under the awnings. At least twenty kids were having a great time swimming and playing in Jordan's pool.

A catering company had been hired and a full bar was set-up doing a brisk business. There were also three wait people, two young men and a one young woman on hand. The three of them were in continuous motion circulating through the crowd and the table areas. Jordan had also gotten lucky with the weather. It was a gorgeous summer day, highs in the mid-eighties, sunny with fluffy cumulous clouds floating overhead.

Rob Judd, holding Maddy's hand, made his way around the pool and through the crowd. Maddy was in a white cotton dress that ended just above her knees with sandals on her feet and was drawing a lot of attention. Rob introduced her to as many people as he knew and they finally made their way to where Corbin Reed and Jordan were standing greeting guests.

Rob introduced Maddy to them and Reed shook her hand then held onto it while staring at her.

"Didn't I see you at Vivian Donahue's party a couple of weeks ago?"

"I was there with Rob," she politely replied while extracting her hand.

"How do you know her?" Reed asked, referring to Vivian.

For some reason this question sounded an alarm bell in Maddy's head. It was an obvious question to ask but something about the way Reed asked it set off the warning.

"Oh, I don't, not really. She's a friend of a friend," Maddy vaguely answered without using Tony's name.

The four of them chatted for a couple of minutes then Rob led Maddy away to a table where several coworkers were seated. Across the pool Ethan Rask stood watching, drink in hand while Reed and Jordan watched Maddy walk away. When they turned back, Rask motioned to Corbin Reed to meet him on his side of the pool.

"Beautiful woman," Rask said when Corbin joined him. The two men were off by themselves under a shady tree watching Maddy Rivers across the pool. The kids in the pool were making so much noise they were confident no one could hear them.

"Yeah, she is," Corbin readily agreed.

"She's also about as dangerous as a pit viper," Rask said.

"What?" Corbin asked. "What are you talking about?"

"She's an ex-Chicago cop and now she's a private investigator here in Minnesota. She's killed two men. Threw one of them out a window of her apartment when he tried to attack her there. Oh, I almost forgot. First she kicked his ass, shot him and then threw him out the window.

"The other one she shot five or six times and blew him off the roof of a building. I'm not sure what happened, but there were no charges ever filed."

"Sounds like a fun girl," Corbin laughed. "You think we should try to warn our guy before he takes out Rob Judd?"

"What the hell are you two talking about?" they heard the voice of Walter Pascal anxiously ask from behind them.

The two men turned around and faced Pascal who had seen them talking and decided to join them. He had not meant to eavesdrop but had heard Corbin's comment about Rob Judd as he approached, unnoticed, from behind.

"Jesus Christ, Corbin. First McGarry and now Rob," Pascal whispered at them. "Where does this stop? I didn't sign on for this shit!"

"Keep your mouth shut, Walter," Corbin ordered. "Listen to me," he continued stepping right up to Pascal, poking him in the chest with a hard finger and snarling into his face. "Did you think we could pull off what we're going to do without some problems? Grow up. Besides, after McGarry it's too late to turn back now."

Rask patted Pascal on the shoulder and softly said, "Relax, Walter. We'll take care of it. You just take care of your end and keep the cash flow coming in."

Pascal shifted his eyes back and forth between them, sighed and said, "Okay, all right. It's just…"

"Not much longer, Walter," Corbin said while thinking about how much more each would end up with by dividing up Walter's share.

FIFTEEN

Tuesday morning after the long holiday weekend, Marc Kadella was at his desk reviewing a police report. It was 10:00 o'clock and his new client, an affluent financial advisor with a Fortune 500 company headquartered in downtown Minneapolis, had just left. Arrested last week for his second DUI in three years, the man was looking at a gross misdemeanor, up to a year in jail, his driver's license suspended and three grand in fines. That was not the worst of it. His securities licenses were also in jeopardy.

He had left a five thousand dollar check on Marc's desk with the hope Marc could do something for him. The client's wishes were dubious at best. From what Marc could tell from the police report, the arrest appeared to be solid.

Marc set the paperwork and check aside. He would give it to Carolyn or Sandy to open a new case file for him and deposit into his Trust account. He leaned back and thought about the past few days with Margaret. He loved her, he was sure about that. But was he in love with her enough to give up the lifestyle he was enjoying to spend the rest of his life with her? That he was not sure about.

Marc also thought about Mackenzie Sutherland, a woman he became involved with while Margaret and he were separated. Mackenzie had definitely lit a fire in him which mostly burned out just as quickly and with good reason. But he still was not quite over her and that was the heart of the matter.

His intercom buzzed and when he answered it Sandy told him Tony Carvelli was calling and it was urgent.

"Hey, what's up?" Marc asked him.

"I just got a call from Owen Jefferson," Tony began referring to a Minneapolis homicide detective they both knew. "Maddy's in some kind of trouble at her boyfriend's place. I'm on my way," he added then gave Marc the address.

"What's going on?" Marc asked trying to remain calm and keep the panic out of his voice.

"Jefferson wouldn't tell me. He just said to call you and for both of us to get there ASAP."

"This is two minutes from me," Marc said referring to Rob's address. "I'll meet you there."

Marc barely hung up the phone before he grabbed his coat and ran through the office. While running to the exit door he managed to yell out something about canceling appointments and he would call later.

Marc ran two red lights as he sped west on Lake Street passed Lake Calhoun. He could see the fifteen story condo building from a half mile away and pulled into the parking lot ten seconds before Carvelli.

There were six squad cars, lights flashing, Jefferson's car and an ambulance in the fire lane by the door. Marc saw Tony and waited for him then the two of them ran toward the building.

"I don't know any more than what I told you on the phone," Tony managed to say.

They were stopped at the door by a uniformed officer and while Marc explained who they were, Tony saw a vehicle from the medical examiner's office pull into the lot and up to the front of the building. The officer stood aside, opened the door for them as Tony poked Marc on the shoulder and pointed to the M.E. vehicle.

Inside another MPD uniformed officer escorted them onto the elevator and rode up to seven with them. He led them down the hall to Rob's condo and before they went in, the cop stopped them.

"It's pretty gruesome in there," he whispered. "Just so you know."

When they got inside the first thing they saw was Madeline sitting on the couch by herself. She was wearing a man's white T-shirt, white cotton panties and nothing else. Her hair was a mess, she had a scared and confused look on her face and her hands were pressed together being held between her knees. What shocked both Marc and Tony was the amount of blood that was splattered all over her.

"Jesus Christ," Tony whispered. "What the hell…"

Before he could finish his thought, Marc was already on his knees in front of her. As soon as she saw them, tough-as-nails Maddy, had burst into tears. Now, despite the blood, her arms were around Marc's neck while he held her. They stayed this way for almost two minutes; Maddy letting it out while Marc gently rocked her like a child.

"Tony," they heard a deep, male voice say from behind them.

Tony turned and saw Owen Jefferson standing in the opening of a hallway leading to the bedrooms. Marc saw him too and gestured with his head for Tony to see what the detective wanted.

While Maddy was gathering herself, Tony followed Jefferson down the hall and saw Jefferson's partner, Marcie Sterling, standing in a bedroom doorway.

"It's a mess in there, Tony," Jefferson said as a polite warning.

"Okay, Owen, let me take a look. Hi, Marcie," Tony said as he stuck his head into Rob's bedroom.

What he saw would have made a normal person vomit almost immediately. Lying on the bed, covered in blood, was the obviously dead body of Rob Judd. The blood had sprayed over almost the entire room. Obviously a fight had taken place. There were items smashed and scattered throughout the large bedroom. There were also two crime scene techs inside. One was holding a camera filming while the other was beginning the job of processing the room.

Tony stepped back, looked at the two detectives, then asked the obvious question, "What happened?"

"He didn't show up for work this morning and one of his coworkers came to check on him. No answer at the door so he got the maintenance guy to let him in and they found this," Jefferson said referring to the mess in the bedroom.

"Maddy was lying on the floor, a knife in her hand and the coworker thought she was dead too," Marcie added.

"They got the hell out, called 911 and a squad showed up. He took a look, thought they were both dead and called it in. When we got here, Maddy was starting to make some sounds, groaning and such," Jefferson said. "We got her up and took her out into the living room. I asked her what happened and she says she can't remember anything.

"Tony right now it looks like there was a fight of some kind, she got a hold of the knife and…" Jefferson said.

"Bullshit!" Carvelli said. "You don't believe that any more than I do. Besides, she wouldn't need a knife to handle this guy."

"Maybe he had the knife and she took it from him," Marcie said.

"Then its self-defense," Carvelli said.

"There's a shitload of stab wounds on the body, Tony. At least a dozen," Jefferson said.

"I'll let her lawyer deal with you guys," Carvelli snarled then turned and walked back to the living room. He found Marc sitting next to Maddy on the couch. Marc had found a blanket and wrapped it around her. Carvelli pushed a chair up to the couch so he could listen in.

"I don't remember anything after the fireworks," Maddy was saying.

"What fireworks?" Marc asked.

Maddy told her two good friends about the party they had been to the previous day. It was pleasant enough if somewhat boring.

"How much did you have to drink?" Marc asked.

"Not much," Maddy said, shaking her head. She still had a somewhat glazed, far-away look in her eyes, which were very dilated. "I remember I had a couple beers before we ate…"

"Bottles or glasses?"

"Glasses," she answered Marc. "I remember they had a keg and I had two small glasses. Plastic cups, probably ten ounces."

"Okay, go on," Marc said.

"Then I had another one when we ate. After that I switched to wine and had a couple small glasses of wine.

"About ten o'clock there was a fireworks show and I remember telling Rob I wasn't feeling well. Oh God," she said as she covered her mouth with her left hand and her eyes began to tear up again. "Rob. I saw him when the police came. Is he dead?"

Marc looked at Tony who took her right hand and quietly said, "Yes, sweetheart, I'm sorry."

For the next minute or so, Tony held her hand and Marc put his arms around her while she cried and quietly sobbed some more. When she stopped, Marc gave her his handkerchief and she wiped her eyes and blew her nose with it.

"Okay," Marc softly said to continue, "you told Rob you weren't feeling well."

Maddy stared across the room for a few moments then said, "And that's it. I swear, I don't remember anything else."

"What do you think?" Marc asked Tony.

Before Tony could answer an obviously distraught Maddy blurted out, "Don't you believe me? You believe me don't you?"

"Of course," Marc said smoothing her hair to soothe and reassure her.

Tony took both of her hands, held them, looked directly into her eyes and emphatically said, "Yes, of course we do."

Still holding her hands, Tony looked at Marc and said, "She was drugged."

"I think so too. Wait here with her. I'll be right back. I need to make a call," Marc said.

Marc came back in less than five minutes and said, "I have a doctor who owes me a favor. I'm going to have him draw some blood and a urine sample from her for testing. We need to find out what you were given."

"The cops will want to test it too," Tony said.

"That's their problem. I need to get her out of here now. Let me talk to Jefferson and see if we can leave."

Marc went down the hall and found Jefferson and Sterling watching the M.E. and the crime scene guys. They knew each other and politely, if somewhat grimly, shook hands.

"I'm going to need your prints and a DNA sample," Jefferson told him.

"What?" Marc asked.

"This entire place is a crime scene and I'm going to need yours, Maddy's and Carvelli's prints and DNA."

"Not without a court order," Marc said. "Look, Detective Jefferson, I don't mean to be a pain-in-the-ass but the bedroom is a crime scene. Nothing happened out here, obviously. I'm a little reluctant to have my DNA and prints in your database," Marc said, even though having served in the Air Force, his prints were already in the government's database.

"I know," Jefferson said. "I was just jerking your chain a bit. When do I get a statement from Maddy?"

"Is she under arrest?" Marc asked.

"Not yet, but she's obviously suspect number one," Jefferson admitted.

"She didn't do this, Owen and you know it," Marc said testing him to see what he would say to that.

"I don't know any such thing, Marc. How well do we know anyone?"

"Okay. Look, I'm going to take her home. I'll think about bringing her in and let you know," Marc said.

"You'll let us know?" Marcie said clearly annoyed.

"Marcie…" Jefferson started to say knowing what was coming from Marc.

"If she's not under arrest, detective, I'm taking my client out of here," Marc sharply told her. "Is she under arrest?"

"No, not at this time," Jefferson admitted while looking at an angry Marcie Sterling.

"Owen," Marc continued much softer, "If you decide to arrest her, give me a call and I'll bring her in. Okay?"

"All right," Jefferson agreed.

SIXTEEN

When Marc, Tony and Maddy exited the building they were confronted by a small herd of reporters. There were only two cops doing crowd control in the front of the building and they evidently needed help. Along with the dozen or so media types, there was a crowd of almost one hundred curious observers milling about. The three of them turned to their left to head toward the parking lot. As they did this, Tony did a quick double take to look back over his shoulder at a couple of men dressed in plain clothes. They were certainly cops, Tony could spot the look, or at least law enforcement from somewhere. One of the men in particular looked familiar but Tony couldn't remember him.

A couple of TV news reporters recognized Marc and, with microphones drawn and cameramen in tow, made a beeline toward him. The fluffy blonde from Channel 3 was a little quicker than the cute and perky brunette from Channel 6.

"Mr. Kadella," the blonde said aiming the mic at Marc's face, "can we have a word?"

Madeline, still quite disheveled, the blanket wrapped around her was being shielded by her two friends. As soon as Marc saw the clamoring herd heading their way, he whispered to Tony to get her to Tony's car.

While Tony was hustling Maddy to his car, Marc stepped up to stop the stampede and take a few questions.

"Mr. Kadella," the Channel 3 blonde started to ask, "what can you tell us about what's going on inside?" She jabbed her mic at his face so quickly his head involuntarily snapped back.

"Nothing," Marc said. "I'm sure the authorities will have a statement to make soon. You should probably wait for that."

"Why are you here? Who is that woman you were with who had the blanket wrapped around her?" the perky Channel 6 brunette asked.

"No comment," Marc said.

"Mr. Kadella," a man that Marc knew from the Minneapolis paper started to ask, "we know there was a homicide that took place and it was quite bloody. Can you elaborate? Was the woman you were with involved and what is her name?"

"How do you know that there was a bloody homicide?" Marc asked. He looked over his shoulder and saw Tony's black Camaro leaving the parking lot by the back exit. "I have no further comment," Marc said and turned to leave. He took several steps ignoring the questions still being thrown at him when he saw two casually but well-dressed men coming his way.

"Excuse me, sir," the younger one said to Marc. "I'm Corbin Reed, I'm with CAR Securities."

Marc tried to ignore the man and keep walking until the man told him he was Rob Judd's boss. Marc stopped, looked them over then introduced himself to Reed and the other man, Ethan Rask.

"It was one of our people who found him," Reed whispered.

Marc noticed the media people heading their way.

"Come with me," he quietly said to the two men.

He took the two CAR executives inside, introduced them to a uniformed cop and asked the cop to call up to Owen Jefferson. Marc then slipped out a back door, got to his car and left. As he drove away he was trying to remember where he had seen the one named Corbin Reed before. He was sure he had but could not remember where.

Across the street from the front of the high-rise condo building, a well-dressed, bland looking man was watching the scene in front. Slightly disguised with hair dye, glasses, a mustache and goatee, he had more than a passing interest in the proceedings.

Shortly after eleven A.M., Owen Jefferson with Marcie Sterling behind him, came out to face the media. Surprised at the attention this crime had already engendered, Jefferson waited a minute for the media to get ready before speaking. This also gave the man in the disguise an opportunity to slide through the crowd to get close enough to hear him.

114

"At this time, all I can tell you is that a man in his late-thirties was found dead by an apparent homicide this morning. No other information can be made available until next of kin have been notified."

The reporters started shouting questions at the two detectives who answered with "no comments" all the way to their car. While Jefferson and Marcie drove off, the man in the disguise took out a flip phone and made a call.

"It is done," he said with a barely discernible Latino accent.

"Thank you," was the only response by Paul Quinones.

While the man Quinones sent to eliminate the problem he and Victor Espinosa had talked about was making that call, another man, one who had blended into the crowd like a chameleon, was hurrying down the sidewalk to get to his car. Charlie Dudek, having recognized Maddy Rivers when she came out, would head for a place to cool out for a few days. In less than ten minutes he was on eastbound I-94 to drive through St. Paul on his way to Chicago.

Seated on his couch in his shorts and a T-shirt, Dale Kubik was grinning like an idiot while watching the 12:00 o'clock news. There was film of Maddy Rivers coming out of the high-rise with two men. By now apparently Rob's next of kin had been notified and the announcer was using his name. When the story was finished, Kubik put his coffee down and stood up.

"This calls for a celebration," he said to himself. With the big smile still on his face, he went to the refrigerator, took out a can of cheap beer, popped it open and downed half of it in one swallow.

"So, what do you think?" Corbin Reed asked Ethan Rask.

The two executives from CAR Securities were in Rask's Mercedes sedan. They had spoken to Owen Jefferson who gave them very little information other than Rob Judd was dead in an apparent homicide. Jefferson did tell them he had been stabbed several times and asked them not to speak to the media. He let the two men know they were about to notify next of kin and did not want them to hear about this on TV. Of course they agreed and used

115

the same back door Marc used to get past the reporters. Plus, they did not want their names associated with what happened anyway.

"Do you think it was our guy?" Corbin continued.

"It must have been. Who else? The man's a genius. Did you see who that was that the lawyer was leading out of the building? The one with the blanket wrapped around her?" Rask asked.

"Yeah, Rob's girlfriend," Corbin answered.

"She spent the night. She's probably the cops' number one suspect."

Corbin turned back to stare out the windshield. The two men remained silent for a couple of minutes while Rask drove toward downtown.

"We'll need to put out some kind of press release," Corbin said breaking the silence. "Once they find out where he worked, they'll be calling."

"That's all right," Rask said. "It was one of our people who found him. We don't have to act as if we didn't know."

"True," Corbin agreed. "I can write something up with the usual bullshit in it. What about the girlfriend? We know Rob talked to her. What if she uses that to bargain with the cops?"

"I was just thinking about that," Rask said. "I'm not sure there is much we can do for now. We'll have to wait and see."

"So, what do you think?" Marcie Sterling asked Owen Jefferson. They were in their department issued Chevy sedan. Marcie was driving and Jefferson was silently staring through the windshield.

Owen Jefferson was a veteran homicide detective who had been with the Minneapolis Police Department for almost twenty years. He was a one-time basketball star at the University of Minnesota with a promising NBA career ahead before knee problems ended it.

A six-foot-five, divorced, handsome, bald, black man with a small gold stud in one ear, Jefferson was a highly regarded, professional homicide investigator. In fact, he had recently made the short list for promotion to lieutenant.

His partner, Marcie Sterling had been thrust upon Owen a couple years ago. Behind their backs, they were known as the Odd Couple. A six-five black man and a five-foot seven-inch white woman did not exactly look right as a pair of detectives.

Originally, Jefferson correctly believed she was a recipient of gender affirmative action in the PD. Jefferson, a little resentfully, took her under his wing and their first case together taught him that with a little training, experience and mentoring, Marcie would likely be Chief Sterling one day. The resentment he initially felt was long gone.

"I don't know what to think," Jefferson answered her.

"Come on, do you think she did it?"

Jefferson looked at Marcie who was watching him with a smirk on her face. They both knew Maddy Rivers. In fact, Marcie was needling him a little bit because of prior comments Jefferson had made about Maddy. Comments that made it clear Owen Jefferson harbored a little thing for her.

Jefferson inhaled a deep breath then said, "My heart and gut tell me no, but I also recognize that could be because I don't want to believe it. On the other hand, my head tells me we don't really know what anyone else is really capable of doing."

He turned to look through the windshield again and continued.

"I hope she didn't do it," he softly said.

Marcie reached over and patted him on the back of his left hand and said, "Me too. I really like her despite how much I envy her."

"We'll see where the evidence goes," Jefferson said. "And take it from there, no matter what."

"I know," Marcie agreed.

SEVENTEEN

When Marc arrived at Maddy's apartment, barely ten minutes from Rob's building, she was still in the shower. Tony had answered the building's intercom and buzzed Marc in. Tony also left the door open for him and when Marc walked in, Tony was sitting on the couch talking on the phone.

"Marc just came in, Vivian. Let me call you back," he heard Tony say.

Marc looked at Tony and nodded his head toward the bathroom.

"She's in the shower," Tony said.

Marc walked back to the bathroom, opened the door about three inches and yelled to her to let her know he was there.

"Are you okay?" he asked.

He heard the shower curtain being pulled back then Maddy stuck her head out. "Yeah," she said. "I'll be a while yet. The shower is helping to clear my head."

"Take your time. We'll be in the living room."

Marc went back to the living room and pulled a chair up to the coffee table in front of Tony.

"You called Vivian?" Marc asked referring to Vivian Donahue, the Queen of the Corwin family.

"No, she called me," Tony said. "She wants to talk to me about something we've been working on. She didn't know about our girl so I told her."

"Oh, geez," Marc replied. "What did she say?"

"I thought she would reach through the phone and grab me by the throat. I got her to calm down and she said if we need anything, let her know," Tony said. "She'd move mountains for Madeline."

"What are the two of you up to?" Marc asked, referring to the project Vivian had Tony working on.

"Hmmm, nothing I can tell you about. At least not without her permission and at this point, the fewer people who know the better."

118

"Oh, well, okay then," Marc said feigning indignation. "Just so you know, if I ever win the lottery, I'm not telling you."

Tony laughed then said, "If you ever win the lottery you won't be able to keep your mouth shut for three seconds."

"Probably true," Marc agreed.

"What about this business?" Tony asked, turning serious, referring back to Rob Judd's murder. "Did you get a look inside that bedroom?"

"Yeah, I did. Thought I might throw up. God it was awful," Marc replied.

"What do you think…"

"I don't think anything, yet," Marc said cutting him off. "I believe she was drugged but we need to get her tested today and keep her away from the cops for now."

"Jefferson is gonna want a statement," Tony said.

"Good for him," Marc said. "I want a lot of things. We'll see if I let her give him one."

"Give who one what?" Maddy asked as she came around the corner of the hallway from the back. She was wearing a large, white terry cloth robe with a white towel wrapped around her hair.

"Give Owen Jefferson a statement," Marc said.

Maddy sat down next to Tony, gave Marc a puzzled look then said, "Was Owen there? I don't remember seeing him."

Marc and Tony exchanged looks then Marc said to Maddy, "Yes, Jefferson was there."

"Oh, God," Maddy said then hung her head and started sobbing again. Tony put his arm around her, she leaned into him and the three of them sat like this for over a minute.

"I can't remember," Maddy said through her sniffles. "And I can't stop crying. I hate this!" She took the handkerchief Tony held for her, blew her nose and wiped her eyes. What if I did this?" she softly said looking at Marc. "What if I did that to Rob?"

Marc leaned forward, elbows on his knees and sternly said, "First of all, do not ever say anything like that to me or anyone else again unless I ask you. Second, I don't believe you are capable of such a thing so put it out of your head. Even drugged I don't see you doing this."

"I don't believe it, either," Tony added.

Maddy weakly smiled at her friends and quietly said, "Thank you."

At that moment Marc's phone rang for about the twentieth time since leaving the office. He had spoken to Carolyn and Connie Mickelson and told them what had happened. The other calls were all ignored. This one, after checking the caller ID, he decided to answer.

"Hi, Gabriella," Marc said when he answered his telephone.

"Is she all right?" he heard from Gabriella Shriqui, Maddy's best friend and reporter with Channel 8. "I'm outside the station in the parking lot so no one can hear me," she continued, the concern in her voice quite obvious.

"She's okay, Gabriella," Marc said. He was looking at Maddy who gestured for the phone. Marc handed it to her and within ten seconds, Maddy, the strongest, toughest woman Marc and Tony knew, was sobbing again.

Marc took the phone away from her and said, "I think she's been drugged and keep that to yourself…"

"Of course, I'll keep that to myself! What do you think I am?"

"Sorry, sorry," Marc stammered. "I'm taking her to a doctor. I'll call you later, I promise."

"My guess is, I think you were definitely drugged with something," Dr. Nathan Lockhart said to Maddy. He was examining the pupils in her eyes with a tiny penlight, clicked it off and slipped it back into the pocket of his white coat.

"We're going to need blood and urine but based on your eyes and what you've told me, I'm pretty certain somebody slipped you something."

"Why both blood and urine?" Maddy asked, a little curious.

"Some drugs show up in one but not the other. Roofies, which is a likely candidate, shows up in urine but not blood. I'll have the lab do a full spectrum analysis."

"Okay, interesting," Maddy said showing signs her mind was starting to clear. "While I'm gone do you want to bring Marc back and tell him?"

"Do you want me too?"

"Yes, definitely. He's my lawyer and he needs to know," Maddy replied as she hopped down from the exam table.

"I'll have a nurse get him and bring him back after she shows you to the lab and bathroom. We'll be in my office when you're done."

"Thanks, doctor," Maddy half-smiled and said.

"I'll have the lab put a rush on it," he told her.

The front doors of the clinic slid open and Marc and Maddy walked into the heat and sunshine of the July afternoon. As soon as they did, they spotted the white van with the Channel 8 logo on the side in the parking lot.

"Oh, shit," Marc quickly said when he saw the reporter and cameraman heading their way.

"Mr. Kadella, Ms. Rivers," Samantha Johnson, the court reporter for the station was calling out to them. Samantha was someone both Marc and Maddy knew. She worked at the same station as Gabriella Shirqui. In fact, Samantha had Gabriella's old job of covering the local courts and crime scene.

Marc and Maddy, trying to ignore her, kept walking toward his car.

"Marc, please, wait a second," Samantha pleaded as she tried to catch up with them.

"You get in the car," Marc said as he slipped the keys into her hand.

"Yes, Samantha," Marc said as he turned to block them from Maddy. "What is it?"

"I would like a quick interview," she said.

"What about?"

121

"Madeline Rivers. You and another man were seen leaving the scene of a brutal murder with her. We have it on good authority that the victim was Ms. Rivers' boyfriend, a man by the name of Robert Judd. Is she involved? What can you tell us about the death of Robert Judd? Why are the two of you coming out of a medical clinic?"

"No comment, no comment, none of your business," Marc said. Knowing Maddy was in Marc's SUV by now, he told Samantha, "Shut that thing off and I'll give you something."

Samantha nodded at the camera operator who shut it off. She then turned her microphone to Marc.

"That too," Marc said. When she shut it off he continued. "If anything comes of any of this, I'll give you an interview."

"Come on," she pleaded, "you can do better than that."

"Nope," Marc smiled thinking the only reason she got that much was because Marc thought the sultry redhead was sizzling hot, which she was.

While Marc and Maddy drove out of the parking lot, Marc had Maddy speed dial a number on her phone then hand it to him.

"Hi Maddy. Are you okay?" he heard Gabriella ask.

"It's Marc," he said. "Tell me you didn't sic Samantha Johnson on us."

"What? What are you talking about? Of course not," Gabriella said, the anger in her voice rising as she spoke. "What kind of person…"

"Gabriella, stop," Marc said. "I didn't believe it but she and a camera guy caught us as we were coming out of a clinic. I just…"

"Well, I didn't send her! What did you tell her?"

"I told her I owed her an interview but nothing today. I'm driving. I have to go, I'll talk to you later," he said then cut off the call before she could yell at him some more.

"I knew it wasn't her. She's a great friend," Maddy said.

"I know and now I'm in trouble with her," Marc said with a sigh.

"Why was there so much media at Rob's building?" Maddy asked.

"Are things starting to come back to you?"

"No, not really. Nothing after the fireworks started last night. I only vaguely remember being on Rob's couch this morning and you and Tony showing up. I still don't remember seeing Owen or Marcie there. Why all of the media?" she repeated.

"I don't know," Marc said. "Probably got a tip from a cop or maybe one of the cops spoke out of school over the radio. They heard it somehow, that it was a bad scene," Marc continued not wanting to make it sound any worse than it was, "and they all came running. Some black gangbanger gets popped and they all just shrug. A well-to-do white guy, well, that news sells tickets. Sorry. I don't mean to be flip about it or upset you." Marc reached over to squeeze her hand. Instead, with tears in her eyes she grabbed his hand and didn't let go until they were back at her building.

EIGHTEEN

Tony Carvelli angle parked his Camaro in the parking area in front of the Corwin Mansion on Lake Minnetonka. He was coming from downtown Minneapolis after a fruitless attempt to extract information about Rob Judd's death from his friend and former police colleague, Owen Jefferson. After leaving Maddy's apartment, while Marc was talking to his doctor friend, Tony made a run downtown to police headquarters. He sniffed around for an hour or so trying to glean anything he could from cops he knew, with no success at all. Jefferson had been polite and professional, as always, but was not forthcoming with anything Tony didn't already know, which was no surprise to Carvelli.

As Tony made the walk from his car to the front doors of the Mansion with Maddy on his mind, he thought about how he had come to know Vivian Donahue.

A black sheep member of the Corwin clan, Robert Corwin, Jr., Vivian's nephew by her older brother Robert, was murdered by two men working for a local gangster. By coincidence, Marc Kadella had represented one of the men, the one that was mostly innocent. The thug who had killed Vivian's nephew got off due to a corrupt judge and Vivian hired Tony to find out the truth.

Vivian Corwin Donahue, annually one of Forbes Magazine's ten richest and most powerful women, and Tony had become part-time lovers. It was through Tony that Vivian had come to know Maddy Rivers and loved Maddy like the daughter she would have liked to have. All of these things passed through his mind as he took the steps leading up to the front door. He hesitated a moment, drew a deep breath then rang the doorbell. Tony was not looking forward to telling Vivian what had happened to Maddy. But he also realized that this woman could move mountains, which might be useful in helping Maddy clear her name.

Tony rang the bell again and in about twenty seconds, Vivian's longtime housekeeper, friend and sometime confidante, Mary, opened the door and warmly greeted him.

124

"Vivian's on the patio down at the lake," she told Tony.

"Thanks, Mary. I can manage by myself," he replied.

Tony took the concrete pathway from the pool area the three hundred feet to the shore of Lake Minnetonka. He found Vivian seated on a cushioned patio chair on the upper level of the dock. There was a boathouse to their right larger than most homes, a one-hundred-foot portable dock extending into the lake and two eighty-year-old oak trees providing shade. It was a very nice way to while away a pleasant summer day.

"Hello, Anthony," Vivian smiled when she turned to greet him.

Tony bent down and kissed her cheek, poured himself a glass of lemonade from the pitcher on the white, wrought iron table and took the chair next to her. Before saying anything he took a large swallow of the ice-cold drink.

"Tell me about Madeline!" Vivian impatiently said. "I saw the news. They had film of the three of you coming out of the building. What happened?" she continued, obviously quite concerned.

Tony held up a hand to politely stop her then said, "We're not sure yet." He then went on to go over all of the details, everything they knew about the death of Rob Judd and Maddy's potential involvement.

"This is dreadful. This is just horrifying," Vivian said practically fighting back tears. "What are we going to do?"

"The first thing we're going to do is presume she is innocent and was setup. I'm pretty sure, because of her memory loss and the way she was acting, she was drugged. We'll know in a few days," Tony said. "I think somebody slipped her something at a party she was at the night before and when I find out who he won't like the result."

Vivian quietly thought about it for a few moments. She watched a small cabin cruiser go by on the lake without really noticing it. Finally, she turned to Tony and said, "Will you call Marc, please? I'd like to talk to him if I can."

"Sure," Tony said. He removed his phone, found Marc's cell phone number and dialed.

"Where are you?" Tony asked when Marc answered.

"We just got back to her apartment," Marc replied referring to Maddy.

"What did the doctor tell you?"

"He said she definitely showed signs of being drugged. He said he'd put a rush on the lab tests and thought maybe we'd have at least some preliminary results as early as a couple days."

Tony looked at Vivian who was leaning toward him with an anxious look on her face. "Vivian would like to talk to you, if that's okay?"

"Sure, put her on," Marc said.

"Marc, hi, how is she?" Vivian asked.

"Better than this morning," Marc replied.

"Is that Vivian?" Maddy asked Marc.

"Yeah, you want to talk to her?"

"Of course," Maddy said as she reached for the phone.

Marc covered the mouthpiece of the phone with his hand, the lawyer in him taking over, and said, "Be careful what you say to her. She can be forced to testify if it comes down to it."

Having been around enough cops, criminals and lawyers in her life, she understood what Marc was saying and why.

"Okay," she agreed and took the phone.

Marc waited patiently while Maddy was on the phone with Vivian. From what Marc could make of the conversation hearing just one side of it, Maddy was trying to assure Vivian that she was all right. After almost fifteen minutes she pulled the phone away from her face to speak to Marc.

"She wants me to come stay with her at the mansion. I told her…"

"That's a really good idea," Marc said.

"…I was all right and it…"

"No, you're not."

"…wasn't necessary," Maddy finished and gave Marc a severe look.

126

"Vivian's right. In fact, Vivian is always right. You shouldn't be alone for the next few days. I have no doubt you were drugged, probably with roofies. You're not all right. Besides, she'll protect you from the media. You can hide out there and Vivian will spoil you like a baby."

"She heard that," Maddy said holding up the phone. She put it to her ear and heard Vivian.

"I did hear that and Marc's right, I will spoil you. Please, dear Madeline," Vivian continued, "it would make me feel better."

Maddy heavily sighed then said, "All right you win. I'll have Marc bring me in a little while. I'll throw some things in a bag and we'll be along."

"Wonderful. I'll see you then."

"CAR Securities," Vivian began talking to Tony when she got off the phone with Maddy. "Have you discovered anything more about the people who run it?"

"I got a picture of the mystery man, this Ethan Rask guy…"

"The one with very little history?"

"Yeah, that one. Anyway, the picture I had wasn't the best but I had my computer guy run facial recognition on it and he came up with a half a dozen possibilities, none of them good."

"What does that mean?" Vivian asked while refilling their glasses.

"It means none of the six possibles he came up with are Boy Scouts. They all have rap sheets for serious things and arrests for violent crimes, including murder."

"Convictions?"

"Some, yes. None for the most serious stuff. The problem is the pictures themselves. They are all possible. They could all be him at various ages and it may be that none of them are him. There's nothing that you could take to court. My guy is running them down now to find out where each of them are and see if we can eliminate any. Could be at least a couple are in jail somewhere."

"Have you discussed this with Marc or anyone else?"

"No", Tony replied shaking his head. "I'll keep working on this Rask guy. The rest of them, the people at CAR, are who they seem to be. Oh, wait a second, I forgot. The guy who looks the most like our Mr. Rask has a couple of interesting things on his record. He's not just a crook, he's a con man. He did time, almost two years about ten years ago in a federal prison in Florida for running some kind of securities scam. I couldn't find out what exactly."

Vivian thought about that news for a moment then said, "That is interesting. And it may help explain what I found out. I checked with several investment people I know and trust, independently, of each other, of course. They all had the same basic things to say about them. Their returns were bordering on too good to be true, but not quite. Although one of them did tell me the Chief Investment Officer, Jordan Kemp, is a mathematical wiz, almost genius level."

"What about their SEC filings?"

"I obtained copies and had them reviewed. SEC filings aren't necessarily very valid," Vivian told him.

"Why is that?"

"Because, dear Anthony, the SEC is a bigger revolving door than Congress. Too many people work for the SEC to make friends with Wall Street firms so they can score a lucrative job when they leave the government. Simply put, corruption is rampant and business filings, especially investment firm filings, how shall I put this," she asked slightly nodding her head from side-to-side with a sly smirk on her face, "are not the most reliable and honest source of information."

"What about the credit rating firms?" Tony asked.

"Same answer," Vivian replied. "Now, it could be that CAR Securities returns are absolutely legitimate. The market over the last six or seven years has been pumped full of cheap, almost free, money. Our economics and business knowledge-deprived president is clueless about how all of this works. Real under-employment and unemployment are still ridiculously high and income for almost everyone, especially the middle class people who have to work for a living, is down. Yet he believes he's doing a splendid job because the market is overheated."

Tony laughed then said, "Stop before you get yourself angry over the guy. I'm sure he's doing what he thinks is best."

"You're right. Still, the man's a fool," Vivian smiled. "Now what?"

"I need to get fingerprints from Mr. Rask," Tony said. "It would be nice to get them from the others as well, but I need Rask for sure. There's something there, in his background," Tony said.

"Cop's intuition?" Vivian smiled.

"Probably," Tony agreed. "Cynical ex-cop."

Tony heard the sound of a car approaching. He stood up and looked across the huge lawn, through the trees and caught a glimpse of Marc's SUV.

"They're here," he said and held out a hand to help Vivian out of her chair.

"That was quick," she said.

Marc pulled up and parked diagonally next to Tony. He turned the key to shut off the engine and unbuckled his seatbelt. As he began to open the door, Marc noticed that Maddy had not moved.

"You coming?" he asked.

She turned in her seat to look at him. With a very troubled look on her face she said, "I have to tell you something."

"Okay, what?"

She hesitated a moment then said, "All day I've been having, I'm not sure what, visions or images like flashes of photographs pop in and out of my head. At first, I wasn't even sure if they were real or what they were. But they're getting clearer. Marc..." she paused.

"What, sweetheart?" Marc softly asked.

"They're images from Rob's bedroom. I see him dead and the blood everywhere. I think I may have done it. I might have killed him."

NINETEEN

Marc peeked through the tiny window in the exterior door of courtroom 1745. He was in the hallway on the court's side of the Hennepin County Government Center in downtown Minneapolis. It was a little after ten A.M. Having finished a court appearance for an incarcerated client, Marc wanted to stop and see Margaret Tennant.

Yesterday, Tuesday, had been a long stressful and hectic day dealing with the drama surrounding Maddy Rivers. Margaret, after seeing the noon news reports, had left a half-dozen messages, the last one with an annoyed tone to it.

Marc continued to look through the little window at the proceeding taking place. He had forgotten but now recalled that Margaret had a trial starting today. A personal injury case where liability was clear but the insurance company refused to pay anything at all. They were employing the usual defense strategy. When you have no case, stall, stall and then stall some more.

Marc checked his watch, 10:13, and believing a break in the trial was coming, quietly slipped in and took a seat in the back row. He patiently waited while the plaintiff's lawyer, a woman Marc didn't know, was making her opening statement. It was pretty obvious who the plaintiff was. It was the man who would spend the rest of his life in a wheelchair. *Evidently one of those frivolous lawsuits conservative TV and radio big mouths are always railing against*, Marc thought. *Those poor insurance companies*, he continued silently thinking, *I practically weep for how maligned they are and how much unjust advantage people take of them.*

Ten minutes after Marc sat down, the plaintiff's lawyer finished up. Marc had spent most of the time waiting, watching the six jurors. Minnesota Rules of Civil Procedure do not specify the number of jurors to hear a civil case. The rules simply state between six and twelve. Being a criminal defense lawyer, the small number of people in the jury box looked a little odd to Marc.

Having seen Marc come in and take a seat, Margaret chose the moment when the plaintiff's lawyer finished to take a break.

Marc stood as Margaret left the bench and waited for the jury to be led out.

Margaret's clerk, Lois, waved Marc forward and when he got to her she warned him. "You're in big trouble, pal."

"Thanks, Lois. Is she really mad?"

"Nah, I'm just pulling your chain. Go on back."

A minute later he closed the door of Margaret's chambers and sheepishly said hello.

"How is she?" Margaret asked as she walked toward him. "What happened?"

They gave each other a brief hug and light kiss then the two of them sat next to each other on her couch.

"I'm not sure," Marc said. "I really don't know what happened."

He then told her, as much as he could without violating attorney-client privilege. If Maddy was ever charged, it would be handled by a judge in this building but it would not be Margaret Tennant

"So she's staying with Vivian for a while?" Margaret asked when he finished.

"Yeah, at least for a few days," Marc replied. "I know she was drugged. Probably at the party…"

"If someone drugged her then Rob was deliberately murdered and she was setup," Margaret said.

"Or, at least that will be a defense," Marc agreed.

"God, this is horrible," Margaret said. "Can we go see her? Maybe this evening? Will you call Vivian and see if it's okay for you to bring me out to see her, please?"

"Of course," Marc smiled. Just then he felt his phone vibrate. He took it from his coat pocket and looked at the screen.

"What is this about?" he muttered out loud while reading it. "What?"

"It's a text from Carolyn. My kids are at my office."

"You'd better go. Something might be wrong and …"

"No," Marc continued, "she says there's no problem they just dropped in to see me."

"Do you believe that?"

Marc thought for a couple seconds then said, "Ah, no. But, it's probably not too bad since they're both there."

Mark poked the screen for the office number and heard Sandy answer it. He told her he was on his way and hung up.

"I'll call Vivian," he told Margaret as he started to leave. "Call me this afternoon when you take a break and I'll let you know what she said. I'm sure it will be okay."

"Hey," Marc said to his son and daughter when he entered the suite of offices. He could actually feel the twinkle in his eye while he watched them stand up from the client chairs they were seated on waiting for him. If there was anything that he was proud of and always brought him joy, it was seeing them, especially the rare site of seeing them together. Sibling rivalry was alive and well.

"Hey, Pops," Eric said.

"Hi, Daddy," Jessica, daddy's little girl said.

They exchanged hugs then Marc asked, "It's a little early but should we get some lunch?"

"You buying?" his son asked.

"Why, do you want to volunteer?" Marc asked with a skeptical look.

"No, no, I'll let you," he grinned.

"I figured you might," Marc replied. "Let me put this away," he continued referring to his briefcase, "then we'll walk across the street."

Ten minutes later the waitress had taken their orders and left to put it into the kitchen.

"Okay," Marc began, "which one of you is in trouble?"

On the drive back from downtown all he could think was, *please don't let Jessica be pregnant. Anything but that,* a father's number one concern for his daughter. Having once been a teenage boy, fathers know what boys were sniffing around for when it came to their little girls.

"Go ahead," Eric told his sister. This statement and the way it was spoken and to whom caused Marc's anxiety meter to take a significant, upward spike.

"Actually, Daddy," she leaned forward and began, "we think it might be you."

"Me?" Marc asked trying to mask his relief. "Why am I in trouble?"

"Mom's been talking about you a lot lately," Eric said.

"Saying really nice things," Jessie added.

"What things and why?" Marc asked with serious suspicion.

"You tell him," Jessie said to her brother.

"Um, well, Mom and Tom, her husband…"

"I know his name," Marc said.

"…aren't getting along too good."

"And?"

"Well, you know, Mom's always felt a little guilty about you and the divorce and how she was," Jessie added.

"No she hasn't. Guilt is not a word in your mother's vocabulary but go ahead," Marc said again looking back and forth at the two of them.

"We think she might want to get back together with you," Eric flatly stated.

"And if you even think about it we'll have you committed and put in a home," his daughter quickly added.

"That's it? That's what you're worried about?" Marc asked.

"We just think you're a lot happier now than when you were married to her," Eric said.

"We love Mom, you know. She's Mom and all but…" Jessie said.

"Relax," Marc told her. "I thought it was something serious like, she wanted more money." He looked at Jessica and said, "Now that you're eighteen and done with high school, the child support stops."

"I know," Jessie said. "She made it a point to tell me."

"That doesn't surprise me," Marc said.

"Don't say mean things about Mom," Jessie admonished him.

"You're right, I'm sorry."

The waitress brought their meals and while Eric started in like he had not eaten in a week, Marc said to his daughter. "So that's why she invited me over this weekend."

"Yep," Jessie said. "Oh my God, I almost forgot, how's Maddy? What happened?"

"She's fine and I can't tell you about it except she's innocent. Just leave it at that," Marc said wanting to avoid that discussion.

The three of them spent the rest of lunch catching up. Marc had not spoken to them since sometime last week. Eric had yet another new girlfriend and Jessie was on a girls' softball team. Marc told her to send him her schedule so he could come to her games. All in all, one of the more pleasant couple of hours he had spent on a workday for quite a while.

Marc was holding Margaret's hand as the two of them climbed the steps to the mansion's front door. When they reached the landing and before he could ring the doorbell, the door opened and Vivian stepped out to greet them.

"How is she?" Marc asked while Vivian and Margaret gave each other a quick hug.

"All right," Vivian replied. "She seems less distraught than she did last night. I gave her a sleeping pill and I think she slept well."

"Are you talking about me?" they heard Maddy say as she came through the open front door.

"Ooops," Marc said and smiled when he saw her. She did look and seem much better than the day before. Her eyes were clear and her entire bearing was much better.

"Hi," Maddy said as Margaret embraced her.

Marc stepped up to her and examined her eyes. The dilation and hazy, confused look were gone.

"Feeling better?" he asked.

"Yeah, physically at least."

"Let's go inside," Vivian said. "Anthony is on his way and when he gets here we'll have some dinner."

Tony Carvelli arrived and Vivian had dinner served on the patio by the pool. The five of them made awkward small talk while eating. The elephant at the table, Rob Judd's murder, was completely avoided. No one was quite sure how, or even if, the subject should be brought up.

Maddy was seated to Marc's left between Marc and Tony. Almost a half-hour went by during which she was conspicuously silent. Maddy poked at her food while pretending to listen to the mundane chatter at the table.

Finally, Marc finished his meal, placed his utensils on the plate and pushed it toward the center of the glass topped table. He reached over and placed his hand on Maddy's forearm. She looked at him and weakly smiled.

"Have you had anything to eat today?" Marc asked.

"Yes," Maddy said.

"Not much," Vivian interjected.

"You have got to eat. I know you're in an emotional hell right now but it's likely going to get worse. You have to eat and sleep and keep your strength up."

"Why do you think it's going to get worse?" she asked.

Marc looked around the table and saw everyone had gone silent and were watching him. Marc took Maddy's hand and gave it a squeeze.

"Owen Jefferson called me today. He wants you in for questioning. I told him I'd think about it and let him know," Marc said.

"So, let's do it," Maddy said.

"And tell him what? That you have no memory of anything? He already knows that. I'm not inclined to cooperate with them," Marc said.

"Are you sure that's the best way to play this?" Margaret asked.

Marc released Maddy's hand, turned to Margaret and said, "People have this belief, or really it's a hope, that if they tell the cops their side of things then the cops will see it their way. They think that somehow the cops will understand how things happened, that it wasn't really their fault, the cops will apologize for the inconvenience and let the whole thing slide."

He turned back to Maddy and continued. "When the police are investigating a crime, they are not your friends. I like Owen Jefferson as a person, too. He's a good man. But he's a professional and right now, he is not your friend. You, as an ex-cop, should know that. How am I doing, Tony?" Marc asked Carvelli while still looking at Maddy.

"Spot on," Carvelli replied.

"I don't see any way you giving them a statement will help you. And I don't know why, but I don't think they're not going to find any fingerprints or DNA in Rob's bedroom except yours and his. We'll see, but I think somebody drugged you to set you up to take the blame for his murder. If that's true, then whoever did it is good enough not to leave anything behind."

"You think I'll get arrested?" Maddy quietly asked.

"Yeah, honey I do. We'll see but I'm pretty sure. Now try to eat."

Vivian woke up with a start and her body involuntarily shook from it. Wide awake, she tossed her head from side to side trying to grasp what it was that awakened her. She looked at the clock on her bedside table which read 2:13 and saw the darkness outside through the window. Suddenly, she heard it again. A sharp, short scream coming from a bedroom down the hall. Only this time it wasn't her subconscious that heard it.

In a flash she flung back the covers and was up and headed for the door. Almost sprinting, she burst into Maddy's bedroom, turned on the light, and found her huddled in a corner. Maddy's knees were pulled up to her chin, her nightgown covering them and her arms squeezing her legs together.

Vivian went right to her and when Vivian got to her, she saw that Maddy's eyes were wide open, unblinking and with a terrified look. Vivian knelt down in front of her and Maddy tried to shrink back farther into the corner.

Vivian reached toward the terrified woman with both hands but was afraid to touch her, "Madeline," she whispered.

"No, no! The blood! What's happening? Make it stop…" Maddy cried out.

Vivian grabbed her shoulders gave her a hard shake and yelled, "Madeline! It's me Vivian!"

It worked. The sudden forceful shaking and the yelling of her name apparently snapped Maddy back from wherever she had been.

Vivian continued to hold her by the shoulders as Maddy blinked several times and silently looked around the room. At first Maddy was breathing hard and it took almost a minute while the two women looked at each other before her breath came back to normal.

"What, what happened? Why am I on the floor? What…"

"You had a bad dream," Vivian quietly said.

Maddy looked directly at her for several seconds then whispered, "No, no. It wasn't a dream. It was too real. I saw Rob and the blood and… I'm not sure."

"What can you remember?" Vivian asked letting go of her shoulders and taking her hands.

"It was…bizarre," Maddy quietly said, trying to recall. "It was… I don't know how to explain it… I saw the bedroom and a dark shape, like a man but I couldn't see his face and I don't know," she said as the tears trickled down her face.

Vivian held her for a couple minutes then said, "Are you okay to go back to bed?"

"Yeah, I think so. Help me up, please."

TWENTY

Marc Kadella was in his SUV eastbound on I-394 toward downtown Minneapolis. He was on his way back from the Corwin Mansion and had Maddy Rivers on his mind. Maddy had two more traumatic experiences over the past three days. Vivian had taken her in for testing and a visit with a psychiatrist. They were waiting for lab results from her blood and urine but so far, no news. The shrink believed she was having some kind of flashback attack and likely, at least, somewhat drug induced.

Marc had called his friend, Dr. Lockhart every day impatiently looking for the results of the samples Maddy gave the day Rob was murdered. Lockhart assured him he would call as soon as he knew.

When Marc got into downtown, he quickly drove through the light mid-morning traffic to the government center. Being a Friday during the summer, he wasn't surprised to find space available in the building's underground parking. County employees were not shy about starting their weekend early.

He was running a little late for a pretrial conference for a minor in possession, first time offense drug case. His client was the son of a business client of Chris Grafton, a lawyer in his office. The spoiled, little snot — Marc couldn't stand the kid — was selling prescription opioids in high school. Because it was a first offense, a plea deal had been made. He received no jail time, probation until age twenty and a stern warning not to do it again. Every time Marc heard a politician blathering about how harsh the justice system was on drug offenders, he got a hearty laugh at their ignorance. The simple truth was, except for serious crimes such as homicide and rape, these miscreants had to work damn hard to get sent to prison.

When his case was resolved, instead of leaving the building to go to his office, Mark took an elevator up to seventeen. He took a look through the window in the door of 1745, saw that the courtroom was empty and went in. He went through the courtroom and into the back hall leading to the judge's chambers.

"Hey," he softly said to Margaret's clerk, Lois, not wanting to startle her.

She looked up from her desk at Marc, frowned and said, "I see I have to call security again. They'll let anybody wander around back here."

"Is she in?" Marc asked ignoring the comment while looking at Margaret's closed door.

"Just a second," Lois said. She picked up her phone, dialed Margaret's extension, put her phone on speaker, and when she answered said. "There's a lawyer out here to see you."

"What does he want?" Margaret asked not knowing who it was.

"I think it's a personal matter."

"Is he tall, dark and handsome?"

"Not really," Lois answered her. "He's not bad and I've heard he has a pretty cute butt."

"Really? Well, send him right back," Margaret laughed.

"You two should take this act on the road," Marc dryly said.

"Hi," she said as Marc came through the door. Margaret was out of her desk and slipping her feet into her shoes. She grabbed her purse and as she walked toward him said, "You're just in time to take me to lunch."

"How about Peterson's," Marc said referring to a coffee shop with good food in the building across the street.

"Sounds good," she replied.

The waitress took their order, a salad for Margaret, cheeseburger and fries for Marc, then left them alone in the booth.

"Did you talk to Maddy or Vivian today?" Margaret asked.

"I went out there, to the mansion," Marc replied. "She's better," he added referring to Maddy. "No waking up in the middle of the night screaming last night at least. Vivian had her in for a complete medical checkup. They haven't found anything but they're still waiting for lab results.

"She also had her see a shrink. He's pretty sure it's some kind of PTSD reaction. Of course, he wants to see her every week for the next ten years or so."

"Don't be so cynical," Margaret said.

"I could've told them it was some kind of PTSD reaction," Marc replied.

"Have you heard back from your guy, doctor what's his name?"

"Lockhart," Marc said. "No, he said it would take a few days to run a thorough check."

"It's been a few days. Have you called him?"

"Yes, every day."

At that exact moment, his phone went off. He checked the caller ID and saw it was from the office.

"Your doctor friend called," he heard Carolyn say. "He has Maddy's lab results."

"And, what are they?" Marc anxiously asked.

"He wouldn't tell me. He said he was only authorized by Maddy to tell you."

"Give me his number, I'll call him," Marc said.

Carolyn told him the number which Marc wrote down on a napkin. He thanked Carolyn, ended the call and started to dial.

"What?" Margaret asked.

Marc told her what it was about while listening to the phone ringing. A receptionist answered and put him on hold. While he waited the waitress came back with their orders and while Marc was munching on French fries, Dr. Lockhart came on the line.

"Nathan, it's Marc Kadella, what did you find?"

"You were right, they found a significant dose of flunitrazepam also known as Rohypnol…"

"Also known as roofies," Marc added.

"Right," Lockhart agreed.

"Enough to make her blackout?"

"Easily. Probably twice the amount needed."

"Now, I have to figure out who, how and why it was done to her," Marc said.

140

"What?!" Margaret anxiously asked. "Someone slipped her roofies?"

"It gets worse, Marc," Lockhart said.

Marc looked at Margaret, nodded his head at her question and held up an index finger to her,

"What?" Marc asked.

"She was also a given a pretty good dose of lysergic acid diethylamide," Lockhart told him.

"What the hell is lysergic acid diethylamide?" Marc asked the doctor.

"LSD," Margaret said from across the table.

"LSD," Lockhart replied through the phone.

"Sonofabitch," Marc quietly muttered. "That may explain some things. Anything else?"

"Isn't that enough?" Lockhart asked. "No," he continued, "so far at least. They're still double checking for other things but so far, that's it."

"Okay, thanks Nathan, I think I owe you one," Marc said.

"Is that bad news or good news?" Lockhart asked.

"Both," Marc replied then ended the call.

They ate their lunch mostly in silence. When they finished Marc called Vivian and told her he was stopping by again.

On their way back to the government center, they walked against a red light on Fourth Avenue. They went inside and got on the escalators to rise up to the second floor.

"You have a defense against murder," Margaret told him as they stood looking at each.

"If it comes to that," Marc said. "I don't believe she did it. Someone spiked her drinks at that party to set her up. I just need to find out who…"

"And why," Margaret added as they stepped off the escalator.

They said goodbye and Margaret walked toward the elevators to take her up to her courtroom. Marc headed for the building's Northeast corner and the elevator to take him down to his car.

"What can you remember?" Marc asked Maddy. The three of them, including Vivian, were in the library and Marc had given her the news. It took almost five minutes for Maddy to calm down and stop talking about a revenge homicide if she found out who did this. She finally got enough control to take a seat on the couch with Vivian opposite the one Marc was on.

"Before the fireworks, what can you remember?" he asked again.

"Pretty much everything," she said. "It had to be one of the bartenders or the waiter. I had two small glasses of beer," she continued, "both of them Rob got for me. Then I had another with dinner."

"Do you think Rob..." Vivian started to ask.

"No," Maddy answered emphatically. "Why would he?"

"That's the question," Marc agreed.

"Besides, I felt fine until later, several hours later. It wasn't until the fireworks started that I began to feel sick."

"What time was that?" Vivian asked.

"Ten o'clock," Maddy said. "I had three small glasses of wine after we ate."

"Did you get them from the bar or did Rob?" Marc asked.

"No, no," Maddy said after thinking about it for a moment. "The waiter. It was the same waiter. A young guy, early twenties, curly brown hair, about five foot seven or eight. Muscular, like he worked out a lot."

"Are you sure?" Marc asked. "It was the same guy that brought you the wine each time?"

"Yes, positive," Maddy replied. "I remember him because he had this funny little smile on his face like he was expecting me to swoon over him. Believe me, I know the look."

"Okay, good, that's a start. We'll get Tony on it," Marc said.

"I'll go find his little ass..." an angry Madeline started to say.

"No, you won't and that's final," Marc declared. "And you know you can't do that. Let Carvelli do it."

After a few moments Maddy took a deep breath, sighed and said, "Yeah, you're right. But I'll tell you right now, when this is over, me and that little shit are gonna have a serious chat."

Vivian, through her laughter, said, "I'll want to see that."

Marcie Sterling was a faster reader than her partner, Owen Jefferson. That and Owen was more thorough and meticulous. Marcie had finished the preliminary autopsy report of Rob Judd two minutes ago. Owen was still checking and rechecking points he had already read while Marcie patiently waited for him.

"Fourteen stab wounds," Owen finally said when he finished and looked at Marcie. "None of which, by itself, was fatal."

"Except for the one in his liver. That would have eventually killed him," Marcie said.

"Yeah, right. I meant none in the heart or lungs to kill him quickly," Owen added.

The two of them were at their desks in the homicide squad room facing each other. The preliminary autopsy had been emailed to them this morning.

"Almost like someone who was stabbing wildly."

"And defense wounds on his hands," Marcie added. "He was fighting her off."

"You're pretty sure it was Maddy Rivers," Owen said.

"You got someone else in mind?" Marcie asked him. "Any evidence pointing at anyone else?"

Owen looked to his right and saw their boss, Lt. Selena Kane approaching. She took a chair from an empty desk, rolled up to her two detectives and sat down.

"Did you read the autopsy?" she asked looking from one to the other.

"Yeah," Owen answered.

"Yes, ma'am," Marcie said.

"And?" Selena asked.

"And what?" Owen replied.

143

"And when do we arrest Madeline Rivers? I just got off the phone with Steve Gondeck," Selena continued referring to the chief felony prosecutor in the Hennepin County Attorney's office. "He thinks we have enough for an arrest and so do I."

"I thought we should wait for the DNA test results from what the crime scene people found in the bedroom," Owen said.

"According to their report," Selena said, "they found nothing in the bedroom to indicate there has been anyone in there except Robert Judd and an as yet unidentified female whom we can reasonably believe is Ms. Rivers since she was found unconscious on the bedroom floor with the murder weapon in her hand. Plus, there were no fingerprints, no hair and no samples of any kind except those of two people.

"Owen, I know she's a friend of yours. Steve Gondeck is heartbroken over this. He knows her and likes her too," Selena said more softly. "Steve told me to tell you to call her lawyer and have him bring her in. We'll keep it quiet, just the three of us and Steve. He can bring her in on Monday. Steve knows her lawyer very well and if he's willing to vouch for her and guarantee he'll have her here Monday morning at nine, we'll give her the weekend. Give him a call."

TWENTY-ONE

Steve Gondeck finished his deli sandwich at the same time he finished reading the story in the morning newspaper about the Judd homicide. The media was starting to turn the heat up wondering why the girlfriend, Madeline Rivers, had not been arrested. This morning's article in the Minneapolis paper decided to drop all pretense and flat out claim it was racially motivated. The reporter had sought out quotes from two local community organizers. Both of them claimed that if Maddy Rivers was black, she would have been arrested at the scene.

Gondeck pushed himself away from his desk, spun his chair around and leaned on his credenza while he stared out of his office window. From the twentieth floor of the government center he had a great view of South Minneapolis including the chain of lakes toward the southwest.

Gondeck had been with the Hennepin County Attorney's office ever since law school. He was a careful, methodical prosecutor who knew how to build a case and convince a jury. And woe be unto the foolish defendant whom Gondeck caught in a lie. Quick on his feet, if you tried lying with him as your prosecutor, he could, and did, crucify you with your own words in less than two minutes.

As chief prosecutor of the felony division it would be his job to prosecute Maddy Rivers. He had known Maddy for several years and was, at least, a friendly rival of her lawyer, Marc Kadella. Aside from the fact his tongue practically fell out of his mouth whenever he saw Maddy, he genuinely liked her. She was a bright, pleasant, reasonable person. And he liked and respected Marc. But as chief prosecutor, he knew his boss would not let him recuse himself.

Gondeck's phone went off and he knew who it was without looking. Lillian Gardner, the Hennepin County Attorney, was about to bite off a chunk of his ass.

"Yes, Lillian," Gondeck said into the phone. "I'll be right there."

145

Lillian Gardner had been selected by the Governor, Ted Dahlstrom, to complete the term of her predecessor, Craig Slocum. Slocum had been forced to resign under a very dark cloud of scandal and misconduct. At the time of her appointment, Gondeck and everyone in the county attorney's office was baffled by the selection. Why would Dahlstrom, a fairly conservative Republican, select her? Gardner was an uber-liberal feminist with no criminal law background. Gondeck also found out the forty-eight-year-old woman had not been in a courtroom in over twenty years. Rumor had it that the Democrats, led by Gardner's friend Mayor Susan Gillette, insisted on her. Gondeck was convinced that Dahlstrom didn't select her as much as he inflicted her on Minneapolis as payback for being overwhelmingly Democrat.

Since she took charge almost twenty-five percent of the lawyers had quit. Also, the cops with MPD hated her and crime in the city, mostly smaller offenses such as theft and burglary, were up almost thirty percent. And the cops blamed her directly. Gardner's attitude, fueled by her own white guilt, was that gangbangers were really misunderstood youths and drug dealers were urban entrepreneurs.

Gondeck sat staring at his phone for several seconds then thought, *Well, let's go see what Old Iron Ass wants.* Iron Ass being a nickname she had earned by rarely leaving her chair. Gondeck had a pretty good idea what her problem was. It was likely she saw the story in the paper and wanted Maddy Rivers arrested, now.

He knocked on her door, entered her large corner office and before Gondeck had a chance to take a seat, without even a polite greeting, she started in on him.

"I just got off the phone with Mayor Gillette," she said. Gondeck could see this morning's paper on her desk with the Judd homicide story prominently displayed. "She had a talk with Chief Watters who had spoken to Lieutenant Kane of homicide..."

"I know who Selena Kane is," Gondeck quietly said.

"Don't interrupt me. Anyway, to cut to the chase, apparently you told Kane's detective that Madeline Rivers could

146

enjoy a nice, pleasant, leisurely weekend then surrender herself on Monday morning."

There was a long pause between them during which Gondeck kept quiet.

"Well?!" Gardner snapped.

"Oh, I'm sorry, you want me to say something," Gondeck irreverently said. "Yes I did."

A clearly annoyed Gardner said, "You call her lawyer, I assume you know who that is…"

"Yes, I do," Gondeck blandly replied.

"…and get Madeline Rivers in here this afternoon. Since she is represented I will extend the courtesy of allowing him to bring her in. But if she's not here by five o'clock you put out a BOLO or whatever those things are and kick the MPD in the ass to go get her. Am I clear?"

"Yes, ma'am," Gondeck again, calmly replied.

"She can spend the weekend locked up."

Won't happen. She'll be out in time for supper, Gondeck thought but knew better than to tell her.

"I'll take care of it," he said. "Then I want to recuse myself from prosecuting this case."

Gardner, caught off guard by that statement, looked at him for a few seconds then asked, "Why? Do you have a personal relationship with her?"

"I've known her for several years and consider her a friend."

"Do you have a personal or romantic relationship with her?"

"Well, no, but…"

"Then the answer is no. You will not recuse yourself. I don't want the media to claim favoritism by this office. Understood?"

"Okay," Gondeck said quietly.

"Besides," Gardner continued, "Your personal knowledge of her could be an advantage."

"And grounds for an appeal," Gondeck said. "What are we charging her with," he added before Gardner could reply.

"Murder two until we get the DNA then take it to a grand jury for first degree. Throw in a couple of manslaughter charges as well."

"So, Iron Ass saw this morning's paper and her liberal guilt went into overdrive and now I have to bring Maddy in today," Marc Kadella said to Gondeck.

"Yeah, that's pretty accurate," Gondeck said into his phone.

"Can we do this without the media being all over it?" Marc asked.

"I doubt it," Gondeck replied. "They won't get it from me but this place, the mayor's office and the police department, leak like sieves. They'll find out."

Marc looked at his watch, did some mental calculations then said, "I'll have her there by three. Assuming I can get a hold of her."

"Marc get her here or I'll have to issue an arrest warrant and have the cops find her."

"I'll see you at three and I'd appreciate it if you were there," Marc said.

"Wouldn't miss it. In fact, I'll be in my office all afternoon. Call me when you're on the way."

"Will do."

After speaking to Gondeck, Marc had immediately called Maddy at Vivian's. He quickly gave her the bad news and told her he was on the way. Less than thirty minutes later he parked next to Tony's Camaro in Vivian's driveway.

All three of them, Vivian, Tony and Maddy, were waiting for him in the library. Marc sat down on a couch next to Maddy, put his arm around her shoulders and kissed her cheek. She had her hands folded in her lap and was nervously squeezing and releasing them over and over.

"Hey, it'll be okay. I promise," Marc told her.

"Why are they doing this? What evidence do they have? What..." Vivian started to ask.

"Vivian," Marc said holding up his hand to stop her. "We've been expecting this all week. I don't know what evidence they have. We'll see. I suspect it's because they lack any evidence involving anyone else.

"Did you see the story in this morning's paper?" Marc asked.

"Yes," Vivian said.

"No," Maddy replied. "What was it?"

"They're trying to make this some kind of white privilege deal. Claiming if you were black you'd already be in jail."

"Is that true?" Vivian asked.

"No, I don't believe that," Marc said. "I know the lawyers in the county attorney's office. I know the MPD detectives. It's not about race, it's about evidence. Hell, Owen Jefferson is a black man and as straight as any cop there is. Their race claims are about selling newspapers.

"They're making her come in on Friday afternoon and they'll try to stall to prevent her from getting before a judge to try to make her spend the weekend in jail. Vivian, here's what I want you to do..."

With Maddy in the back seat and Tony riding shotgun in front, Marc drove around both the Old City Hall and the Hennepin County Government Center across Fifth Street. He was looking for something he didn't want to find but found it anyway. On the north side of the Old City Hall, parked along Fourth Street, were vans from every local TV station.

"I figured they would pull that stunt and get the media out," Marc said.

"I wonder if Gabriella's here," Maddy said.

Tony turned in his seat to look at Maddy and said, "I doubt it. They'll send a reporter. But she'll have to cover it. At least one of these jackals will be fair to you."

149

Marc parked across the street in the underground government center lot. The three of them took the tunnel under Fifth Street and when they reached the police booking area, the herd of reporters began to circle them.

Tony shielded Madeline from them and stood with her while Owen Jefferson read her the Miranda warning. With Jefferson were Marcie Sterling and Steve Gondeck.

Marc held the media at bay and made the usual defense lawyer claims about his client's innocence. He gave the standard answers about the prosecutors being pressured to make an arrest and their weak case. Satisfied that they had enough film and quotes, they backed off and left Marc to go attend to his client.

Marc joined Tony, the cops and Gondeck, while the deputy was about to lead Maddy away.

"Deputy," Marc politely said to the man who loosely held Maddy's arm. "After you're done booking her, we'll need her in a conference room."

"Sorry, lawyer. Our jail doesn't work on your schedule," the man replied with an evident attitude just as Gondeck joined Marc.

Before Gondeck could intervene, Marc's eyes narrowed and he snarled at the deputy, "Do you really want to explain to Chief Judge Jennrich why you took it upon yourself to deny my client her Constitutional right to counsel?"

The startled man stuttered, "Well, uh, no, I guess not, sorry."

"And be quick about it," Marc added.

"Yes, sir," the chastened man said.

Marc and Gondeck watched the deputy lead Maddy away to be booked. Gondeck said, "Why do we need a conference room?"

Marc turned to answer him then saw an elderly gentleman approaching from the direction of the tunnel Marc, Maddy and Tony had walked through. He was in his mid-sixties, had thinning white hair, wore a slightly rumpled, charcoal gray suit and no tie. He was also very well known to the prosecutor.

150

"For him," Marc said nodding his head toward the man.

Gondeck turned and saw him coming then whispered to Marc, "How did you do this on a Friday afternoon?"

"Pays to know people," Marc whispered back.

"Good afternoon, your Honor," Gondeck said when the man reached them.

"Thanks for coming, Judge," Marc said.

"No problem," Judge Harold Jennrich, Chief Judge of the Hennepin County District Court said. "My court reporter will be along in a few minutes."

Barely two minutes later two more men arrived both a little frazzled from running the media gauntlet. One of the men was the judge's court reporter and the other looked like either a corporate lawyer or an accountant. He was wearing a three-piece suit with a bowtie and introduced himself as Vivian Donahue's representative, the man who was there to make Maddy's bail.

An hour later, Marc, Tony and Maddy were back in Marc's SUV on their way back to Vivian's.

"Thank you," Maddy told them both for at least the tenth time.

Finally, Marc said over his shoulder to her, "Don't thank us yet. That was the easy part."

TWENTY-TWO

"What part of 'give this case a priority' don't you people understand?" Owen Jefferson said as calmly as he could into his telephone. He was talking to a lab supervisor at the Minnesota Bureau of Criminal Apprehension about the DNA analysis from Rob Judd's bedroom. Owen was squeezing the handle of his office phone so hard Marcie Sterling thought he was going to break it. Marcie was watching the vein on Owen's temple throb while doing her best not to laugh at his discomfort. Owen had good reason to be angry but Marcie knew if she laughed it would only make it worse.

"I don't give a damn how many samples you have to test! For Christ's sake, it's been over a week…"

Owen stopped to listen and looked at Marcie who covered her mouth with her hand. Owen continued to listen, gave Marcie a hard look and waved an admonishing index finger at her.

Owen moved the phone's mouthpiece below his chin and said to Marcie, "He's checking. Don't you dare laugh."

"I'm sorry," Marcie said barely containing herself.

"It's not funny," Owen growled. "Okay, it's a little funny but don't…Yeah, I'm still here," he said into the phone. "They're done?" he continued more calmly. "And?"

He listened to the man for a moment then said, "Okay. Get us the official report this morning and thanks."

Jefferson replaced the phone handle in its cradle, rubbed his face with the palms of both hands then looked across their desks at Marcie.

"Well?" she asked.

"DNA from Robert Judd and one unidentified female. We need to get a sample from Madeline Rivers for a comparison." While he was saying this, Jefferson was dialing his phone.

"Steve, it's Owen Jefferson," he said to Steve Gondeck.

"What did you find out, Owen?"

"What we thought," he sighed. "They've found DNA from Robert Judd and a female who has to be…"

152

"Maddy Rivers," Gondeck finished for him. "I'll call her lawyer and see if he'll let us get a sample from her. Why do I feel so shitty about this?"

"Because we don't want it to be true," Jefferson replied.

Three hours later, Marc and Maddy were in his SUV westbound on I-394 to go back to Vivian's home. They were leaving downtown Minneapolis after having a lab tech swab Maddy's mouth for a saliva sample. Gondeck, Jefferson and Marcie were all there. While the tech did his thing, Gondeck had taken Marc into a room where they could talk.

"I'm sick about this," Gondeck confessed.

"So hand it off to someone else," Marc said. "There are other…"

"She won't let me," Gondeck said referring to his boss.

"Sucks to be you," Marc replied. "What do you want, Steve?"

"We're going to take this to a grand jury for first degree."

"Okay," Marc shrugged. "Do what you have to do. I can't stop you."

"Gardner's pissed that you were able to get Jennrich down to the jail to get her arraigned, have bail set and released right away. Off the record, how did you do that?"

Marc thought the question over for a moment then said, "Might as well tell you, you'll know soon enough anyway. Vivian Donahue thinks of Maddy as the daughter she would have wanted to have. She called Dahlstrom," Marc continued referring to Minnesota's governor, "and he called Jennrich. I guess they're golfing buddies."

"So Lillian Gardner, in an election year for the county attorney's job she wants as a stepping stone to Washington, just made an enemy of Vivian Donahue," Gondeck said with a huge smile. "I'll have fun watching that ton of bricks drop on Gardner's head."

"Don't tell her," Marc said.

"No chance," Gondeck replied. "It'll be too much fun standing by watching it happen. I just wish it was Craig Slocum," he added referring to Gardner's predecessor.

Turning serious, Gondeck said, "I just want you to know, I'll put my personal feelings aside and prosecute Maddy to the best of my ability."

"You better, it'll be your ass if you don't," Marc said.

The two adversaries shook hands. As Gondeck reached for the door to leave, Marc stopped him.

"Hey, just for the heck of it, what if I got her to spend a week in Hawaii with you? You know, just a little get away from the wife and kids kind of thing."

Gondeck looked at him, pursed his lips in thought then said, "You're getting warm." He paused and continued with, "Nah, Beth would cut my balls off and feed them to me."

"Might be worth it," Marc said smiling.

"Stop reminding me how much I like your client. It won't do you any good," Gondeck laughed.

"Worth a try," Marc said still smiling.

"And I'll have a nice fantasy before I fall asleep tonight," Gondeck replied.

"Why did you make them get a court order to get my DNA?" Maddy asked Marc while they cruised west on 394.

"There's a case out of Georgia heading toward the U.S. Supreme Court about this. If it gets there at all, it will be there in about two years. If the Democrats keep the White House and appoint more Supremes, they might overturn the law and say the cops need more grounds to get a DNA sample," Marc answered.

"Really? You think it will happen?"

"No," Marc said shaking his head. "It's a long shot at best. Getting a DNA sample isn't very intrusive, but you never know. This way, making them get a court order preserves it for appeal."

"In case we lose," Maddy quietly said.

Marc reached over, patted her arm and said, "Relax, we're a long way from that."

"God, I'm such an idiot," Maddy said. "I've been meaning to tell you something that may be important."

"What?" Marc asked looking back and forth between Maddy and the road.

Maddy adjusted her seatbelt and turned to face Marc. "Before the party, on Thursday the night before the weekend of the Fourth," she began.

"Yeah?"

"Rob and I were having dinner and, as usual, he was a thousand miles away. Something was bothering him and had been for weeks."

"And, go on," Marc said.

By the time they were turning into the long driveway to the Corwin Mansion, Maddy had told Marc everything Rob had told her about CAR Securities. She told him what Rob had said about the mortgage securities, the secret room across the hall and even the death of Patrick McGarry and his girlfriend.

Marc was making the turn onto the Corwin property driveway as he said, "Rob went to his boss about what sounds like it could be securities fraud a few days before he was killed?"

"Yes. He was very concerned and his boss, Walter something, I can't remember his name, wasn't the least bit concerned," Maddy replied.

"And someone else who also died was the one who first told Rob about this?"

"Yes, that's what he told me, but McGarry's death was ruled an accident."

Marc silently thought this news through as he finished the drive and parked the car.

Maddy, who had continued to look at him asked, "Something? Nothing? Maybe something? Am I grasping at straws?"

"No, definitely something," Marc said.

Maddy abruptly turned in her seat and silently stared through the windshield.

"What?" Marc asked.

"No DNA in Rob's bedroom except his and mine," she softly said.

"That doesn't mean anything," Marc reminded her. "A pro wouldn't leave a calling card like that. Besides, we'll get the pictures, the report of the blood spray and I have my guy coming tomorrow to go over the scene himself. We could still find evidence of a third person in the bedroom. I'm going to drop you off..."

"When can I go home?"

"You don't like it here?" Marc asked.

"I love it here but it's not my place," Maddy said.

"How about a couple more days?"

"Okay, two more."

"Maddy," Marc said, "look at me."

She turned her head to him.

"You didn't do this. Even drugged you couldn't do this. You were set up and we'll find out who did it and why. What you told me about CAR Securities is a good starting point. Someone wanted Rob dead..."

"Oh, that's another thing," Maddy said. "That same night at dinner, in the restaurant, there was a man by himself at another table. I caught him looking at us three or four times."

"Was he just checking you out?"

"No, I don't think so. I think he was looking at Rob. When I asked Rob if he knew who he was, Rob told me he didn't but I got the feeling he was lying that he didn't know the guy."

"Would you know him again if you saw him?"

"Yes, I think so. I was almost certain I had seen him before," Maddy answered.

Marc looked past Maddy, through the passenger window and saw Vivian slowly walking toward them. Marc waved to her and used his window button to put Maddy's window down.

"Am I interrupting?" Vivian asked through Maddy's window.

"No," Marc said. "It went fine," he continued referring to the DNA swab. "I'm taking off. Take care of our girl."

"I will," Vivian replied.

"I'm gonna call Tony," Marc said to both of them. "I'll talk to him about what you told me," he told Maddy.

"Can I tell Vivian?"

"Sure. Did you find out who catered the party she went to on the Fourth?" Marc asked Vivian.

"Not yet. I have a friend still looking but so far, no luck," she replied.

Back on 394 now eastbound back toward downtown, Marc retrieved his phone from his coat pocket and punched the number for Carvelli. It took six rings but the P.I. finally answered.

"What's up?" Tony asked.

"You got time to meet me? I need to talk to you about Madeline," Marc said.

"Sure, when and where?"

"Where are you?" Marc asked.

"Five minutes from downtown," Tony replied.

"Great, I'll meet you at Peterson's in ten minutes."

Carvelli arrived first, ordered a Diet Coke and waited for Marc. He was in a booth facing the entrance and waved to the lawyer when he saw him arrive as the waitress set Tony's soda on the table. Marc ordered a regular Coke from her then sat down.

"At your age, you should be watching your calories and drink a diet soda," Tony smiled.

"What?"

"Getting a little soft around the middle," Carvelli teased him.

"Oh, kiss my ass, gangster. Besides, that diet shit will kill you."

"Everything is bad for you these days. Even the water," Carvelli said.

"Nonsense. The water's cleaner than it's ever been."

"What's up?" Tony asked getting to the reason for the meeting.

"Thanks," Marc told the waitress. He watched the teenager walk away and said, "They're getting younger all the time."

"No, they're not," Tony said.

"Thanks for the reminder. Anyway I need you to start an investigation into Rob Judd's employers. It's an investment firm called…"

"CAR Securities Management," Tony said cutting him off.

"Yeah, you know them?"

"Hang on a minute," Tony said. For the next minute or so Tony was obviously on the phone with Vivian getting her permission to tell Marc what they knew about CAR Securities.

"Yes, I knew you would be okay with it but I still, ethically, have to get your permission. I'll call you later with an update," Marc heard Tony say into the phone as he looked at Marc and shook his head.

Marc had a leather folio with him with a small legal pad in it. For the next half-hour the two friends exchanged all of the information they had on CAR Securities.

"What do you think?" Tony asked Marc when they finished.

Marc looked over his notes for a minute before answering. "Something's not right with this outfit. I'm not a securities guy but I do know enough about them to know I'd like to get my hands on those documents Rob Judd went to his boss with, this Pascal guy," Marc finally said.

"Vivian's pretty sure there's some fraud going on there. Did you tell her about these securities Judd was worried about?" Tony asked.

"No, you can. As far as fraud in the securities industry, that's not exactly a newsflash. For small investors, you're about as well off to go to Vegas with your money. The gambling there isn't as crooked as it is on Wall Street or as rigged.

"But we need to keep digging," Marc continued. "All I need is reasonable doubt. A way to show a jury someone else had a motive to kill Judd. We may be on to something here," Marc said.

"What about Maddy being drugged? What did Jefferson and Gondeck have to say about that?"

"I haven't told them," Marc replied.

"Seriously? Why not?" a surprised Carvelli asked him.

"That goes more to diminished capacity. At best, it would knock it down to manslaughter. We're going on the theory she was set up, a pro did this and made it look like she did it. If we can come up with someone else that isn't based on conjecture and speculation, something more concrete than what we have now, then I can tell them and use it as an alibi."

"A pro huh? Working for who?" Tony asked.

"Whom," Marc corrected him.

Tony gave him an annoyed look and scratched his nose with his middle finger.

Marc laughed then said, "We've got one candidate, maybe. CAR Securities. If there's fraud going on, there must be at least several people involved. The more possibles we find, the better."

"Okay," Tony nodded. He held up his glass of Coke, the two of them clicked their sodas together then Tony said, "Let's get to work. Our pal's in trouble."

TWENTY-THREE

The two men in almost identical black, pinstriped suits, white shirts and striped ties marched in step down the hallway, the subordinate of the two, careful to stay one pace behind his boss. When they reached the glass enclosed conference room, the younger man waited silently for the older man, the younger man's security guard, to open the door for him.

They entered the room and ignored the people seated at the table. The one in charge took his seat at the head of the table while his security guard sat behind him in the corner. The younger man, in fact the youngest one in the room, looked over those already seated.

"It's been, what, twelve days since your informant was murdered, what was his name?" he asked looking at a man seated to his right.

"Robert Judd," the man replied.

"So now what?" the U.S. Attorney for Minnesota, Winston Paine asked, in his usual arrogant fashion to the two FBI agents, the Deputy U.S Marshall and the Assistant U.S. Attorney. These four people had been waiting almost forty minutes for Paine to make his appearance. Winston Paine, who never missed an opportunity to remind people that his long dead relation, Robert Paine, was a signer of the Declaration of Independence, made sure he was late to every meeting. It was his not so subtle way of reminding everyone who was the most important person in the room.

"Well, after making us wait for forty minutes for you to grace us with your presence, maybe we can get on with it," FBI Special Agent Mike Anderson irreverently replied. Anderson was pushing thirty years with the Bureau and generally hated arrogant, political appointees and Winston Paine in particular. Anderson worked for the FBI not the U.S. Attorney and he never missed a chance to let Paine know it.

"Mike..." Joel Dylan the Assistant U.S. Attorney started to say. It was his boss that Anderson had verbally slapped which inwardly delighted Joel but he still wanted to keep the peace.

"I was on an important call with the Deputy Attorney General," Paine said, as close to an apology as he would ever utter.

"Did you tell him about your dad, the guy who signed the Declaration of Independence?" Anderson asked.

At this, a beet-faced Paine turned to Joel Dylan and asked, again, "Where are we with your investigation?"

"Well, we got enough information from Keegan's guy to keep digging," Dylan said referring to Deputy U.S. Marshall Keegan Mitchell, seated across the table from him. "And…"

"All right, good," Paine said cutting off his subordinate. Paine abruptly stood up and went to the glass and chrome conference room door.

"Keep me informed."

Paine's underling bodyguard who shadowed Paine everywhere, opened the door and the two of them left.

"That's it," Anderson said looking at Joel. "We wait forty fucking minutes for this dipshit for that?"

"Sorry, Mike," Dylan said. "He was supposed to tell you to pick up Walter Pascal. We have enough from what Judd told us the other day to start squeezing him. I think he's the weak link at CAR."

"I could've been told that with a phone call, Joel," Anderson said.

"I know, sorry. Holly," he continued looking at Holly Byrnes, Anderson's partner.

"It's okay," Holly smiled. "It's nice to get out of the office. Besides, it's always amusing watching Mike get his rocks off on your boss."

Keegan Mitchell, unable to contain his laughter any longer finally said, "That's perfect. She knows you well, Mike."

Anderson looked at the pretty, short-haired blonde and the Marine in him growled, "Yeah, a little too well."

Holly laughed, blew him a kiss and stood up to leave. "We'll pick him up tonight, after he leaves work."

"We'll bring him in for a little chat this evening," Anderson added. "You want to be there, Keegan?"

161

"Yeah, I would," the deputy said. "Maybe, I should tag along when you grab him."

Anderson shrugged the said, "You can if you want to but I can give you a call after we get him."

"Okay," Keegan replied.

"Call me, too," Joel Dylan said.

"I was going to. We'll see you guys this evening."

Anderson and Holly Byrnes were in their Fed car parked across the street from the Lasalle Building. Holly had called CAR Securities fifteen minutes ago, and asked for Walter Pascal. When he answered, she hung up so they knew he was still there. They also knew what he drove, a three-year-old Mercedes, its plate number and parking spot. Holly had verified the Benz was parked in the correct spot and they waited for it. There was only one exit from the ramp and the two agents were staring right at it.

"Ten minutes to six," Holly said.

"It was a quarter to six just five minutes ago, when you told me that," Anderson teased her. "Plus, I can see the clock myself. Be a little patient, my child," he said to the younger woman.

"I know," she replied. "I don't know if I'll ever have the patience for stakeouts."

"You have a date tonight?" Anderson asked. Anderson was over fifty and Holly was still in her early thirties. They had been partners for four years and Anderson looked at her as the daughter he would have liked to have.

"What's a date?" she joked. "There he is," she quickly added then she started the car.

Holly waited for two cars to go by then pulled out to follow him.

"If he turns right on Ninth he's probably going home," Anderson said. "If he does, we'll follow him there and let him park his car so we don't have to mess around waiting for a tow truck."

"And the paperwork," Holly added.

162

Thirty minutes later the two agents followed Walter Pascal right into the two car garage of his townhouse. Holly drove in so close Walter couldn't close the garage door. Anderson was out the door and on top of a terrified Pascal before he could get his car door open. Walter looked at the hulking form of Agent Anderson and visions of being murdered flashed through Walter's brain. He was so frightened, he was on the verge of emptying his bladder in his car when Anderson opened his door and stuck his FBI shield in his face.

"Mr. Pascal, my name is Anderson. I'm an agent with the FBI. Step out of the car, please."

"Oh, my God," a very relieved Walter Pascal muttered as he leaned forward and rested his forehead on the steering wheel. He stayed like this for three or four seconds until he started breathing again. By this time Holly Byrnes had joined her partner and held her credentials out as well.

"Mr. Pascal," Mike repeated. "Please step out."

"Oh, yeah, sure, um. You just scared me," Pascal said as he swung his legs out and stood up. "You're, ah, with the FBI, huh?"

"Yes, sir," Anderson said.

"What do you want?" a more composed Walter asked.

"We need you to come with us. We have some questions to ask," Anderson replied.

Walter Pascal, although startled by what had happened, was an intelligent, educated man. He was totally composed now and said, "And if I don't want to?"

"We'd rather not turn this adversarial, sir," Holly quickly said before Mike verbally slapped the man.

"Maybe I should call a lawyer," Pascal said.

"Why?" Holly smiled. "You're not under arrest. If you haven't done anything wrong, you shouldn't need a lawyer."

"I don't know," Walter said. "I don't think I want to go with you."

Anderson who stood a good six inches taller and was forty pounds heavier than the smaller bond salesman, leaned into him and said, "You got three seconds to get your ass moving, Wally. Then I slap you in cuffs and we haul your ass out of here, Three, two…"

"Okay, I'll come along. Relax."

Holly Byrnes looked at her watch and noted it was now 7:30. Mike Anderson, Holly, Deputy U.S. Marshall Mitchell and Joel Dylan were standing together watching Walter Pascal.

"How long has he been in there?" Dylan asked.

"Forty, forty-five minutes," Anderson answered him.

The four of them were looking through a two-way mirror into an interrogation room. They were in the Minneapolis office of the FBI in the suburb of Brooklyn Park, just north of the city.

"Hey! How many goddamn times do I have to demand to talk to a lawyer?" Pascal yelled for at least the tenth time. He had been locked in this room by the two agents who brought him in almost an hour ago. They had not even allowed him to use the restroom, which he had requested, and he was getting a little uncomfortable.

"At least come tell me why I'm here," he yelled again looking at the mirror on the wall.

"Time for a little chat," Anderson said, "before he wets himself."

TWENTY-FOUR

Walter Pascal stood at the urinal and felt a single drop of sweat slide down his nose. He hoped the FBI agent waiting in the men's room for him didn't notice it or how shaky his knees were. What had him the most worried was Rob Judd. What did they know? No one said a word and all he could think about was, *If this isn't about Rob, then what? Again, what did they know?* One thought brought him some comfort. Murder is a state crime and these guys are all feds.

Walter finished wiping the water from his hands and tossed the paper towels in the trash. Now that he felt better, he decided to try something.

"If I'm not under arrest, I'm leaving. If I am under arrest, I want a lawyer," he told Mike Anderson.

Anderson gave him a little smile and said, "Wally, you don't mind if I call you Wally..."

"I prefer Walter," Pascal said trying to sound tough.

"Wally," Anderson said again still wearing the same smirk, "you're not going anywhere. What you need to do is get back in that room across the hall, sit down, shut up and listen. I'm gonna do you a favor. So just cut out the tough guy act and listen to what we have to say."

The two men went back to the interrogation room and Anderson held the door open for Walter. He reentered the room and found three other people waiting for them. One he recognized as the female FBI agent who brought him here. The other two, one dressed in a business suit the other in jeans and a nice golf shirt with a badge of some sort clipped to his belt, were two men Walter did not recognize. The female agent and the casually dressed man were leaning on the wall by the mirror. The man in the suit was seated at the table. Walter sat back down in the same chair he was in before.

Anderson sat at the table across from him and silently stared at him for almost a full minute. None of the others said a word while they waited.

"Who are you?" Walter nervously asked the man in the suit.

"I'm Assistant U.S. Attorney Joel Dylan," the man answered.

Before Walter could respond, Anderson said, "Wally, do you think it's a coincidence that we picked you up?"

"I have no idea…" Walter started to say.

"That we just plucked your name out of the phone book to bring you in for a little chat?"

At first, Pascal said nothing, hoping his nervousness was not too obvious.

"Does the name Robert Judd ring a bell?" Anderson asked.

"Of course," Walter responded. "He worked for me." He said this while thinking, *I had nothing to do with his murder.*

Anderson continued to stare at him, obviously trying to intimidate the man. Dylan reached down into the briefcase he had on the floor to his left, removed a manila folder and handed it to Anderson.

Anderson removed a two-inch stack of paper and set it on the table in front of Walter and asked, "Does this look familiar?"

Walter silently stared at it, knowing exactly what had been placed on the table. It was a copy of the computer printouts Rob Judd had given him showing the defaults of the CAR Securities' mortgage backed bonds. Walter said nothing but a bead of sweat broke out along his hairline.

"We have you for securities fraud right now, Walter," Joel Dylan interjected. "Our forensic accountants went through this."

"And we know Rob Judd told you about this and you know what's in here. He came to us on the Friday before the Fourth of July," Anderson said, "a few days before he was murdered. In fact," Anderson continued, placing his hand on the documents in front of Wally, "some people might think this could be a motive for murder."

"That's crazy!" Walter said. "They made an arrest. It was the girlfriend."

166

"The Minneapolis cops don't know about this," Anderson said.

Dylan reached down again and removed another folder from his briefcase. He handed this one to Anderson also.

Before he opened the new folder to show Walter the contents, Anderson folded his hands and placed them on top of it.

"You and Victor Espinosa took a one day vacation to visit with some friends in Panama a few weeks ago," Anderson said, a statement not a question. "Must have been a long day with all of those different flights you had to take. Are you wondering how we know?"

Walter didn't answer the question. He sat silently shifting his eyes about the room looking for a friendly face. All he found were stone-faced looks staring back at him.

Anderson opened the folder removed an 8 x 10" color print, reversed it and slid it front of Walter.

"This gentleman here," Anderson said poking his finger on a man in the photo, "the one shaking hands with your pal Victor Espinosa, is a Latino gent we know by the name of Carlos Rodriguez. And that's you standing next to Victor isn't it Wally?"

Again, Walter sat silently while Anderson continued.

"Mr. Rodriguez is a known associate of a fellow by the name of Javier Torres, also known as El Callado, the Quiet One. A mean, nasty bastard if there ever was one.

"This next picture," Anderson continued showing Walter the next photo, "was taken earlier that same day. You can see the date and time stamp on it. Anyway, it's a shot of that same Mr. Torres taken at a villa outside Panama City. He's conversing with a man whose name is Pablo Quinones. Quinones is the number two guy in this particular drug cartel the U.S. Government is interested in.

"This next photo is you and Victor and your friend Carlos later that day walking toward that very same villa. And here is a shot of you and Victor at the door shaking hands with Pablo Quinones, at the front door of the villa. Have a nice chat with the fellas in Panama? Don't tell me, let me guess. You were discussing financial transactions, transactions we like to call money laundering, for a drug cartel, weren't you Wally?"

"You can't prove…"

"Don't even try that," Dylan jumped in to say.

"I want a lawyer," Pascal weakly said.

"No, you don't, Wally," Anderson said. "Because if you do, we'll lock your ass up right now, no deals and you do twenty years in a bend-over-in-the-shower federal prison. No country club for you, Wally. You and your pals get the real deal."

"Have you ever heard of the acronym RICO?" Dylan asked. "It stands for Racketeer Influenced and Corrupt Organizations. It's a federal law that allows us to go after you and your pals the same way we go after the Mafia. And you do life in sunny, pleasant vacation spas like Leavenworth, Kansas. Or…"

"Or?" Walter asked after a long pause.

"Or, guess what," Anderson replied.

"I go to work for you against my friends and partners," Walter weakly said.

"You got it," Anderson answered him.

Walter sat silently thinking it over. He again looked around the room searching for a friendly face while he did so.

"I don't know," he finally said. "I think I should talk it over with a lawyer."

"Told you so," Holly Byrnes said as she sprang from the wall. She walked behind Walter who nervously watched her remove a pair of handcuffs from her belt.

"Get up sleazebag," she said. She grabbed Wally's right arm and started pulling him out of the chair.

"Sorry, Wally," Anderson said.

"You're under arrest and I just won fifty bucks. I knew you were too weak and stupid."

"Wait, wait," Walter whined, struggling to remain seated. "Okay, I'll do it. But," he continued looking at Dylan. "I want a complete walk. No jail time. And I want it in writing."

Holly stood behind him dangling the handcuffs alongside his face. Walter looked back and forth at the serious expressions coming from Anderson and Dylan.

"I don't think so, Walter," Dylan said. "We got you by the balls right now. Why should we deal?"

"Because you don't know the half of it," Walter said with a lot more confidence than he felt.

"Okay," Dylan agreed. "I'll put it in writing for you. But you screw up one time, hold anything back or lie to us, and all bets are off. You got it?"

"And we are going to want everything and I mean everything," Anderson added.

"You know," Walter said. "I feel relieved. I feel like a five-ton weight has been lifted off of me. But, it will take some time. They don't tell me everything. I think I can find out what all they're up to, but I'll need some time,"

"What all who is up to?" Dylan asked. "Who's running the show?"

"Corbin Reed and Ethan, Ethan Rask," Walter answered.

Anderson looked at Dylan who nodded his head then Anderson looked at Holly.

"Are you sure about this?" Anderson asked Holly.

"Yeah, it'll be fine," Holly said.

"Here's the deal, Wally. The lady standing next to you with the handcuffs, she's your new girlfriend."

"Without the fringe benefits," Holly added,

It was almost midnight by the time Anderson and Holly dropped Walter Pascal back at his townhouse. Dylan had found a computer to type up the grant of immunity. They had spent another two hours going over the ground rules and what was expected of him. Walter also told them everything he knew about the illegal activities of CAR Securities. At least that's what he claimed. All he really did was more or less confirm what they already knew.

When they were about finished, Dylan startled him with a question.

"What can you tell me about the deaths of Patrick McGarry and his girlfriend, Lynn Mason?"

"What?" Walter asked looking genuinely surprised. "It was an accident. They were hiking somewhere up North and slipped on a trail and fell."

"We don't think so," Anderson said. "Rob Judd told us McGarry came to him with concerns about CAR, the same concerns Judd talked to you about."

"Then Judd gets killed too," Dylan added.

"I don't know anything about that," Walter insisted. "McGarry was an accident and Rob's girlfriend went nuts. I don't know…"

"Find out," Dylan said.

Walter paused, looked around the room and then said, "Okay. I'll see if I can find out anything. But I don't think these guys would do something like that. I mean, murder? I don't think so."

When Walter got home he mixed himself a stiff scotch and soda. He stood in front of the bay window in the living room in the dark sipping his drink. *This could work out better than I planned,* he thought to himself.

TWENTY-FIVE

Tony Carvelli sat by himself at end of the bar where it made a left-hand turn to complete its L shape. He was in the Rendez Vous Piano Bar of the Leamington Hotel in downtown Minneapolis. The Leamington was the last of the city's old-style Grand Hotels from a bygone era of class and elegance, rarely found in today's mass marketed, chain hotels.

Tony loved this old place, its understated style and grace. It was a comfortable and warm place where women unashamedly wore dresses and heels and men were still expected to be in a suit, tie and polished shoes.

The man at the piano was playing a tune Tony didn't recognize but knew, somehow, it was from the forties. It was quiet and serene like the Grand Old Dame that was the Leamington herself.

While he watched Rask and waited for the bartender, Tony thought about his other problem. Vivian Donahue was trying to use her contacts to find out who catered the Fourth of July party for CAR Securities. Tony was certain it was one of their employees, the waiter Maddy described, who spiked her wine with the drugs. So far, Vivian was not having any luck finding them.

A good crowd for a Wednesday evening, Tony had been tailing his quarry, Ethan Rask, for three straight days now. The first two days, Rask went right home after work and did not leave. Being a veteran cop, Tony was used to the need for patience. When he saw Rask park in the lot across the street then scurry across Nicollet to the hotel, he started to believe tonight was the night he would get lucky.

Rask was seated at a table by himself, his back to the bar and Tony, sipping a cocktail. Tony's eyes were focused on the glass Rask held trying to decide how best to steal it. The best way would be too bribe the waitress but he didn't know which one had served him. Before long, one of the four waitresses working the bar stopped at Rask's table, smiled while he reordered then hurried off to get the man his drink.

Tony started to get up to go to the waitress' service area of the bar when Rask stood up to greet a very attractive, younger woman. Rask took the woman's hand, kissed her on the cheek then held her chair for her.

When Tony saw this he dropped back onto his barstool, his mouth half-open and thought, *I'll be damned, Gretchen Stenson. I wonder what name she's using these days?*

Ethan Rask would never be mistaken for a George Clooney. Pushing fifty, thirty to forty pounds overweight and a hairline that was rapidly receding, Rask's chances of attracting a woman of Gretchen's caliber was somewhat less than zero. Except Gretchen was a high-end prostitute that Tony had known for almost twenty years. He first busted her as a seventeen-year old high school girl turning tricks and running three of her high school friends.

As Tony watched, he was impressed that even though she had to be pushing forty, she looked twenty-five and was still gorgeous and likely a thousand-dollar a night entrepreneur.

Tony caught the bartender's eye, a young man in a white-shirt, black bowtie and black vest, and motioned to him. The bartender came over to him, both hands on the bar and leaned toward him.

"Yes sir?" the young man asked.

"Who's the woman that just sat down with that older guy?" Tony asked turning his head toward Rask and Gretchen?

The bartender stood up straight and stuttered, "I'm ah, not sure, ah..."

"I'm not a cop and I know what she is," Tony said. "I want to know what name she's using these days. I used to be a cop and I know her from back when, but how do I get in touch with her now?"

The young man looked around, held up his right index finger to indicate to Tony 'wait a minute', then walked off. He served a couple customers, made another vodka tonic for Tony and walked back to him.

He set the drink down and discreetly slid a business card to Tony who took it and slipped it into his pocket. With the index finger on his left hand, Tony slid a fifty-dollar bill to the young man then casually waved that hand to indicate he could keep it.

The waitress returned with Rask's second drink, leaned down and placed it on the table while listening to Gretchen order something. Rask drained the glass he was holding and set it on the waitress' tray. When Tony saw that, he knew he had his chance. He stood up and headed down the bar to intercept her.

"Excuse me," he said to the young woman just before she got back to the bar. "This may sound a little crazy but I'll give you fifty dollars for that glass."

The waitress did a quick look around to see if anyone was watching then said, "You got it, sir," and she reached for the glass to hand it to Tony.

"No, no, don't touch it," Tony frantically whispered. He took her arm and gently led her away and when they were by the door, Tony pulled two, large, Ziploc bags from his pocket.

"I need it untouched," he explained.

"You a cop?" she asked him.

Using a napkin to hold the glass, Tony poured the ice and what was left of Rask's drink in one bag and sealed it. He then placed the glass in the other bag and sealed that also.

"Private," he whispered. He peeled off two twenties and a ten, placed them in her hand and said, "This is between you and me, okay?

"No problem," she smiled. "Anytime you need to buy any dishes just let me know."

Tony laughed then said, "At these prices I can't afford it."

While Tony was leaving he turned and read the name by the bar's entrance. *Rendez Vous bar is exactly right*, he thought with a smile while thinking about Gretchen and Rask.

As Tony walked back across Nicollet to where his car was parked, the muggy July weather made him take off his light tan, silk jacket. Once in his car, he removed the business card from his pocket. On it was the name Audrianna, a phone number and website address. That was it. No information of any kind.

Tony started the car to get the A/C going then retrieved his phone from the jacket he had tossed on the Camaro's passenger seat. He held it in his hand for a couple of minutes while he stared through the windshield.

"That's it," he quietly said to himself when he remembered the number he had searched for in his memory. He quickly punched in the number and listened while it rang. After the third ring, a familiar voice answered.

"Garrett," the man said.

"Hey, Alfonso," Carvelli said. "It's Tony…"

"Carvelli, you reprobate," the man finished for him. "How the hell you been?"

"I'm good Al. And you? How are you, Jodie and the boys?" Tony asked referring to the man's family.

"Everybody's good, Tony. Doing fine. You should come to dinner. We'd love to see you again. What's up?"

"I'm looking for some information on a hooker," Tony said. "And, of course, I thought of you, immediately, because of your intimate knowledge of them."

"Very funny, smartass." Al laughed.

Al was Sergeant Alfonso Garrett with MPD Vice and a long-time friend of Carvelli's. "What's her name?"

"I got a card here," Tony said. "First name only. Audrianna."

"Our girl, Gretchen Stenson," Al said. "Sure, I know her. She's been around a while."

"I know. I knew her years ago," Tony said. "I want to know where she's living now. Is she working for someone or…"

"No, I don't think so. She's been on the high-end call girl list for years. Very discreet and very expensive. She does most things, straight sex and even S & M, but only as a dominatrix. Hang on a minute, I got her address here."

When Al told Tony about Gretchen being a dominatrix Tony got an image of Rask being tied up and punished, an image that made Tony wince.

Al came back on the line and read Tony the woman's address. When he finished, Tony asked him, "You guys bust her lately?"

"Not for years," Garrett admitted. "She quietly does her thing and she has some very well-to-do clients. As long as she stays off the streets we pretty much leave her and others like her alone. What do you want with her?"

"It's a private matter," Tony said.

"Hey, Carvelli, forget it. You can't afford her." Garrett laughed

"No kidding," Tony agreed. "Thanks, Al."

After he finished his call with his vice cop friend, he quickly dialed another number, this time off of his phone directory list. The man he was calling answered before the first ring finished.

"Hey, it's Carvelli," Tony said. "I have what I talked to you about. Can I swing by with it yet tonight?"

"Sure, come on over. I'll get it done while you wait."

An hour and a half later, Carvelli backed his car down the driveway of the man he had come to see. He was a fingerprint specialist with the MPD who did a little moonlighting on the side, out of his home. His name was Galen Fisher and Tony had used him many times in the past. At home, without anyone looking over his shoulder, he could work, undisturbed, lift latent prints and get Tony a clear set very quickly and at a reasonable price.

While Tony waited in Galen's living room watching a Twin's game on TV, he called his computer hacker, Paul Baker. Like most internet nerds, Baker was a total night owl. Twenty minutes after Tony left the home of the fingerprint guy, Baker fed the photos of Ethan Rask's prints into his computer. He then hacked into AFIS, the FBI's fingerprint data base. A few minutes short of a half hour, Baker had the information Tony wanted.

TWENTY-SIX

Tony padded barefoot across the polished oak, hardwood floor of his living room. He owned a small, older house by Lake Nokomis in South Minneapolis that he used for living space and his office, which was in one of the upstairs bedrooms.

It was early for Tony, shortly after eight A.M. After leaving Paul Baker's house with the information about Ethan Rask, he had driven to the luxury high-rise where Gretchen Stenson lived. Her condo was on the third floor and he could see it from the street. Tony sat in his car across the street watching the only window, he guessed the living room, with a light on, reminiscing a bit about the kid he had busted many years ago for solicitation, hoping she had not had a rough life. Just before he drove off, he thought, *she seems to be doing okay.*

Now, the next morning, wearing his normal morning ensemble of a pair of old, gray sweats and a plain, white T-shirt, he opened the front door to retrieve the paper. When he did, the early morning heat and humidity hit him like a sauna.

"Wow, looks like a steamy day," he quietly muttered as he picked up the paper.

Tony looked at the front page, above the fold headlines.

P.I. Girlfriend Indicted By Grand Jury.

He began reading the article as he closed the door by pushing on it with his butt. He had the paper in one hand, a cup of coffee in the other as he walked back into the kitchen and the breakfast nook.

Tony was about half-way through the story when his phone rang. It was on the counter by the sink where he had left it to recharge. He got it from its recharger, looked at the caller ID, sighed and answered it.

"Yes, I've seen it," he said to Vivian without saying hello.

"I'm surprised Marc hasn't called," Vivian said.

"He probably doesn't know yet. He will soon."

"How could he not know?" Vivian asked.

"I know he got a letter from the country attorney to let him know Maddy was the subject of a grand jury investigation. That was a couple weeks ago. They got their indictment then leaked it to the media. They're starting their campaign to taint the jury pool," Tony said while he sipped his coffee. "They probably didn't send him a copy before giving it to the news people."

When he finished saying this he heard another call come through on his phone. Tony looked at the screen then said, "Maddy's calling. Let me talk to her and I'll call you back. Or, have her call you."

"Do that, thanks," Vivian replied then ended the call.

"Hi, sweetheart," Tony softly said to Maddy.

"Have you seen the paper?"

"Yeah, I have. We knew it was coming."

"I know," she said. "But seeing your name in the paper indicted for first degree murder…"

"What are you doing?"

"I'm curled up on my couch hoping the world will go away and leave me alone. Hoping I'll wake up and this will all be a bad dream. On top of it Marc's in court already this morning and I can't get a hold of him."

"Maddy," Tony firmly said. "We'll get you through this, I promise."

"What if I did this?" she whispered.

"Stop it!" he said. "You are not capable of that. Okay? Tell you what, your picture's not in the paper…"

"It's on TV," Maddy said.

"Let's go get some breakfast. I have some news. I'll meet you at Sir Jack's on Fifty Third and Chicago in half an hour."

"Make it an hour and I'll be there," Maddy said.

"Give Vivian a quick call, before you do anything else. I'll leave a message for Marc," Tony told her.

Tony waved to Maddy from the corner booth he was seated in, waiting for her. She saw him and without removing her sunglasses, she made her way through the crowd to Tony. He stood up, hugged her and kissed her on the cheek.

When they were seated she leaned onto the table and said, "See, everybody's looking at me because…"

"Everybody always looks at you," Tony laughed. "I thought you were used to it."

"I guess I'm just being paranoid," she said.

"Marc called me back," Tony said. "He told me to meet at his office at eleven. He hadn't seen the news so I told him."

"What did he say?"

"Not much. He wasn't happy about them leaking it but wasn't surprised either," Tony replied. "Did you call Vivian?"

"Yes," Maddy said.

The waitress arrived and they ordered. When she left, Maddy continued.

"She wants me to move back to the mansion. She said it will protect me from the media. I already got a half a dozen calls, my number's listed so…"

"Not a bad idea," Tony said.

"What news do you have?" Maddy asked ignoring Tony's comment.

"I found out who this Ethan Rask guy is," Tony said.

"The mystery man of CAR Securities?"

"Yeah, him. It's not good," Tony replied. "Or, for us, maybe it is."

While they ate, Tony explained what he had done the previous evening and what he had learned.

When he finished, Maddy, with raised eyebrows and a sly smile asked him, "So, who's this high-priced hooker friend of yours, Carvelli. This is a story I want to hear."

"No, I never did," Tony said to stop her inquiring stare. "She was a high school kid, homecoming queen, pretty, popular girl the first time I busted her. She was turning tricks at age seventeen and had three other girls working for her.

"I took her home, upper-middle class family in Burnsville. I thought she straightened out but I was wrong.

"A few years later, I ran into her again and found out she was still working but learning the trade as an upper-end call girl. Not on the street, no drugs, no pimp, nothing like that. I lost track of her after I retired. Apparently I don't travel in the right circles.

"Anyway, I saw her last night with Rask. She looks great. Looks like she's still twenty-five though she's got to be pushing forty."

"And your heart did a little pitter patter," Maddy teased him.

"Very funny, but yeah. I liked her she was always a good person. I talked to a friend with vice last night. They know who she is but leave her alone because she's clean, discreet and honest. I am going to track her down and have a little chat with her about Rask. You ready?" Tony asked as he looked at the check. "We should go."

"Ah, the hooker with a heart of gold. How touching," Maddy said.

Tony reached the parking lot door to the Reardon Building and waited for Maddy. She stepped onto the concrete stoop and Tony opened the door for her.

"Marc's back from court," she said referring to his SUV in the lot.

"I see that," Tony agreed.

The two of them went up the backstairs side-by-side. About half way toward the top, Tony stopped and turned to Maddy.

"Hey," he softly said. "Have you thought about getting some counseling?"

"For what?"

"You're pretty obviously depressed and with good reason."

"What's a shrink going to tell me? 'Don't let it get you down that you might have murdered your boyfriend and will go to prison for twenty-five or thirty years.' I'm not sure that would help."

Tony frowned at her and she said, "I'll think about it. Okay?"

"Let's go."

"Hi," Maddy said to the staff when they entered the suite of offices.

As soon as she saw her, Carolyn practically jumped up and ran to Maddy with her arms outstretched. They held each other for almost fifteen seconds then Carolyn kissed her cheek and let go.

"You didn't do this," Carolyn said holding Maddy's shoulders and looking her directly in the eyes. "I absolutely know you could not. You got it?"

"Yes, Mom," Maddy sadly smiled.

"Hey, kid," Maddy heard a raspy, female voice say from behind her.

"Hi, Connie," Maddy said.

"C'mere, give us a hug," Connie said. After it, Connie said, "Carolyn's right. You didn't do it and we're all gonna work to get you off. Don't worry about it."

"Marc's on the phone but he said you should go right in," Carolyn told Tony.

Tony knocked once then opened Marc's door. He then stepped aside to let Maddy go in first. Marc, with the desk phone to his ear, waved them forward.

"This is bullshit, Steve," they heard Marc angrily say. "We've known each other long enough now for you to extend me the courtesy of…"

The man on the other end interrupted him. Marc listened for a few seconds while Maddy and Tony sat down.

"Okay, fine. You didn't know, you didn't do it, blah, blah, blah. Get it to me please and I'll talk to you later."

He listened for a moment again then said, "I don't care. Fax, email, messenger whatever. Thanks, goodbye."

Marc looked across the desk to Maddy, seated to his right, then Tony next to her.

"Hi. That was Steve Gondeck. It's always fun to chew a prosecutor's ass for something. This time for not getting me the indictment before it hit the papers."

"How bad is it?" Tony asked.

"I don't know," Marc shrugged. "I haven't seen it yet. How are you holding up?" Marc asked.

"Okay," Maddy said. "I feel better being around friends."

"You should move back to Vivian's. She'd love to have you," Marc said.

"I know. I'll think about it. What am I charged with?" she asked.

"I'm not sure. We'll see when we get the indictment. At least one count of first degree which is overcharging," Marc said. "They'll try to get a plea to second degree or manslaughter."

"I might take manslaughter…"

"Stop right there!" Marc almost yelled. "We're a long way from that."

"Relax," Tony said patting her right arm. "I have some news," Tony said looking at Marc.

"About?"

"CAR Securities and one of their main guys, Ethan Rask."

"Tell me," Marc said visibly curious.

"His real name is Anatoly Brodsky, born in Brooklyn, New York to Lev and Riva Brodsky."

"Russian Jews," Marc commented.

"Yep. Forty-eight years old," Tony continued. "Also known as, David Carter, Dominic Reznick, Martin Cameron and Edward Mallory.

"He's done two stretches in prison. Once in his late-twenties he did eighteen months in New York for theft by swindle. Second time he did three years in Atlanta courtesy of the feds for, you ready?"

"Yeah, sure."

"Securities fraud," Tony announced.

"He's a con man," Marc said.

"He's also been arrested twice for suspicion of murder and three times for felony assaults. None of which stuck."

"Well, well, well, well," Marc said with a smile. "I see the beginning of reasonable doubt."

"Do you think so?" Maddy hopefully asked.

"Oh, yeah," Marc said. "If you're going to claim some other dude did it, it's always good to have some other dude to point at."

"Because of what Rob told me," Maddy said, "CAR Securities had motive."

"And it was their party where you were drugged," Marc reminded her.

Maddy leaned forward and reached across the desk to take Marc's hand. "I feel better already," she said.

"We still have a lot of digging to do, but we have a theory now. Something we can use."

"Yeah, by the time I'm done, we'll know everything about these guys," Tony said. "And it looks like we may have some shady dealings of theirs to start with."

Maddy let go of Marc's hand and as she started to lean back in her chair, she glanced at the newspaper on Marc's desk. She picked up the Metro section of the Star Tribune, looked at a picture then started reading the article.

"What?" Marc asked her.

"Wait," she answered him while she continued to read. Ten seconds later she pointed at a picture of a young man with dark, curly hair above the article and showed it to Tony.

"That's him!" Maddy said. "That's the waiter from the party. I'm certain of it."

Tony leaned forward to look at the photo and after a couple seconds Maddy showed it to Marc.

"I remember now, he had on a name tag. The name on it was Kirk, the same as this guy. How many Kirk's are there that look like this? I'm positive it's him."

"He's missing. He hasn't been seen since the Fourth of July," Maddy said.

TWENTY-SEVEN

While Marc read through the written copy of the indictment which had come in via email, Tony asked Maddy to hand him the newspaper. Believing he meant the section with the story about the missing waiter, she gave him that section only.

Tony read the entire article then said to Maddy, "You're sure about this?"

"Yes, absolutely," she nodded.

"It says he was a student at the U. It doesn't say where he worked. I'll start on this today. I'll check with the Minneapolis cops first and see what they have. I should be able to find out where he was employed. Find out who the caterer was," Tony said. "He's been missing since the Fourth."

"He's dead, isn't he?" Maddy asked Tony.

"Probably," Tony agreed. "We can still look into him and maybe find out if he drugged you and why."

Marc put the indictment down and Maddy stood up, reached across the desk and snatched up the document.

"Don't read it. I'll tell you what's in it," Marc said.

"Do I tell the cops why I'm interested in finding this kid?" Tony asked Marc.

Marc thought about the question then said, "No, not yet. I'm not ready to tell them she was drugged."

"First degree murder? How can they say this was first degree?" Maddy asked holding the indictment.

"Give me that," Marc said holding out a hand to her. "They get pretty graphic describing the crime scene. You don't need to read it.

"As far as first degree," Marc continued as Maddy handed him the document, "they're overcharging. They'll shoot for first degree and hope the jury gives you second degree, or at least first degree manslaughter.

"You seem pretty calm," Tony said.

"I'm a wreck," Maddy said. "When do they want to arraign me on the new charges?" she asked Marc.

"I told Gondeck to set it up for a couple days from now. They'll want to make sure the media's in full attendance," Marc answered her.

"Have you heard back from Jason Briggs?' Tony asked wanting to change the subject. He was referring to a professional, independent criminalist, CSI type, Marc hired to go over the crime scene.

"Yeah, he called late yesterday. He's done with the crime scene. Now he'll get his samples to a lab and have them analyzed. It'll be at least two or three weeks," Marc answered Tony.

"What did he think?" Maddy asked.

"He had no opinion about anything, yet," Marc said. "Hopefully he'll come up with something to argue there was a third person there. Just because the crime scene unit didn't find it doesn't mean he won't."

"The CSU people aren't really as good as what you see on TV," Tony added. "Especially if they believe you did it because they found you there. They may have gone into their investigation with blinders on, not really looking for any other evidence."

Tony felt his phone vibrating in his coat pocket. He took it out, looked at the screen, said, "Vivian", then answered it. Tony listened for a minute while she told him something.

"I'm at Marc's office with him and our girl. I'll bring her along and see you in twenty minutes."

Tony looked at Marc and said, "She has information about the guys at CAR Securities."

"Mind if I tag along? I got nothing better to do. I might as well hear about this, too," Marc said.

"Sure, come on, let's go. She'll feed us lunch, too," Tony replied.

Carvelli drove his car and Marc had Maddy ride with him and leave her car in the lot at Marc's office.

"I have someone you should see," Marc said a few minutes into their journey. "You need to get into some counseling."

"Will it help my memory?"

"I don't know but it will help your depression and anxiety."

"I've been thinking," Maddy said turning in the passenger seat to face Marc. "Maybe I should get hypnotized. Maybe I can find out what happened through hypnosis."

"No," Marc emphatically declared.

"Why, I want to find out…"

"I don't," Marc said turning his head to her as he drove. "I don't want to know anything we might have to turn over to the prosecution. Dr. Butler can't be forced to testify. There's no such thing as a hypnotist privilege."

"Unless it's from a doctor. If the hypnotist is a doctor," Maddy said.

"You know an MD who does hypnosis therapy?"

"No, but we can find one," Maddy said.

"No we can't and we're not going to look," Marc said unequivocally. "Besides, for the purposes of a trial, we're better off not knowing. Look, Maddy," Marc continued more softly. "I don't believe for a second you did this. But you may have, in your subconscious, convinced yourself that you did. If some hypnotist quack brings that out and we have to give it to the prosecution as discovery, you're hosed. No, we're going to defend this with the very rational belief you were set-up because that's what our investigation is finding."

Maddy sat silently staring out the windshield thinking over what her lawyer had said. After almost a full minute, realizing he was right, she finally, softly said, "Okay."

Marc and Tony, walking together, followed Vivian and Maddy through the large, open foyer of the mansion. Vivian had her right arm around Maddy's shoulders as the four of them passed through the building to the large French doors leading to the patio. One of the patio tables, with an open umbrella in its center, was set with excellent Chinaware for four people.

"Mary has whipped up an excellent chicken salad for lunch. You two guys especially, look like you should start eating a little healthier," Vivian said with a sly wink at Maddy.

"Getting a little soft around the middle, fellas," Maddy added with a smile.

While Maddy took her seat, Marc tilted his head and looked at Maddy's backside. "I'm not so sure you should be talking there, wiseguy," Marc said.

"Ahhh! What do you mean?" Maddy practically squealed as she tried to swivel her head to look at her butt. She then gave Marc a dirty look and slapped him hard on the shoulder. "That's not funny," she said.

"See how they are?" Marc asked Tony.

"Yep, they can dish it out but they can't take it," Tony replied.

"You two are living dangerously," Vivian told them.

Marc looked at Vivian and said, "I just like saying things like that to her because they're not true. But it won't matter. She won't eat anything but carrots for a month."

This good-natured banter and teasing continued for a few more minutes while Mary served their lunch. Mary also got in on it, taking a couple of well-timed, verbal pokes at Carvelli.

They all began eating and a couple minutes in, Vivian started.

"The guys at CAR Securities," she began, "are pretty much what you see. The three from Wall Street," she continued removing a small notebook from the pocket of her slacks, "Corbin Reed, Jordan Kemp and Walter Pascal, all met while working at Bear Stearns before the crash.

"Pascal and Kemp seem to be pretty straight. Corbin Reed has a history of having several different employers. Rumor has it that he was ethically challenged. He didn't have a problem putting customers into high risk investments for higher fees for himself."

"Gee. Wall Street guys putting themselves ahead of their customers. What a shock," Marc sarcastically commented.

"Kemp is a math and analytical genius. Pascal is an excellent bond trader. Combine that with what we now know about Ethan Rask and we have what may be a Ponzi scheme taking place," Vivian said. "My nephew is going to get his money out as soon as possible."

"There's another guy, what's-his-name…" Tony said.

"Victor Espinosa," Vivian said. "Not much on him. By all appearances, he seems legitimate."

"He got hooked up with those guys for a reason. We'll keep digging," Tony said.

Marc, eating too fast, finished his lunch, set it aside and said, "With what we know about this Rask character, the question I have is, can we point a finger at them and claim they had a motive to kill Rob Judd?"

"He went to his boss, this Walter Pascal and warned them about some securities. Something about mortgages, I can't remember exactly what," Maddy said.

"Mortgage backed securities?" Vivian asked her.

"Yes! That's what he called them, mortgage backed securities. Rob told me they were not what they should be. They weren't backed by mortgages with a good enough rating."

"Oh my God, you're kidding," Vivian said. "What exactly did he tell you?"

"Let me think," Maddy said. She paused for a moment to gather her thoughts then continued. "He said, legally, they were supposed to be triple A and double A mortgages but they weren't. They were much worse. I think it was double or maybe triple B and lower. I can't remember for sure. I know it was some type of B rating," Maddy answered her.

"Good God," Vivian said tossing her linen napkin on the table in disgust.

She looked across the table at Marc who looked back at her, shrugged his shoulders and said, "They haven't learned."

"Too big to fail," Vivian sighed.

"What?" Tony said looking first at Marc then at Vivian. "I'm just a dumb cop. What's going on?"

"Do you remember the financial industry melt down of '07 and '08?" Vivian asked Tony.

"Sure," Tony said.

"What caused it was this very thing. Between greedy mortgage companies, greedier Wall Street crooks and stupid, do-gooder politicians, they almost crashed our economy.

"First, the politicians, in their never-ending quest to con people into voting for them, decided it was a good idea to get home loans for people who couldn't pay for them. A few very powerful members of Congress pressured Fanny Mae and Freddie Mac, government mortgage insurers, to get mortgages for people of low income and poor credit. Those were B level rated securities at best. And the companies who rate these things were in on this scam up to their eyeballs.

"Then Wall Street packaged these things up in mortgaged backed securities and sold them. You buy the security, you get the interest payments when they come in. They are pretty much the same thing as bonds but supposedly backed by no risk or low risk mortgages.

"Do you remember AIG, the giant insurance company?" Vivian asked Tony.

"Yeah, I do. The government bailed them out for like eighty billion. What did they have to do with it?"

"AIG wrote insurance policies for these mortgage backed securities," Vivian continued. "This was a complete scam designed to generate billions of dollars of fees for Wall Street firms. It was based on the assumption that the real estate market would continue to grow at eight to ten percent every year. There were people who were warning these guys that the housing market was a bubble about to burst but no one listened. No one wanted to believe it and these guys had been crying wolf over this real estate bubble for at least ten years. Which is why no one believed them. If you yell fire over and over and there's never a fire, it won't be long before people stop listening. But if you say it long enough, sooner or later there will be a fire and then you can brag that you predicted it.

"Finally, in '07 and '08, the bubble did burst, the real estate market started to decline and these entire mortgage backed securities that were backed by too many bad loans, collapsed. Wall

Street losses sky rocketed and AIG didn't have the money to pay all of the insurance claims in the meltdown."

"And they're at it again," Maddy interjected.

"Maybe," Vivian agreed. "Even probably."

"How much did Rob say CAR Securities had invested in these low rated mortgage backed securities?" Marc asked Maddy.

"I'm pretty sure he said it was three hundred and forty or fifty million and the default rate was getting too high," Maddy answered him.

"That doesn't sound like much in an economy as big as ours," Tony said.

"No, you're right," Vivian agreed. "If that's all there is. But CAR Securities did not package these securities themselves. They bought them on the market. Probably from the big boys who still have their gambling habit.

"Do you remember did Rob tell you what the default rate was?" Vivian asked Maddy.

"I think he said it had gone over six per cent," Maddy replied.

"If it gets to even nine or ten percent, it could happen again," Vivian said looking at Marc.

"Their cash flow from these things is higher than they're reporting, I'd be willing to bet," Marc said.

"High enough to show investors a rate of return better than what should be in this market. And if they are using money from new investors to pay interest payments to other investors, we have a classic Ponzi scheme," Vivian told him.

"How do you know all of this?" Tony asked Marc.

"I have a Business Degree from the U for my undergrad degree. Plus I have read news reports about what happened in '07 and '08," Marc told him. "Is three hundred plus million enough to murder someone to shut him up?" Marc asked, the answer very obvious.

"How do we prove it?" Tony asked. "We can't put Maddy on the stand to tell a jury this without proof."

"No, we can't," Marc agreed. "We need to get our hands on some documentation to prove it."

TWENTY-EIGHT

July 27th, a Wednesday, started off warm and humid and the weather geeks reported it was going to get worse. Marc had left his apartment early, before 7:00 o'clock. It was already eighty degrees and muggy. Now, seated at his desk, he checked the clock on the wall which read 9:10.

He swiveled his chair around, opened the window behind his desk and involuntarily flinched at the blast of hot air that hit him. The high was predicted to be 98.

"Must be climate change," Marc muttered to himself as he closed the window.

His intercom buzzed at the same time there was a knock on his door. Marc answered the intercom and was told Maddy had arrived at the same time she walked through his office door.

"I see that. Thanks," he told Sandy.

He looked over Maddy as she stood in his doorway. Marc had told her to dress nice but simply, which she had done. A simple white blouse, navy blue slacks and plain, low-heel, black pumps. Maddy could wear sackcloth and she would still look great.

"Maybe we should put a burqa on you," Marc said with a smile.

"Shut up, I'm nervous enough as it is," she said.

"You know what's going on here today. It's…"

"Never, as the guest of honor."

"…an arraignment on the indictment. We've been all through this."

"What if the judge won't allow bail? You said Gondeck is going to ask to remand into custody. What if the judge agrees?"

"Graham? Margaret says he's okay. I was in court with him once," Marc was saying as he grabbed his leather, satchel briefcase and suit coat. He continued as they headed across the office toward the exit door to a chorus of 'good lucks' from the office personnel.

"He had this idiot gangbanger in front of him with a street thug attitude. He even called Graham 'bro' but only once."

"Is Graham African-American?" Maddy asked.

"Yeah, but he sure as hell didn't appreciate that level of disrespect."

Marc held the door for Maddy and he continued as they started down the stairs.

"Graham proceeded to read into the record this guy's adult criminal record, all of it. It took the judge almost ten minutes. Graham then ripped this guy a new ass and put him in prison for six years on multiple drug charges."

Maddy stopped three steps from the bottom, looked at Marc and said, "And how is this story supposed to make me feel better?"

Marc looked back at her, his mouth hanging partially open, and said, "Ah, well, um, he's a fair judge. He'll set bail. The story is meant to show you he doesn't play favorites."

Maddy rolled her eyes up then said, "I'm hoping he does, dummy."

"Well, maybe you should have worn a mini-skirt."

"Oh yeah, that helps," she said.

"Or you could unbutton three or four…"

"I'm going to hit you," she snarled.

Marc laughed, walked down to the back door, opened it and said, "Come on, you'll be fine. Let's go," he said smiling while she scratched her cheek with the middle finger of her right hand as she walked past him.

The hearing was scheduled for ten A.M. and the two of them stepped off the elevator at 9:40. Waiting by himself, away from the mob by the courtroom, was Tony Carvelli. He gave Maddy a warm hug, put his arm around her shoulders and started to lead her to the security doors. Tony had slipped a court deputy he knew twenty dollars to stand by and let them in through the back. Tony rapped a couple of times on the frosted glass door. His deputy friend immediately opened it and ushered them in.

"There's a good size gaggle of media out front in the hall. They haven't opened the doors yet to let them in," Tony told them as they walked toward the courtroom.

Marc looked ahead and saw both Steve Gondeck and Steve's main assistant, Jennifer Moore leaning against the wall. They were standing next to the door to Judge Graham's chambers. Marc continued down the back hallway while the deputy took Tony and Maddy into the empty courtroom.

"Sneaking in the back," Gondeck said as he shook hands with Marc.

"I guess there's a mob out front," Marc said. He turned to Jennifer, extended his hand and said, "I hear congratulations are in order. Why wasn't I invited?"

"It was a small ceremony, Marc. Very few people. It's a second time for both of us so we kept it small. But thanks," she smiled.

"Well, I hope it works out and you're happy. If not, Connie Mickelson will handle your divorce and suck out all of his internal organs. Is he a lawyer?"

"No, he's a dentist with a good practice," Jennifer said.

"Well, then you have a chance." Marc then turned to Gondeck and asked, "What's going on?"

"Graham wants to see us," Gondeck shrugged. Graham's clerk stepped out and asked, "Everybody here? Good, go on in," she said without waiting for a reply.

Gondeck and Jennifer Moore took their seats as the judge stood extending a hand to Marc.

"I don't believe we've met. Derek Graham," he said shaking Marc's hand.

"Once, your Honor," Marc replied. "About a year ago."

"Sorry, I don't remember it. Please, have a seat. "We have a high publicity case," Graham stated when Marc was seated. "I'm already getting requests for cameras in the courtroom. What are your opinions?"

"No," Gondeck quickly said.

"Marc?" the judge asked.

"I hadn't given it any thought," Marc said. "Normally, I'm not a big fan. Too much risk of lawyers, jurors, witnesses and, pardon me, your Honor, even judges playing to the camera."

"Have you seen his client?" Jennifer said. "She's enough of a distraction without putting her on TV."

"Oh? How so?" Graham asked Marc.

"She's an attractive woman your Honor," Marc looked at Jennifer and said, "I promise I won't let her wear a swimsuit."

"Damn, I was hoping," Gondeck muttered.

Graham looked at Gondeck, smiled, shook his head and said, "I take it you've met her. I'll put off the question of cameras for now. But I'm not inclined to allow them." He looked at Marc and continued. "I agree, they tend to create a little too much acting and drama.

"This morning," Graham said continuing, "bail was previously set by Judge Jennrich at a prior appearance, before the indictment. You're opposing bail entirely, Mr. Gondeck?"

"That is correct, your Honor."

"And you want to continue what has already been paid?" he asked Marc.

"Yes, your Honor."

"Okay. We'll put the arguments on the record and I'll rule. I'll be out in a couple minutes."

The first appearance or, in Minnesota, the Rule 5 hearing, is basically to tell the defendant the charges, read her the *Miranda* rights, enter a plea and set bail.

Marc waived reading the indictment. Maddy agreed, on the record, that she had received a copy through her lawyer, understood the charges and entered a plea of not guilty. There is also a Rule 8 hearing that is little more than a second appearance for mostly the same reason as the Rule 5. These are normally, by agreement, combined into the first appearance to save time. This was also read into the record.

Marc requested an Omnibus hearing to force the prosecution to satisfy Judge Graham that there is probable cause to proceed to trial. It forces the prosecution to present most of its evidence through witnesses. This gives the defense an opportunity to get a good look at their case before the trial. This hearing must, by rule, take place within twenty-eight days of the combined Rule 5 and Rule 8 hearing. Marc also informed the court his client would not waive her right to a speedy trial. A trial date would be set at the Omnibus hearing.

"Bail application, Mr. Gondeck," Graham stated toward the end.

Marc again swiveled his head around to look over the media. For some reason, they had all crowded into seats behind the prosecution table. That is, all except for one older gent who worked for the paper across the river, the St. Paul Pioneer Press. He had the front row behind Marc, Maddy and Tony all to himself.

Gondeck stood up and said, "The state requests that the current bail be revoked and the defendant remanded to custody. This is a horrible, heinous crime, your Honor. She is originally from Chicago, has minimal ties to the jurisdiction and is a threat to others and a flight risk."

After Gondeck sat down, Graham turned to Marc and said, "Mr. Kadella?"

Marc stood and said, "Ms. Rivers moved here permanently several years ago. She has been an upstanding, law-abiding citizen whose every intention is to use the trial to clear her name. There is no indication she will flee and no evidence she is a risk to anyone. As to the crime itself, it is no worse now than it was when Judge Jennrich set the original bail. The only difference is the state convinced a grand jury to grossly over charge it. Bail should be continued."

Gondeck stood again and said, "Your Honor. She is responsible for the deaths of two men..."

"Objection!" Marc yelled as he jumped out of his chair. "Mr. Gondeck knows perfectly well one of those men was trying to rape and murder her in her own home. The other was about to murder her best friend. Both were ruled justifiable homicides."

"Is that true, Mr. Gondeck?"

"Well, ah, yes, your Honor," Gondeck meekly replied.

"Then don't bring it up again. Bail will remain as set. Has your client surrendered her passport?"

"Yes, your Honor," Marc answered.

"Your Honor, her bail was paid by a very wealthy friend of hers, Vivian Corwin Donahue. No amount of bail will…"

"Stop," Graham politely said. "It's irrelevant who paid her bail, Mr. Gondeck. The questions are: is she a flight risk or is she a danger to the public? I am satisfied, as was the Chief Judge, that she is neither of those things."

"Then she should at least wear a monitoring ankle bracelet," Gondeck said.

"I disagree. Ms. Rivers," Graham said looking at Maddy. She stood up next to Marc and Graham asked, "You going to run out on us?"

"No, your Honor. I am innocent and I am going to fight to clear my name."

Graham turned to Gondeck and said, "For now, I'm satisfied and apparently Chief Judge Jennrich was satisfied. Plus, those things tend to hinder a defendant's ability to meet with counsel and help in their defense. You can always reapply if you have grounds, Mr. Gondeck. If there's nothing else," he paused and looked at both lawyers, then said, "We're adjourned. I'll see counsel in chambers." With that, he fled.

"Thanks," a relieved Madeline said to Marc as she hugged him.

"What does he want to see you for?" Tony asked.

"Set a date for the Omnibus hearing. You can wait for me in the hall in back. This won't take long then we'll get some lunch," Marc said.

"I'll call Vivian while we wait," Maddy told him.

Javier Ruiz Torres, El Callado, the godfather of the Del Sur drug cartel walked out the front door of his Panamanian villa. He turned to his left and slowly made his way along the sidewalk toward the concrete patio surrounding the diamond shaped swimming pool. A slight breeze coming off of the Pacific Ocean barely ruffled the palm fronds in the trees overhead.

When he reached his destination, a padded lounge chair alongside the pool, he gently eased his bulky frame onto it. While he did this, two young women hurried to set up a small table with a snifter of Remy Martin King Louis Cognac. At over three thousand dollars a bottle, it was meant for people who could appreciate it. El Callado was not one of them. He could have been served ten bucks a gallon rotgut and this peasant would not have known the difference. Also on the table was an expensive Waterford ashtray and a fresh Montecristo. The man might not know fine Cognac but he did know his cigars. The older of the two girls, sisters, held the cigar lighter for him. When the man she secretly loathed was satisfied, he waved her off with a flick of his hand and she scurried away.

The fat man with the spindly legs sticking out of his shorts relaxed in the chair, smoking his cigar, sipping his Cognac. He ignored the gorgeous day and beautiful scenery, the clear blue, sunny sky and the ocean lapping softly on the white, sandy beach barely two hundred meters from him. El Callado had a problem and he was waiting for his tardy counselor so the cartel boss could ask him about it.

It was almost a half hour since he sat down that El Callado heard the car pull up behind him in front of the villa. A minute later, he was joined by Pablo Quinones. Quinones pulled up a patio chair next to the table, sat down in it, crossed his legs and waited for his boss to speak.

Torres exhaled a large cloud of smoke from his second cigar that the breeze quickly dissipated. "Where've you been?" he asked Quinones in Spanish.

"You know where I was, boss," Quinones replied to the man he secretly believed was far beneath him. "I was in Texas at a skydiving competition."

"I thought you would be back yesterday," Torres growled. "I do not understand this foolishness of jumping out of a perfectly good airplane. You risk your life too much. And this swimming under water with sharks? Why do you do this?"

"It's exhilarating," Quinones answered with a smile. "I told you many times, when I was in the army I fell in love with jumping."

"We have a problem in Minnesota," Torres said abruptly changing subjects.

"I know," Quinones agreed.

"Why am I finding out about this from people other than you?"

"Because it came up while I was gone and right now is the first chance I've had to discuss it with you," Quinones calmly replied. "And I already went to Minnesota and discussed the situation with our people."

This last statement was a lie. He had not traveled to Minnesota. Quinones had spoken to Victor Espinosa on the phone about it and was satisfied their plan was still in place and on schedule.

The younger of the two sisters arrived with a fresh drink for Torres. She also had a bottle of Evian water and a glass of ice for Quinones. A she walked away, Quinones saw the lustful look on Torres face as he watched the young girl, barely fifteen, hurry off. Disgusted, Quinones tried to take his boss' mind off of her.

"What do you want to do?" Quinones quickly asked.

"I want to pleasure myself with that child," Torres said without turning his head. "See to it."

"I'm talking about the money in Minnesota," Quinones said ignoring the order to pimp for his boss.

"How much do we have with them?" Torres asked turning back to his counselor.

"A little more than one hundred million," Quinones replied.

"One hundred and three million, six hundred eighty seven thousand," Torres said.

Annoyed but not daring to say it, Quinones repeated his question, "What do you want to do?"

"You are sure my money is safe?"

"Yes. The returns are very good and everything is fine," Quinones reminded him.

Torres knocked the ash off of the cigar, picked up the lighter and relit it before answering him.

"Very well but keep a close eye on the situation and do not fail to keep me informed," he said as he puffed away to keep the cigar going.

TWENTY-NINE

"This is getting to be bullshit," Mike Anderson said. He was at his desk in his office. His feet were resting in a desk drawer he had pulled out and was talking to Assistant U.S. Attorney Joel Dylan and Holly Byrnes.

Anderson turned his head to look out the large window behind his desk. He stared for two or three seconds at the wet, windy weather that was knocking the leaves off of the trees. Autumn was upon them and in Minnesota it was always a portent of things to come, namely real winter.

"Patience, Mike," Dylan replied. Joel Dylan was sitting to Anderson's left on the cloth-covered couch. Holly Byrnes was seated in one of the barely comfortable government-issued chairs in front of Anderson's desk.

"These things take time," Dylan reminded him.

"I get that, Joel," Anderson said. "But it's almost November. It's been almost three months and this asshole Pascal hasn't given us dick."

"He's right, Joel," Holly agreed. "He's stalling. I think he knows more than he's telling us."

"We need to put a wire on him," Anderson said.

"Can we get a court order to bug their offices?" Holly asked looking at Dylan.

"Probably," Dylan said.

"But it won't do us any good if Pascal is right when he tells us they sweep their offices regularly and randomly," Anderson reminded Holly.

"How can you do something both regularly and randomly? Isn't that a contradiction in terms?" Dylan said with a smile.

Anderson looked at Dylan, snarled then flipped up the middle finger on his left hand which made Dylan laugh.

"I hear the case against Rob Judd's girlfriend is moving toward trial," Dylan said. "Her lawyer has subpoenaed records from CAR Securities. There's a hearing on it in a couple days."

"What's he looking for?" Anderson asked.

"The stuff Judd turned over to us; the securities fraud documents. I think he's trying to show that CAR Securities had a motive to kill Judd to shut him up," Dylan said.

"They did," Holly added. "Are we sitting on exculpatory evidence?" she asked.

"That's not our problem," Dylan said. "Keep your eye on the ball, Holly. Our case is our case and we don't have any legal or ethical obligation to help out a defense lawyer on a state murder trial."

"Seems wrong," Holly said.

"It's called the law. Besides from what I hear the prosecution has a very good circumstantial case against the girlfriend. She snapped and butchered the guy. Her lawyer's just trying to muddy the waters with bullshit. He has no proof that anyone else could have done it. It's not our problem."

"I think maybe it's time to bring Walter in for another chat. He needs to get us evidence of the money laundering we know is going on," Anderson said getting them back to the subject at hand.

Holly Byrnes opened the door to the same interrogation room Walter Pascal was put in the first time he was brought to this building. He appeared to Holly to be a lot more nervous than what he actually was. So far, Walter had been able to stall and put them off. He also knew why he was being brought in again. They were going to try to browbeat him into stepping things up.

"I'm trying my best," he pleaded as Holly stood aside for Walter to go in.

"Get in, Walter," she said, letting her annoyance show. "Sit down and shut up. Stop your whining. I'm tired of it."

Holly closed the door behind him, locking him in. Walter took the chair facing the mirror and looked nervously around the room. While he did this he thought, *We're going to play this same, silly game again where they make me wait trying to intimidate me. Fortunately, I used the toilet before I came here this time.*

Holly went into the observation room behind the mirror where Mike Anderson and Joel Dylan were watching Walter. Holly joined them at the window.

"How long do you want to wait?" Dylan asked.

"We'll see…" Anderson started to say.

"I don't think sweating him will make much difference," Holly said. "We can probably go in now."

"Let's do that," Dylan agreed.

"We think you're jerking our chain," Anderson said to Walter.

Pascal sat by himself on one side of the cheap table. Anderson and Dylan were opposite him and Holly was sitting on the end to Pascal's left.

"It's been almost three months and all you've done is confirm what we already knew," Dylan interjected.

"We think you're stalling, Wally," Anderson said.

"No, I swear I'm not. Look, I told you I work in bonds. I went to Panama with Espinosa because no one else wanted to. I was ordered to go by Corbin. All we talked about was how much money they were going to send. I don't know anything about how it's done or any other details."

"Why haven't you come up with anything about who this Ethan Rask guy is?" Anderson asked.

"What?" Walter said looking nervously between his three antagonists. "I told you who he is. He's a guy Corbin knew. Corbin brought him in. He's the…"

"Compliance officer," Anderson said.

"That's right," Walter agreed.

"Bullshit. What's his background? Where did he come from? Who has he worked for?" Anderson asked.

"I don't know. I've tried to find out and was not too politely told to mind my own business. I've told you this. I can't find out what they won't let me know," Walter said.

"Who killed Robert Judd?" Holly abruptly asked.

Startled by the suddenness of the question, Walter's eyes shifted about before he said, "Ah, his girlfriend. What's-her-name? The chick being brought to trial on it. It's been in the papers. That's all I know about it."

Holly Byrnes stared directly into Walter's eyes, while he said this. Holly was a former NYPD detective and had been with the Bureau for three years. An experienced and very capable investigator, Holly trusted her instincts enough to know when someone was lying to her. At that moment she had no doubt Walter Pascal was lying. He knew more about the murder of Robert Judd than he was admitting.

Mike Anderson knew exactly what had just taken place between Pascal and his partner. He saw Wally's eyes fidget and the look on Holly's face told Anderson she believed Pascal had lied to her. Anderson knew he and Joel Dylan were going to get an argument from Holly. Quickly he decided to get the discussion back to where it should be.

"Wally, we want you to wear a wire," Anderson said.

"No way. Not a chance. I'll never be able to pull it off," Pascal answered. "I'll find out what you're looking for, I promise. I just need more time. I know what's going on and I'll find out how and what. You'll see. These things take time."

"Get us a copy of Rask's fingerprints or DNA," Anderson said.

Pascal looked over the three of them with a concerned look on his face. "How am I supposed to do that? Go up to Ethan and say 'Put your fingers on this inkpad so I can get a set of your prints'? That won't look too suspicious," he added sarcastically.

"Get a coffee cup or a glass or a piece of paper he's handled, dummy. Anything will do," Anderson growled at him.

"Oh, yeah. Okay, I get it. But I don't work with him. I'm not even in the same part of the office as him. But I'll see what I can do. I'll come up with something sooner or later," Walter assured them.

Holly, who had continued to stare at Pascal throughout this exchange, said, "Bullshit. He's full of it. I say we lock his ass up right now, get a search warrant and go after the place."

"That will be our next step," Dylan said.

Thinking quickly, Pascal said, "The things you're looking for might not even be on the premises. With computers, it's easy to store information anywhere in the world. You're better off letting me find it for you. I don't want to go to prison. I'm doing my best," he pleaded.

"Get on with it," Anderson said. "Our patience is at an end."

"I know what you're going to say and don't bother," Anderson said to Holly when she came through his office door.

Holly had escorted Walter Pascal back to his car when they were done with him. In the meantime, Anderson and Joel Dylan had retreated to Anderson's office to wait for Holly to return. Both men knew what she was going to come at them with as soon as she got back.

Holly, annoyed her partner would say that to her, dropped down on a chair across from the two men. They were seated around a small, round table.

"Oh, and what was I going to say, Mr. Clairvoyant?" she asked.

"You were going to say Pascal knows more about the murder of Robert Judd than he's admitting. That maybe the boys at CAR Securities had something to do with it."

"And?" she said now even more annoyed because Anderson was right.

"And we're not going to blow our investigation by running to the defense lawyer for the girlfriend with conjecture and speculation," Dylan told her. "We have no legal or ethical obligation to help him and we're not going to."

"How about a moral obligation?" Holly asked. "How about the fact that she is likely innocent?"

"You don't know that," Dylan said.

205

"You may believe it but we have no evidence of any kind to back it up."

"And if we find evidence?" Holly asked Dylan.

"We'll see," he said. "But I'll tell you right now, I probably won't change my mind. Our case is our case and we are not involved in the murder of Robert Judd."

Holly looked at her partner and asked, "Do you agree with that, Mike?"

"Keep your eye on the ball, Holly. Joel's right. We work for the federal government. Not the state of Minnesota."

"That is…"

"Relax, Holly," Dylan said. "We'll see how it goes, okay?"

"No, it's not okay, but we'll see," she said.

THIRTY

Tony Carvelli parked the Camaro in front of his internet hacker's house, turned off the wipers and shut down the big engine. Before he got out, Tony took a few seconds to sit and look through the windshield at the weather. Another wet, windy, late-October day. *I already miss summer and it's going to get a lot worse before it gets better,* he thought.

Tony turned up the collar of his full-length, black leather coat, opened the driver's door and, when he got out, ran up the house's sidewalk, his head scrunched in like a turtle's. When he reached the four stairs leading to the front door, he jumped two steps to get to the stoop, pressed the doorbell twice and impatiently pounded several times on the door.

Paul Baker had called Carvelli a half hour ago and told him he had more information. Just before Tony was to pound the door again, Baker opened it for him.

Tony quickly stepped into the house as Baker said, "Shitty day out there today."

"Yeah." Carvelli said as he slipped off the heavy coat and shook the rain from it. "What do you have?"

Baker led the way into the living room and let Tony sit on the couch.

"Ah," Tony said, his head tilted back while he sniffed the air. "The aroma of a fine blend of cannabis. How refreshing."

"Screw you, Carvelli. It's my house...."

"Open a window, Paul. Let some air in."

"It's cold and raining out there."

"So?"

"I did more digging into the guys at CAR Securities," Baker said getting to the point. "I came up with some stuff I thought you should know. I'm not sure it will help, but that chick you're trying to help is too hot to go to prison."

For the next twenty minutes, Baker explained to Carvelli how he did what he did in more detail than Tony wanted. While he talked, about every two minutes, Carvelli would give him an impatient look and rotate one of his hands in a gesture to indicate to step it up and get on with it.

"I typed it up for you, too," Baker said pointing to a stapled document on the coffee table between them.

"Good," Tony said. He picked up the six pages and quickly leafed through them. "Look, Paul," Tony said after looking them over. "I know you like to brag and let me know how smart you are and," Carvelli stopped and held up a hand to Baker when he started to protest, "I appreciate all you do. I really mean that. But when you type it up, you can just give me what you found. I don't understand all of this internet, techno, gibberish anyway."

"Okay. What do you think? Is it something you can use?"

"Maybe, yeah, I think so. I'll get it to her lawyer. It's worth a couple grand and I'll make sure you get it," Tony promised. "I don't have it on me..."

"Hey, I trust you and thanks. I'll keep digging and see what I can come up with."

Carvelli stood up, put on his overcoat, folded the papers and placed them in the inside pocket of his coat. As he was leaving, just before he opened the front door, he turned back to Baker.

"Do something for me. When you get a chance, check out a guy that worked at CAR Securities. His name is Robert Judd, with two d's."

"Who is he?" Baker asked.

"He's the victim in our case. It just occurred to me, we need to check him out, too. See what you can find."

"I'll do that," Baker said.

Carvelli scurried back to his car and when he got in it made a call from his cell. He talked to Carolyn, who told him Marc was on the phone but he would be available when Tony arrived.

Ten minutes later, Tony parked behind the Reardon Building. The rain had almost stopped so he walked less hurriedly to the back door of Marc's office.

"So what did your mystery hacker come up with?" Marc asked Tony after the two men had taken seats in Marc's office.

Tony removed the report from his coat Paul Baker had typed up for him. He laid it on Marc's desk, then sat back.

"You can take your coat off," Marc said.

"I'm still cold," Tony replied. "Why is it that forty degrees in October is freezing your ass off time but by February forty degrees will feel like a miracle?"

"Minnesota weather. We like to think it keeps the riff raff out," Marc answered.

"If only it did," Carvelli said. Tony stood up, removed his leather overcoat and placed it on the other client chair.

"Okay," he began when he sat down. "My guy dug a little deeper and he came up with more interesting little tidbits.

"At the end of May, a couple of the CAR guys took a one day trip to Panama. Victor Espinosa and Walter Pascal."

"A one-day business trip to Panama? Raises some questions, but by itself, not incriminating," Marc said.

"I'm not done. He also found out that Espinosa went to college at the same place and time as a guy by the name of Pablo Quinones. Quinones is known by the DEA as the number two guy of a southern Mexican drug cartel run by a sociopath…"

"Aren't they all?"

"…by the name of Javier Ruiz Torres, aka El Callado, the Quiet One. Sounds like he's watched *The Godfather* a few times.

"When Victor Espinosa and Walter Pascal made their quick trip to Panama, my guy found out that Pablo Quinones and his boss were there at the same time.

"Cynical ex-cop that I am and cynical lawyer that you are, neither one of us believes this is a coincidence," Tony said.

"They're washing money for a Mexican drug cartel," Marc said.

"Looks like it," Tony agreed.

"That's living dangerously," Marc added.

"Which makes me wonder if Rob Judd found out about this and…"

"We would have another possible motive to kill Rob Judd," Marc said.

"Unlikely," Tony said. "If the cartel did it, Maddy would be dead, too. They wouldn't leave a witness and they wouldn't take the chance that Rob told Maddy about it."

"I don't care," Marc said leaning back in his chair. "I just want another possibility to point at to create reasonable doubt. It's not my job to figure out who did it for sure."

"Is a judge going to let you bring this in without more than just a plane ride for these guys?"

"That's the question," Marc said. "Probably not. I need to get one of these guys on a witness stand. This Pascal guy would be the one. He's the one Rob went to with the problems about the securities fraud. He went to Panama, also. He would know what's going on."

"I thought you hit him with a subpoena to testify at your hearing coming up," Tony said. "What's it called?"

"A motion to compel. I want those records Rob showed this Pascal guy to show they had motive to kill him. CAR Securities and Gondeck are both fighting it."

"What do you think?" Tony asked.

"I think we're going to lose," Marc said. "I can't prove any of it without Maddy testifying. Even then, it would be pretty thin. 'My dead boyfriend told me about this.' I'm not sure that would be good enough."

"It looks like you're fishing."

"I am fishing," Marc admitted. "Anything on the waiter?"

"Nothing new. The cops found a thousand bucks in twenties in an envelope that he had in his dorm room. Certainly looks like the payoff he got to drug Maddy. But I haven't found anyone who can substantiate it. What about the doctor?"

"The doctor can testify she was drugged. We need Maddy to get on the stand to testify that this kid was the waiter at the party who served her. A few days later, he's dead and the cops found the money. But without Maddy to testify, to draw the link between being drugged, his disappearance and murder and the money, I don't see Judge Graham even allowing it in."

"Maddy may have to testify," Tony said.

"Even if she does, that doesn't mean she didn't go nuts and stab and kill Rob. That's what Gondeck will argue. We need solid motive for our 'some other dude did it' defense."

"We're running out of time," Tony glumly replied. "Can we continue it?"

"I don't think so. I already got one continuance. Gondeck opposed it and made the point that I was the one who wouldn't waive Maddy's right to a speedy trial. He said he was ready to go. I'm not sure Graham would go along with it."

"Now, what?" Tony asked.

"Madeline may have to take the stand and that's a bad idea. Steve will easily show that everything she says is speculation. She was the one found with the knife in her hand covered in Rob's blood. And they have pictures," Marc said. "The rest of it will look like defense desperation."

"Which is exactly what it is," Tony said.

"Which is exactly what it is," Marc agreed.

THIRTY-ONE

Marc, Tony and Maddy were let into the back hallway of the courtroom by Tony's court deputy friend and the twenty dollar gratuity. When the three of them passed through the security door they almost ran into Steve Gondeck and Jennifer Moore who were also sneaking in the back way. What could have been an awkward moment passed with relief for everyone when Maddy put her hand out to Gondeck.

"Hi, Steve," she said.

As they shook hands, Maddy added, "I hope you don't mind if I don't wish you good luck."

Amid the mild laughter, Gondeck smiled and started to say, "I just wish I didn't..."

"It's okay. I understand," Maddy said. "Let's just leave it at that."

Maddy turned to Jennifer, said hello and shook her hand as well.

When they were in the courtroom and seated at their table, Marc turned to Maddy.

"That was pretty classy," he whispered.

"Oh, not so much," Maddy whispered back. "I want him thinking about how much he doesn't want to do what he has to do."

"You sly little devil," Marc smiled. "It probably won't work..."

"But it can't hurt," Maddy finished. "Besides, you didn't see it but I gave him my best bedroom eyes, FM look. That will give him something to think about."

Marc laughed then said, "You are devious. Remind me to stay on your good side."

Marc swiveled around in his chair to look at the prosecution's side. Besides Gondeck and Moore, there were four more lawyers seated at or behind them along the rail. He also noticed two men in business suits in the front row behind them. One of them was Corbin Reed who was leaning forward talking to one of the lawyers. The other, looking more than a little anxious was

Walter Pascal, the man Marc had served with a subpoena to be here today to testify.

Marc heard the doors open and turned to see the small mob of media rushing in. None of the seats had been set aside for them which brought on a mad scramble to get up front. A couple of the more optimistic ones rushed to the rail behind Marc, then shoved microphones at him and tried to ask questions. Marc smiled, gave them his 'no comment' and turned back toward the bench.

"All rise," the court deputy intoned when Judge Graham came through the door behind the bench. It was 9:20 and the normally punctual Graham took a moment to apologize for being tardy. Marc and Steve Gondeck stole a quick glance at each other surprised by Graham's contrition. It was rare indeed that a judge would apologize for being late onto the bench.

Graham read the case name and court file number into the record. The lawyers all spoke their names and whom they represented, also for the record.

"We're here on a defense motion to compel discovery from a nonparty business, CAR Securities Management. Is that correct, Mr. Kadella?"

Marc stood and affirmed for the judge that he was correct.

"I have read your pleadings and memorandums and am thoroughly versed in the facts and law of this matter," Graham continued. "I understand you want to call a witness, Mr. Kadella."

When the judge said this, Graham's eyes flicked upward to the courtroom's entrance. A woman with short, blonde hair slipped in and quietly took a seat toward the back. Holly Byrnes had arrived to keep an eye on the FBI's CAR Securities' snitch.

Still standing, Marc confirmed that the judge was correct.

"Okay. Before we get to that does either side have any new or additional facts or case law not contained in your pleadings?"

"No, your Honor," Marc said. Reading Graham's almost indifferent attitude, Marc was getting a bad feeling about how this hearing was going to go.

"Mr. Gondeck?" Graham asked.

"No, your Honor."

"Mr. Kadella, have you taken this witnesses statement or deposition?"

"No, your Honor. He has not cooperated."

"Is he here?" Graham asked looking over the small crowd.

"Yes, your Honor," Marc replied.

"Well, let's get him up here and find out what he has to say."

Marc called Walter Pascal who stood up along with two other men in fairly expensive business suits. They all came through the gate and Graham held up a hand to stop them.

"Which one of you is Mr. Pascal?" Graham asked.

Walter acknowledged he was and Graham waved him forward.

"You gentlemen must be lawyers for Mr. Pascal and the company he works for along with these others," Graham said.

"Yes, your Honor," the older one answered.

"I've read your briefs, all two hundred and sixty pages, and now you want to put your objection on the record. Go ahead."

For the next ten minutes the older man prattled on basically repeating the same argument presented in the brief submitted to the court. Marc spun around in his chair to face him. The man was barely three feet away, still standing in front of the gate. Marc stretched out his legs, laced his fingers together on his stomach and stared at the lawyer as if he was giving Lincoln's second inaugural address. Steve Gondeck saw this and quickly turned away to avoid laughing. All the while Judge Graham was acting attentive but thinking, *please shut up and sit down.*

When he finally finished, Graham politely said, "Thank you, I'll certainly take that into consideration." While thinking, *if I can remember any of it.*

Graham looked at the deputy as the two interlopers returned to their seats.

"Okay. Swear him in and let's get on with it."

For the next half hour, Marc and Pascal sparred over Pascal's knowledge of mortgage backed securities being held by

CAR Securities Management. Pascal denied everything. He denied that Rob Judd had ever mentioned a problem to him. He denied any knowledge or evidence that these securities were not backed by the appropriate mortgages. And, he denied Patrick McGarry ever mentioned a problem to him or anyone else at CAR Securities.

Finally, a very frustrated Marc Kadella asked, "Isn't it true that CAR Securities Management has a serious problem with these mortgage backed securities?"

"Asked and answered, repeatedly," Gondeck objected.

"Sustained," an impatient Judge Graham ruled.

"Isn't it true," Marc continued, deciding to roll the dice one more time. "CAR Securities had a significant motive to silence both Patrick McGarry and Robert Judd?"

"Your Honor!" Gondeck almost yelled jumping out of his chair.

"That's it!" Graham loudly proclaimed. "Don't answer that," he told Pascal. "Mr. Kadella, you're done."

"Mr. Gondeck, do you have any questions for this witness?" Graham asked.

Still standing Gondeck thought about it for a moment then said, "No, your Honor."

Pascal was excused and smugly walked back to his seat.

Graham looked at Marc and said, "I am unconvinced that you have made the case that your client's defense will be harmed if you are not allowed to review what are clearly proprietary documents from CAR Securities. Defense motion to compel compliance with their subpoena duces tecum is therefore denied. I'll see counsel in chambers."

Graham left the bench and the media made a scramble for the door. While Walter Pascal was leaving flanked by his two-lawyer escort, he made eye contact with Holly Byrnes. Knowing he had perjured himself, Pascal quickly looked away from her. Even though she was there to make sure he kept his mouth shut, her contempt for him was palpable.

Marc had whispered to Tony and Maddy to wait for him. He then swiveled in his chair to follow the judge.

215

"You may be in for an ass-chewing," Gondeck said with a big grin while looking down at Marc, still seated at the defense table.

Marc stood up, shrugged his shoulders and said, "Won't be the first and won't be the last time either. I'm sure you've had your share, too."

"Oh, yeah," Gondeck nodded his head still smiling. "They're always more fun to watch, though."

As the two of them, along with Jennifer Moore, were walking through the courtroom, Marc whispered to Gondeck. "Forget the week in Hawaii with her. The deal's off."

"Damn. And I was counting on it."

As Gondeck and Moore were taking their seats, Marc preemptively said, "That man committed perjury at least a dozen times, your Honor."

Graham had removed his robes, was sitting behind his desk and said, "Okay. Bring me proof and I'll put him in jail. You didn't make your case, Marc."

"You're not going to bite off his ass for what he did in your courtroom?" Gondeck asked showing his disappointment.

"No," Graham replied smiling. "You know why?" he asked rhetorically. He pointed at Marc and said, "Because I believe him. I think your guy was lying his ass off in there. How did our Mr. Kadella know these things? You think he just made it all up? His client told him and Rob Judd told her."

"Your Honor," Gondeck solemnly began, "if you're biased I'll have to ask you to recuse yourself."

"Relax, Steve," Graham said. "This case will be decided by what happens in that courtroom. Not by what anyone, especially myself, believes. Okay?"

"Yes, sir," Gondeck said.

"Now, the reason I brought you back here, I heard from the court of appeals on the TV cameras in the courtroom. I got their decision just before court in an email. That's why I was late." While saying this, Graham handed a copy to each of them.

"I'm going to appeal," Marc said.

"Go ahead, but I'm not granting a continuance. They ruled we could not show prejudice so the cameras are in."

"Great, I'll have to get a haircut and shave every day," Gondeck joked.

"You can use my makeup," Jennifer told him.

"He certainly could use some," Marc zinged him. "I have something else," Marc said pulling several documents from his briefcase. He handed copies to Graham and the prosecutors.

"And this is?" Graham asked.

"Discovery," Marc said. "The night of Robert Judd's murder, my client was surreptitiously drugged. She was slipped a large dose of roofies and LSD, enough to knock out a horse. She was physically incapable of attacking Robert Judd."

THIRTY-TWO

"No way, no way!" Gondeck loudly proclaimed. "How long have you been sitting on this? No way is this to be allowed."

"You'll excuse me, Mr. Gondeck, if I'm the one who asks those questions and makes those decisions," Graham icily said.

"Sorry, your Honor," a calmer, chastened Gondeck said.

"What about this, Marc? How long have you been sitting on this?" Graham turned to Kadella and asked.

"Since the murder," Marc shrugged. "I took her to a doctor that day. They took blood and urine samples and had them checked."

Gondeck and Jennifer Moore both looked like they were going to say something. Graham held up a hand to stop them.

"They could've done the same thing. They still can. I made sure my guy got enough samples and preserved them for additional testing. You can send them to your lab anytime you want, Steve," Marc replied trying to act as innocent as possible.

"There isn't enough time," Jennifer said knowing this argument was weak.

"Yes, there is," Graham said.

Graham folded his hands together and looked down at his desktop pondering the problem. After a minute he looked up.

"I'll allow it to come in but as I see it, you have a problem. Unless you can get someone to testify how she was drugged, it's likely your client is going to have to take the stand. Have you thought about that?" Graham told Marc. "Unless you can bring in the person who drugged her."

"Yes," was Marc's one-word answer. He wanted it to sound like he had solved this problem and was holding back. He did not want them to know he had no idea how to show she was drugged without Maddy's testimony. Plus, he wanted to keep the news about the waiter's murder to himself, for now.

Still steaming, Gondeck sarcastically asked, "What other little surprises are you sitting on?"

"If I told you that they wouldn't be surprises now would they?" Marc said knowing that would needle his opponent even more.

Graham laughed, looked at Marc and said, "Touché."

"Your Honor!" Gondeck protested.

"Relax, Steve. There's no court reporter or jury here," Graham said. He turned back to Marc and said, "But he does have a point. Anything else?"

Marc pulled another manila folder from his briefcase and removed three, two-page copies of a report from it.

"I have a report from my criminalist, Jason Briggs," Marc said as he handed each of them a copy. "The gist of it is, he believes the blood splatter patterns in the bedroom show a third person in the room. I just got the report yesterday," he added looking at Gondeck.

"Mr. Gondeck?" Graham said.

Gondeck said, "My guy says no, there wasn't anyone else in the room."

"And their CSU guys have never missed anything," Marc added.

"That's enough," Graham said. "Anything else?"

"I'm not done with CAR Securities, your Honor. It was them and I'm going to find it," Marc replied.

"I'm not going to let you put these people on a witness stand and go fishing. You better have something solid against them. Do I make myself clear?" Graham said.

"Yes, your Honor," Marc answered him.

Marc told the hostess they would like a booth to sit in. The three of them, Marc, Maddy and Tony had been joined by Margaret Tennant. They were at Peterson's across Fourth Avenue from the government center for an early lunch. The hostess grabbed four menus and led them to a booth in the far corner.

"I'm not surprised Graham ruled against you," Margaret said after they had been seated. "It looks like a fishing expedition. You need someone who knew Rob went to his boss with his concerns. Otherwise they'll do what they did; close ranks and lie."

"You believe me?" Maddy asked Margaret.

"Of course," Margaret smiled.

"So does Graham. He even said he believed Pascal was lying but needed proof," Marc sighed.

"Now what?" Tony asked.

"We keep digging," Marc answered.

The waitress came and took their order and when she left, Marc told them what happened in chambers.

"They're pushing to allow TV cameras in the courts more often," Margaret said. "They claim it makes things more transparent."

"That seems to be the trendy word these days, transparent," Tony said. "Except every time I hear a politician use it, you can be sure they're hiding something."

Margaret looked at Marc and said, "Well, get your hair cut and buy a couple new suits."

Marc looked at Maddy, opened his mouth to say something but before he did, she cut him off.

"I'm not wearing a bikini. Forget it."

Marc's shoulders slumped and he muttered. "Damn there goes that idea. I was going to try for an all-male jury, too."

Holly Byrnes parked her FBI issued car in one of the spots reserved for them. After leaving the court hearing, she had driven straight back to the FBI offices. Mike Anderson had asked her to call him for an update when it was over but Holly felt physically ill after watching Walter Pascal's performance. She needed a little while to get over it before she talked to her partner, or anyone else.

Once inside, instead of going to Anderson's office, Holly went straight to her cubicle. Anderson saw her walk by and before she had dropped her purse and hung up her coat, Mike was there.

"I thought you were going to call. What happened?" Anderson asked.

Holly finished hanging up her coat then quietly said, "Let's go in your office."

220

Anderson barely had the door to his office closed behind them when she started.

"That lying little bastard! I sat there listening to him while he calmly committed perjury over and over," a boiling-over angry Holly Byrnes let loose while stomping around Anderson's glass enclosed space.

Anderson had taken the chair behind his desk to wait for her to finish.

"Goddamn, I thought I would throw up."

She looked at her partner who patiently waited for her. After another minute of cursing and stomping about, she finally stopped and sat down.

"Feel better?" Anderson asked.

"No," she said.

"You never once stretched the truth while testifying against someone you knew was guilty?"

"This was different," she protested.

"Yes, it was. You knew he would lie. In fact, we made him lie," he said. "Holly," he continued more softly leaning forward on the desk, "we have our job to do and case to make…"

"That doesn't make it right, Mike, and you know it. He enjoyed it. He enjoyed his little act. You know what I think? I think Rivers' lawyer is right. I think these guys did it to shut up Rob Judd and the other guy, too, Patrick McGarry and his girlfriend. They did it and they set up Madeline Rivers to take the fall for it."

"These guys aren't that clever…"

"Yeah? Ethan Rask? After what we found out about him you don't think he knows people who know people who could pull this off?"

"All of the evidence points to the Rivers woman. They had some kind of fight and she went nuts. It happens. And your opinion about what else might have happened better stay in this room. For your sake, you don't take this stuff outside the Bureau. Not if you value your career. Ever."

"Okay," Holly quietly agreed.

"I'll call Joel and let him know how it went. When does the trial start?"

"Three weeks they said. November fourteenth," Holly told him. "I think that's what's bothering me. Is our case and our careers more important than Madeline Rivers' life? If that's true, then what have we become?"

"Joel Dylan would remind you to look at the big picture. Yes, our case is more important than a state homicide case. We may be able to roll up a Mexican drug cartel and..."

"We'll never touch them and we both know it," Holly interrupted.

"Our case is our case and that's our job."

"I know. I'm on board and you know I am," Holly agreed.

"I do, yes."

THIRTY-THREE

Marc sat quietly staring through the open window behind his desk. Maddy's upcoming trial was causing sleepless nights and he was in the office early because of it, again. He looked down at the traffic on Charles, both vehicle and pedestrian, without really seeing it at all, his mind somewhere else.

A gust of wind brought a wave of cold air and moisture through the window which felt good and brought him back to reality. Marc poked his head out and looked up at the low-hanging cloud cover dropping a mixture of rain and snow to remind Minnesota of what lay ahead.

"Good morning, sunshine," Marc heard Carolyn say from the doorway. "Coffee's ready. You want some?"

"Sure," Marc said as he wheeled around and held up his cup to her.

"Where's the goddamn coffee?" they heard Connie Mickelson yell out.

Carolyn looked at Marc, smiled and yelled back, "In here Miss Congeniality."

Connie appeared in Marc's doorway, cup in hand which Carolyn quickly filled.

"How you doing?" Connie asked Marc then sipped the coffee.

"All right," Marc shrugged.

"Bullshit," Connie said.

"Truth be told," Marc continued. "I'm pretty worried. Maddy's trial is in two weeks and I don't have much of a case."

"Oh, shoot," Carolyn said. "I just remembered. John asked me to tell you to call him. He said he has something to tell you about Maddy's case. I'll get his cell number for you."

While Carolyn went to write down her husband's phone number, Connie sat down in one of Marc's client chairs.

"What do you have?" Connie asked referring to Maddy's case.

223

"She was drugged. And my expert will testify the blood spatter shows evidence of a third person in the bedroom. Their expert will say it doesn't. Plus, we can put on a bunch of people who will swear Madeline never used drugs. And there was no way she could have done this because of the amount of roofies in her system."

"Is that enough? Should be," Connie said.

"That's optimistic."

"You get the witness list?"

"Yeah. I got Tony and some of his guys chasing them down. Thanks. I'll call him," Marc said to Carolyn who was back and handed a slip of paper with the phone number.

"He said it was important," Carolyn said.

"I got work to do. Let me know if I can do anything," Connie said as she rose to leave.

"Hey, John," Marc said into his phone. "It's Marc Kadella. What's up?"

"I have something to tell you. Have you had breakfast?"

"No, ah…"

"I'm in Highland Park. There's a Bakers Square just across the Ford Bridge. I'll be there in five minutes."

"Okay," Marc replied. "I'll come right over," he finished referring to crossing the Mississippi into St. Paul.

Marc walked into the restaurant and saw Carolyn's husband wave to him from a booth. The host approached him and Marc pointed to John and headed toward him as the host nodded in recognition.

"So, what's up?" Marc asked when he sat down in the booth across from the St. Paul police detective.

While Marc poured himself coffee from the carafe on the table, Lucas started in. "I've heard something through the cop grapevine you might find interesting."

"Okay," Marc said then opened a small creamer and poured the contents into his cup.

"A couple guys I know were out the other night after bowling and they stopped at Stout's up in Roseville afterwards."

"That's nice, John," Marc said with mild sarcasm when Lucas paused to take a drink. "Did they have a nice time?"

"Very funny, smartass. You want to listen? They ran into an acquaintance of yours. An ex-cop named Dale Kubik. Ring a bell?"

"Yeah it does. So?"

"Kubik was booted from the job because he's a drunk, a junkie and bad cop. But he takes no responsibility for it."

"Those types never do."

"Yeah, true, but my friends told me he was a little drunk and talking trash about a female P.I. of our acquaintance he blames for it."

"Maddy?"

"Yep. Pretty mouthy. Calling her a name I won't use because it's disgusting and Carolyn would kill me. He also was bragging that he got even with her. Claimed he set her up and she's going to take a hard fall."

"Are you serious?"

"That's what they told me."

"Would they be willing to testify?"

"Before you get too excited," Lucas continued. "I don't believe a word of Kubik's bragging. Kubik isn't that clever. No way could he pull off something like that and he doesn't have the balls. He's all mouth."

"I don't care if he did it or not. I don't have to prove he did it. I just need somebody else to point at. Will your guys testify?"

"Lawyers," Lucas said shaking his head. "You don't care who did it…"

"It's Madeline, John. Do you believe she did this?"

"No, you're right. I'll check to see if they'll talk to you."

"John, if I have to, I'll put you on the stand and force you to give me their names then I'll subpoena them," Marc said, leaning forward on the table and staring into his eyes. "It's Madeline," Marc repeated.

"I'll talk to them and call you yet today," Lucas said.

"Are they detectives?"

"Yeah," Lucas nodded. "Straight shooters, both of them. I'm sure they'll cooperate. Nobody owes Dale Kubik anything. He disgraced the job and deserves whatever he gets."

"He'll deny it," Marc said. "I don't care. I can still use it."

"You know two St. Paul detectives named Raphael Suarez and Greg Dugan?"

Marc was in his SUV on the phone with Tony Carvelli. Marc was on his way back after meeting with the two cops and John Lucas.

"Doesn't sound familiar," Carvelli said. "I can quietly check them out. Why?"

Marc took a couple minutes to explain to his friend what he had been told.

"John thinks they're okay?" Tony asked, referring to John Lucas.

"Yeah, he brought this to me," Marc answered. "Why?"

"I don't know," Tony continued. "Something doesn't smell right. I know Kubik and he's an asshole and a loser but I don't think he's so stupid he'd run his mouth like that. Maybe, but I'm not sure. Before you get carried away with this, let me do some digging. We got another problem."

"Now what?"

"We've found a dozen or so people on their witness list who are going to testify that Maddy and Rob had a big fight in a restaurant a couple weeks before the murder. She got mad enough to get up and stomp out of the restaurant and left him sitting there."

"Come on pal, push down on the right hand pedal so we can get where we're going," Marc said.

"Who're you talking to?"

"The guy ahead of me. I swear slow driving is becoming an epidemic in this town," Marc replied. "Come on you old geezer. Squeeze thirty-five out of your little Ford Pissant. You can do it," he continued sounding very frustrated. "Get me the names of these witnesses and what they said. In fact, come by the office, can you?"

"I'll be there before you. I'll give Max Cool a call. You remember him?"

"Yeah, the detective from the Sutherland case. Will he talk to you?"

"Yeah, he's a good guy and a professional. Don't worry about it. I'll see you in a little while."

"Hello, gorgeous," Tony said. He had silently come in through the exterior door of the law office then peeked into Connie's office, the closest one to the door.

"Screw you, Carvelli, you no-account deadbeat," she came back at him with a smile.

Tony leaned against the doorframe, smiled back and said, "When are you going to dump your most recent husband and run off with me?"

Connie rolled her eyes at the ceiling and said, "Could be any minute now the way things are going. But you need a lot more money than you have to get me to run off with the likes of you."

"Hey," Tony said holding out his hands in protest. "I was thinking maybe a weekend and you could pay."

"In your dreams, gumshoe. Besides, you're too old. You couldn't keep up with me," Connie laughed at the much younger Carvelli.

"Did you find out something?" Carvelli heard Marc say from Marc's office doorway.

Carvelli tilted his head back to look at Marc and said, "Yeah. I'll be right there," He looked back at Connie and said, "You're probably right. I need my rest."

"And little blue pills," Connie added.

On his way to Marc's office, Tony said a quick hello to the office personnel. He went in, closed the door and took a seat.

"I talked to Coolidge. He had nothing good to say about Dale Kubik. His partner was there too."

"Anna something as I recall," Marc said.

"Finney. She was partnered with Kubik for a while. She said he was a good cop then divorce, money problems, booze and drugs got him. But neither one of them believes he could have pulled off something like this."

"I don't care if he did it," Marc said. "Would he shoot his mouth off about it in front of people and what are these other cops like? The ones who heard him."

"Max and Anna both said that Suarez and Dugan are all right. Good cops and straight shooters," Tony replied.

"I didn't think cops would stick it to other cops," Marc said.

"Kubik's not a cop and he burned a lot of bridges in St. Paul."

"What about these restaurant witnesses?" Marc asked.

"They all say pretty much the same thing," Tony began. "Maddy and Rob were at a table having dinner and seemed to be arguing. Maddy got up, obviously very angry, and stomped off. Their words. Angrily stomped off."

"How do they remember this?" Marc asked.

"Maddy's pretty noticeable, remember? We're used to her so we don't notice it so much. When she's out in public in a situation like that, people will notice it. Plus, her picture's been in the news for a while."

"Okay, yeah, I get it," Marc said. "But so what? So they had an argument. Big deal."

"One of them ends up murdered a couple weeks later and the other is accused of it."

"Get after some people who spent time with them at that party on the Fourth of July. Start with Rob's coworkers. Let's see if we can find a few rebuttal witnesses who will testify that they were getting along fine."

"That was next on my list. Give me a couple days. Have you turned over your witness list?"

"It's not too late. I can amend it," Marc replied.

THIRTY-FOUR

"You may call your first witness, Mr. Gondeck," Judge Graham said.

It was the afternoon of the fifth day of the trial, Friday, November eighteenth and the judge was already annoyed. Graham had allocated two days to select a jury and it had taken four. Graham had hoped to get the trial in before the Thanksgiving holiday which was coming up next week. Before court this morning, in chambers, Gondeck had brought a motion to have the jury sequestered. Marc was absolutely opposed to it. Forcing these people to spend a holiday weekend away from their families would not sit well with any of them. There was a very real risk they would want to take it out on someone and the only one they could take it out on would be the defendant. Fortunately, Marc barely had to say a word before Graham denied Gondeck's request.

Marc had done everything he could to have as many young men on the jury as possible. The more of them he could get paying attention to Maddy and not the trial, the better. At least, that was his theory.

During the jury selection process, Marc had hammered home the concepts of innocent until proven guilty and the standard of guilt beyond a reasonable doubt. He had also obtained a promise from every juror to keep an open mind and not decide the case until all of the evidence had been submitted by both sides. Because of this, Marc had deferred giving his opening statement. The defense had the option of waiting until the prosecution had finished presenting their case before giving their opening.

Jennifer Moore had given the opening for the prosecution. She had done a very thorough, professional and easy to follow presentation of the evidence the jury would receive. Doing so, Jennifer had used up most of the morning session.

Gondeck stood and said, "The state calls Detective Owen Jefferson."

Jefferson came in from the hallway and in less than a minute was sworn in and took the stand. Having been thoroughly prepared and being a veteran detective with many trials under his belt, Jefferson's testimony was extremely smooth.

Gondeck started slowly by having Jefferson tell the jury about his years as a cop and homicide detective. They spent almost a half hour going over the awards and commendations he had received to implant in the jurors' minds the obvious information that Owen Jefferson knew his business and could be trusted.

The entire afternoon was taken up by Jefferson explaining to the jury and the cameras, how the investigation had been conducted. Normally this would be done in a sensible, chronological order. The detective's arrival at the crime scene would be delivered right away and in great detail, including a photo display of what was found.

Instead, Jefferson, with Gondeck's prompting, barely touched on it at the beginning of his narration. When this happened, after Jefferson's testimony had moved on, Marc found himself looking at the wall clock. Knowing what was coming at the end of the afternoon, Marc thought; *Very clever Steve.*

When 4:30 rolled around, Gondeck went back to the crime scene. "Detective," he began, "Let's go back to the crime scene. Please describe for the jury what you found in the bedroom when you arrived at the victim's apartment."

"It was the most gruesome scene I had ever come across in all my years as a homicide detective," Jefferson began.

For the next ten minutes, he methodically explained in horrific detail the interior of Rob Judd's bedroom. When he finished, Gondeck, over Marc's objection, used the large screen TV to display six photos of various angles of the room to visually imprint the bloody scene in the jury's memory.

In every homicide trial, these photos are a subject of intense scrutiny, debate and heated argument. The prosecution wants to show the jury every horrible detail in large, blown-up, high-definition color. Of course, the defense does not want any of that shown to anyone. More than one-hundred photos of Rob Judd's bedroom were taken and Judge Graham had pared down the number to the six showing, plus one more. Two of the six were shots of the mutilated, bloody corpse of Rob Judd lying on the bed.

A few minutes before 5:00, Gondeck and Jefferson got to the seventh photo, the one Marc had been waiting for with dread.

"Detective Jefferson," Gondeck began as the final photo came up on the TV screen which caused a stir in the jury box. "On the screen is a photo marked States Exhibit Seven. Do you recognize this photo?"

"Objection," Marc said as he stood to address the court. "It is my understanding that Detective Jefferson did not take this picture. He should not be allowed to testify about it."

Graham knew Marc would object for the record. He patiently waited for Marc to finish then politely overruled him.

"Yes, I do," Jefferson said.

"Describe it for the jury, please."

"It is a photo of how and where the defendant, Madeline Rivers, was found on the morning of the murder of Robert Judd. That is her, unconscious, lying on the bedroom floor of Robert Judd's apartment. She is dressed in a white t-shirt we subsequently found belonged to Mr. Judd and white, cotton panties. The red substance splattered all over her and her clothing is Mr. Judd's blood."

Marc reached under the table and took Maddy's hand. She squeezed his hand so hard it actually hurt. The two of them were able to look at Jefferson and act as if this was the most natural, normal testimony they had ever heard.

"What is that in her hand?" Gondeck asked.

"It is a kitchen knife with a seven inch blade. It was one that matched a set we found on a counter in the kitchen apartment. It was the one used…"

"Objection. Lack of foundation," Marc said without standing.

"Overruled," Graham said.

"It was the one used to stab Mr. Judd fourteen times," Jefferson said finishing his statement.

"Your Honor," Gondeck stood and said to Graham. "It's after five and I am at a good place to break…"

"Very well," Graham said. "We'll adjourn and pick up with this witness at nine A.M. Monday morning." Before formally adjourning, the judge gave the jury a stern and explicit warning to avoid any and all news coverage of the case. He then rapped his gavel once and walked out.

The jurors all stood to be escorted out. Marc watched them and every one of them glanced at Maddy as they were leaving the jury box, including the four alternates. None had a sympathetic look on his or her face.

Marc swiveled his chair toward Maddy and silently watched her for several seconds until the jury was gone.

"We knew he was going to do that," Marc quietly said referring to Gondeck. Marc had anticipated that the bloody photo of Maddy, unconscious on the floor of Rob's bedroom would be the last one shown today. Being Friday afternoon, Gondeck had planned Jefferson's testimony so that picture would be in the jurors' minds all weekend. Marc would have done the same thing.

"I'm okay," Maddy finally said with a weak smile.

"Come on," Marc said. He placed a hand on her arm and continued, "Connie told me to call when we finished for the day. She's ordering in pizza. Everyone's waiting."

Maddy paused for a moment then said, "I am hungry."

"That's a good sign," Marc said.

"What were your impressions of the first day of the trial, Victor?" Pablo Quinones asked Victor Espinosa. Pablo was relaxing alongside the pool at his boss' seaside villa outside Panama City. El Callado was in a lounge chair a few feet away smoking a cigar and listening to his counselor's side of the conversation.

"I was not in the courtroom myself. We have someone there watching the proceedings. Are you getting it on a satellite TV feed?" Espinosa replied.

"Yes, we are," Quinones acknowledged. "But I don't have time to sit and watch it on TV all day. Plus it is boring most of the time."

"Our man says it went very well. The pictures that were put on the TV were very graphic, very gory," Espinosa told him

"They were not shown on TV," Quinones said.

"I know, but he had a seat in the courtroom that had a good view of them. The first day definitely went well for the prosecution."

"Good. Good. Very good," Quinones said nodding his head at his boss. "Take care, my friend. We'll be in touch."

Charlie Dudek was home in his suburban Kansas City house and had spent the entire day watching the trial. Charlie loved court TV. He watched trials on it as often as he could. There was something about the real life drama taking place that he found almost irresistible. Probably because deep down in his psyche, he knew he would likely be the guest of honor at one someday. Plus, over the years, he had learned a lot about criminal procedure and admissibility of evidence, pointers Charlie had picked up that helped him in his business.

There was something about what Charlie had seen during the trial that was bothering him. Something in the back of his mind that was causing a physical reaction, a tugging sensation in his chest.

Charlie shut off the TV then retrieved a beer from the refrigerator. He returned to the living room and silently stared at the blank TV screen without really seeing it. It took almost a half hour before he was able to understand what it was that was bothering him.

Over the years, Charlie had dealt with his sexual yearnings mostly by visiting prostitutes. Charlie had learned at an early age that he was sexually straight but emotionally unable to connect with females. He did not dwell on it because it did not bother or affect him at all. It was simply part of who he was. Charlie was emotionally detached from everyone, except young children. For some reason, he understood that they needed and must have adult protection. He had never once come close to harming a child. Women, men, lovers or friends were not in Charlie's DNA.

Charlie looked up at the ceiling and said, out loud, to himself. "Wow. So this is what it's like to be attracted to a woman. Interesting. God I hope she gets off."

Madeline Rivers, without her knowledge of course, had managed something no one else had ever done. She had jabbed a theoretical finger through Charlie Dudek's shield and touched his heart.

Dale Kubik was angry and getting angrier with each shot of whiskey he tossed down. Kubik had also watched the opening day of testimony on TV. At the end of the day he was almost giddy from what he had seen and heard. Several times the camera panned over the courtroom to give the viewers a close up of the Rivers woman. She tried to look calm and in control but Kubik wasn't buying it. He had been involved in enough trials himself to know the photos the jury saw would be devastating.

An hour ago, there was a knock on his door, which caused Kubik's good mood to evaporate. When he opened the door a man in an inexpensive suit handed him a piece of paper. Dale Kubik had been given a subpoena to appear as a witness for the defense at a date and time to be determined.

"I'm at the office, why?" Marc said into his cell phone. Tony Carvelli was on the line.

"I got some information today I need to talk to you about. Is Maddy with you?"

"Yeah, everybody's here. The whole office except Chris. He had to leave. We just got back from court. Connie ordered up pizza. If you hurry you can get some."

"I'll be there in ten minutes. Don't start without me."

When Tony arrived, the pizza delivery man was walking through the building's back door on his way out. Tony hurried up the backstairs and went right in.

After filling a paper plate with slices of sausage and pepperoni and opening a beer, Carvelli settled into a chair next to Marc. Everyone, including the staff, Connie and Barry Cline, another lawyer, were seated in the staff work area waiting for Tony's news.

"Well, what did you find out?" Marc asked.

"How did today go?" Tony asked while setting down his beer.

"About as expected," Marc said after swallowing. "What?" Marc asked again.

By now, everyone in the room was quietly eating, waiting for Carvelli's news.

"I had my guy do a search on Rob Judd. He called today with what he found. We owe him some money, by the way."

"Whatever," Marc said. "He can get in line."

"What he found wasn't much," Tony said.

"That's the big news? Didn't find much," Marc said.

"You don't understand. He didn't find much at all. Not nearly as much as you would find for someone like him. He found his securities licenses, Series Seven and a couple others but not much else. He has a degree from some small college but no résumé, very little employment history, no parents, siblings nothing."

"What the hell?" Barry Cline said.

"Exactly," Tony replied looking at Barry. "I've seen this before from a witness protection guy. The feds are getting lazy about the backgrounds they're making for these guys."

"You think he's a Witsec guy?" Maddy asked.

"Don't know, sweetheart. But I'll find out," Tony answered her.

THIRTY-FIVE

"Let me remind you, detective, you're still under oath," Judge Graham quietly reminded Owen Jefferson.

"Yes, your Honor, I understand."

Gondeck picked up where he had left off on Friday afternoon. Before he started Jennifer put the photo of Maddy lying unconscious, knife in hand on Rob's bedroom floor back up on the TV screen. Marc was on his feet in an instant objecting to it. Before he could finish, an angry Judge Graham ordered it removed. Gondeck insincerely apologized but the damage had been done.

Jefferson's testimony took up the entire morning session and half of the afternoon. Gondeck used him to talk about almost every piece of evidence to be introduced whether he personally gathered it or not. Marc objected to all of it and Graham made sure the jury understood that each item had to be connected by the person who obtained it. It was almost 3:30 before Gondeck finished and turned Jefferson over to Marc for cross-examination.

Marc stared at Jefferson for several seconds all the while not a sound was heard throughout the courtroom. Normally this would likely make a novice witness nervous, waiting for the hammer to come down. Owen Jefferson was nobody's fool and knew exactly what Marc was up to.

"Mr. Kadella, do you have any questions for this witness," Graham finally asked to get things moving.

"Yes, your Honor. Detective Jefferson, did you even attempt to investigate anyone else for Robert Judd's death, yes or no, detective?"

"No, we did not."

"You knew Madeline Rivers before this case didn't you?"

"Yes, I did."

"When you arrived at Rob Judd's apartment were you surprised to find her there?"

"Yes, very much."

"Did she seem to be the same person you knew? Was she calm, collected, in control of herself?"

"No, she did not."

"In fact, she looked lost, confused and not at all like the Madeline Rivers you know, isn't that true?"

"Yes, I would say that's true."

"Isn't it also true that your first reaction was that you did not believe she could have done something like this, yes or no detective."

"Yes, that's true," Jefferson admitted.

"Did you test her for drugs?"

"No, we didn't get a chance to."

Steve Gondeck had not asked Jefferson anything about the drugs that were found in Maddy's system. Marc could only speculate that was because Jefferson had not investigated anything surrounding the drugs and how she may have ingested them. Gondeck did have the samples Marc had saved tested and had found the same thing Marc's doctor had found. The lab tech who tested the samples for the prosecution would testify later.

"As a veteran police officer and detective, would it be fair to say you are familiar with street drugs?"

"Yes, I am," Jefferson said.

"Explain to the jury what roofies are, if you know detective."

Jefferson did as he was asked and turned to the jury for a five minute lesson on Rohypnol and its effects. The date rape drug is what he called it.

When he finished, Marc used this as an opening to go after him and try to show his investigation had not been very thorough at all. For the next twenty minutes the two of them verbally sparred about what Jefferson and his partner did not do and what he did not look into. It was weak and Marc knew it. He also knew exactly what Gondeck would do as soon as he finished.

"Redirect, Mr. Gondeck?" Graham asked when Marc finished.

"Briefly, your Honor," Gondeck said. "Detective Jefferson, why didn't you do all of the things suggested by defense counsel?" Gondeck asked.

"There was no evidence to indicate any of that was necessary. We went where the evidence took us."

"Do you now believe the accused did in fact commit this crime?"

"Objection..."

"He opened the door, your Honor," Gondeck quickly said.

"Yes, you did. The witness may answer," Graham ruled.

"Yes, I certainly do," Jefferson said looking directly at the jury. While he said this, Marc sat silently horrified at the mistake he had made by asking for Jefferson's initial opinion about Maddy's guilt.

The elevator doors from the building's underground parking garage opened and before Carvelli could exit, three rude people, in a hurry to get home, entered the car. At least five more were waiting to get on, forcing Carvelli to literally elbow his way past them. Quitting time at a government building was not the best time to arrive unless you wanted to be trampled. As he hurried across the building's atrium Tony heard and felt his phone go off in his inside coat pocket.

"Carvelli," he said into the device as he continued toward the elevators that would take him up the court side of the building. He was in a hurry to get up to the courtroom to catch some of the proceedings before they finished for the day.

"Mr. Carvelli?" he heard a female voice ask. "You probably don't remember me but my name is Gloria Metcalf. I work at CAR Securities. You talked to me a couple weeks ago about Rob's death."

"Actually, I do remember you, Gloria. Sandy-blonde hair, about five foot six, blue eyes, late twenties," Tony said.

"Wow, that's pretty good."

"What can I do for you?" Tony asked. His curiosity grabbed ahold of him and Carvelli was standing still as the crowd of office workers hustled past on their way out.

"Well, um, I ah, I think I have some information for you. I didn't tell you before but I think I need to. Can we meet somewhere?"

"Sure, Gloria. When and where? You tell me and I'll be there," Tony assured her.

Metcalf gave him the location of a Caribou Coffee shop in a suburb north of Minneapolis. They agreed to meet that evening.

"This might be something," Carvelli quietly whispered to himself as he replaced the phone in his pocket. Less than two minutes later he stepped off an elevator on the fifteenth floor. He arrived at Judge Graham's courtroom just in time to greet the crowd of media types rushing through the door on their way out.

Carvelli entered the courtroom and saw that it was almost empty. The few remaining members of the audience were quietly moving to the exit. The judge, jury and prosecutors were all gone leaving Marc and Maddy still seated at the defense table. Carvelli looked at the TV camera and saw the red light was off indicating the camera was no longer turned on.

"Hi, where have you been?" Maddy asked Carvelli as he came through the gate. Desperately needing and happy to see a friendly face, Maddy stood and they quickly embraced.

"You okay?" Tony asked.

"Yeah, I'm all right," she said with a weak smile. "It was a tough day."

"I may have something," Tony said. He sat on the edge of the table and looked down at Marc. "What's wrong with you? Is the trial over?"

"I did something stupid," Marc said. "I opened the door to allow Owen Jefferson to give the jury his opinion that Maddy was guilty."

"So what? He wouldn't be on the stand if he didn't believe that," Tony said.

"What's done is done," Maddy said,

"You're right," Marc agreed. "We'll move on."

Marc said, "The worst is probably over. The photos of you in the bedroom is the worst visual the jury will see. Maybe the autopsy photos, but you're not in those. What do you have?"

Tony quickly told them about the phone call he had received downstairs.

"I'm pretty sure she's on our witness list," Marc said. He opened his laptop, found the witness list on it and quickly found her name listed on it.

"Yeah, Gloria Metcalf, CAR Securities. We didn't serve her yet," he continued referring to a subpoena, "but we still can. She didn't say what she wanted?"

"No...." Tony started to say.

"She worked with Rob," Maddy said. "I remember meeting her at the party. Sort of pretty but she seemed a little, I don't know, mousy, I guess. Quiet. I remember Rob said she was really smart and had great phone sales talent. Kind of off for someone who seemed kind of quiet and soft spoken. What do you think she has?"

"I'm guessing something about CAR Securities," Tony said. "I'll find out."

At precisely 7:30, the exact time they had agreed to meet, Carvelli walked into the coffee shop. Seated at a small table for two, as far from the door as she could get, he saw Gloria Metcalf waiting for him. She raised a hand and lightly waved at him and Tony nodded his head in recognition. He made a drinking gesture with his hand and she shook her head and held up her cup to indicate she did not need anything.

Carvelli looked over the menu located behind the counter on the wall. He did not recognize a single thing on it. Finally he gave up, looked at the smiling young girl patiently waiting and shrugged his shoulders.

He held up both hands, palms up, and said, "Can I just get a cup of black coffee? Do you serve that?"

"Sure," the girl laughed.

Less than a minute later he joined Gloria at the table.

After greetings and handshakes Tony quietly said, "You seem a little nervous. Are you okay?"

Gloria heavily inhaled then said,, "Yeah, I'm okay. It's just, I don't know, I'm not sure I'm doing the right thing. I mean, I guess I know I am but I just, I don't know."

Tony reached across the small wood-topped table, gently squeezed her hand and said, "It's okay. We'll take it slow. I won't bite, I promise."

Gloria weakly smiled, inhaled heavily again and said, "Okay." She exhaled and began.

"Something's going on at work, at CAR. Something's not right. I didn't tell you this and I should have. I'll be honest," she continued. "I had a huge crush on Rob. He was so hot and such a great guy and, well, anyway I was a little jealous of Madeline Rivers, his girlfriend."

"It's okay," Tony said. "You're human. It happens."

"And, I believed she did it. I believed something happened and she killed him. And the TV and newspapers made it sound like she did it. Now, I'm not so sure."

"Why? What happened?" Tony asked.

Gloria turned her head to stare out the window for several seconds before answering. She turned back to Tony and said, "Rob told me, a little bit at least, about problems with the mortgage backed securities that CAR held for their customers. He told me they were not what they were supposed to be. That they were not backed by the risk level they were legally required to be. He said he went to Walter with them, that's Walter Pascal, our boss. He said Walter told him he would look into it. That was a few days before the party on the Fourth of July. He also told me Pat McGarry knew about this, too. He told me Pat told him he was going to talk to Walter about them, too."

"Did Pat talk to Walter about them?"

"I don't know. Rob didn't know, either. Rob wasn't so sure Pat's death was an accident. I'm not so sure now, either."

"Why?" Tony asked.

Gloria picked up a small leather folio she had placed on the floor next to the wall. She pulled out a small stack of papers from it and handed them to Carvelli.

"These are computer printouts of a sample of the mortgage backed securities held by CAR. About fifty-million-dollars-worth. They show that there are a lot of B grade mortgages in them and there shouldn't be. They are supposed to be triple and double A only. Do you know what I mean?"

"A little bit," Tony said. "I can get these to people who do."

Tony casually looked over the sparse crowd in the coffee shop. Satisfied that no one was paying any attention to them, he turned back to Metcalf and continued.

"Gloria, if what you're saying is true, then you need to get out of there, out of CAR Securities. If they find out what you've done, your life could be in danger."

"I know," she said. "And I still don't know if I'm doing the right thing. As far as I know, Madeline Rivers is probably guilty..."

"She's not," Tony leaned forward looked her directly in the eyes and said, "I've known her for years and she could not do this. And, you probably don't know this, but she was drugged at that party. We think someone paid a waiter to drug her with roofies and LSD..."

"Oh, my God!"

"...and the waiter was found murdered right after that."

"Oh, my God!" she repeated.

"You're right, something's going on at CAR Securities and with what you gave me, we might be able to get to the bottom of it and find out what."

"Oh, my God," she said again more quietly looking around with a dazed expression. She looked at Carvelli and said, "I can't go back to work, can I?"

"No, you shouldn't," Tony agreed.

"What am I going to do?" she asked, tears forming in her eyes.

Carvelli again reached across the table and took both of her hands in his.

"Relax," he smiled reassuringly. "You're not going back to CAR Securities. I know someone willing to help and when this is over, find you a better job. Trust me, okay?"

"I'm not sure I have any choice."

"It will be all right," Tony said.

He reached in his coat, removed his phone and found the number he wanted. He dialed it and it was quickly answered.

"Hi, hon," Tony said. "I have a huge favor to ask for Maddy. I need to bring someone out to see you, tonight."

He listened for a moment then said, "Good. We'll see you in a little while. Thanks, Vivian."

THIRTY-SIX

It was after 1:00 o'clock on the Wednesday before Thanksgiving when Graham adjourned for the lunch break. As the jury was being led out, the judge motioned to the lawyers to come up to the bench.

"Are you on schedule?" Graham asked Gondeck.

"Yes, your Honor," Gondeck replied. "I have the medical examiner as my last witness this afternoon. I am anticipating one or two rebuttal witnesses to call during the defense case but that's it."

"Mr. Kadella?" Graham looked at Marc.

"I'm going to want to make my opening statement when he's done, no matter how late it is."

"My witness will take a while, your Honor. The jury is going to want to get home for the holiday," Gondeck said.

"Your Honor, he wants the autopsy photos to be the last thing they see before the weekend. In fairness to my client..."

"I agree, Mr. Kadella. In fairness to the defendant he gets to make his opening today. Unless you want to come in tomorrow?" Graham said looking at Gondeck.

"I'm willing," Gondeck said knowing the jury would be angry at the defendant for ruining their long weekend.

"Your Honor! They'll want to take it out on my client..."

"Relax, Marc," Graham said. "We're not coming back until Monday. But," he continued looking at Gondeck, "he gets to make his opening today so, move it along. If the jury thinks you're dragging it out, well..." he shrugged.

Marc noticed Tony Carvelli come into the courtroom. Tony walked up to the gate and waited for Marc.

"Your Honor," Marc said. "One moment, please."

He quickly walked to where Carvelli was waiting and the two of them quietly conferred. Marc pointed at a chair next to Maddy, who was anxiously watching them, and Carvelli took a seat next to her as Marc went back to the bench.

"Your Honor, I need to revisit another matter. We have a witness who can verify that the owners of CAR Securities had a motive to murder Robert Judd..."

"No, no, no," Gondeck emphatically shook his head while saying, "we've been around this block already judge."

"I don't need his permission, your Honor. She's on my witness list. I also have an independent expert to call to back up what she will say," Marc said. "I want to subpoena their records and the owners, or, at least, one of the principals."

"I strongly object, your Honor," Gondeck said.

"Tell you what," Graham said looking at Marc. "What's her name?"

"Gloria Metcalf," Marc replied.

"Okay. Have Ms. Metcalf in here at ten. on Friday morning and your expert too. Let's hear what they have to say without the jury present. Then I'll decide about a subpoena for their records."

"Nice try," Marc said to Gondeck as they walked back to their tables.

"Will you leave the autopsy pictures up while you give your opening?"

"Sure and I'll have Maddy change into a bikini while you're M.E. is testifying and when you do your close," Marc replied.

"Might be worth it," Gondeck replied.

"You two are disgusting," Jennifer Moore said barely containing a laugh.

"I was thinking we could dress you up in a French maid outfit," Marc said to Jennifer.

"You know I have a permit to carry a gun, right?" Jennifer said with a serious, grim look.

"She's good with it, too," Gondeck said.

Maddy heard this last comment and asked Marc, "Good with what?"

"A gun," Marc replied.

"What did you say to her?" Maddy severely asked. "You have my permission to slap him," Maddy told Jennifer.

"He needs it,"

"I'm leaving," Maddy said.

Over lunch the three of them Marc, Maddy and Carvelli discussed Gloria Metcalf's testimony. Carvelli had brought the news that a certified financial planner from an investment advisor firm had reviewed the documents Metcalf had obtained from CAR Securities. What they came up with verified what Metcalf and by extension, Rob Judd, had found. The mortgage backed securities were not the quality they should have been.

"There is a problem here," Marc said. "The documents Metcalf took with her are stolen, proprietary reports. We can probably get her to tell what she knows on a witness stand but Graham might not let the documents themselves into evidence. And what she claims Rob told her is hearsay although there is an exception to the hearsay rule. Graham should allow that."

"What about this afternoon?" Maddy asked. "I'm a little worried about it. I don't want to see Rob's autopsy pictures."

"Try not to look at them," Marc said. "Graham's only letting them show two of them to let the jury see the stab wounds. Most of his testimony will be done using a drawing of the outline of a man's body. Knowing Steve, he'll get those photos up on the TV right away and leave them there as long as he can."

"And then their case is done?" Carvelli asked.

"Yeah, of course," Marc continued looking at Maddy, "he'll use the picture show again during his closing argument."

"Maybe I should wear a bikini," Maddy said with a grim smile.

"That's not a bad idea," Marc seriously said.

"I'm joking, Marc. I don't think the judge would allow it."

"No, remember what we did during the Fornich trial?"

"Yes, I do!" Maddy said lighting up. "You think..."

"Let's think about it," Marc said.

"Okay, I'm game," Maddy agreed.

"You think this is a good idea?" Carvelli asked.

"I don't know. Let me think about it. We'll see," Marc said.

"How's Metcalf doing?" Marc asked Carvelli.

"She's fine. Bored but okay," Carvelli said. Vivian Donahue was funding the trial and picking up the expense of hiding Gloria Metcalf in a Bloomington hotel with round the clock security. The security was being provided by several retired-cop friends of Tony.

"Her family is in Philadelphia, so she wasn't going home for Thanksgiving anyway. I'll bring her to Vivian's tomorrow."

"Yeah, I know," Marc said. "I'll take her to a room at the mansion and prepare her for Friday. We should get back," he continued looking at his watch.

The prosecution wrapped up their case with almost four hours of testimony from the medical examiner, Clyde Marston. Marston was a long-time veteran of the M.E.'s office and virtually a professional witness. He barely needed any preparation before testifying. Just wind him up and let him go. He could explain his procedures and get to the cause of death in a way a ten-year old would understand him. And he would not come across as condescending or patronizing in the least. Plus, it helped that he looked like everyone's idea of a favorite uncle.

What took so much time was Gondeck's inability to control his witness. There are times when a professional witness can be a problem and now was one of them. Because of the TV camera Marston took it upon himself to savor the limelight. Despite Gondeck's best efforts, and he truly tried to move his witness along, Marston decided he needed to graphically show and explain to the jury each and every stab wound. All fourteen of them.

During this phase of his testimony, after the preliminary of his qualification and years on the job, he put up a photo of Rob Judd lying on an exam table. Rob was shown naked from the waist up. Fortunately this photo was taken after being prepared for the autopsy but before it was performed. Each of the wounds in his torso was cleaned and clearly visible but sterile. While it was a real photo of a real homicide victim, every juror had seen much worse things, many times, on TV and in the movies.

On an easel set up next to the TV was a life-size outline of a man. On that Marston had displayed every stab wound and numbered them in the order he believed they were inflicted.

Using a pointer he went through each one pointing first at the outline on the easel, then the corresponding wound on Rob's body. And for each one he spent anywhere from five to ten minutes explaining the damage the wound had done to Rob's internal organs.

Marc was tempted to object two or three times. Instead he looked over the jurors and it was not long before he saw obvious signs of boredom. One older man actually nodded off, so Marc kept quiet and let Marston go.

"Your honor," Marston said after the fifth or sixth wound he described, "it would be useful if I could put up photos of the actual organs I'm talking about."

Marc had stood up to object but the judge beat him to it.

"Not a chance, Dr. Marston," Graham told him. "This is graphic enough."

When Marston finally finished, he returned to the witness stand.

"Dr. Marston," Gondeck began delighted to get this show moving again, "in your expert, medical opinion, what would you say was the actual cause of death?"

Not wanting to waste a second of his time on TV, Marston paused as if thinking it over.

"Well, I'll tell you, it was blood loss. And if that hadn't killed him, the tissue damage would have."

"What caused the blood loss?" Gondeck asked.

"Fourteen stab wounds," Marston said as if speaking to a child eliciting a round of good natured laughter from the entire courtroom.

"Was it any one particular stab wound that caused the blood loss that led to Robert Judd's death?"

"No, actually, that's a good point," Marston answered. "There were five or six that would have done the job by themselves if left untreated but not one single wound could be said to be the sole cause of death."

"Did he die right away?"

"No, no, he laid there and bled out probably in tremendous pain..."

"Objection, speculation and prejudicial with no probative value," Marc said trying to put a stop to the image of Rob lying on the bed slowly dying a painful death.

"He's an expert and can give his opinion," Gondeck said.

"Overruled," Graham ordered.

"In your expert opinion, Dr. Marston," Gondeck continued, "how long would it have taken Robert Judd to bleed out and die?"

"At least fifteen minutes and could have been as long as an hour."

With that, Gondeck ended his direct examination and turned Marston over to Marc.

"Isn't it true, doctor, you have no idea who did this, do you?"

"No, no medical evidence of who did it," he agreed.

"Was it one person or two or maybe three people who stabbed him?"

"Likely one, unless they took turns because the wounds were all done using the same knife," Marston chuckled at his wit.

"Isn't it true, Robert Judd could have done this himself?" Marc asked trying to move on from the mistake he had just made.

"Well, I don't..."

"Yes or no, doctor," Marc said.

"Yes, it's possible," Marston reluctantly replied.

Marc kept at him for a while finally realizing he had gotten all he could from the M.E., an admission he did not know who did this, Marc ended his cross examination.

Having entered every piece of information and evidence he had, Gondeck rested his case. Marc went through the formality for the record of requesting a directed verdict from Judge Graham. Graham quickly denied the request then spoke to the jury.

"I understand the hour is getting late and you're all anxious to get home for the holiday weekend. However, I have promised the defense the opportunity to make an opening statement first. We'll take a quick ten minute recess then Mr. Kadella will address you. Thank you for your patience."

When court resumed Marc stood in front of the jury and started out by profusely thanking them. He also assured them he would be brief and to the point. A promise he kept.

Normally an opening statement is to be used to tell the jury what the lawyer was going to present for his or her case. It is also an opportunity to indoctrinate them.

Marc spent very little time telling the jury what his witnesses were going to tell them. Gondeck had already put on an expert to explain the drugs found in Maddy's system. The prosecution's expert also made it clear that in her opinion, with the level of roofies and LSD in her system Maddy could have committed the murder. The roofies would not have knocked her out before she could have done it and the LSD would have likely helped her do it.

Marc had been thoroughly educated by his drug expert how to go after the prosecution's witness. He was able to score several points and came close to getting her to admit she was stretching reality with the claim Maddy could have done it as drugged as she was.

Now Marc told the jury his expert was going to tell the jury it would be extremely unlikely anyone could do this with the amount of drugs Maddy had in her system. And he reminded them that Gondeck had not addressed the question of how Maddy became drugged in the first place. Still uncertain about letting her testify, Marc was careful not to over promise and tell them he would fill in that gap. He did give them the information that the defense had several witnesses who had known the defendant for years and she

250

was not a drug user. He clear attempt to imply she was surreptitiously drugged.

"Finally, ladies and gentleman," Marc said wrapping up. "Remember before the trial started each of you swore an oath to keep an open mind. Each of you promised not to decide this case until you had heard all of the witnesses and seen all of the evidence."

Marc stopped, took a couple of small steps to his right and looked at each and every one of them. Several actually nodded their heads and they were all paying close attention.

"So far, you've only heard one side of the case. Yes, Robert Judd was brutally murdered. There is no point in denying it. But the one thing the prosecution has failed to deliver is motive. A squabble in a restaurant two weeks before this happened is hardly enough to prove any level of animosity between them. And, we will present witnesses to counter that claim anyway. No, the real issue here is: Why was he murdered? Keep that question in mind because you're about to find out."

That last statement was a promise Marc sincerely hoped he would be able to keep.

When Marc finished speaking and Graham excused the jury, Charlie Dudek clicked off his television set. He had never had any feelings while watching a televised trial before. Charlie, without really understanding why, was having ambivalent feelings about it. He knew he should not care how it came out, in fact, he knew he should be pulling for a guilty verdict. At the same time he was totally fixated on the defendant. Charlie found himself hoping she would win and was troubled by why he felt that way. And, on top of that, he was sorry the show would not be on for several more days. It was going to be a long weekend for him.

"It is going well," Victor Espinosa said into his private cell phone. "Our man in the courtroom believes it will take a minor miracle to get her off."

251

"Yes, that seems to be true," Quinones replied. "But we've only seen one side. It does appear to be that the prosecution has made a serious case."

"The picture of her holding the knife is damning. The jury will get more of that, before it is over," Espinosa said.

The two friends chatted about other things, money things, for another few minutes. Quinones wished his friend a Happy Thanksgiving then ended the call.

THIRTY-SEVEN

"Mr. Gondeck, do you have any questions for this witness?" Judge Graham asked.

"Not at this time, your Honor," Gondeck answered.

Graham looked down at Gloria Metcalf and said, "Thank you, Ms. Metcalf. You may step down."

It was after eleven on the Friday morning following Thanksgiving. Gloria Metcalf had been on the stand in the closed empty courtroom, under oath, telling Judge Graham her story. Marc had prepared her the day before and she did an excellent job. She handled herself smoothly and most importantly, credibly.

"Anything else?" Graham asked Marc.

"I have an expert waiting in the hall who has been through the documents Ms. Metcalf obtained..."

"Stole," Gondeck interjected.

"...from CAR Securities."

"That won't be necessary, Mr. Kadella. I believe her but it's irrelevant. I'm not going to allow those documents to be admitted into evidence. Mr. Gondeck is right. They contain confidential, proprietary information and they are stolen. But, I will allow Ms. Metcalf to testify about those securities and what Robert Judd told her. Also, I will allow you to subpoena Walter Pascal and put him on the stand."

Tony Carvelli was sitting with Gloria Metcalf in the first row of the gallery directly behind the defense table. As soon as Graham said he would allow Marc to subpoena Pascal, Tony sent a brief, four-word text message. 'Serve Walter Pascal only!'

Five minutes later a well-dressed, professional looking man in his late fifties walked into CAR Securities office. He was one of the retired cop friends of Carvelli's who had been watching Walter Pascal and knew he was in the CAR offices.

"Hi," he politely said to the receptionist. "Walter Pascal, please."

"Do you have an appointment?" she politely asked.

"No, but it's very important and I just need to talk to him for a minute. It's sort of an emergency," Tony's guy said.

She placed a quick call and barely thirty seconds later a curious Walter Pascal appeared.

"Are you Walter Pascal?" the gentleman asked.

"Yes, what's the emergency?"

The man smiled, handed Walter a piece of paper and said, "You've been served, pal. See you in court." He then turned and calmly walked out leaving a steaming Pascal staring at his back.

Out in the hallway outside the courtroom, Marc, Maddy, Tony and Gloria Metcalf were huddled together.

"Now what?" Maddy asked Marc.

"Without the CAR documents proving the securities were a fraud, it's going to be more difficult to prove Pascal is lying."

Marc looked at Gloria and asked, "Is there any other thing you have that we can use against Pascal?"

"Just my word. Won't they believe me?" she asked.

"It's hard to say," Marc said. "Pascal will say you're a disgruntled employee out to make trouble. Gondeck will come after you for not coming forward sooner."

"I was scared," she said.

"I know and it's okay," Marc assured her. "Do you know anyone else at CAR that Rob or the other guy, Pat McGarry might have talked to?"

"I have a couple names to check," Tony said. "I'll get them this weekend."

Tony's phone rang, he answered it and had a brief conversation.

"My guy served Pascal," he told Marc after ending the call.

"Okay, let's get some lunch then Tony will take you back to the hotel," Marc said to Metcalf.

"I need to go by my townhouse and pick up some things first," she said to Tony. "Is that okay?"

"Sure, no problem," Carvelli replied.

254

While Gloria punched in the security code to unlock her front door, for at least the fourth or fifth time she apologetically assured Tony it would not take long. "I just need a few things," she said again.

Smiling, Tony replied, "Gloria, relax, we have all day. In fact, take your time and make sure you're getting everything. I'm just sorry you have to go through this."

As they walked through the entryway, Gloria turned to look back at Carvelli and said, "Me too but I think it's the right thing to do."

She took one step into the living room and yelled, "Oh my God!"

Her home looked like a biker gang had thrown a party in it. Every piece of furniture was smashed. The couch torn to shreds, the pictures and photos on the walls had been used for Frisbees and thrown around the room.

Carvelli grabbed the shocked woman's arm and pulled her back to the door. While he did this he urgently whispered, "We have to get out now. Someone might still be here."

Carvelli got her outside and back into his car. He retrieved a .40 caliber automatic from his glove box and called 911.

While the two of them waited for the police, Carvelli stood guard by his car, gun in hand. Gloria sat in the passenger seat in stunned silence.

Carvelli had identified himself to the 911 dispatcher as ex-MPD. It helped because in barely a minute, the first patrol car arrived. There was a lone MPD sergeant in it who Carvelli was acquainted and friendly with. By the time Carvelli explained to the man what was inside, two more cars with four more cops arrived. The sergeant sent two of the newcomers around back to check the patio while he led the other two, with Carvelli trailing, into the house. Five minutes later, with guns drawn, the cops had cleared every room and were satisfied no one remained inside.

Back outside, the sergeant, Ed Rollins, called it in and requested a CSU team and detectives. A half-hour later, while the

CSU team began going over the ruins inside Metcalf's home, Carvelli was explaining things to a detective he knew.

"You think this might have something to do with Maddy Rivers' trial?" the detective, Sam Booker, asked Tony.

"Sam, I don't know any more than you do. It does seem a bit too coincidental that this happened to a witness I'm babysitting," Tony replied.

Booker looked Carvelli in the eyes with a skeptical look on his face. "I'm open to suggestions," Booker said.

"I told you, Sam. You're guess is as good as mine," Tony said.

"Bullshit. I know you too well. You're pulling my weenie, Carvelli, and I know it," Booker said poking Carvelli in the chest with a finger.

At that moment, Booker's partner, Carl Sweet came out of the townhouse with Gloria Metcalf. Gloria was doing her best to fight back the tears in a losing battle. When she reached Carvelli, he held her while she cried into his chest.

"The place is totally trashed," Sweet quietly told Booker and Carvelli.

"All my stuff is destroyed," Gloria sobbed. "If..." she started to say then Carvelli put a finger to her lips to stop her before she blurted out the name of CAR Securities.

Gloria stepped back, wiped her eyes and sniffled while looking inquisitively at Carvelli.

"Are you done with us?" Carvelli asked Booker.

"What were you going to say, miss?" Booker asked ignoring Carvelli.

Gloria's eyes shifted between the detective and Carvelli. She understood Tony wanted her to keep quiet so she said, "Ah, if I find out who did this, well, they're going to pay."

"Uh, huh," Booker skeptically replied. He turned to Carvelli and said, "If you know who did this, I want to know. I don't want you getting in the way of a police investigation, Carvelli."

"Sam! Would I do that?" Carvelli innocently said.

256

"Yes, I know you would," Booker said. "And I'll put your ass in jail if you do."

"Look, she's obviously upset. Your guys are inside doing their thing. We're gonna take off. If I think of anything, I swear I'll call you right away. In fact, give me your card with your cell number, okay?" Carvelli said.

Both detectives handed Carvelli a business card. Carvelli shook their hands then hustled Gloria into his Camaro and they got out of there as quickly as possible.

While he drove off, Booker said to his partner, "He knows what's going on here."

"Will he tell us?" Sweet asked.

"Yeah, we'll find out. When he's ready," Booker replied.

Carvelli was seated in his car in the underground parking garage of a high-rise condo building off of downtown Minneapolis. He had a clear unobstructed view of the two-year-old Cadillac XTS that belonged to the subject of his surveillance.

When he and Metcalf left her townhouse, Carvelli called Vivian Donahue and told Vivian what happened. Of course, Vivian told Tony to take Gloria shopping for anything she needed which he did. On the way to a suburban mall he called Marc to let him know what was going on also.

Reasonably suspecting that CAR Securities had a hand in vandalizing Metcalf's home, Tony decided what his next move should be. Several hours later he was now waiting to talk to an old acquaintance.

A few minutes before seven P.M. the building's elevator doors on Tony's right opened. A tall, well-dressed, attractive, elegant looking woman stepped off the elevator. Tony watched her with a slight smile on his face as she came toward him in the well-lit garage. Without noticing him sitting there she strolled past his car headed toward the Cadillac.

Tony quietly exited his Camaro and said, loud enough to be heard, "Hello, Gretchen, it's been a while."

The woman let out a shriek, spun around toward the noise and stumbled backward a step and a half while clutching her heart. Barely breathing she stared at the source of the greeting for several seconds before recognition finally came to her.

"Tony? Is that you? My god, what's it been, fifteen years?" she exclaimed. "And what the hell are you trying to do, give me a goddamn heart attack? Come here you big lug," she said holding out her arms.

Tony walked over to her and they gave each other a warm embrace.

Tony stepped back and said, "I'm sorry, sweetheart. I didn't mean to scare you. You look fabulous."

"Thanks," she smiled. "You look pretty good yourself." She paused, looked him up and down then said "Wait a minute, you're up to something. Why are you here waiting for me and what do you want?"

Tony nodded his head once then said, "I need a favor from you and you're the only person I can get to help me with this. Are you working tonight?"

"No, in fact I was going out for a bite to eat," she replied.

"Let me buy you dinner and I'll explain what I need," Tony said.

THIRTY-EIGHT

The waiter sincerely thanked Carvelli and Gretchen for their orders, took the menus, turned away and walked off to place their order. They were in an Italian restaurant called Zelo on Eighth and Nicollet in downtown Minneapolis. Gretchen was well known there and despite her profession, always welcome.

"So, Tony Carvelli, how the hell are you? God, it's good to see you again," Gretchen said reaching across the table to squeeze his hand.

"You, too," Tony smiled. "But this isn't a coincidence."

"I gathered that," Gretchen said then sipped her wine. "You need a favor. How did you find me?"

"I'm a cop, or more accurately an ex-cop. We know everything," Carvelli smiled. "Actually, I was at the Leamington a while back and saw you there with a client."

"You could've stopped to say hello," she admonished him.

"No, I couldn't. It was your client I was interested in."

"Oh, I see," Gretchen softly said. "And who was he?"

"His real name, or at least the one he's using now, is Ethan Rask," Tony said then described Rask to her.

"That's a guy I know as Edward. Not one of my favorites," she said. "He can be a bit of an arrogant ass, and he's cheap. He always insists on taking me to dinner then bitches about the bill. Like he expects me to pay for half of it. Plus he's getting to be a little rough. I don't mind dishing it out for the right client, if you know what I mean, but I'm not gonna take it."

"I do," Tony said. "So, you might not mind losing him as a client?"

"No, not at all. I've been thinking about dumping him anyway. What do you have in mind?"

"When do you see him again?"

"Tomorrow night, in fact. We're going to a new Mexican restaurant on Hennepin."

"Perfect," Tony said. "I have something for him. Slip it into a Margarita to cover the salty taste. Here's what I want you to do…"

Carvelli was sitting in the back seat, passenger side, of a Ford van waiting for Gretchen. With him were two other ex-cops, Jake Waschke and Dan Sorenson. Both men, also friends of Maddy Rivers, were fully versed on what to do and were 100% in favor.

It was the Saturday night of the Thanksgiving weekend, the night Gretchen had her 'date' with Ethan Rask. Tony had given her a very illegal drug to slip into Rask's drink that would knock him out and make him very easy to handle. They were parked in a neighborhood in South Minneapolis where the residents minded their own business and were reluctant to call the police.

Headlights appeared through the van's back window and the car they belonged to parked behind the van.

"This must be her," Carvelli said as he opened his door.

Within a minute, Sorenson and Waschke were struggling to cram an inert Ethan Rask into the back of the van. While they were doing this, Carvelli and Gretchen were getting back into Rask's Mercedes so Tony could take her home.

"Don't start the party without me," Carvelli said to his two partners.

Sorenson quietly closed the van's back door as Waschke said to Carvelli, "We'll see you in a bit. I don't think he'll be ready to do the deal before you get there anyway."

On the drive back to Gretchen's condo building she asked Carvelli "What are you going to do with him? I don't want to be a part of anything serious."

"Don't worry about it," Carvelli smiled while turning his head from the road to look at her. "He'll be fine. We're just going to have a serious chat with him."

"He's a tough guy, Tony. He may not tell you what you want to know."

"Then he doesn't," Tony shrugged. He took his right hand off the steering wheel, patted her hand and said, "Don't worry. We're not going to hurt him. Much."

Carvelli parked the Mercedes next to Sorenson's van behind a small, empty warehouse. The owner was a man who owed Sorenson a favor and let him have the keys to the place for the evening. Of course he received a hundred dollar bill courtesy of Vivian Donahue through Carvelli. Fortunately, Vivian knew nothing about what these guys were up to.

Carvelli went in through the open back door and found Rask handcuffed to a chair in a corner with three powerful, very bright lights on six feet tall metal stands pointed at him. A fourth man, another ex-cop by the name of Tom Evans was holding smelling salts under Rask's nose. After a few seconds Rask's head snapped back, he made a couple of grunting sounds, shook his head a couple times and came back to reality,

Evans, wearing a Halloween mask of a zombie, walked away and joined the other three behind the lights. The four ex-cops stood next to the lights so Rask could see them in silhouette but be unable to identify them.

They waited in silence for almost two minutes while Rask struggled with the fuzziness in his head and the handcuffs. He finally gave up trying to free himself, settled down and moved his head around in an effort to see where he was. The lights in his face made that impossible.

"Who are you and what do you want?" Rask broke the silence by asking.

"Who we are is not important," Jake Waschke answered him. It had been decided that Jake would do the questioning to lessen the odds Rask would recognize his voice. "What we want is the truth and we're going to get it."

"Are you cops? Nothing I tell you like this could be used in court so fuck you!" Rask snarled in defiance.

"Are you going to make this difficult or easy? The harder you make it, the longer it takes, the more unpleasant for you," Jake said.

At that moment, Evans with the zombie mask and Sorenson wearing a skull mask stepped forward to let Rask see them. Rask tried his best to appear calm. Inside he was a quivering bowl of Jello. Even as a child he was terrified of physical pain. He could dish it out but he could not take. He knew he might as well cooperate since it would not take much for these very serious guys to get it from him anyway. He acted like a tough guy but in reality he was like all bullies; an insecure coward.

For the next thirty seconds, while sweat broke out on his forehead, Rask's eyes nervously shifted from the two men in masks to the two in silhouette. He licked his lips several times and again pulled on the cuffs holding him in his chair.

"All right, I'll tell you what you want to know," he conceded.

"Are you out of bed yet?"

"Carvelli it's almost 10:00 o'clock. I've been up for three hours," Marc said into his phone.

It was Sunday morning and Marc had spent the night at Margaret Tennant's. Despite it being a football Sunday, Marc had trial preparation to do for Monday's testimony and was planning on spending the afternoon in the office.

"Have you had breakfast?" Carvelli asked.

"Yeah, Margaret made waffles. They were great. Why? What's up?"

"I have some information for you. Meet me at Sir Jack's on Chicago. I don't want to do this over the phone," Carvelli said.

"Can I bring Margaret along?"

"No! This is definitely not something for a judge to hear. Say hello for me then I'll see you soon."

When Marc arrived at the popular local eatery Carvelli was finishing what looked to be a large Sunday morning breakfast. The waitress brought a fresh carafe of coffee and poured both men a full cup.

"Man, that hit the spot," Carvelli said while emptying two creamers into his cup. "I was hungry. I missed supper last night."

"What's so important you couldn't tell me over the phone?" Marc asked.

Tony leaned on the table and whispered, "Me and some friends had a little chat last night with that Ethan Rask guy from CAR Securities."

Knowing Carvelli, Marc rubbed his temples with both hands then said, "Do I want to know how this came about?"

"No, you don't. So I won't tell you. Don't worry, he's not going to say anything to anyone and even if he did, he won't be able to identify anyone. We were very careful."

"Jesus Christ," Marc softly said. "How many felonies did you guys commit? On second thought," he quickly added, "don't tell me, I don't want to know."

"Do you want to know what we got or not?" Carvelli asked.

Marc sipped his coffee, sighed and said, "Sure, why not?"

"He confessed to all of it. Rob's murder, the guy up north, the Ponzi scheme, the money laundering, you name it. He folded like a cheap suit. He even admitted he and a guy he hired were the ones who trashed Gloria Metcalf's townhouse. They were looking for documents from CAR Securities."

"What did you do to him?"

"Nothing. I swear," Carvelli continued holding up his right hand. "We didn't lay a hand on him. Didn't have to. He was scared shitless."

"Can we use it?"

"Not a word of it," Carvelli shrugged. "At least I don't see how. It was totally coerced. In fact, we'd all go to jail. But at least we know what happened."

"How did they kill Rob Judd and set up Maddy?" Marc asked.

"They, or more accurately Rask, hired a pro through some guys he knows in Chicago. Rask doesn't even know the pro's name. Except that he's very good."

"Obviously. And the other guy and his girlfriend, McGarry?"

"Rask did that himself. He followed them up North and caught them on a hiking trail and pushed them off."

"Are you serious? Jesus," Marc said.

"That's what he claims," Tony replied.

"Okay, now I want to know. How did you pull this off?"

Tony took a minute to quickly tell him about Gretchen and slipping a 'Mickey' into Rask's drink.

"He's going after her," Marc said. "He'll know it was her."

Tony shook his head and said, "I don't think so. We warned him about that. Made it clear if anything happened to her we'd find him. I don't think he'll bother her."

"What did you do with him afterwards?"

"We gave him a hypo, a shot, with a sedative that would put him out for an hour or so. Then we packed up and left him. We unlocked his handcuffs, put his car keys in his lap and left a light on above the door. Unless somebody stole his car, it was waiting for him when he woke up."

Marc leaned forward and asked, "Where do you get all of these drugs?"

"We're cops. Cops know where to get everything. Haven't you ever heard the old saying, cops have the best dope?"

Marc sat back in the booth they were in and silently thought over what Tony had done. Carvelli refilled their cups and sipped his while waiting for Marc to speak.

"Why did you do this?" Marc asked with an admonishing look on his face.

"I wanted to get to the bottom of it," Tony shrugged. "Somehow, we're going to use this to get Maddy off. Now that we know for sure what happened, she's going to get her life back. We'll figure out something."

"I don't know what. I guess I can try to go after Walter Pascal when I get him on the stand. Did Rask say if Pascal knows about this?"

"He said they all did. All the principals of CAR Securities. Especially about the first guy, McGarry and the girlfriend, what's-her-name?"

"Ah, Lynn, something," Marc said. "Mason, Lynn Mason. Let's think about this. I still think we have a pretty good shot at an acquittal. I'll go after Pascal but I'm not sure what Graham will let me accuse him of. He'll deny everything but at least he'll be shocked when I hit him with it. You think Rask will tell the others what happened."

"No way. He said if the guys at CAR find out he'd be next. He says Corbin Reed is a sociopath. He has no conscience and would kill Rask himself. Although I got the feeling he was keeping something from us, but I couldn't say what."

THIRTY-NINE

Having driven downtown together Marc and Maddy stepped off the crowded elevator on the fifteenth floor a few minutes before 8:00 A.M. It was Monday morning and Marc was set to begin presenting his case. Tony Carvelli would arrive with his first witness just before 9:00. Waiting for them with lights ablaze and cameras whirring were several members of the local media.

"What can you tell us about what's taking place in the courtroom?" the bubbly, bottle-blonde from Channel 3 quickly asked, stabbing her microphone at Marc.

"Brenda, get that thing out of my face," Marc irritably said while shielding Maddy. "I don't know what's going on in there. Excuse me," he kept repeating as the two of them marched through the small crowd.

At the courtroom was a young sheriff's deputy guarding the door to keep spectators out. When he saw Marc and Maddy, he said a pleasant good morning while brightly smiling at Maddy and opened the door for them. When they passed through the door, they found the same group of lawyers as had appeared before on behalf of CAR Securities milling about the prosecution's table. Passing through the gate in the bar Marc nodded toward them and said an all-inclusive good morning.

"Why are they here?" Maddy whispered to Marc when they took their seats at their table.

Marc looked at the lawyers and replied intentionally loud enough for them to hear him, "They're here to try to quash the subpoena we served on Walter Pascal. Apparently we're onto something. Obviously CAR Securities has something to hide."

While he was saying this they were all looking at him. When he finished he looked them over and they all turned away or looked down, not wanting to make eye contact.

Marc turned back to Maddy and more quietly said, "It's too bad the jury didn't see that reaction."

While Marc was setting up the table with his case file, laptop and other items, Steve Gondeck and Jennifer Moore arrived.

They also said a perfunctory good morning to the CAR lawyers. Gondeck then looked at Marc and silently pointed to the conference room door by the jury box.

"What's this all about?" Gondeck asked Marc when the four of them, including Maddy, got behind a closed door.

"I assume they're out to quash the Pascal subpoena," Marc answered.

"Did you know about it?"

"Did I have notice? No. But I figured they'd try it so I'm not surprised. Apparently you didn't know either," Marc said.

"No, we didn't," Gondeck said. He looked at Jennifer who shook her head then Gondeck said, "Marc, I'm not going to help them but I won't oppose it, either. That's the best I can do."

"That's okay," Marc said. "I'm not worried. Graham will throw them out."

"You're probably right," Gondeck agreed.

Almost literally throwing them out is exactly what Judge Graham did. Back in his chambers, Graham listened with growing impatience for more than a half hour to their arguments. Already annoyed with having his Sunday interrupted the previous day with the phone call requesting this impromptu motion and then served with an eighty page 'brief' at his home, his irritation was obvious.

When they finished Graham looked at his court reporter and asked, "Did you get all of that?" The man nodded his head in the affirmative.

"Denied," Graham quickly said. "The defense has made an offer of proof and I am satisfied Mr. Pascal has information pertinent to the case before the court. You gentlemen will now excuse us. I need to discuss something with case counsel."

One of the older, more expensive lawyers tried to make an objection and Graham quickly slammed a verbal door in his face. He then requested that the trial be continued to give them a chance to appeal. Graham silently stared at the man for several seconds as if to say, "You're crazy if you think that will happen." Instead he politely denied that as well.

"Good day, gentlemen," Graham said with obvious finality.

When they had sullenly filed out, Gondeck asked, "What did you want to see us about, Judge?"

"Nothing. I just used that as an excuse to get rid of them," Graham replied. "You ready to go?" he asked Marc.

"Yes, your Honor. My first witness is on the way and probably here," Marc said.

"You may call your first witness, Mr. Kadella," Graham said after taking the bench.

Marc stood and replied, "The defense calls Gloria Metcalf, your Honor."

Tony Carvelli came through the exterior door first and led Metcalf up the aisle. He stepped through the gate, held it open for her and smiled and winked at her as she passed by. Tony then took a seat behind Maddy in front of the bar along the railing.

To ease her nervousness Marc got Gloria going by having her tell the jury a little bit about herself. Who she was, her education to establish credibility, where she worked and what she did. Gradually, he moved her into what she knew about Rob Judd and the things he told her.

Metcalf explained to the jury what Judd told her about his concerns at CAR Securities. Before she was able to get into it, Gondeck vehemently objected because it was all hearsay. Among the numerous exceptions to the rule disallowing hearsay testimony is one where the declarant, Rob Judd, is unavailable. Obviously since he is dead, he is no longer available to testify himself. Graham overruled Gondeck's objection and allowed Metcalf to continue.

"Ms. Metcalf," Marc continued, "bearing in mind that I'm a lawyer and need things explained so even I can understand it, please explain to me what a mortgage backed security is?"

This admission of ignorance by Marc elicited mild laughter and a large smile from Gloria Metcalf. Of course, having thoroughly rehearsed this ahead of time, Metcalf knew exactly what to say. She turned her head to the jury and calmly, efficiently, without sounding condescending or patronizing, explained what these financial instruments are.

"Did Robert Judd tell you if he had any concerns about these securities being held by CAR Securities for its customers?"

"Yes, he did," she answered.

"When did that take place? When did he tell you his concerns?"

"It was the Thursday before the Fourth of July weekend, June thirtieth.

"What did he tell you?"

Metcalf again turned to face the jury and told them what Rob had found. She explained the difference between the various risk levels, called tranches, assigned to mortgages from the best, triple A down to much riskier double B and single B securities.

"Why is that important?" Marc asked.

"Because the securities CAR held were far riskier than they were telling their customers. They marketed them as risk free, triple A backed and they were not."

"How did Mr. Judd know this?"

"Because he told me he had checked every one of them, all three hundred and forty-million dollars worth."

"Did he show them to you?"

"No, he said he went to our direct supervisor, the head of the bond department, Walter Pascal, and told him about it. Rob told me Walter was surprised and would look into it."

"To your knowledge, did Mr. Pascal do anything about it? Did he look into it?"

"Not that I'm aware of," Metcalf admitted.

Gondeck stood up and said, "I'm sure this is all very interesting your Honor, but I fail to see the relevance."

Silently Marc thought, *thank you Steve*.

"It is the defense's contention that others had a strong motive to silence Robert Judd, your Honor. That CAR Securities had three hundred and forty million reasons," Marc replied.

"Overruled," Graham said.

"Did you have occasion to discuss this with Robert Judd again?"

"No," Metcalf answered. "The next time I saw him was at the Fourth of July party at Jordan Kemp's home. The next day Rob was dead."

When she said this, there was a noticeable stirring in the jury box and gallery. Several of the jurors glanced at Marc and Maddy with what Marc hoped were sympathetic looks.

"Let's go back to these securities again. Explain why, if it is, is it a big deal to have higher risk mortgages in them?"

"Well, first of all, because we were selling them as risk free this was fraud…"

"Objection," Gondeck said. "Calls for a legal conclusion she's not qualified to make."

"Sustained," Graham said. He looked at Metcalf and said, "Don't use the word fraud. That's a legal term."

"Yes, sir. Selling them as risk free is a lie," she continued.

"That's better," Graham said smiling.

"And second it's also illegal. These high-risk mortgage backed securities were probably the main reason for the financial industry meltdown of '07 and '08."

"Could three hundred forty-million dollars-worth of these cause that to happen again?" Marc asked.

"No, it would take a lot more than that. CAR Securities bought them from somewhere else. If CAR bought them, they're probably being sold to others," Metcalf blurted out before Gondeck could object.

"Do you have any personal knowledge that these securities are as Robert Judd described them to you?"

"Yes, I checked fifty-million dollars-worth myself and what I found was worse than what Rob told me."

"In your opinion, would it be safe to say CAR Securities would not want this information to get out?"

"Objection, speculation plus she has no idea what someone else might think," Gondeck rose and said.

"She can give her opinion," Graham said. "The jury can decide for itself what that is worth."

"Absolutely," Metcalf answered.

"Ms. Metcalf, where are you currently living?"

"In a hotel. I'm in fear of my life," she replied.

Marc glanced over at Gondeck expecting an objection. When one did not happen he continued.

"What happened this past Friday afternoon?"

Metcalf described being taken to her home and what she found when she got there. When she finished, there was more stirring and another murmur that went through the courtroom.

"Just a couple more questions. When you saw Robert Judd at the Fourth of July party was my client, Madeline Rivers, with him?"

"Yes, she was."

"How did they seem to you? Were they getting along all right?"

"Yes, they seemed very happy together."

With that Marc turned her over to Gondeck.

Gondeck politely but quite forcefully as well, went right at her. He wasted no time with preliminary questions. Instead he used yes and no questions to get her to admit she had no evidence of any kind as to the guilt or innocence of Maddy Rivers. In fact, he went over it so much Marc finally objected and Graham told Gondeck to move on. Then Gondeck went into an area Marc had hoped he would.

"Ms. Metcalf, why didn't you go to the police with this? Why did you wait so long?"

"Because the newspapers were so sure Madeline Rivers did it. I didn't think the things Rob found at CAR had anything to do with it. Plus," she paused and looked around feeling a little awkward, "I had a bit of a crush on Rob and, well, I was probably a little jealous of Madeline Rivers and was maybe a little angry at her and hoped she'd go to jail."

Having been slapped with an answer he did not expect and having obtained her admission that she had no real knowledge of the case, Gondeck ended his cross-examination.

"Redirect, Mr. Kadella?" Graham asked.

"Yes, your Honor. After coming forward and finding your townhouse trashed, what do you think of Madeline River's guilt now?"

"Objection..."

"Overruled."

"Now, I don't believe it."

"Nothing further, your Honor."

FORTY

Tony Carvelli had interviewed several more employees of CAR Securities over the weekend. Only a couple of them would even speak with him. One of the salesmen from the bond department, Turner Smith, told Carvelli the word was out from their bosses. If you value your job, no one is to cooperate with the defense in the Rob Judd trial. Smith did say that neither Rob nor Pat McGarry ever spoke to him about any problems they suspected. As he was getting ready to leave, Carvelli warned Smith without saying why, to get out of CAR Securities.

Unable to find anyone to corroborate Gloria Metcalf's story, Marc put Dale Kubik on the stand after the lunch break. Marc wanted the jury to hear from another witness, this time the actual source, that others had a motive to kill Rob Judd.

Kubik was Marc's witness and ordinarily Marc would not be allowed to ask leading, yes and no, type questions. It took less than ten minutes for Kubik's hostility to be made very apparent. Because of this, Graham agreed to allow Marc to treat him as hostile and allow him to use leading questions.

Marc methodically walked him through the case that caused Kubik's downfall; the drug case Marc defended when Kubik planted drugs on a young man. Kubik did his best to deny any wrongdoing until Marc focused in on his dismissal from the St. Paul Police Department. By that point it was obvious that Kubik had an axe to grind against both Marc and Maddy Rivers.

"It's fair to say, Mr. Kubik, that you blame Madeline Rivers for being fired by the police department, isn't that true?"

"Well, her and..." he stammered.

"Yes or no, Mr. Kubik."

"In part, yeah," he replied.

"Before I ask this next question, Mr. Kubik, let me warn you, you are still under oath and I have the names of two St. Paul police detectives who were there and heard you say this.

"Isn't it true, you were at Stout's, a bar in Roseville, bragging that you had gotten even with a certain private investigator, a woman that you referred to as a word that rhymes with punt?"

"I don't recall," Kubik nervously answered.

"Okay, I'll bring the detectives in and..." Marc started to say.

"Okay, yeah, I guess I did."

"You also said you did something to get even with her, something really bad that she was going to take a hard fall for, yes or no?"

Kubik hesitated and glared at Marc as if he wanted to leap over the rail and go after him. Marc sat impassively staring back at him waiting for an answer.

"Your Honor, please have the witness answer," Marc said after a long fifteen seconds of silence.

"Yeah, I guess maybe I did but..." Kubik said before Graham could order him to answer.

"Thank you, Mr. Kubik," Marc said abruptly cutting him off. "I have nothing further."

Gondeck spent less than fifteen minutes on his cross-exam of Kubik. He asked him to explain his behavior on the night he was at the bar bragging and just let him go. A very relieved Dale Kubik readily admitted he was drunk, running his mouth and there was nothing to it.

"Did you ever meet Robert Judd?" Gondeck asked.

"No, I had never heard of him until the day she murdered..."

"Objection!" Marc jumped to his feet.

"Sustained. The jury will disregard that last statement," Graham ruled. He looked at Kubik and said, "As a former police officer, you should know better."

"Sorry, your Honor."

"Did you murder Robert Judd and frame Madeline Rivers for it?" Gondeck asked.

"Of course not," Kubik answered.

Gondeck ended his cross and Graham asked Marc if he wanted to redirect.

"Isn't it true, Mr. Kubik, you were dismissed by the St Paul Police because you planted drugs on a suspect, you have a drinking problem, use drugs yourself and were found to be unfit to be a police officer, yes or no?" Marc forcefully asked.

"Well, I..."

"Yes or no!"

"I suppose, yes," Kubik admitted.

"In fact, you hate both myself and Madeline Rivers, don't you?"

"Objection. Argumentative," Gondeck said.

"Goes to credibility, your Honor," Marc replied without moving his stare from Kubik.

"Overruled," Graham said.

"Don't bother," Marc told Kubik. "We all know the answer."

Special agents Mike Anderson and Holly Byrnes walked through the door of Joel Dylan's office. The two FBI agents greeted the Assistant U.S. Attorney, then took chairs in front of his desk.

"What are we gonna do about Walter testifying in this trial?" Anderson asked Dylan.

Dylan shrugged his shoulders then held up both hands, palms up and said, "I'm open to suggestions."

"Can we go to the judge and try to get the subpoena, what's the word?" Holly Byrnes said.

"Quashed," Dylan replied. "And no, I don't see how, not without giving up our case."

"He's going to get on that witness stand and lie like hell," Holly said. "Commit more perjury. That doesn't sit well with me."

"It doesn't sit well with me either, Holly," Dylan said. "But it's not our problem."

"Better he lies than tells the truth," Anderson said.

"And help put a woman in prison who may be innocent?" Holly asked.

"We don't know that," Dylan reminded her. "In fact the evidence points right at her. The question here, for us today is: what

275

can we do to keep him off the stand? I could get a federal court order to prevent it, but it would get out and these guys at CAR Securities..."

"Or the Mexican cartel people they're dealing with," Anderson put in.

"...would probably kill him."

"And blow our case," Anderson added. "The bigger worry is if he gets on the stand and the lawyer goes after him and gets him to admit something."

"Like what?" Holly asked. "You guys think they murdered Robert Judd?"

"It doesn't matter what we think or even if we know they did it," Dylan said. "Our case takes precedence."

Pablo Quinones was admiring his naked body in the full length mirror. Always a vain man, he had done an impressive job, at least to his eye, of taking care of himself over the years. Even in his mid-forties he looked great and never met a mirror he didn't fall in love with. On the lengthy list of reasons he secretly despised his psychopath boss, El Callado's hedonism and slovenliness were near the top.

While he finished brushing his hair he heard his private phone go off in the living room. Although there was no one else in the Cancun beach house, he quickly wrapped a towel around his waist while hurrying to take the call.

"Yes, Victor, what happened?" he quickly asked without even saying hello.

Quinones knew about the subpoena for Walter Pascal. He also knew that lawyers for CAR Securities were going to see Judge Graham this morning. Quinones had been waiting for Victor to call with the news.

"The judge turned them down. Pascal will have to testify. But they did learn from the county attorney herself that any documents this Metcalf woman had will not be admitted into evidence. And Metcalf testified and said nothing about our arrangement. I believe she knows nothing about it."

276

"Yes, I know. I watched her myself. What can we do about Walter Pascal? Should we simply eliminate the problem? That's what Javier will want to do."

"That would be a bad idea. At this point it would cause too much suspicion, bring too much attention. Better to let him testify and deny everything. Without the documents to back up Metcalf's story, it's her word against his," Espinosa replied.

"I agree but with Javier, well, he only sees one solution to every problem. He is also starting to grumble about pulling his money out of your business. So far, I have convinced him not to but...." By now Quinones was standing in front of the huge, bulletproof bay window overlooking the Gulf of Mexico.

"We're not ready yet, are we?"

"No, we're not. At least not on my end. Could you do what you need to do?" Quinones replied.

Espinosa remained silent while thinking over the question. Finally he said, "I could probably get some of it but not all. It would be noticed and ring alarm bells up here. So, it is best to stay on course. Your end is the most important. We would have no place to hide."

"I agree. My plans are made, I'll be ready," Quinones said. "What about Pascal?"

"Corbin and Ethan Rask had a serious talk with him. I was there but only listened. Rask scares everybody but I'm beginning to think he's just a bully. All talk. Walter will lie his ass off, don't worry."

"Yes, he'll lie, but will the jury know he's lying?" Quinones asked.

"Pablo, he knows nothing. He doesn't know you sent someone to silence Rob Judd. What can he say? Have you heard from your man?"

"No, he goes to ground for several months after a job. He's very cautious, very professional."

Espinosa heard Quinones deeply inhale, heavily sigh then say, "There's nothing we can do now. Don't worry, I will handle Javier, el cerdo, the pig," Quinones said.

"Be careful my friend," Espinosa said

"Adios, amante," Quinones replied.

Marc opened the hallway door and let Maddy enter the offices first. Marc walked in with Carvelli trailing him and said, "See, I told you they'd all still be here."

"Because we love you," Carolyn told Maddy as she gave her a warm hug.

Maddy said to Connie," More pizza?"

"There's no such thing as too much pizza," Carvelli said walking to the table where the still-warm pizza boxes were waiting.

When everyone had filled a plate and found a seat, Barry Cline sat next to Marc and asked, "How did it go today?"

Marc shrugged, swallowed, took a drink from his Pepsi, "Who knows? You know how this goes. We'll see. I have a reasonable 'some other dude did it' claim to present. Will the jury buy it? That's always the question."

"How are you holding up, kid?" Connie asked Maddy.

"Okay except for the fact that I'm a nervous wreck and scared to death. Once, when I was a cop in Chicago, I was in a gunfight and I wasn't this scared. I don't know how you do it."

The last statement she made while looking at her lawyer.

"We don't normally represent people we care about," Marc said. "At least not this much. Trust me, I'm not sleeping very well."

"Is that supposed to give me confidence?" Maddy smiled.

"Normally," Barry interjected, "you do your job. Set aside your personal feelings, do your very best and when it's over you can look yourself in the mirror and know you gave your client the best representation you could. And if you lose, which is almost always the case despite what you see on TV and what the media tells us, then well, you lose. Go home, hug your kids and be glad you're not the one going to jail."

"Wow," Sandy said, "that is really cynical."

"Sandy," Marc said to her "you can't live their lives for them. You do your best to help them. That's all you can do. If you bleed for every one of them, you're in the wrong business.

"As for you," Marc continued looking at Maddy, "When it's over, you're going to get your life back. You'll see."

FORTY-ONE

"I thought you were going to put Walter Pascal up next," Maddy said.

It was the morning of the second day of Marc's case. They had arrived at the courtroom a little early and except for a couple of deputies who came in, looked around and left, they were alone.

"I changed my mind," Marc replied. "I'm going to put him on last."

"Wouldn't it have made more sense to put him on today right after Gloria Metcalf testified?"

"Maybe, probably, I don't know," Marc said. "There's some guesswork involved in this, sometimes. I decided I wanted him to be the last witness the jury hears from. If I can get them to believe he's lying, well, we'll see."

"What if he takes off?" Maddy asked.

"I have Tony and his guys on him round-the-clock. He's not going anywhere. Relax, it'll be okay."

"Easy for you to say," Maddy said.

At 9:05, before Judge Graham was on the bench but after the gallery had filled up, a large, bald, older black man, with the look of a cop came into the courtroom. Most of the spectators turned to watch him as he quickly went through the gate and to the defense table. He leaned down and whispered to Marc.

"Everyone's lined up and ready in the order you wanted. I got them all out in the hall ready to go," Franklin Washington, another one of Tony's ex-cop buddies said.

"Thanks, Franklin," Marc replied.

"Hello, sweetheart," the man said to Maddy flashing a big smile. "How you holding up?"

"Okay, Franklin. Thanks for your help," she replied.

Still looking at Maddy he said, "Anything you need, we'll be there."

At that moment Graham came on the bench. When Graham told everyone to be seated, Washington quickly went back through the gate and left the courtroom.

The people Franklin was referring to were CAR employees who were in attendance at the Fourth of July party and saw Rob and Maddy together.

The morning session was taken up by them testifying that Maddy and Rob Judd were getting along splendidly. Two of them, women about the same age as Gloria Metcalf, testified they seemed to be very much in love and both of the women witnesses even admitted to a twinge of jealousy.

Marc also had each of them testify that CAR Securities had a secret office across the hall. Each admitted that they believed there was something odd about this. All had previous employment histories with other investment and financial firms and had not seen anything like this before; a secret room where employees were not allowed to go or know what took place in them. Marc tried to elicit speculation from them as to what might be taking place across the hall in room 2007 but Gondeck's objections stopped him every time. Marc knew his prodding into the secret coming and going of room 2007 would be objected to and sustained. He didn't care. He accomplished what he wanted just by bringing it up and planting another seed of suspicion on CAR.

"Have you decided if I'm going to testify?" Maddy asked Marc. They were in Marc's car driving south on Lyndale to get back to Marc's office. The trial was recessed for the afternoon. Graham had previously blocked out the afternoon session to attend a conference for young black lawyers. Graham had been invited to speak and was looking forward to the opportunity.

"Yes, I have," Marc replied.

"And?" Maddy asked leaning toward him but restrained by the seatbelt.

"I think not," Marc replied. "You can't get on the witness stand and absolutely deny doing this. Gondeck knows this. Or, at least, because you were drugged, he can get you to admit that you are not positive you didn't do this."

"How are you going to make the connection between the drugs and the waiter?"

"Each of our witnesses from the party testified that you seemed fine, remember?"

"Sure," Maddy answered.

"I have another one to testify that Rob told him he was taking you home because you weren't feeling well. Arnold Beyer. Remember him?"

"No, and why didn't you tell me before?"

Marc glanced over at her and said, "Tony talked to him this weekend and I forgot to mention it, sorry. I've had a lot on my mind."

"Is he on our witness list?"

"Yes he is. Just in case, I put the names of all the employees of CAR on our witness list.

"I think I can make the connection between the drugs and the waiter through Tony. Putting you on the stand is a bad idea. Do you want to testify?"

Maddy thought about the question while staring through the windshield. Finally after more than a minute, she said, "Yes, no, maybe, I'm not sure. I'm sure the jury would like to hear from me and deny I did this. I'm worried about what they will think if I don't."

"Then the answer is no, you're not getting on that stand. We will deal with what the jury might think with jury instructions."

The next morning, Marc's first witness was his expert criminalist, Jason Briggs, a man Marc had used before with very good results. A criminalist is basically an independent CSI type investigator. Briggs was in his early fifties, though he looked older because of his bald head, gold-rimmed glasses and diminutive frame. He earned a Baccalaureate degree in forensic science from Northwestern and a Masters from Boston University. Briggs then spent ten years with the Chicago police department and six more in the Chicago office of the FBI. He had watched many people of lesser ability making a lot more money as independent agents and over ten years ago he decided to go that route himself. Because of his reputation from the CPD and FBI, he immediately tripled his income and worked less doing it.

Briggs job was essentially twofold; first to show the jury evidence that a third person was in Robert Judd's bedroom and second, to go over the investigation by the Crime Scene Unit of the MPD and cast doubt on their thoroughness.

Briggs skillfully used his photos and the photos taken by the CSU team to explain why he believed they missed some things. He also used the CSU team's written report, the autopsy and medical examiner's report to lead the jury around the bedroom and visualize the attack. By doing this, he was able to prove that Judd was not lying helplessly in bed. He was on his feet facing his attacker. The purpose was to give Marc the testimony to use, in his closing argument that this six foot four inch, two-hundred fifteen pound man was not likely stabbed fourteen times by a smaller person such as a woman.

Both the M.E. and the prosecution's CSU witness testified the first stab wound occurred while he was lying in bed. The difference was in how the blood spatter was interpreted. The claim by the CSU blood spatter expert was weak and there was no reason to believe the claim Judd was lying down except that it fit in better with the prosecution's claim that Maddy first stabbed Rob Judd while he was on the bed. Briggs used the same CSU photos themselves to show he was on his feet facing his attacker. Plus, there were multiple defensive wounds on his hands. The prosecution would argue the first stab wound did not kill him. The M.E. also testified to this. The defensive wounds on his hands came after the first stabbing when he got to his feet. Briggs gave the jury a very plausible reason to believe Judd was already on his feet when he was first stabbed. It could easily come down to which expert would the jury believe.

Jason Briggs was on the stand through the normal lunch hour until well past one o'clock. Marc had assigned Maddy the task of keeping an eye on the jury. If they looked bored or restless, she was to let Marc know while he examined Briggs. Amazingly, not once did any of the jurors show any symptoms of mental fatigue. Jason Briggs, being a professional witness, was not only informative but came across as candid, personable and even a little charming. Like a favorite uncle people respected and liked to listen to.

The weak part of his analysis was the third person in the bedroom testimony. He used two photos of blood-spatter to point out two places that could be the shape of a human's shoeprint caused by the blood spray. It was not solid let alone definitive but the argument for reasonable doubt could be made.

Following a late lunch break Gondeck went after Briggs like a shark to blood. Apparently Gondeck had decided to treat this witness as nothing more than a professional, paid, witness-for-hire.

Briggs' many years and multiple trials worth of experience allowed him to handle this attack smoothly. No matter what side he testified for, and he had testified many times as a prosecution witness, the other side always used this tactic. Attack the messenger as a paid witness. At the end it would come down to whether or not the jury believed him and found reasonable doubt.

"How's Gloria Metcalf dong? I feel terrible about what happened to her," Maddy asked Tony.

The four of them, including Jason Briggs, were having dinner at Jason's hotel.

"She's fine. She's on a cruise ship and will dock in Rome in a few hours. Vivian and I decided to get her out of town until after the trial is over to keep her away from the boys at CAR Securities. She's having a leisurely cruise around the Mediterranean."

"Have you talked to her? She's okay?" Marc asked.

"She's having the vacation of her life," Tony said. "How did today go?"

"Good," Marc replied. "We got what we wanted, what we needed, into evidence. It's always building your story one piece at a time. Perry Mason is the only one who got the guilty guy to break down on the stand. The rest of us just stumble along."

"I'm sorry I couldn't do better with the footprints in the bedroom," Briggs told Maddy.

"You did fine," Maddy answered with a smile. "We'll be okay."

"Hey," Marc said turning to Carvelli. "I just remembered, have you found out anything more about Rob Judd's background or being in Witsec?"

"Nothing more on his background," Carvelli replied. "I checked with a couple sources with the Feds and they tell me nothing shows up about him with Witsec."

"Hmmm, well, okay," Marc said. "Onward we go."

FORTY-TWO

The next day Tony Carvelli was called to the witness stand following the afternoon break. During the morning session Marc had Dr. Nathan Lockhart testify about drawing blood and getting a urine sample from Maddy. Next up was the lab tech who took entirely too much time in the limelight. Instead of looking at the jury the way he had been told, he could not resist performing for the camera in the back of the courtroom.

It took the better part of two hours to get through it but Marc finally steered him to his conclusion. Madeline Rivers was drugged at the Fourth of July party the night before the murder. In his opinion, based on his professional judgment, the 'roofies' would have rendered her incapable of attacking Robert Judd and stabbing him fourteen times.

Marc then called a CAR employee, Arnold Beyer. Beyer basically verified what the lab tech had said. Beyer had sat at the table with Rob and Maddy while eating, as the other CAR employees testified, and Maddy was fine. Later he spoke to Rob when they were leaving who told him Maddy was not feeling well. He also testified seeing her obviously distressed. So much so that Rob had to help her walk.

Marc asked him about Maddy's alcohol intake. Beyer said he saw her drink a couple of small glasses of beer over three or four hours, hardly enough for her to be intoxicated.

Jennifer Moore did the cross-examination and got him to admit it was possible she took some drugs both before they came to the party and after he saw her during dinner. Beyer admitted he did not watch her all night so it was possible she could have drugged herself and drank a lot more than what he saw. It came across as a little weak.

For credibility purposes, Marc and Tony spent the first half-hour going over Tony's police career. Before this, Marc had never discussed these things with his P.I. friend. Unknown to Marc, Anthony Carvelli had a very distinguished career with the MPD. He had been the recipient of numerous awards for bravery, lifesaving and, best of all, twice awarded the Investigator of the Year honor.

When they moved into Carvelli's investigation on behalf of Maddy, Marc tossed him a couple of easy questions and then let him go.

"I believed the source of the drugs must have been from one of the caterer's people," Tony said when he got to that part of his investigation.

"Why do you believe she didn't take the drugs herself?"

"I've known her for years," Tony answered. "She rarely drinks alcohol and I've never had reason to believe she does drugs. No, in my opinion, somebody…"

"Objection," Gondeck said. "He's not qualified to give an opinion about how she came to have drugs in her system."

Graham thought about it for a moment then said, "No, he's known the defendant for many years. He can give his opinion about this, if that's where you're going, Mr. Carvelli. Overruled."

"I believe somebody slipped them into a drink she was served."

"What did you do next?"

"I obtained the name of the catering service and got a list of their employees who worked the party," he answered careful not to draw a hearsay objection by admitting Maddy saw the guy's picture in the paper.

"I then proceeded to quietly start checking them out. It didn't take long for me to discover that one of the staff who worked the party was missing."

"Who was that?" Marc asked.

"One of the waiters, a young man by the name of Kirk Jankovic."

"Did you find him?"

"Sort of," Tony answered.

"What do you mean, sort of?"

"He'd been murdered a few days after the party."

This revelation caused an explosion in the courtroom. Gondeck practically jumped up on top of the table to yell his objection. The media and spectators, rumbled like a herd heading for water and it took a gavel-pounding Judge Graham almost two minutes to restore order.

"Recess. In my chambers, now," Graham said to the lawyers.

A minute later, Graham turned on Marc, "What the hell is this about?"

Marc, looking as innocent as possible, merely shrugged and said, "One of the wait staff," he said, "who just happened to be the one who served my client," he continued turning to Gondeck and Moore, "disappeared and was found murdered. We found out about it. If they didn't," he said referring to the prosecution, "that's not my problem."

"It clearly taints the jury and has no probative value on the issue of guilt or innocence, your Honor," Jennifer Moore said. "So what if he slipped her something? She still could have done it."

"I'm not done," Marc said.

"Well, Ms. Moore, you make a good point and you can certainly argue that in your closing. But," Graham said then turned to Marc, "I am a little troubled. Is it your theory she was drugged and set up? If so, where's the connection?"

"The police found an envelope in his apartment with a thousand dollars in cash in it. His roommate has no idea where he got it," Marc replied.

"He could've gotten it in tips," Gondeck said.

"And you can make that argument," Graham told Gondeck. "I'm going to let it in. The jury can infer whatever it wants to."

Back in the courtroom, Carvelli testified about the money found in the waiter's apartment and his questioning of the roommate. Obviously whatever the roommate told Tony was hearsay but Gondeck did not object. Knowing Marc could easily bring the roommate in to verify what he told Carvelli about the cash, he decided to let it slide.

Gondeck did the cross-examination of Carvelli and did an excellent job. Tony had no choice but to admit the entire thing about the waiter's murder and cash was nothing more than speculation and conjecture.

"So, Mr. Carvelli, you admit that Mr. Jankovic's death may have absolutely nothing to do with the case against the accused is that correct?"

"Yes, that's true," Tony admitted.

"Merely a coincidence?"

"Yes, could be," Tony agreed.

This series of questions had been anticipated by Marc and his officemate, Barry Cline, when they had prepared Carvelli. Marc was also ready for redirect.

"Redirect, Mr. Kadella?"

"Yes, your Honor. Mr. Carvelli do you believe Mr. Jankovic's death was a mere coincidence, as the state suggests?"

"No, I do not."

"Why not?"

"Because of my experience as a police officer, detective and now a private investigator. In fact, ask any cop with more than a year's experience and they'll all tell you, in police work there's no such thing as a coincidence."

Gondeck started to rise to object, thought better of it and sat down. When Graham asked if he wanted to re-cross examine he hesitated for a moment then passed. He had obtained about all he was going to from Carvelli.

Another piece of reasonable doubt had been put in place.

As soon as the doors of the elevator were closed, a smiling Maddy Rivers practically jumped on Marc. She squeezed him as hard as she could and kissed him smack on the lips. She then turned on Carvelli and did the same thing.

"I haven't felt this good in months," Maddy exclaimed pumping both fists. "I think we hit a home run today!"

"Easy, tiger," Marc said. "This isn't over…"

"I know, I know," Maddy said. "I do think we scored today."

"Probably but you never know. I hate to rain on your parade..."

"Then don't," Maddy said as she looped an arm through one of Marc's and one of Tony's. "Let me enjoy the moment. Maybe I'll sleep tonight."

Before the trial Marc had prepared a list of more than a dozen character witnesses to testify on Maddy's behalf. Obviously the jury would get bored listening to that many witnesses extolling the virtues of Madeline Rivers. Instead, he pared the list down to just two people.

The first one up the next morning created almost as much buzz, especially among her media brethren, as the murdered waiter bombshell. Gabriella Shriqui, the well-known, very recognizable host of a popular local TV show, came into the courtroom and onto the witness stand.

Gabriella's testimony was actually a bit of a risk. She could and did testify about how well she knew Maddy and what a terrific person she was. Of course, with Gabriella's well-known celebrity, this was likely to carry some weight with the jury. Especially her emphatic claim that Madeline Rivers did not use drugs.

The risk was two-fold. First was the fact Maddy had shot and killed someone to save Gabriella's life. Gondeck would try to use this to show Maddy as a trigger-happy killer. Marc easily took most of the steam out of this by having Gabriella fully explain the circumstances. The man Maddy shot was an obsessed co-worker and child serial killer. He was holding a knife on Gabriella and wildly threatening to use it. If Gondeck wanted to try to twist that to make Maddy look blood thirsty, Marc would wish him luck. The second issue was more problematic. Having saved her life, did Gabriella feel she owed Maddy something? Again, rather than allow the prosecution to go after this, Marc dealt with it and brought it out himself. Gabriella could and did deny that it influenced her but a jury could easily believe otherwise.

290

Gondeck's cross-examination covered all of the areas Marc anticipated. Being an experienced prosecutor, he was able to show, in an unobjectionable way, his skepticism. It was very effective and Gondeck had enough to at least argue that Gabriella was obviously biased.

Gondeck finished and the court took a short recess. Before anyone could get through the hallway exit, the door opened and Marc's next witness came in. Even the people who did not know who she was instinctively stepped aside to let her pass.

"Excuse me, thank you," Vivian Donahue pleasantly repeated as she strolled up the center aisle to the front row behind the defense table.

Marc looked over at Gondeck who was glumly watching Vivian. When he noticed Marc, he gave him a little sneer then scratched the side of his face with his middle finger.

Marc stood up, stepped over to Gondeck and whispered, "I'm looking forward to you trying to cross-examine her and then see if you can keep your job. Go ahead, go after her, piss her off and see how it works out."

"Thanks, I appreciate your concern," he whispered back.

Marc used up the rest of the morning session with Vivian. With a character witness like her, he had to be very careful not to flaunt her wealth in front of the jury. Instead of focusing on that and the family's political clout, he focused on her philanthropy. By the time they finished, she came across as a wealthy Mother Theresa, at least enough to give the jury the impression she did good things for people with her money. Plus, and this part was truly genuine, Vivian herself gave off the effect as someone who could enjoy a beer and hotdog at a ball game. Someone the jury could like despite her wealth. And, of course, Maddy was the daughter she wished she had.

Seeing his career flash before his eyes if he went after this woman too hard, Gondeck completely passed on any cross-exam. He wasn't going to get much out of her anyway so why try?

When Vivian was excused she went straight to Maddy and gave her a well-rehearsed, sincere hug before taking her seat in the front row next to Carvelli.

Graham recessed for lunch and before he was off the bench, Marc turned to Carvelli and said, "Go get him."

"I got two guys on it including your old pal, Jake Waschke," Carvelli said.

"Come on," Marc replied, "don't say that like that."

Carvelli smiled and said, "Relax, he genuinely likes you, as much as he can like any lawyer."

FORTY-THREE

Carvelli set his coffee cup on the coaster on the coffee table. He looked at it and remembered it was one of a set that was a gift Maddy had given him. He smiled when he recalled how she had chastised men in general and Carvelli in particular for being so indifferent about the care of their furniture. He then thought about the predicament she was in and his heart dropped to his stomach.

Carvelli looked at the television. He had the latest sixty inch wide-screen, high-definition set situated directly in front of him in his living room. It was a few minutes past eight A.M. and he was killing time before he left for court. Watching a local morning news show, he was waiting for the daily report on Maddy's trial when his phone rang. Tony looked at the caller I.D. and saw the number was blocked. Curious about who would be calling him at home so early, he answered it despite the blocked I.D.

"Tony?" he heard a man's voice ask. "It's Russ Simmons with the DEA. Do you remember…"

"Russ Simmons! Now there's a voice out of the past I haven't heard for a while. How the hell are you Russ?"

Russell Simmons was a DEA agent Carvelli had worked with while he was still a detective with the MPD. Carvelli and several other MPD members had been assigned to a joint, local/federal task force investigating an Upper Midwest drug and prostitution ring. Carvelli had joined the task force toward the end of the investigation and was on it for a little over three months. During that time he had become good friends with Simmons.

Russell Simmons was also a bit of a character. Doing undercover work with the DEA will do that to you. At the time he was still undercover acting as a member of a biker gang and looking very much the part. Long hair, a beard, biker boots, tattoos, T-shirts and a leather vest, he had easily infiltrated the meth and hooker ring they busted.

"You got time to meet this morning?" Simmons asked.

"You're back in Minnesota?"

"Yeah and you need to see me."

"About what?"

"Some stuff I've been seeing on TV," Simmons cryptically replied. "It's worthwhile."

"Okay. Can you meet me now? There's a place on Fifty-Third and Chicago called Sir Jack's. Can you find it?" Carvelli asked.

"I'll be there in twenty minutes," Simmons said.

When Simmons came through the door of the restaurant, Carvelli saw him but paid no attention to him. Tony had the morning paper on the table and after checking the man out, went back to the sports section he had been looking over.

"Hey, Tony, how you doing?" Simmons said as he slid onto the booth's seat opposite Carvelli.

"Russ?" Carvelli asked an uncertain look on his face.

The man Carvelli was looking at bore no resemblance whatever to the Russ Simmons, undercover DEA agent, he had known years ago. This one was short-haired, clean shaven, noticeably grayer and dressed like a grown-up.

"Oh, that's right, I should have warned you," Simmons laughed as he reached across the table to shake Carvelli's hand. "I'm not undercover anymore. I'm too old. So they make me look and dress like a government employee now," he explained while holding up the cup Carvelli had for him as Carvelli poured from the plastic carafe.

After spending almost twenty minutes on small talk, catching up on each other's lives, Carvelli got to the point.

"What do you want to see me about?"

Simmons filled both cups again then looked around to make sure no one was paying any attention to them.

He leaned forward, as did Carvelli, and quietly said, "We're looking at CAR Securities. We're thinking they are a cleaning service for a Mexican cartel."

"Russ, that's not news. We know a couple of them made a one-day trip to Panama. We also know one of the guys who went is connected to a guy high up in the cartel…"

294

"Pablo Quinones," Simmons said.

"Yeah, that's him." Carvelli acknowledged.

"We also have information to believe," Simmons continued, "Quinones sent an assassin he uses who goes by the name Michael Stone after Robert Judd. Then a couple weeks later, Judd is murdered."

"Jesus Christ, Russ! We need that to show Maddy Rivers got set-up. Are you sure?"

"Yeah, positive. I can't positively say this Stone guy did it but he's good enough to pull off something like this.

"We also have photos to prove that the two guys from CAR Securities met with Quinones and his boss, a psycho asshole by the name of Torres, in Panama.

"Here's the deal, Tony. I'm willing to testify that Quinones sicced this Stone on Robert Judd. I think the girlfriend got set up. But I can't testify about anything else. We have an investigation to protect. I'm sticking my neck out two miles just doing that."

"Are you going to get jammed up?"

"No." Simmons shook his head. "I talked to my boss about it. She agrees the jury should know about this but I have to be very careful."

"Let me talk to Kadella, the lawyer. Be ready to go first thing tomorrow morning. Can you do that?" an excited Carvelli asked.

"Call me," Simmons said. He wrote his cell phone number on the back of his business card and gave it to Tony.

When Carvelli arrived at the courtroom the lawyers were at the bench discussing something with Judge Graham. Tony quietly went past the crowded gallery, through the gate and took a seat along the rail behind the defense table. He smiled at Maddy and whispered a hello to her. While patiently waiting for the bench conference to end, he again wondered how anyone could sit and watch this on television. To Carvelli, trial veteran that he is, trials move at a snail's pace rarely having an exciting moment and are normally quite boring.

The meeting finally broke up and when Marc got back to his table, Carvelli whispered to him they needed to talk.

"Your Honor," Marc stood to address the court, "the defense requests a brief recess."

Graham looked at the wall clock and said, "It's a good time for a break. Fifteen minute recess," he ordered.

When Carvelli finished telling Marc about Russ Simmons, Marc immediately went up to Graham's clerk. Steve Gondeck was right behind him.

"Natalie, we need to see Judge Graham in chambers, on the record, right away, please," Marc said.

"Okay, I'll tell him," she replied as she picked up her phone.

Gondeck pulled Marc away and quietly, so the few people who remained in the courtroom could not hear him, said, "What kind of defense lawyer bullshit are you trying to pull?"

"Don't talk to me like that," Marc snarled back at him as he pulled his arm from Gondeck's hand.

The stress of a trial was starting to get to both of them.

"You can go back," Natalie told them.

Back in chambers Gondeck took a chair. Jennifer Moore was upstairs in the county attorney's offices and not in attendance and Marc remained standing, his hands resting on the back of one of the chairs in front of the judge's desk. They waited in silence for Graham's court reporter to finish setting up. When he was ready he said so to Graham.

"All right, gentlemen, what's up?" Graham asked.

"I need to add a witness your Honor," Marc said.

Before Gondeck could object Graham held up a hand to stop him and said, "One at a time, Mr. Gondeck, please."

Marc then carefully, for the court's record, explained to the judge what had transpired that morning.

"This man can clearly provide us with exculpatory evidence your Honor. Evidence we could not have discovered with

296

a reasonable effort before this. Evidence the jury must be allowed to hear," Marc concluded.

"Did you know about this?" Graham asked looking at Gondeck.

"Of course not," Gondeck indignantly replied. "Besides," he continued looking at Marc, "does he have any evidence that this alleged hit man actually completed the assignment?"

"I don't know," Marc admitted.

"Prejudicial and proves nothing," Gondeck said to Graham.

"I'll tell you what," Graham said again looking at Marc, "get him here in the morning and we'll meet with him in chambers. If I am satisfied as to who he is and how credible he is, I'll let him take the stand."

"Your Honor," Gondeck started to protest.

"If you want a continuance to prepare your cross-exam, I'll grant it. We'll see how it goes. But if what Mr. Kadella says is accurate, I think the jury should hear this."

A half hour after the in chambers meeting was over and court resumed, Russ Simmons and his boss, Candace Green, arrived at the offices of the local U.S. Attorney. A few minutes later they were ushered into the office of the AUSA Joel Dylan. Waiting for them were Dylan, Mike Anderson and Holly Byrnes from the FBI.

"Hi, Candace," Dylan said as he rose from his chair behind his desk. "Thanks for coming. Please take a seat," he said gesturing to the two empty chairs to his right.

"What's going on here?" Green curiously asked looking over the other three people.

"This isn't an inquisition, Russ," Mike Anderson said. "But we need to know why you talked to Tony Carvelli in the restaurant this morning."

"Before you answer," Dylan said moving a tape player on his desk closer to Green and Simmons then turning it on. For the next minute they listened to part of the conversation between Simmons and Carvelli.

"What the fuck...!" Simmons, his blood practically boiling, almost yelled as he started to come out of his chair, "You've been following me, Mike?"

"Of course not," Anderson quickly replied. "We've been keeping a loose eye on Carvelli. We just happened to be on him when you met."

"And who else?" Green asked glaring directly at Dylan. "The lawyer, Kadella? His client? What the hell are you guys up to?"

"So," Dylan calmly began, "I take it you knew about this," he said tapping the tape player. "You knew Simmons was going to offer to testify at this trial?"

"What of it?" Green angrily asked.

"Can't happen, Candace," Anderson said.

Simmons leaned forward in his chair, looked to his right at Holly Byrnes and said, "What do you have to say about this, Holly?"

"I just follow orders," was all she said.

"Have you been subpoenaed?" Dylan asked Simmons.

"No, I haven't," Simmons replied, his anger still unabated.

"Russ, you can't testify," Anderson quietly said. "We have serious, classified investigations going on that we have to protect. I'm sorry. I hate to blindside you like this but we had no idea you were going to meet with this Carvelli. Sorry."

The room went silent for a couple of minutes, no one knowing quite what to say. Finally, Candace Green spoke up looking directly at Dylan..

"You could have let us know you were investigating CAR Securities. So are we."

"You didn't have the need to know," Dylan said.

"God I hate that 'need to know bullshit'. Joel, you should have called me in to talk to me about it. Find out if we had an interest in it. This is why people think their government is such an inefficient clusterfuck. We keep running around tripping over each other wasting more time, money and resources than should be necessary."

"That's why you're here now, Candace," Dylan said cutting her off. "We're going to bring you and your investigation in and roll it into ours, with your involvement, of course. This is straight from the Attorney General and is non-negotiable," Dylan lied.

"As for you," Dylan continued as he reached into his desk drawer, removed a plain, white, letter-size envelope and handed it to Russ Simmons, "Holly is going to take you home, you'll pack a bag and get out of town for a few days. There's a plane ticket and accommodations for you all paid for in there," he said referring to the envelope. "Have a nice trip."

FORTY-FOUR

Maddy reached over and placed her right hand on Marc's left to stop him from nervously tapping his fingers on the tabletop. Marc looked at the clock on the courtroom's wall then compared that time to the time his watch had. Both read the same: 9:22. Barely two minutes more than the last time he checked.

Judge Graham's clerk, Natalie, answered her phone. Marc watched her as she whispered something into the phone, nodded her head and then hung up. She looked at Marc and motioned for him to come up to her chair. Steve Gondeck went with Marc and before they got to Natalie, Steve gently nudged Marc and with a smirk on his face pointed at the clock.

"Judge says he'll give you ten more minutes to produce your witness then he's coming out."

"Tell him we can put Pascal back up, he's here," Marc replied.

"Okay, I'll call back to him," Natalie whispered.

Before Marc got back to his table, Tony Carvelli came through the hallway door. Marc looked at him with an inquisitive look on his face in response to which Carvelli shook his head and shrugged his shoulders.

The gallery impatiently stirred as they watched Carvelli walk up the center aisle.

"What's going on?" a reporter in the front row asked Marc.

"Shut up, Ben," Marc answered him obviously irritated.

Knowing something was wrong with Marc's case, this exchange elicited a round of laughter from the three rows of media members, including Ben.

"He's gone," Carvelli whispered to Marc and Maddy at their table. "No answer on his phone and I called their office and got stonewalled."

"What the hell…" Marc started to ask.

"Don't know. Something tells me somebody doesn't want him on the witness stand."

"How…?"

"I don't know," Carvelli said cutting him off. "I tried finding him last night, too. No luck."

"Mr. Kadella," Natalie said.

"One minute," he replied holding up his left index finger.

"Get Pascal in here," Marc said.

Marc drove out of the underground parking garage to be greeted by barely moving rush hour traffic. As predicted, a heavy snow storm was rolling across Minnesota. The snow had started coming down shortly after 1:00 o'clock and by the time Marc left the courtroom at 3:30, there was already three inches of wet, slick, sloppy snow bringing the start of rush hour traffic to a crawl.

The testimony had ended in the morning with a very mild cross-examination of Walter Pascal by Steve Gondeck. With no more witnesses to produce, Marc rested his case and requested a dismissal of the charges by Judge Graham which was promptly denied. Knowing the snow was coming, Graham, after meeting with the lawyers, released the jury for the weekend. Closing arguments would take place first thing Monday morning.

After lunch Marc sent Maddy home with Carvelli. His afternoon was taken up in chambers with the judge and prosecution arguing about jury instructions. At 3:00 o'clock Graham stood up, stretched his arms over his head, looked out his window at the new Vikings' stadium and decided to call it quits.

"It's coming down pretty hard," Graham said after turning back to the lawyers. "Let's get out of here. I'll go through your requested jury instructions over the weekend and have them ready by Monday. I want your closings done Monday and we'll charge the jury Tuesday."

While Marc was creeping along with traffic he tried to move his head from side-to-side. His neck, shoulders and back were sore and as tight as a drum.

"God, could I use a massage," he tiredly whispered to himself.

Instead he turned on the SUV's radio and punched the button for a classic rock station. The babbling idiot on the radio finally shut up in time for Led Zeppelin to pound the car's interior with their classic hit, 'Rock and Roll.'

"Perfect," Marc said and turned up the volume to let the music blast the stress out of his head.

For the third morning in a row, Marc was the first one into the office. Sleep had come fitfully at best since the jury began deliberations. Today would be the third day they had the case. Usually or at least in theory, the longer they took the better for the defense. Were there a couple of holdouts for acquittal that could get him a hung jury? Maybe.

Also for the third morning in a row, after arriving early, Marc sat staring out the open window behind his desk. Exhausted due to little sleep, stress and worry, he was unable to keep his concentration long enough to get any work done.

"Still replaying the trial?" he heard Connie Mickelson ask from his doorway.

"No," Marc answered Connie as he closed the window and swiveled around to face her. "At least not as much."

"You know better than to second guess yourself," she said as she sat down in one of the client chairs.

"You two want some coffee?" they heard Carolyn ask when she came through Marc's open door. She filled their cups from the pot she carried with her then said to Marc, "I'd tell you to go home but it wouldn't help."

"No," Marc agreed, "it wouldn't. Sorry I'm not being very social…"

"It's okay," Connie quietly said.

"We get it," Carolyn added.

"I've never felt like this, I'm scared down to my toes. What if I screwed this up and they find her guilty? She'll go to prison and I'll never forgive myself."

"Stop it!" Connie demanded. "Did you do your best?"

"I don't know," Marc replied. "I guess so, I suppose so but…"

"It's our girl whose ass is on the line," Carolyn said. "Not some stranger who was probably guilty anyway."

"Let me talk to him alone," Connie said to Carolyn.

"Sure, I have work to do anyway," Carolyn replied then left and closed the door behind her.

"Get a grip," Connie started off. "If they come back with a guilty verdict, it's not over and you know it. We know what really happened and we'll figure out a way to get those guys."

Marc had told Connie about Tony Carvelli's clandestine and extremely illegal talk he and his pals had with Ethan Rask.

"I know, I've thought of that," Marc said. "I'm thinking maybe we go to Owen Jefferson. I'm not sure how…"

The intercom on his phone buzzed and Marc stopped to answer it.

"Okay, put her through," he told Sandy. "Maddy," he said to Connie.

Connie started to stand up to leave and Marc waved her back into her seat.

"Hey, how are you today?" Marc asked.

"Fine," Maddy replied. "In fact, last night was the best night's sleep I've had in months. I feel great. Whatever happens, well, we'll deal with it. I have great friends. They'll help me."

"You have great friends who love you and will never stop fighting for you," Marc added.

"I know. Anyway, call me as soon as you hear something. I'll be home!"

Maddy's phone call and cheerful attitude eased the stress Marc had brought on himself. Because of the trial, there were over a dozen case files piled on his desk needing his attention. He dug into those and was able to get some work done and put the jury deliberating his friend's fate out of his mind, for a while. At 11:30, he got the call from Graham's clerk.

"They're in," she told Marc. "The judge wants everybody at 2:00 o'clock."

"Thanks, Natalie," Marc replied.

Without hanging up the phone on his desk, he quickly dialed Maddy's number and gave her the news. Marc would pick her up and the two of them would meet Carvelli for lunch then go to court.

Marc stopped in the office's common area to announce to everyone what he had been told. As he was putting on his overcoat Connie came out of her office.

"Mind if I tag along?" she asked.

"No, not all. Grab your coat."

Marc turned back to the staff and said, "2:00 o'clock, courtroom 1540. You're all welcome to come and sit with us. I think Maddy would like that."

"We'll all be there," Chris Grafton replied.

"Absolutely," Barry Cline chimed in.

Marc looked over at the prosecution table and wondered where Steve Gondeck was. Jennifer Moore had come in, said hello and was quietly sitting by herself.

Behind Marc, Maddy and Connie at the defense table, seated in chairs in front of the rail, was the entire office staff. Best of all was the presence of Vivian Donahue seated next to Carvelli. Tony had called her after getting the news from Marc. Maddy's eyes had started to tear up when they all filed in.

"Hey," Marc quietly said to Jennifer over the murmuring of the gallery, "where's your boss?"

Jennifer used her head to indicate Marc should join her.

"He's not coming," she whispered when Marc got to her table. "He thinks they'll find her guilty and he doesn't want to be here for it. I don't either but…" she shrugged.

"All rise," the deputy intoned. Everyone stood as Judge Graham took his seat. "Be seated," he told the audience. He then looked at the deputy standing next to the jury room door and nodded his head.

While the jurors filed in, Marc watched them carefully. It is believed that if the jurors look at the defendant, that it is a good sign for the defense. Is this true? No one really knows. In this case, some of the jurors looked at Maddy and some did not.

Graham asked the foreman, a thirty-six-year-old, divorced insurance salesman Marc had wanted on the jury, if they had reached a verdict. The man answered affirmatively then handed the deputy the jury form. The deputy brought it to Graham who took a minute or so to read it over. He then sent it back to the foreman.

"We the jury, in the matter of the State of Minnesota vs. Madeline Elizabeth Rivers…"

This was all Maddy remembered hearing as Marc gently held her hand after easing her back into her chair.

"It's not over, I promise you, it's not over," he repeated several times.

Her friends seated in the chairs behind her were too stunned to move. Even Carvelli, who was usually in total control of himself and every situation, was in a daze.

Only Vivian Donahue was able to grasp the situation. She immediately went to Maddy, got down on one knee, wrapped both arms around her and held her as Maddy quietly began to weep.

FORTY-FIVE

It was past midnight when Marc inserted the key to the front door of his apartment, turned it to open the lock, then gently thumped his forehead against the door. He stood in the hallway like this trying to shake the image of Maddy in jail. After ten or twelve seconds he opened the door and went inside.

Marc kicked off his shoes at the entryway closet, went into the living room, tossed his overcoat on a chair and his suit coat on the couch. He flopped down on the couch, put his stockinged feet on the coffee table, stared at nothing and fought back the tears while replaying the day.

The jury foreman started to read the verdict form and gave the defense initial good news. Not guilty to the charge of first-degree murder. The optimism was very short-lived.

"As to the count of murder in the second degree we find the defendant guilty," he had said.

The Foreman continued with the lesser included charges and repeated 'not guilty' for each of them.

Despite being verbally kicked in the groin, Marc had enough presence of mind to immediately request that Maddy's bail be continued until sentencing. Because of the seriousness of the crime, Graham denied the request. Maddy would be jailed immediately. While Maddy was being handcuffed and taken away, the gallery crowd, quiet and seemingly surprised, began to file out of the courtroom. Even the media members, not always behaving as paragons of decorum, were acting with suitable restraint. A couple of them approached the defense table but walked away when Marc looked at them and simply shook his head. The atmosphere had the definite feel of a funeral.

Ten minutes after Maddy had been taken away, it was Vivian Donahue who broke the silence speaking to Maddy's small group of supporters in the otherwise empty courtroom. "All right, we need to get together and figure out what we're going to do to fix this," Vivian said in a commanding voice. "Marc?"

"She's right. This isn't over. Let's all go back to the office and put our heads together," Marc said to the people sitting behind his table. "You, too," he told Vivian.

"I've never been to your office," Vivian commented.

"Well," Connie replied standing up and putting on her coat, "You're in for a real treat. Do you need a ride?"

"I'll ride with Anthony, but thanks, Connie," Vivian replied.

Barry Cline and Chris Grafton, having driven downtown together, stopped at a liquor store for a case of Grain Belt Premium beer on their way back. At the office, everyone, including Vivian was served a bottle and they all found chairs in the common area.

"I didn't know you drank beer," Tony said to Vivian.

"There's a lot you don't know about me," she answered. Vivian looked at Marc and asked, "What is she looking at when she is sentenced?"

Graham had scheduled a sentencing date for after the holidays, January third.

"The sentencing guidelines," Barry Cline said to answer her, "call for twenty-five years with a criminal history score of zero."

"She would have to do almost seventeen before being eligible for parole," Marc said.

"My god, this can't be happening," Vivian said.

"First we ask Graham for a new trial. He'll deny it. Then we start the appeal process," Marc said. "Connie," Marc continued, "who's the best appellate lawyer in Minnesota?"

"Criminal?" Connie rhetorically asked. "I'm not sure. Probably Julian Bronfman."

"Isn't he a professor at the U law school?" Chris Grafton asked.

"Yeah, teaches Con law and criminal procedure," Connie replied referring to Constitutional law.

"Can you get him?" Vivian asked. "Money is no object."

"You don't want to say that to a Jewish lawyer," Connie said eliciting a much needed laugh. "Yeah he goes to my synagogue. I'll talk to him about it. Especially when I tell him that we know for certain she's innocent."

"And how do we know that?" Carolyn asked after hearing the tone of certainty in Connie's voice.

"We do," Marc said. "Just leave it at that."

Carolyn looked at Marc who shifted his eyes toward Vivian as a signal to keep quiet about it.

"I know all about it, Marc," Vivian said when she saw him make that gesture.

With a stern expression, Marc looked at Tony Carvelli and said, "And how does she know that? Never mind, but it's a problem if she had to testify about it."

"Not if we make her part of the defense team," Barry interjected.

"Okay," Marc said. He looked at Vivian and added, "You are now a member of my staff and covered by privilege. No talking to anyone," he turned to an embarrassed Carvelli, "else about this for now."

Carvelli took Vivian home then met Marc for dinner at a place on Lake Street. Neither of them were very hungry and the meal was picked at by both men. Tony apologized for telling Vivian about his chat with Ethan Rask. Marc brushed it aside as spilled milk. They then drove back downtown and met with Maddy for more than an hour.

The guard brought her in and at Marc's insistence, removed the cuffs and leg shackles. Maddy then quickly exchanged long embraces with both men.

"You're not supposed to make physical contact with inmates," the guard, an older man hanging on for retirement tried to tell them.

Knowing who the guard was, Tony snarled at him, "Give me a break Turner. You think what, we're gonna slip her a file to cut through the bars?"

"Look, Tony, I'm just doing my job," the man said apologetically.

"You told us now beat it. We'll call you when we're done," Carvelli said. After the guard left Carvelli said, "The guy was an elementary school principal for twenty years. Now he's on the government tit for another pension."

"Double dipping," Marc said.

"Yeah, he's gonna spend his whole life with his face in the taxpayer's trough slurping up other people's money," Carvelli said. "Plus he's an asshole."

"How are you doing?" Marc asked Maddy.

"I'm okay. The other women are pretty much avoiding me. One of them, a really nice, older black woman in for beating up her husband, told me they know who I am and are a little afraid of me."

"I must admit," Tony said, "you even look good in orange."

Maddy smiled but said, "That's not funny."

Tony reached across the table, squeezed her hand and said, "It's a little funny. It got a smile out of you."

The three of them talked about everything except the actual verdict. Since there was nothing to be done about it no one wanted to bring it up. Oddly, Maddy did not ask about what her sentence would likely be. As they were getting ready to leave, Tony asked her why.

"Because I know you guys will fix this and get me out. In my heart I have absolute faith that you'll find a way."

While driving toward his apartment, Marc took a call from Margaret Tennant. She had tried calling and left messages six times since the afternoon.

They chatted for a few minutes, Margaret expressing her sadness. She had known Maddy as long as Marc and could not believe, even drugged, she could do this.

"We'll get her out of this," Marc said toward the end of the conversation.

"Do you want to come over?"

"I think I need to be alone tonight," Marc replied.

"I understand. If I can do anything for you or Madeline, please call."

"I'll call you tomorrow," Marc promised.

Marc ended the call as he pulled the SUV over and parked in front of the Lake City Tavern, a neighborhood bar on Lake Street. Marc had been in the place only once before to meet a client. It was perfect for his mood; a quiet, seedy joint where everybody minded their own business. A half-hour later, after three shots of Jack and three small chasers, Marc decided pouring conscience relief down his throat was not the answer and was not going to help either himself or his client.

Still sitting on his couch, his feet on the coffee table, Marc looked at the clock on the cable TV box.

"12:40," he quietly said to himself. "Time to go to bed and try to get some sleep."

The next day Charlie Dudek opened his business email account to check for any new inquiries. He was across the river from his home in Kansas City at the West Wyandotte branch of the Kansas City, Kansas public library using one of their computers. Charlie had a PC of his own at home but never used it for this particular email account. If anyone ever checked his home computer, — police — they wouldn't find anything incriminating on it. Instead he used computers in the public libraries of both Kansas City, Missouri and across the river in Kansas.

There was only one email and as luck — and good timing — would have it, it had been received just fifteen minutes ago. It was from a Russian Mafia boss located in Brighton Beach, N Y, a psycho thug named Dimitri Kirilov.

As little as Charlie normally felt emotionally about anyone, he truly hated the Russians. Charlie was a professional and a businessman. He understood that his particular business was, to say the least, out of the mainstream. But he still took pride in his work and went about it in an unemotional, objective, professional manner. The Russians were anything but professionals. In fact,

Charlie considered them to be little better than bloodthirsty animals. After serving honorably in the Army Charlie considered himself a patriot. He despised the fact that these Russian gangsters were in America for one reason only; to rob and steal as much as they could. At least the Italian Mafia came here to be Americans.

Charlie opened the attachment that came with the email. In it was everything he needed, including the contract amount, two hundred thousand dollars. Kirilov knew Charlie's standard price and added an extra fifty grand to that. Instead of simply accepting the job, Charlie emailed back demanding an additional fifty thousand.

Thinking he might get a quick reply, Charlie reviewed the target's information. There was a recent photo along with the man's name, address and usual hangouts; all in New York. He began printing off the attachment and Kirilov's answer came back while Charlie did this. Kirilov had accepted the amount and had wired the first half into a Cayman Island bank account. Kirilov wanted this man gone in a vicious way to send a message in the process.

When Charlie returned home, as he always did when accepting an assignment, he sat down and wrote out a thorough list of everything he needed. The list, of course would be almost one hundred percent the same every time. Charlie took pride in his professionalism and the fewer things he had to purchase after leaving, the better.

Two hours later, after notifying the neighbor he was on a business trip and shutting down the house, Charlie was ready to go. As he was going over his to-do list one last time before burning it, he remembered he had not checked on the trial in Minneapolis. He quickly got on line, found the news story and saw the verdict. When he finished reading the story from the Minneapolis paper, Charlie's heart sank and he felt furious; sensations he had never experienced over something like this before.

He shut down the computer and while staring at the blank screen, quietly said to himself, "After New York, it looks like I'm heading back to Minnesota."

FORTY-SIX

The short, slender, frizzy-haired man with a salt and pepper mustache and goatee quietly closed the hallway door behind himself. Without a sound he poked his head into the open door of Connie Mickelson's office and for seven seconds, watched her working at her desk.

"Hello, Connie," he finally said.

"Goddammit, Julian," Connie shrieked as she rose, startled, three inches out of her chair. "Jesus Christ," she continued, "you just took five years off of my life which I can't afford. I wish people would stop doing that to me."

"Sorry," he said holding back laughter.

"You are not," Connie calmly replied as she stood up to greet the man. The two of them exchanged a quick, friendly hug. By this time, after hearing the startled Connie bellowing through her open door, everyone in the office was aware they had a visitor.

Marc, who had been waiting for the man, was the first one to greet him.

"Marc Kadella, Professor Bronfman. Thanks for coming," Marc said as they shook hands.

"Please, call me Julian. I don't even let my students call me professor."

"May I take your coat?" Carolyn asked.

As Bronfman was removing his coat and scarf, Carolyn asked, "Can I get you some coffee?"

"Tea would be nice, Earl Grey if you have any," he replied.

"Coming right up," Carolyn said.

With Connie leading the way, they went into the office's conference room, situated between Connie's and Marc's personal offices. Waiting for them were Tony Carvelli, Vivian Donahue and Barry Cline. After introductions were made and Carolyn had delivered Bronfman's tea, they all took chairs around the table.

"I hope you don't mind my being here," Vivian politely said.

312

"Not at all, Mrs. Donahue," Bronfman replied. "It's my pleasure to meet you. If Marc believes there is something to be covered by privilege…"

"We've hired her as office staff," Marc interrupted. "She's technically covered."

"Well, I hope they're paying you sufficiently," Bronfman said with a sly smile.

"A dollar a year. It's the first job I've had in years."

Bronfman had an expandable, canvas briefcase with him. He removed a stack of paper and a legal pad from it and placed both on the table.

"Might as well get started," he said. He laid a hand on the stack of paper and said, "I've been over the transcript a couple of times and, Marc, I don't understand why they found her guilty or, more accurately, how the jury failed to find reasonable doubt."

"It was the photo, I believe," Marc said. "The one of Maddy lying on the bedroom floor covered in blood, with the knife in her hand."

"So you think she's innocent?" Vivian asked showing obvious optimism.

"I didn't say that," Bronfman replied. "I said I'm surprised they didn't find reasonable doubt."

"But you think you can convince the Court of Appeals the jury was wrong?" Vivian said.

"Unfortunately, no, that's not their job. The Court of Appeals won't retry the case. They aren't supposed to second guess a jury. That's not what they do. They review the judge's rulings to determine if he made any mistakes, if he didn't apply the law correctly or acted outside the scope of his discretion.

"Now, we will certainly slide in evidence to suggest the jury was wrong. These people, the appeals justices, are human. Maybe," he continued holding his hands out, palms up, "if they believe she should have been found not guilty, they'll find a way to rule in our favor."

"But that's not what they're supposed to do," Marc quietly said to Vivian. He looked at the professor and said, "What do you think? Are there grounds?"

"Of course," Bronfman smiled at Marc. "There are always grounds. We can challenge every ruling he made that didn't go in our favor. The first one is that very photograph you referred to. In my opinion it is highly prejudicial and has no probative value beyond shocking the jury. The question is: was Judge Graham wrong in allowing it to be shown and entered as evidence?"

"You don't think a photo of the accused passed out at the crime scene holding the murder weapon helps prove she did it?" Carvelli, the ex-cop asked.

"In reality world, of course it does," Bronfman replied with a wink at Tony. "But in a legal world, we can argue that it really doesn't. They didn't show how she stabbed him or how she came to be lying unconscious on the floor.

"Look," he continued moving his eyes around the rectangular table to make contact with each of them, "I'll be honest. A winning appellate decision in this case is, well, the odds are not in our favor. What you need to do is prove her innocence."

"I thought Justice Scalia said, rather infamously," Barry Cline said, "that a finding of innocence doesn't matter in the appeal process."

"And he was absolutely correct," Bronfman said. "It's not up to an appeals court, even the U.S. Supreme Court, to determine guilt or innocence. But if we can really prove she did not do this, sooner or later we'll find a way to get her out. Until then, we'll have to start the process."

He looked at Marc again and said, "I'm putting together a group of students to work on it. I need our client's permission to do this. Will you get that for me?"

Bronfman handed Marc a single page document with signature lines on it and Marc said, "Sure, I'm going out to see her tomorrow. Ineffective assistance of counsel," Marc said.

"It's on the list. Sorry, even though I thought she should've gotten off because of you, we'll argue you were incompetent..."

"Tell them I was drunk every day and fell asleep," Marc said. "I don't care. Do what you have to do. Would you like to ride along and meet her tomorrow?"

"Yes, I would but I can't. I do need to meet her and soon. We'll set something up."

The next morning at 8:00 o'clock, Marc and Carvelli were driving south on 35W out of Minneapolis. Since they were heading in the opposite direction of rush hour traffic they were making good time. The day before, following the meeting with Julian Bronfman, Marc had called ahead to arrange a meeting with Maddy. The administration of the Shakopee Correctional Facility, the prison for women, assured him she would be waiting.

The prison in Shakopee is about twenty-five miles driving distance from Marc's office. Since Maddy's transfer to it from Minneapolis a month ago, Marc had made the trip at least three times each week.

"Been a pretty mild winter so far," Carvelli said breaking the silence between them.

"Yeah," Marc muttered in agreement.

"Probably means more snow in July," Carvelli said wondering where Marc's head was.

"Might happen," Marc absently agreed.

"Hey!" Carvelli said.

"What?" Marc replied turning his head to look at him.

"Snow in July. Even in Minnesota it doesn't snow in July."

"Who said it does? What are you talking about?"

"Where are you? She's okay you know."

"Twenty-five years, Tony. Twenty-five," Marc quietly repeated as he slid his SUV to the right to take the ramp on Highway 13 in Burnsville to go to Shakopee. "And we know she didn't do this."

"We'll get her out. You'll see."

"I've been thinking about sitting down with Steve Gondeck and let him know what we know."

"Be careful, we don't need more people in jail, especially me. Although I'd trade places with her in a heartbeat if I could. What can Gondeck do?"

"I don't know. It's something I've thought about. We'll see."

When the two men reached the prison, Maddy was waiting for them. The facility, opened in 1986, is almost a college dormitory. In fact, it wasn't until the Spring of 2016 that a fence was built around it. And instead of the normal grey concrete wall with razor wire, the fence is a chic wrought iron with attractive brick columns. If you had to go to prison, there are a lot of worse places. But no matter how modern the facility or comfortable the amenities, it is still a prison. Your life is theirs, not yours.

"How are you doing?" Marc asked her after their greetings. The three of them were in a comfortable, private conference room used by attorneys to meet with clients.

"I'm okay," she shrugged forcing a smile.

"I told you," Carvelli said, "you find the number one bad-ass chick in the place, walk right up to her and punch her in the face."

"Carvelli, you've been watching too many movies," Maddy laughed. "It's not like that. I'm fine. Besides, word spread pretty quick about who I am. Court TV is one of the most popular shows in here.

"You know what though?" she continued turning back to Marc. "The next time you hear someone, especially some big-mouth, nitwit politician, talking about how good inmates have it in prison, tell them they're full of shit. You get up when they tell you, go to bed when they tell you, eat, shower, you name it when they tell you. Yeah, it's okay in here but it's still prison. There's no freedom at all," she finished then wiped a tear that had trickled down her cheek.

"I know," Marc softly replied and took her hand. "I've been in just about every jail in the metro area and the prison here and the ones in Oak Park Heights and Stillwater. They're no country club.

"Anyway, let me bring you up to speed. We met with Connie's pal, the guy handling your appeal, Julian Bronfman. He's a bit of a character, you'll like him, but a really smart guy…"

A little before noon, after hugs and kisses and reassuring Maddy, they were going to get her out, Marc and Tony went out to the parking lot. Neither would admit it but both were fighting back tears of their own.

FORTY-SEVEN

Tony Carvelli was walking toward his car while turning on his phone to check for messages. He was leaving the corporate headquarters of the 3M Company in Maplewood, Minnesota, a suburb east of St. Paul. Carvelli carried the weight of Maddy's incarceration 24/7 but had other clients to look after, including his best one, 3M. And he still had to make a living. As he approached the Camaro in the visitor's lot, he noticed a call from an unusual source. It was a woman he had not seen or spoken to in a couple of years. Tony stood next to the driver's side door while listening to the message. When it finished, he pressed the dial button to return her call as he got into his car.

"Hey, Paulette," he greeted her when she answered, "it's Carvelli calling back. What's up?"

Paulette Horne worked in the medical examiner's office in Minneapolis. The two of them had what would best be described as a fling several years ago. Paulette was going through a divorce at the time and the affair ended when she reconciled with her husband.

"Hey, Carvelli. It's great to hear your voice again," she said. Like a lot of people in and around the MPD who knew him well, she never called him Tony. It was always Carvelli, as if he only had one name.

"You too, sweetheart. How are you? Still married?"

"Ah, no at least not to Darren anymore. But probably yes again pretty soon," she replied.

"You mean I missed my chance?"

Paulette went silent for several seconds then said, "I don't want to go down that path. I have very fond memories of you, Carvelli. Can we just leave it at that?"

"Of course, hon," Tony softly said. "So, why did you call?"

"Okay," she began getting back on track. "Something strange happened yesterday. Do you have time to swing by the office?"

"I guess," Tony said. "Is it important?"

"Yeah, at least I think so. You'll have to decide but I think you'll want to see this."

"All right. I'm in Maplewood but I'll come right over. Half an hour?"

"Good. Have them buzz me and I'll come get you."

Paulette closed the door to her office while Tony took a chair. She sat at her desk and began.

"Yesterday, something kind of odd happened. I was in the storage area, where we keep our guests, the bodies, when a couple of guys in suits showed up with a federal court order for us to release a body to them."

"Who were they after?"

"Robert Judd," she answered.

"He's just now being released for burial? And why would...."

"Let me finish. These weren't just two guys," she said.

"Feds?"

"U.S. Marshalls."

"Seriously? Why would U.S. Marshalls want to have the remains of Rob Judd released to them?"

"Don't know. But I remembered seeing you on TV working for the defense in the trial of his girlfriend and I thought you might want to know. Let me show you something," Paulette continued as she turned her laptop so Tony could see the screen. Having prepared for Carvelli's visit she only needed to hit one key and a video image came up.

"This is the security footage of the two of them. Do you recognize them?"

Tony stared at the frozen screen for a while then quietly said, "Yeah, I do. I saw them outside the condo building on the morning after Judd was killed. I don't know who they are but I remember thinking they look like cops. Or law enforcement from somewhere. Did you get their names?"

"Just this one," Paulette said pointing a finger at one of them. "His name is Keegan Mitchell."

319

Tony removed a small notebook from his pocket, flipped it open to a blank page and wrote down the name, date and time on the screen and a note to go along with it.

Ten minutes later, following a few minutes of small talk about Paulette's new beau, an MPD lieutenant of Carvelli's acquaintance, Tony exited the building. A pleasant, fairly warm winter day, Carvelli's black, full-length leather coat was open and flapped as he ran across Chicago Avenue to his car. He had lied when he told Paulette he did not know why the U.S. Marshall's had picked up Judd's body. At least he had a pretty good idea, a rational theory of why this happened.

Carvelli wheeled the Camaro into the light traffic on Chicago then turned west on Seventh Street. While driving down Seventh toward downtown he made a call on his cell to let Vivian know he was on the way. A few minutes later he was through downtown and onto I-394 westbound to go to the Corwin Mansion. Tony needed some information from a shady source that Vivian, his friend with benefits, had access to.

Vivian Donahue stood on the top step of the semi-circular granite stairs looking out over the front grounds of the estate enjoying the beautiful winter day. She decided to get out of the house for a while. Normally, during January, February and March, she would be staying at any of several homes the family had in much warmer climates. Because of her love for Madeline Rivers, she had stayed in Minnesota just to be near her to help in any way she could. Anthony's phone call, while somewhat cryptic, made her realize something was up.

Despite the temperature still below freezing, the sun was shining, there was no wind and Vivian wore a light, almost spring-like jacket and slacks. Vivian heard the Camaro's low growl coming down the mansion's long driveway then looked to her left and saw it through the trees. Vivian descended the steps and held up a hand to have him stop at the bottom. She got in the car, settled into the passenger seat reached over to gently kiss him, then buckled up.

"I need to get out of the house. Let's go for a drive. We can talk in the car."

"Okay," he replied. "How about we drive around the lake? We'll stop somewhere for a bite to eat."

Tony talked while he drove and brought her up to speed on where the investigation was. When he got to the part about the U.S. Marshall's retrieving Rob Judd's remains, she twisted in her seat to look directly at him.

"What? I don't understand. Why would U.S. Marshalls show up with a federal court order and claim his body?" she asked.

"There's only one reason I can think of: Judd was in witness protection," Tony answered.

"Anthony, that's preposterous," Vivian exclaimed. "I met him with Madeline, remember? So did you. He was no mob gangster."

"Vivian," Tony calmly replied, "you don't have to be a mob gangster to get put in witness protection. He could have been a witness to something or any number of reasons. I need you to give your old pal on the East Coast a call and have him check around. See if he can find out anything. Will you do that?"

"Certainly," she replied. "In fact, I'll fly out myself and see him in person."

"You don't need to go see him in person," Tony said with more than a touch of irritation n his voice.

"I don't mind," Vivian said.

"It's not necessary for you to go see him," Carvelli said a little more forcefully.

Vivian leaned forward as far as the shoulder strap would allow, turned to a now obviously annoyed Carvelli and looked at his face.

"Why, Anthony," she said with a mischievous smile, "are you jealous? That's wonderful!"

"No, I'm not..."

"You are too and it's very sweet. Relax, that ended between us decades ago," she said which irritated Tony some more. She patted him affectionately on the knee and said, "I know him. He'll take me more seriously if I see him in person. Stop up ahead here at Fletcher's. I'll buy lunch."

When Vivian was in college many years ago, she, along with several girlfriends, made a trip to New York City. While there she met a handsome, very charming, young Italian man. At first the young man identified himself as Paul Renaldi. Vivian, smitten with first love, came home only to be confronted by her protective father. Dad had her followed in New York and came up with the true identity of Vivian's Italian lover. His real name was Dante Ferraro, the son of a capo in the DiMartino crime family. To make things worse, two months later Vivian and her mother were on an airplane to Switzerland. The family never again discussed the abortion she had obtained while there.

Over the years the two young lovers continued their affair even though Dante followed his father into the family business. As they grew older the flame died out but they remained good friends. If anyone could come up with information about Rob Judd being involved in witness protection, it was Dante Ferraro, even though he was now semi-retired. His name still carried a lot of weight with all of the family members.

The Corwin Family Gulfstream set down at the Teterboro airport shortly after eight P.M. The plane had barely stopped when the door opened and Vivian went down the steps to a waiting limousine. Inside the shiny Cadillac was the man she had flown a quick one thousand miles to see. Delighted to see her, despite the lateness of her arrival, Dante had arranged an evening out across the river in the city.

After attending the huge Broadway hit, *Hamilton*, they were escorted to a private room with a view of the East River at the Riverpark restaurant. A ridiculously priced, grossly overrated meal was served after which Vivian finally had the chance to explain to Dante what she wanted.

"Do you have a photo of this young man?" he asked when she finished.

"Yes, I do," she replied. She retrieved a 5x7 print from her purse and handed it across the table.

Ferrero put his cheater's on and stared at the smiling couple in their photo.

"It was taken last summer at a party at my place," Vivian said.

"And this beautiful girl sitting next to him, that is your Madeline?"

"Yes, it is," Vivian said with sadness in her voice.

Vivian opened her mouth again as if to say something then thought better of it. She was about to tell him that she knew for certain how Anthony and his friends had obtained the truth about Rob Judd's death.

"You were going to say something," Ferraro said.

"She's innocent. I know it for certain. We have to prove it and get her out of this. Please don't ask me how I know," Vivian replied.

"Fair enough. Your word has always been good enough for me. I am a little offended you don't trust me," he shrugged.

Vivian looked him in the eye, sighed then said, "You're right. I do trust you." She then proceeded to tell him the story of how Carvelli found out the truth about Rob Judd's death.

"I'm impressed," Ferraro said. "Your Mr. Carvelli is a resourceful man. If he ever needs a job I know people who could use such a man."

"Leave it alone, Dante," Vivian mildly chastised him.

Ferraro placed the photo in the inside pocket of his suit coat and said, "Then I will do whatever I can to help you. It will be my pleasure to help get this beautiful girl out of prison. And now, my love, it is getting late for this old man. Let me get you to your hotel and I will personally drive you back to the airport tomorrow."

"You won't personally drive me anywhere, you old fraud," she laughed. "But I'll enjoy the company."

FORTY-EIGHT

While Vivian and her ex-lover were enjoying — in Vivian's case, not enjoying — the hip hop musical, Charlie Dudek was sitting in his car across the river in Brooklyn. Specifically, he was situated outside a bar in Brighton Beach trying to find his quarry. This was now the end of his second week in and around New York and so far, no luck. His employer had informed him, via email, the man had been warned about the contract taken out on him. Charlie had also found out by listening to bar talk that his employer was also in hiding. Apparently the hunted was also hunting.

Dimitri Kirilov, the man who hired Charlie, was the head man of a U.S. branch of a Russian mob. His boss was back in Moscow and had tentacles that reached into the highest levels of the Russian government. Rumor had it that the man, Constantin Sokolov, had Vladimir Markoff, the Russian president, on speed dial.

Charlie had also discovered why Kirilov wanted the mark eliminated. Andrei Dernov was the number one hitman for a rival gang. But more importantly Kirilov had proof positive that this psychopath had a sexual taste for young girls. Kirilov, a monstrous sociopath, was the proud father of three young girls himself. Normally there was no such thing as a depravity unacceptable to Russian gangsters. This particular inclination of Dernov's was too much. Plus the contract had the additional bonus of ridding his rivals of a valued employee.

When Charlie found out that Dernov was a pedophile, he could feel the blood rising and heating his face. He had decided that Dernov needed a particularly nasty departure from this life and Charlie knew just how to provide it.

Charlie was growing increasingly impatient. The Russian needed to be dealt with harshly and soon. He also had unfinished business in Minnesota and was anxious to get back at it. After going online and copying the bios of the CAR Securities principals,

324

Charlie had gone over them so many times he could recite them from memory. He smiled a sinister smile thinking about his upcoming visit with them.

When two A.M. rolled around Charlie decided to pack it in for the night. The bar he surveilled was a small, neighborhood joint whose clientele was mostly Russian working-class men. Charlie had overheard a man who was an associate of Dernov mention it while Charlie was eavesdropping in another bar. This was the second night he had looked for Dernov here with no luck.

As Charlie yawned and thought about calling it a night, two men walked out of the bar's side door and into an alley. There was a light above the door that illuminated the men while they stood for a few seconds. Charlie quickly placed his binoculars to his eyes, focused in on the men and a chilling smile made his lips curl. Andrei Dernov was standing in the alley urinating while talking to his friend.

"Hello, Marc what can I do for you?" Steve Gondeck said into his desktop telephone. Gondeck had been paged about a call from Marc Kadella while seated at his desk over a minute ago. He liked Marc whom he considered to be a decent guy and fairly straight criminal defense lawyer, at least as much as prosecutors believed any of them to be straight. Uncertain of why Kadella was calling but believing it had something to do with Madeline Rivers, he was hesitant to answer the phone. Instead he sat and stared at the tiny, blinking red light for a full minute hoping it would stop. Gondeck finally surrendered and answered the call.

"Hey, Steve," Marc replied, "I need to talk to you about something."

"Okay, I'm listening," Gondeck said.

"Not on the phone. Can we meet?"

"Marc, if this is about Maddy, I…"

"Steve," Marc interrupted, "trust me on this, okay? Just meet me and hear me out, please."

"Okay," Gondeck said with obvious reluctance in his voice. "When and where? Not downtown," he added.

"Can you come out here to my office? There's a diner across the street..."

"I know it," Gondeck said. "You can buy me lunch," he added after looking at his clock.

"Deal," Marc said. "See you in what, a half-hour? I'll get a booth."

"Sure, see you then."

The waitress picked up their menus then turned and walked away to place their lunch orders. Both men watched the shapely twenty-year-old walk away, then Marc began.

"You know, you might want to eat a salad once in a while. The waist on those pants looks to be getting a little tight," Marc chided him.

"Is that what you wanted? You wanted me to come here so you could insult me. Like, I don't get enough of that at home," Gondeck replied. "Besides, you're not one to talk there, slim."

"It's our age and what we do," Marc said. "We work too much, eat poorly and never take time for regular exercise. It's a wonder any of us lives past sixty."

"Don't forget the stress," Gondeck added. "So what's up, Marc?"

"Before I get to that, let me ask you, do you think I made reasonable doubt for Maddy?"

"The jury said no," Gondeck replied.

"What did you think?"

"The truth? I thought it was fifty-fifty."

"All right, I'll let it go, for now."

"Good. Let's eat. I need to get back to work."

"I need to tell you something, I'm not sure what you can do about it but," he shrugged and held up his hands, "I figured I'd give it a try."

"About Madeline," Gondeck said, a statement not a question.

"Yes, but I need your word this is between us for now."

"I'm not sure I can do that."

326

"I know but I think you'll be okay with it once I tell you. Plus, I won't give you any details except I, personally, had no knowledge of any of this beforehand. Okay?"

"Okay, go ahead," a now very curious Gondeck replied.

Marc leaned forward as did Gondeck to be sure they could not be overheard.

"Before I start, I'll take your word for it that you're not recording this."

"What? Of course not. You've been watching too many cop shows. No, I am not recording this."

"Even if you do, you won't get anything incriminating."

"What the hell is going on?"

"Steve," Marc whispered, "I know for an absolute fact that Maddy did not kill Rob Judd. She was set-up. And I know who did it and why. How I know this is privileged and I won't tell you, but Ethan Rask, one of the CAR Securities guys...."

"I remember," Gondeck said.

"...confessed everything."

"And you didn't bring this up before because it was illegally obtained," Gondeck said.

"Well, ah, yeah, slightly."

"Slightly my ass. I'm not even gonna mention names but I have a pretty good idea who was involved."

"No one was hurt. No one laid a hand on him. That's all I can tell you," Marc assured him.

Gondeck leaned up against the back of the booth's bench seat and silently looked at Marc for several seconds.

"Do you believe me?"

"Let's say I do," Gondeck said with a shrug. "I don't know what we can do about it."

"I know," Marc sighed. "I just thought it was time to tell you. Think about it, okay? Let me know if you come up with..."

"Marc, I'm on the wrong side in this. I adore Maddy, you know that. But the evidence was there and..."

"I'm telling you positively she is innocent."

Gondeck heavily sighed then said, "All right, I'll think about. Thank God I'm not involved in the appeal."

"Come on in," Corbin Reed said when he opened his front door and found Jordan Kemp waiting for him. The five CAR principals were meeting at Reed's luxury townhouse to make the final arrangements for the liquidation of CAR Securities.

"Is everyone here?" Kemp asked while stepping into the foyer.

"Not yet, we're still waiting for Walter. He had some bullshit deal he had to attend for one of his kids. He called a couple minutes ago and said he'd be along pretty soon," Reed replied as the two men entered his living room.

Kemp walked across the plush, white carpeting then stepped down into the sunken living room. Waiting were Ethan Rask and Victor Espinosa. They were sitting in matching, off-white chairs, each on one side of the large, gas fireplace set into the wall. Kemp heartily greeted both men with a huge smile. Kemp had never let his feelings show but he absolutely despised both of them. He hated Rask because he was so sleazy that every time Kemp shook his hand he wanted to take a shower. He could barely stand to be in the same room with Espinosa because Kemp was a closet bigot and believed all Latinos were drug-dealing gangsters who would slit your throat for amusement. It did not help that Espinosa was involved with people who fit the stereotype. Of course, unknown to Jordan Kemp, both Rask and Espinosa felt the same way about him.

Kemp flopped his bulky body down on the sectional couch opposite Rask and Espinosa. "Getting close to zero hour," Kemp said to the two men.

"What do you want to drink?" Reed asked Kemp. While Kemp greeted the two co-conspirators Reed went to the bar to freshen his cocktail.

"A scotch and soda, Corbin," Kemp said. "And make it the good stuff for once."

Ethan Rask impatiently looked at his watch and growled, "Where the hell is that idiot Pascal?"

"Relax, Ethan," Kemp said with a smile. "He'll be along."

Walter Pascal, if anyone was watching, appeared to be driving aimlessly through a residential area of South Minneapolis. He almost laughed at his own paranoia but also remembered the old saying, *You're not really paranoid if people are really out to get you.*

Ever since he became caught between the FBI and CAR Securities, Walter believed he was being followed. In case they had attached some type of tracking device to his car, he had driven to a rental agency and with a fake ID Ethan Rask had acquired for him a long time ago, rented the Buick he was currently driving. Tonight's meeting was one the FBI should not find out about.

Forty-five minutes after renting the car, satisfied he was not being followed, he parked in the small lot by Corbin's townhouse. A minute later he was greeting the men waiting for him in Reed's living room.

When all five of them were settled into their chairs, Jordan Kemp started the discussion. He removed a document of several pages from his suit coat pocket, unfolded it and handed it first to Victor Espinosa.

"Here it is. This is the plan, in detail for each of us. Look it over, especially your end of things, and make sure it looks right."

After Espinosa read it over and acknowledged its accuracy, he handed it to Ethan Rask. For the next twenty minutes, while they all waited in silence, each man in turn read the contents of the document and passed it along.

Corbin Reed, the last one to look it over, finished reading it and said, "Looks good." He handed it back to Jordan Kemp then stood, held up his drink and said, "Gentlemen, to a long and luxurious life."

The others stood, joined him in the toast and amid smiles and mild laughter, downed their drinks.

FORTY-NINE

Vivian Donahue's one-time illicit lover, Dante Ferraro, was seated in the kitchen breakfast nook drinking the strong, Sicilian coffee he loved. Dressed in a black, silk bathrobe and matching silk pajamas he was in his million dollar Brooklyn Heights home. His housekeeper/cook, Consuela Madera, a sassy Puerto Rican who had been with him for over ten years, again chided him for drinking too much of the heavily caffeinated drink. And again, Ferraro ignored her and poured more from the sterling silver carafe.

Unlike Vivian, the years had not been kind to the old gangster. Barely seventy, he was at least eighty pounds overweight, his once jet black hair, what was left of it, gone completely gray and his health was that of an eighty-five year old. Semi-retired now, Dante Ferraro took comfort from the fact he would die in his bed and not a prison cell.

"Animals," he growled. Ferraro was reading the Daily News story about a body found in Barreto Point Park in the Bronx. The victim's name had not been released but the reporter revealed the tattoos on the body clearly identified the man as a Russian mobster.

"Who are animals?" Consuela asked. She was standing next to him, her right hand lightly resting on his left shoulder while she looked down at the paper.

"Russians," Dante answered her.

"What time are your friends coming by?" she asked him.

"Ten o'clock," he replied.

"You should get ready. It's almost nine," she said. She patted him on the shoulder and turned to continue her duties.

"I can still tell time," he growled. "But you're right."

At precisely ten A.M., not one minute before, not one minute after, the front doorbell rang. Consuela opened it and found three tough-looking men in their forties standing on the stoop.

"Good morning, Consuela," the oldest of the three, the one nearest the door said. "Is the boss in?"

"Yes, he's waiting for you in the little room," she replied. Consuela knew who and what these men were. When she first came to work for Ferraro, they frightened her down to her toes. Since then, she had come to realize they lived outside the law but were always polite and even kind to her.

Ferraro had a small, sparsely furnished, windowless room in a corner of his home. It had been specially built with only one amenity, a wood-burning stove in one corner. There was a small, cheap, wooden conference room table that could accommodate only four with four comfortable chairs around it.

Dante Ferraro had never aspired to become head of the DiMartino family. The last two had both died in prison and the current one, the one the tabloids loved, would likely end up the same way. It was Dante Ferraro who secretly, quietly, brought the family into the legitimate world. It was he who, behind the scenes, made dozens of partnerships with legitimate businesses, all of whom were happy to be involved with him. He cut out competition, consolidated the businesses and made all of them operate more smoothly. And they all made more money with a lot less hassle from the government. Because of this, Ferraro was still treated with great deference and respect. When he summoned you to meet with him, it was still considered an honor.

His three guests entered the meeting room and found the old man seated at the table's head. Each of them silently took his hand and affectionately pressed their lips to it. They did so silently because in this room, words were never spoken out loud.

The three men were all capos with family crews to manage. Ferraro never met with any underlings of these men. To begin the meeting, Ferraro took a slip of note paper and wrote out a question, then passed it to each man who read it in turn. These were the men Ferraro had ordered to find out what they could about Rob Judd. For the next half hour all four of them silently wrote notes to the old man and each other about this and a couple of minor problems to bring to Ferraro's attention and counsel. At the end of the meeting, Ferraro had no more information for Vivian than he had before. So far, they had come up with nothing even from their contacts in the federal government law enforcement agencies.

Silently showing his displeasure by the look on his face, the last note written was his order to the three of them to keep digging. He made it clear they were to leave no stone unturned. There must be something out there somewhere and Ferraro did not want to disappoint Vivian Donahue.

When the meeting adjourned, Ferraro gathered all of the slips of paper and tossed them into the stove. He took a can of lighter fluid from a shelf, sprayed the flammable liquid over the papers then closed the iron grate. He struck a wooden match, tossed it in through an opening in the grate and a brief 'whoof' occurred when the fluid ignited. Being this careful was a significant reason why Dante Ferraro, despite being ratted out by several turncoats, had never been convicted of a crime. No evidence, no convictions.

At about the same time, Ferraro was having his morning coffee and grumbling about what animals Russians were, Charlie Dudek was driving across the New Jersey state line into Pennsylvania. Charlie had completed his task in New York the previous night — Dante Ferraro was reading about it in the Daily News — and was on his way to Minnesota.

Charlie was westbound on I-80 heading toward flyover country. The driving distance being approximately 1200 miles, Charlie could do it in a day if he wanted to push himself. Being the careful sort that he was, Charlie would watch his speed and get a motel room outside Chicago and be back to Minneapolis by tomorrow afternoon. Charlie had confidence the people he was going to meet with would still be there. Plus, this would give him time to think about exactly what he wanted to do. He had never, not once, done anything like this before. This was a personal score to settle. The question he was having so much difficulty with was: *how can he do this and help Madeline Rivers?*

FIFTY

Marc, Connie Mickelson and Julian Bronfman were all seated in the same meeting room at the women's prison that Marc always used when he came there to meet Maddy. They had arrived early and were waiting for her to be brought to them. There was silence between the three lawyers, all of the small talk having been used up on the drive. Ten minutes after being let into the room, they saw Maddy and a guard through the door's window walking toward them.

"My goodness," Bronfman said as he watched her approach. "You didn't tell me that about her."

"Julian, behave yourself you old dog," Connie mildly chastised him. "She's too young for you."

"My eyes still work," he said smiling at Connie.

The female guard unlocked the door and let Maddy go in. Marc introduced her to Julian and they all took seats.

"I wanted to meet you and tell you where we are with your appeals. I have a half dozen very good students working on your brief, with my close supervision, of course. The brief is due next week at the court of appeals and it will be ready."

"How does it look?" Maddy asked.

"It's too early to tell. I'll know more when I get the documents from the state so I can see what they have to say," Bronfman replied.

"That's your polite way of saying it doesn't look good," Maddy said with a chagrined smile.

"Not necessarily, no," Bronfman quickly said.

"Don't get down on yourself," Connie added. "We're going to win and get you out."

Connie reached over and squeezed Maddy's hand who said, "Thanks, Mom," and smiled a genuine smile.

Bronfman went over every aspect of the appeal process and Maddy's particular case. He also regaled her with numerous stories of long-shot cases he thought were total losers that he eventually won. By the time he finished, he even had Connie and Marc believing he would prevail.

While buckling up their seatbelts when they were back in Marc's SUV, Marc turned to Bronfman in the backseat.

"Okay, bullshit aside, what do you really think?"

"I make our chances at maybe twenty percent. Judge Graham did a good job. He was fair and impartial in his rulings and I think it's a stretch to say he went outside the scope of his discretion. Our best chance is to continue to investigate and try to prove she's innocent."

When Bronfman said this, Connie looked at Marc and said, "Tell him."

Marc nodded his head slightly, turned back to the professor and said, "She is innocent. We know it for certain. But we found out in a way that can't be used." He then proceeded to explain exactly how they knew and how they found out. The only thing he left out were the names of those involved.

"Are you serious? Wow! That's the greatest story I've ever heard," Bronfman joyously replied. "It's like something out of a movie. It's fabulous."

Connie turned in her seat, looked directly at him and said, "Julian, I can't tell you how many felonies were committed."

"Oh, quite a few," he said using his right hand to give Connie a dismissive wave. "He wasn't hurt, this man Rask?" he asked Marc.

"No, he's fine. Folded like the proverbial cheap suit. Told them everything."

"And you didn't know about it ahead of time?" Bronfman again asked Marc.

"No, of course not, I…"

"Then it's no problem. Ethically, we're covered. Relax. But what do we do with it?" Bronfman said.

"That's the question," Marc replied as he started the car's engine.

334

"You're not going to tell me who it was that helped your investigator, Tony Carvelli, do this, are you?" Bronfman asked.

"Tony who?" Marc said peeking at Bronfman in the rearview mirror. "I don't know what you're talking about."

"What we need to do is figure out a way to tell this, legitimately," Connie said looking back at Bronfman as Marc drove out of the parking lot.

"Yes," Bronfman sighed. "That's the problem."

Joel Dylan, Mike Anderson and Holly Byrnes were, once again, seated at a conference room table. They were in the office of the U.S. Attorney for Minnesota, waiting after being summoned by the man himself. The investigation of CAR Securities was coming up on a one year anniversary and Winston Paine wanted an update. As usual, the three of them had been waiting almost a half-hour for Paine and his shadow/bodyguard to grace them with his presence.

Anderson and Holly Byrnes were seated along the side of the table side-by-side. They had their backs to the sixth floor window opposite the room's entryway door. Dylan was at the far end of the table to their left.

"Please, Mike," Dylan said. "Don't say anything. Just let it go."

This was said in response to Anderson checking his watch for the third or fourth time in the last five minutes.

"I have to live with this guy, okay?" Dylan added.

"Hopefully, not much longer," Anderson growled. "We get a new president, he'll likely head back east for a big bucks firm."

"I keep praying," Dylan said.

A few minutes later, Paine came through the door held open by his bodyguard.

"How many death threats do you get?" Anderson asked Paine.

"What?" Paine asked looking at the FBI Agent.

"I'm just wondering why you think you need a bodyguard with you all the time, especially in your own office? Do you get death threats from the staff? That wouldn't surprise me," Anderson said. He also sneaked a quick peek at the bodyguard who had taken a seat in the corner. The man was obviously suppressing a smile.

"We're here to discuss your investigation," Paine said ignoring Anderson and looking down the table at Dylan. "When can we expect some indictments?"

"Very soon," Dylan replied.

"When is very soon?" Paine asked.

"We'll be able to take the case to a grand jury within the next four to six weeks," Dylan said.

"That's not what I'm hearing from the guys in forensic accounting, Joel. They're telling me what you have so far is not very conclusive."

"Our informant tells us he is on the verge of obtaining definite proof that CAR Securities is laundering drug money and operating a Ponzi scheme."

"These guys are running a Ponzi scheme using Mexican cartel money? That's living dangerously," Paine said somewhat skeptically.

"No, they're not running a Ponzi scheme on the cartel," Anderson interjected. "They're making money laundering the cartel money and using legitimate money to keep the cartel money coming in. At least that's the way it looks to our informant."

"And he's on the verge of getting us what we need. Plus, they're dealing in fraudulent securities. We are going to have a RICO case, Winston. We just need a couple more months," Joel Dylan said.

"You're sure?" Paine asked.

"No, we're not sure," Anderson said. He placed his forearms on the table, leaned forward and added, "We'll know when we get the evidence. We have our informant and he's running scared. These things take time."

"Do you have enough for a search warrant?" Paine asked looking at Dylan again.

"Maybe, but it's a little thin. If we get one and we don't come up with enough, well, there are some pretty prominent people with money invested with them. If we go crashing in there and grab everything and we're wrong, they'll howl like hell and it could be your ass, Winston," Dylan told him.

The thought that a botched investigation could potentially tarnish him, personally, caused Paine to stop and think. The room went silent for a minute while he did so.

"Yes, I see what you mean. Probably best to proceed with caution and be sure of ourselves. How about putting a little heat on this informant," Paine said looking at Mike Anderson.

"Man, that's a great idea, Winston. I wish I'd thought of it. We'll get right on that," Anderson disingenuously replied which went right over Winston Paines' head. "I'll see what we can do."

"Good, good Special Agent Anderson. Well, very productive meeting," Paine said looking at his watch. "I'm running late so, well," he continued as he stood and looked at Joel Dylan, "keep me informed."

"Yes, sir," Dylan said trying not to laugh.

The door to the conference room barely closed when Holly Byrnes said, "Why do I have to come to these things?"

"Why do any of us?" Anderson asked.

"It's now Thursday," Dylan said. "Get a hold of Pascal and get his ass in here on Monday with something."

"Monday's Presidents' Day," Holly reminded him.

"Okay, Tuesday. We'll meet at your office. Set it up, will you Mike?"

"Sure, I'll get to him today or tomorrow."

"Did anybody ask why we're shutting down the office for the weekend and giving everybody Friday off?" Corbin Reed asked his small group of conspirators.

The five men, the principals of CAR Securities, were meeting in the private conference room across the hall in suite 2007. It was after 6:00 on the Thursday evening before the Presidents' Day weekend. This had been their target date all along and they were right on schedule.

"Sure," Jordan Kemp replied to Reed's question. "But they seem satisfied that we just decided everybody needed an extra day

337

for a long weekend. The markets are always slow on Fridays before a holiday so, it won't raise any alarms."

The other three men, Rask, Espinosa and Pascal all nodded their heads in agreement.

"What do you have left to dump?" Reed asked Pascal.

"Not much. Less than eighty million," Pascal answered him.

Reed turned to Kemp and asked, "Will that raise any flags?"

Kemp shrugged and said, "Maybe but the holiday weekend should cover for it. Nobody will want to ruin their weekend making a fuss about it. If anyone notices, it will sit until Tuesday morning. By then it will be too late."

"What about the rest of it, the other accounts? Everything set to make the transfers?" Reed asked the group in general and Kemp in particular.

All four men nodded their heads and said yes to the question.

While the after-hours meeting in 2007 of CAR Securities was breaking up, Charlie Dudek was in an elevator on his way to his hotel room. In order to be closer to downtown, he was checking into the Radisson near the University of Minnesota. Paying with cash would have raised some eyebrows so he used the only credit card he had, a Visa card in a fake name. Of course, he also had a Missouri driver's license to go with it. Charlie wasn't thinking about that as he rode up to his room. He was mentally going over the plan he had come up with on the drive back to Minnesota.

FIFTY-ONE

Despite the stiff-upper-lip façade Maddy put on when Marc, Connie and her new lawyer, Julian Bronfman visited, her heart felt like a stone in the pit of her stomach after they left. Every time someone came to see her, when they left, she always had the same feeling of despair. Sooner or later, their efforts to get her out were going to end. Over time, their lives would catch up with them, they would be defeated, move on and she would still be here, her life no longer her own.

The prison itself was not the nightmare that terrorized most people's imaginations. At least the facility itself was not. Her 'cell' was a good sized room with two real beds, a table and chair for each inmate and it even had separate closet and drawer space for each of them. Her cellmate was a forty-eight-year-old African American woman named Viveca Brown. Viveca, Maddy found out, was doing six years for first-degree manslaughter. One night she buried the claws of a hammer into the top of her very abusive, junkie boyfriend's head while he slept. Charged with murder, she had pled down to manslaughter because it was obvious she was not in immediate danger while the man slept. That and the only record of violence between them was an event that occurred two weeks prior when the cops had intervened and found the two of them going toe-to-toe throwing punches at each other.

Maddy's first night was the worst. Lying in bed, unable to sleep a wink, she was determined not to breakdown. While Viveca softly snored in the bed next to her, Maddy spent the entire night lying on her back staring at the ceiling. What drove her into an almost crushing feeling of hopelessness was the overwhelming sense of loneliness. Despite the fact she had numerous friends very close by that she knew would visit soon, she had never felt more alone in her life. It went through her mind like a video on a loop. How could she possibly keep her sanity and how could she not become institutionalized if this was what she would deal with for the next seventeen years? Maddy would walk out of this place a bitter, angry, hard, old woman. Despite her best efforts the tears still leaked out of the corner of eyes for much of the night.

Because of her status as an ex-cop and her level of education, Maddy was assigned to soft duty in the library. This caused her serious concern because she did not know how the other inmates would respond to such preferential treatment. After not speaking a single word to her for the first three days, Viveca finally broke the ice with her about this.

"You get the library because everybody knows who you are. You're that hot, white chick on the TV that did her boyfriend, ain't you?" Viveca flatly said.

It was the morning of Maddy's fourth day. She had finally slept the previous night and was now lying in her bed staring at her cellmate. Viveca was sitting on the edge of her own bed looking down at Maddy when she spoke.

"I did my boyfriend, no account, black-ass junkie that deserved it and here I am," she added.

"I didn't kill him," Maddy quietly answered her.

"Innocent, huh? You and just about everybody else in here," Viveca replied.

Maddy tossed the blankets aside, reached down and touched her toes to stretch. She turned her head to look at Viveca and said, "Don't believe me then, I don't care. It's true, I didn't do it."

"It's okay, honey," Viveca said only this time she had a friendly smile. "Someone looked you up online and found out who you are. You already got a rep as a bad-ass. No one gonna fuck with you, believe me. There's some bitches in here but they ain't as bad as they think they are. You be okay. My name is Viveca," she continued and extended her hand to Maddy. While shaking hands, Viveca added, "Looks like we gonna be roomies for a while."

Maddy had finally made at least one friend. Before that same day was over, she would find there were a lot of women wanting to have her on their side. On the fifth day, she took some haircut advice from one of her library co-workers, a young woman

340

barely in her twenties doing time for acting as a drug mule, her fourth conviction.

Her name was Cheryl and at one time she had been as pretty as Maddy. A homecoming queen and the most popular, hot-chick of a south suburban high school not far from where she was doing time. Drugs and the people involved in it destroyed Cheryl's idyllic life and here she was, rock-bottom.

Under the watchful eye of a female corrections officer, Cheryl was allowed to use a scissors on Maddy's hair. When she finished, instead of the locks flowing over her shoulders and down her back, it was barely long enough to cover her ears.

After Marc and the others left, she spent the rest of her day like every day; going through the monotony of life on the inside. For someone like Maddy, the boredom, drudgery and tedious repetition was mind-numbing. In just a couple of months it was already making her a little stir crazy. Fortunately, the library was decently stocked and she figured if she were in here for the full sentence, she would read every word of every book in it.

That evening she sat with a couple of friends, including Viveca, in the common area watching TV. Every once in a while she still caught herself reaching to comb her hair with her fingers then catching herself when there was nothing there to comb. Cheryl, who had latched herself to Maddy, caught her doing it again now and teased her about it.

"Like everything else in here, honey," Viveca said, she always referred to her as honey, "you'll get used to it."

"I hope not," Maddy quietly replied.

Maddy's little support group was seated at a table away from the TV behind a set of chairs. As usual the chairs were occupied by the same seven or eight women who normally sat in them. This bunch was about as close to being a 'gang' as there was in the prison. Their self-appointed leader, a tough-looking, tattoo covered, motorcycle mama named Beverly was in the middle of the couch directly in front of the TV. So far they had mostly ignored Maddy. The word Maddy heard about this was there was a story going around about Maddy and a serial killer who had attacked her in her apartment. The true story was bad enough, but as it made the rounds of the prison grapevine, the embellishment had made it significantly more colorful. Between that and her friendship with Viveca, who had plenty of friends of her own, the Dyke Gang, as they were called behind their backs, had kept their distance, so far.

"Keep looking, you crazy bitch," Viveca quietly said when Beverly turned around to look at Maddy. She smiled and winked at Maddy then slowly turned back to the TV.

"Sooner or later, honey," Viveca said to Maddy, "you gonna have to deal with that."

"We'll see," Maddy said with a resigned shrug.

Viveca's prediction of sooner or later turned out to be sooner — much sooner. The very next day Maddy was working in the library pushing a cart filled with returned books up and down the aisles. She was placing them back on the shelves in their appropriate places, a tedious task but one that at least gave her something to do.

There were seven or eight women in the library scattered about the tables quietly reading. All of a sudden Maddy noticed a mild commotion and looked out at the reading area and saw all of them pack up and scurry toward the exit. Maddy was standing in-between two tall bookshelves and could not see what was going on. With a premonition of what just happened, Maddy placed the two books she was holding back on the cart and calmly walked out into the reading area. She looked at the exit just as her young friend Cheryl looked back with a frightened expression on her face. Maddy lightly waved a hand to her to indicate she should leave, which she quickly did.

Maddy stood still, her heart jumping a bit feeling the adrenaline flowing into her. She silently watched as Beverly and her pals came toward her. As her gang members spread out in a semi-circle around Maddy, Beverly plopped down on a table seven or eight feet in front of her. For several seconds, they all waited silently while Maddy calmly looked at Beverly who leered back at her with a sinister smile.

342

"You sure are a tasty looking little piece," Beverly said breaking the silence.

"What do you want, Beverly?" Maddy flatly asked eliciting some snickers from Beverly's friends.

"Ah, come on, princess. We just want to be friends. Everybody needs friends in here," Beverly replied with that same smile and attitude.

"All right, mama cow," Maddy snarled turning Beverly's smile into a serious frown. "Let me tell you and your merry band of calves here how this is going to go. There are seven of you and you can probably get me and hurt me. Even hurt me bad. But," here Maddy paused and looked over Beverly's six pals, "at least two or three of you will leave here in a lot more pain than when you came in. Bleeding and broken bones, too. Especially you," she said staring at Beverly. "Count on it."

She looked over the now uncertain little gang then turned back to the leader of the pack and said, "As for you, sooner or later I'll catch you alone. And when I do, I'll beat your fat ass into the tub of goo that you are then I'll pitch you out a window just to see if you can fly."

Beverly, with a much more cautious, worried, uncertain expression silently stared back. This aggression from a would-be victim was not something she had ever experienced and made her pause, not sure what to do.

"Yeah, princess," Maddy mockingly said to her, "that story you heard about me is true. And he was a lot tougher than any of you are. So," she paused and again looked at the other six women, one at a time, directly in their now worried eyes. "Any of you want to find out if you can fly after being tossed through a window?"

Maddy waited five or six seconds then said, "I didn't think so." She took a short step toward Beverly who stood up and nervously tried to back away.

Maddy jerked a thumb toward the exit and derisively said, "Waddle your fat ass out of here and take this," she stopped and waved a finger at the others then said, "gaggle of morons with you and don't bother me again."

343

As Beverly started to silently back away, Viveca and four other women, all black except for Cheryl, came into the library. Without a word passing between the two groups, Beverly led her bunch through the door.

"What happened, honey?" Viveca asked Maddy after Beverly and her followers had left.

As soon as Beverly was out the door, Maddy had collapsed into a chair. She was staring straight ahead not even acknowledging her cellmate for several seconds.

Viveca and the women who came in with her were all looking down at Maddy waiting for her to say something.

"What happened?" Viveca repeated.

Maddy finally looked up and over all of their expectant faces and said, "I can't believe I did that."

She then told them exactly what went down.

"That story is true?" one of Viveca's friends said. "That story about you throwing that man through a window, that's true?"

"Yeah, it is," Maddy quietly said.

"Girl, I'm glad you're on my side," the woman replied.

FIFTY-TWO

Charlie Dudek waited patiently in his car in the above-ground parking lot of Ethan Rask's condo building. Not knowing the type of car Rask drove, Charlie was on station before six A.M. looking out and waiting for him. Being Friday morning and what Charlie assumed was a normal workday, he expected Rask to have left for his downtown office long before now. It was now after 9:00 and he was growing increasingly concerned that he had missed him.

While on his way to New York, Charlie had checked with his source in Chicago, the man who had originally put Rask in contact with him. Charlie demanded to know who had hired him. Normally, this man would keep such a thing confidential but Charlie made it clear this was not an option.

Realizing Charlie meant business, the Chicago wiseguy gave up Rask without a second thought. Unfortunately for Ethan Rask, this information put him first on Charlie's list.

While waiting for Rask to appear, Charlie let his mind drift back to his confrontation with the Russian and his last night in New York. After seeing Andrei Dernov in the alley, he watched the two men until they eventually split up. He followed Dernov to an apartment building in the Bronx and saw him go in when a woman opened the door. Charlie waited in his car across the street parked behind Dernov's BMW. The street was quite dark, the only light coming from the doorway Dernov went through, an excellent place to take him.

A few minutes later, Charlie realized what Dernov was up to. Angry now, he almost broke his car door exiting the vehicle. He ran across the street. Charlie went up the steps to the door two at a time then kicked the door open, shattering the frame. The noise it made caused the woman who met Dernov to open her apartment door to see what happened. Charlie ran three steps then blew through the open door, grabbed the scruffy looking, strung-out junkie by the throat and snarled, "Where is he?"

345

Charlie heard a noise coming from a room in the back of the apartment and before the terrified woman could answer, tossed her on the floor. He ran toward the noise and without slowing down, put a shoulder into the door where the noise came from and made it explode into a filthy, small bedroom. In it, he found exactly what he feared he would find, Andrei Dernov, naked on top of a small, naked girl no more than ten or eleven years old, a younger version of the woman on the floor.

Charlie was on Dernov before the pedophile had a second to react. One punch to the side of Dernov's head and the Russian was out cold.

The little girl had been knocked to the floor then crawled into a corner. She sat with her knees up covering her naked little body, her red-rimmed eyes wide with terror.

"Get dressed sweetheart. I won't hurt you," Charlie told her still straddling the tattoo-covered, naked, unconscious Russian.

"Do you have some place you can go?" he asked her while she quickly dressed.

"You can't take her," the girl's mother screamed from the doorway.

In a flash, Charlie had a gun in his hand pointed right at the woman's head.

"Shut your goddamn mouth, you disgusting bitch! One more word and I'll blow your fucking brains out!"

The terrified woman backed away and Charlie turned back to the girl.

"My grandma's," she said. "My dad's mom. Please take me there."

"Do you know where she lives?"

"Yes, not far. I'll show you."

It was then Charlie noticed the shackle marks on the girl's wrist and the chain attached to the room's radiator. He looked at the mother again and said, "You better start running or I'll come back."

An hour later, after dragging the naked Dernov out of the building and into the trunk of his car, Charlie parked in Barreto Point Park, a public park in the Bronx. He had found the girl's grandmother, dropped her off and was now getting ready to deal with Dernov.

It was after 1:00 A.M. and Charlie had found a secluded spot with a tree he needed. Dernov, still naked and with his hands, feet and mouth duct taped, was defiantly staring up at him when Charlie opened the trunk. Normally, being a professional, Charlie would not act in a cruel way. He would do the job required and be done with it. But for the sick, twisted Russian, Charlie decided to make an exception.

Mentally snapping back to his current post, he saw a beige Mercedes exit the Rask's condo building's underground parking lot that Charlie was watching. It was Ethan Rask's beige Mercedes and it brought Charlie back from his daydream about the Russian. As he had done with every car, Charlie checked out the driver with his binoculars.

"And there you are," he softly said to himself.

As Rask pulled the luxury sedan out of the lot onto West 69th, Charlie wrote down the make model and license plate of the Mercedes. There was very little traffic so Charlie sat still watching as Rask drove up to the corner of 69th and York. Rask's left turn blinking light came on which told Charlie he was headed toward the Crosstown Freeway then likely downtown to his office. Charlie let Rask get a block away then drove after him, confident he knew where Rask was going.

"Exactly how long do you think this will take?" Corbin Reed asked Walter Pascal.

All five of the CAR owners were in the private suite, 2007, across the hall from the main office. They were the only ones in on this Friday morning. The idea to close the office and send all of the employees off on a long weekend had been a great idea. They didn't need any employees hanging around the office today. What these men were up to might raise some eyebrows at the SEC. Doing it on a Friday before a holiday weekend would likely minimize the risk. Even if an SEC investigator did pick up on it, it would likely be set aside until Tuesday of next week. By then it would be over, they hoped.

"All day," Walter replied. "We still have a considerable amount to liquidate into cash. That needs to be done as carefully as possible…"

"That's all set up," Jordan Kemp interjected.

"Yeah, but we still don't want to wave any flags to anyone about it. The more time we have to clear out…"

"The better," Rask said.

"Then once it's all turned into cash, probably around 1:30 or 2:00 our time this afternoon, we start bouncing everyone's shares around the globe for the next couple of days."

"And the cartel's money? That will go back to them?" Corbin Reed asked.

"Corbin, relax," Victor Espinosa calmly told him. "It's all set."

"Yeah, yeah, I know. I just don't want that crazy bastard coming after any of us. The rest of these assholes, well, who cares?"

"Hey, you getting cold feet?" Kemp asked Corbin.

"No, no," Reed said shaking his head. "No, it's just, well, now that we're actually here, I just want to be careful."

"You're about to become a very rich man, Corbin," Rask said.

"You're right. Rock and roll," Reed laughed and slapped his hands together. "Let's do it."

That evening, after waiting all day for him, Charlie had followed Ethan Rask back to his condo building an hour ago. This time Charlie was waiting in his car in the underground parking garage for him. He had backed into a visitor's spot approximately fifty to sixty feet away from Rask's car which was parked in its reserved spot. He was as close as he could get and his view was partially blocked by a concrete support pole. It was also poorly lit in this section of the garage. Even so, Charlie was confident he would see Rask get off the elevator and come to his car. He just hoped the man was not in for the rest of the evening.

Ethan Rask stepped onto the empty elevator on the building's eighth floor. As he descended toward the garage he was tempted to check his pulse. Between the events at CAR Securities earlier in the day and his destination this evening, he was pretty sure his heart rate was racing. Plus the two lines of cocaine he had done in his apartment did not help calm him down.

Rask was hurrying toward a pleasant several hours with his current high-class hooker of choice. Rask had developed a taste for prostitutes almost twenty years ago. At the time, while still in his twenties, he was heavily involved with a young Jewish woman. Like most young women at that age, she wanted marriage. Rask finally agreed. For the next six months, the girl and her mother planned every detail of the wedding. A few days before the big event, a friend told Rask — at the time he was still Anatoly Brodsky — that if he wanted to know what his wife would be like, check out the mother. The next day Anatoly Brodsky was on his way to Florida and never looked back.

Seconds before the elevator reached the garage, he again thought about Audriana. Of all the prostitutes he had known, she had been his absolute favorite. Too bad she had given him up. Once again he thought about the guys she gave him up to: *at least they weren't cops.*

Thinking about where he was off to and not paying attention to where he was, after he settled into the driver's seat of his car, Rask started to close the driver's side door. Suddenly, seemingly out of nowhere, a large, dark shadow appeared and blocked the door open. Startled, Rask turned his face toward the intruder and barely had time to say, "No" when a silenced gunshot permanently turned out his lights.

Blood, brains and bone particles were splattered all over the car's interior. What used to be Ethan Rask was slumped over the console and gear shift. The dark shadow quietly closed the car door and quickly walked away. Although the handgun, a .357 magnum, had a sound suppressor attached, the shot still made a considerable noise in the closed environment.

FIFTY-THREE

Corbin Reed was smugly relaxing on his semi-circular, white, sectional couch. He was enjoying a second glass of Cognac, staring at the soothing gas-flames of his large, wall-inset fireplace, imagining his future. Corbin's arrogance and narcissism were in overdrive while he relived in his head, the events of the past year. Everything, with the possible exception of Pat McGarry and Rob Judd, had gone exactly as planned. Even the speed bumps of McGarry and Judd had not proven to be much of an obstacle. *Too bad about Judd's girlfriend*, he thought reflecting on Maddy Rivers. *It's a shame a woman such as her should be wasting away in prison.*

"But," he began to say as he sipped his drink, "sometimes little people have to be sacrificed for the good of the more deserving," he smiled.

Corbin downed the rest of the brandy and decided he owed himself another one. Tomorrow was going to be a long, busy day. Once he was sure the money was where it should be, he had a plane to catch for a warmer climate and a life of luxury.

He stood up and stepped out of the sunken living room to go to the bar. As he did so he chuckled and said, "Hot chicks and thong bikinis. It will be a great life."

On his way back to his seat on the couch, he felt, more than heard, the patio door behind him open. He turned, saw the man standing there and started to say, "What the hell…"

The last thing Corbin Reed heard, if he lived long enough to be aware of it, were three long, rapid sounds. Woomp, woomp, woomp. All three bullets hit him squarely in the chest from barely ten feet away. The brandy snifter he was holding went flying and the impact drove Reed tumbling over the back of the couch.

The intruder took a few steps forward and looked down at Corbin. Satisfied, the man quickly exited the townhome the same way he came in closing the patio door behind him.

There was an asphalt walkway on the other side of the privacy fence surrounding Reed's patio area. The killer went through the gate, turned right and replaced the handgun at the small of his back. He stood still and waited for two or three seconds, listening for evidence of a neighbor overhearing what he had done. He quickly but not hurriedly, went down the walkway back toward the parking area.

Along the walkway, behind the townhouse buildings were a significant number of fir trees to lend privacy. As the killer went past the closest tree to the walkway, he felt a cold piece of metal pressed up against the back of his neck. Knowing what it was, he immediately stopped and raised his hands.

"You've been a busy boy, Walter," Charlie Dudek whispered as he quickly frisked him and found the gun. "It's time we had a little chat."

"Who are you?" Walter Pascal quietly asked.

Charlie placed Walter's silenced handgun in his coat pocket, jabbed his own gun in the small of Walter's back and said, "Put your hands down and walk slowly. Don't try anything stupid. I'm a professional and you won't get away from me."

"Who are you and what do you want?" Walter asked again, his voice cracking.

"All in good time, Walter. Let's go."

Charlie opened the trunk of his car and silently motioned for Walter to get out. His mouth was covered with duct tape and his hands were taped together. Charlie was parked in a small, off-street parking area a hundred or so feet from Walter's home.

Charlie jabbed his gun into Walter's back again and quietly said, "Let's go inside and we'll get acquainted."

A couple of minutes later the two men were in Pascal's living room. Walter was seated on his couch in front of the front bay window. Charlie had removed the tape from his hands and mouth then placed it in a plastic bag to take with him. The drapes on the window were closed and there was only one lamp lit on an end table next to Walter.

"I was in the parking garage of Ethan Rask's condo. I was waiting for him myself," Charlie quietly said. He was in an arm chair that matched the sofa sitting opposite Walter. Charlie had his right leg casually crossed over his left and held his gun in his right hand. It was resting on the chair's right arm pointing directly at Walter.

"Are you eliminating your partners?" Charlie asked.

Charlie waited for Walter to reply and when he did not, Charlie continued. "What about Jordan Kemp and Victor Espinosa."

"Who are you and what do you want?" Walter asked again only this time very nervously.

"Relax, Walter. If I wanted to kill you, you'd already be dead. Tell me what you're up to. What about Jordan Kemp and Victor Espinosa?"

Walter licked his lips and shifted his eyes about. He stared at the extremely confident man holding the gun then decided cooperation was likely his only option.

"Jordan Kemp is dead. I got him as he was driving home. I caught up with him in my car and signaled to him that I wanted him to pull over so we could talk. There was a motel parking lot right there so we pulled in. It was dark, no one was around and so," Walter shrugged, pointed the thumb and forefinger on his right hand at Charlie and motioned as if he was shooting a gun.

"He's still there. Probably won't be found until morning."

"Victor Espinosa?"

"Victor is probably in Mexico by now. He got out of town this afternoon. He told me he had it all set and was going to catch a flight to Houston, then Cancun. He may still be in the air but he's gone. I couldn't catch up with him."

"All right, that accounts for everyone. Now, what the hell are you guys up to?" Charlie asked.

Walter squirmed in his seat and was slow to respond. Obviously, thinking of a way to avoid it.

Charlie lifted the gun, pointed it at him then made a couple of motions with it to indicate to Walter to get on with it and tell him.

"Come on, Walter. I don't have all night."

"Who are you?" Walter again asked.

"We'll get to that when I'm ready. I still have the guns, Walter."

"Okay," Walter said with a resigned sigh. "We liquidated CAR Securities today. We've been planning this for a couple of years. We sold off everything then emptied all of the client and firm accounts. We had set up a series of electronic transfers all over the globe. The money got split up and sent out automatically through bank accounts we had in countries that aren't too cooperative with U.S. law enforcement. It will be done sometime tomorrow. Then it's all supposed to be split up into five accounts, one for each of us. But I knew they were going to screw me out of my share so I screwed them first. The money is going to end up in five accounts, all right. But only I know where they are."

"How much?"

"A little over two point six billion," Walter reluctantly answered him.

"Two point six billion! Billion with a B billion?" Charlie said.

"Yeah, billion with a B," Walter acknowledged. "Now, tell me who you are?"

"You mean you don't know? You don't know who I am? I'm surprised," Charlie replied. "I'm an off-the-books, independent contractor, employed by CAR Securities for a special job."

When he heard that, the light went on in Walter's head and he realized who Charlie was.

"You're the guy Rask hired. The guy he…"

"Yeah, I am," Charlie pleasantly answered him.

Now thoroughly terrified Walter Pascal nervously chattered, "Tell me what you want. I'll give you half. You'll have more money than you dreamed of. But only if you keep me alive."

"Wow, that's very tempting, Walter," Charlie said with mild sarcasm. "But, I'll tell you what. I wouldn't touch that money with a hundred foot pole. Two point six billion. How stupid and arrogant are you guys? Do you really think you can steal that much money and get away with it? I'm sure you ripped off some important, rich people didn't you?"

"Yeah, I guess," Walter reluctantly agreed.

"Do you think the feds are going to stop looking for it? They'll never stop. Sooner or later and probably sooner, they'll find it and you. No thanks, Walter. I'm not that greedy and I'm not that stupid. I want nothing to do with it. No, Walter, you're on your own."

"There are countries that don't have extradition treaties with the U.S." Walter said.

"So? You think that will protect you. Believe me if they have to, they'll kill you to get the money back. No, good luck."

"You're not going to kill me?"

Charlie stood up and placed his own gun in his coat pocket and removed Walter's silenced .357 from the other pocket.

"You know, I don't think so," Charlie said while rolling the gun over and over in his gloved hands. "Nice piece," he said referring to the handgun.

"God, thanks," a very relieved Walter said as he exhaled and sat back on the couch.

In a split second, before Walter had a chance to realize what was happening, Charlie pointed the gun and pulled the trigger. 'Woomp!' it loudly went off. The bullet hit Walter directly in the forehead, blew out the back of his head and lodged in the window sill behind him.

"Sorry, Walter," Charlie said. "I guess I changed my mind."

Charlie stepped up to the glass-covered chrome coffee table and placed the gun on the table in front of Walter. He looked at Walter's bloody corpse and said, "The cops will want to have that."

Before he left, Charlie had one more task to perform. In the kitchen he rummaged around through the cupboards until he found what he needed. He then went back into the living room and slipped a plastic bag over both of Walter's hands and tied them closed at the wrist.

"There Walter, now you're all set for the cops to find you."

FIFTY-FOUR

MPD Detective Owen Jefferson parked his department issued Chevy outside the taped-off crime scene. With his partner Marcie Sterling hurrying to keep up with the long-legged Jefferson, they went under the yellow-tape toward the uniformed sergeant.

"Morning, Norm," Jefferson said to the patrol sergeant, Norman Anderson. "What do we have?"

"Guy's name is Jordan Kemp. His wife has been calling all night," Anderson said as he handed Jefferson the man's wallet. "Looks like a single, large-caliber, gunshot wound to the forehead."

Jefferson removed the driver's license from the wallet and held it so both he and Marcie could read it.

"Jordan Kemp," Jefferson quietly said. "Why does that name sound familiar?"

"I don't know," Marcie replied, "but you're right, it does."

"And his address, he lives in Coon Rapids," Jefferson said referring to a suburb north of Minneapolis. "What was he doing here?"

They were standing in the parking lot of the University Inn, a motel across the river from downtown.

"Trolling for hookers?" Marcie asked.

"Maybe," Jefferson replied. "Let's take a look. Morning, Clyde. What brings you out on a Saturday morning?" Jefferson said to the man leaning into the car over the body.

"My weekend, Owen," Clyde Marston, a pathologist with the medical examiner's office said as he stood up and turned to face the two detectives. "Hi, Marcie."

"Us, too," Jefferson said referring to it being their weekend to work also.

"Take a look," Marston said then stepped aside.

Both detectives carefully looked over the body and the car's interior. When they finished they stepped away to let the M.E. go back to work.

"He knew him," Marcie said. "He was sitting in his car and looked right at whoever did this."

"Yep, I think you're right. That's why the neat hole in his forehead with the gunpowder stippling around it. He was right on top of him but our victim never expected it."

Marcie's hand-held radio beeped and she placed it to her ear. She listened for a moment, walked to a car parked nearby, removed a small notebook, placed it on the car's hood and wrote something in it.

"That's Edina," Marcie said into the radio. "Why are we…"

The dispatcher gave her more details and Marcie listened.

"How was the body found?" she asked to have the dispatcher repeat it.

"Okay," she said. "We're on our way."

"What?" Jefferson asked.

"Got another one," Marcie answered him. "And it sounds identical to this one. They want us to go check it out."

"What do you mean, identical?"

"Single, large caliber gunshot to the head of a guy sitting in his car. I got the address."

Three blocks away from the second crime scene, Marcie looked at her notes again.

"Ethan Rask," she quietly said looking through the windshield. "Ethan Rask and Jordan Kemp." She turned and looked at Jefferson and said, "Weren't they two guys that worked at that securities place that was involved in Maddy Rivers' case?"

"CAR Securities," Jefferson said. "Yeah, I think you're right. That's why the names sound familiar." Owen glanced over at Marcie with a puzzled expression. "If that's who they are what the hell is going on?"

Mike Anderson and Holly Byrnes trudged up the steps leading to the front door of Walter Pascal's home. Anderson impatiently rang the doorbell several times then waited barely three seconds before pounding on the door.

357

"Just what I wanted to do," Anderson grumbled, waiting for a response from inside. "Spend a Saturday of a holiday weekend trying to find this nitwit."

"You had other plans?" Holly asked the divorced Anderson.

"Don't start," he said to her then hammered his fist on the door several more times.

"I wonder where he could be?" Holly rhetorically asked.

"What's this about?" Anderson said. He was looking at an MPD patrol car stop at the end of Pascal's driveway effectively blocking their car from leaving. A lone MPD uniformed officer exited the car and walked toward them.

"Good morning, officer," Anderson said as he and Holly came down the front steps toward the man.

"Morning," the cop warily replied.

"We're with the FBI. I'm going to remove my ID from my inside pocket for you," Anderson told him.

The two feds gave their FBI credentials to the officer who looked them over. Satisfied he handed them back.

"What are you doing here?" the cop asked them.

"I guess I'd ask you the same thing officer Stanton," Anderson said reading the man's name from his name tag.

"You know Owen Jefferson?"

"Sure, I know Owen," Anderson replied.

"I got a call from downtown. There's been a couple homicides last night. I'm not sure about the details. I was just told to check on this guy, this Walter Pascal at this address."

"Holy shit!" Anderson almost yelled.

Both Anderson and Byrnes turned and sprinted back up the steps. Without slowing down, Anderson ran a shoulder into the door and blew it open.

"Hold it, wait, wait..." Stanton was yelling after them as he followed them up the stairs and into Pascal's living room. When he got there he found both feds silently staring at the body of Walter Pascal still sitting on the couch.

"Everybody, outside," Anderson said as he turned to leave.

"I need to clear the house," Stanton told him.

"You're right, sorry. Holly, will you give him a hand? I need to make a call."

Anderson went back out front while Holly and Stanton, guns drawn, split up to make sure the house was empty. Ten minutes later they joined Anderson in the driveway.

Anderson looked at Stanton and said, "Call it in and get me Owen Jefferson's cell phone number, please. I need to speak to him right away."

"Yes, sir," Stanton said as he removed the radio mic from his shoulder.

"We have a gigantic mess on our hands," Anderson said to Holly. The two of them had walked several steps away from the cop for privacy.

"What the hell is…" Holly started to say.

"I don't know yet. I called Joel Dylan at home. Told him what we found. He's going to get a warrant to go in and shut down CAR Securities today. For now, keep that to yourself."

"Agent Anderson," they heard Stanton say, "I have Jefferson's phone number for you."

Less than a minute later, Anderson told Owen Jefferson what they had found. Jefferson also told him about finding Jordan Kemp and Ethan Rask.

"Why were you at Pascal's, Mike? What the hell is going on?" Jefferson asked him.

"Owen, not now. I can't get into that right now. You need to find the address for Corbin Reed and Victor Espinosa and get cars out to check on them, too."

"Already done. We're waiting to hear from them," Jefferson told him. "We need to have a little chat, Mike."

"I'll tell you what I can, when I can," Anderson answered him.

"You stay at that crime scene," Jefferson said. "You're a witness. I'm on my way."

"What the hell?" Holly asked after Anderson ended the call with Jefferson and told her what they talked about.

359

"I don't know," Anderson replied.

"Did you see the gun on the coffee table in front of Walter? And somebody bagged his hands. Why?"

"Well, he didn't commit suicide by shooting himself in the forehead then putting the gun on the table. The only reason I can think of is because that is the gun used to kill Rask, Kemp, Walter and maybe Espinosa and Reed. And his hands are bagged…"

"To preserve the GSR," Holly said.

"Yeah," Anderson agreed.

"Which means Walter shot Rask and Kemp…"

"Maybe," Anderson said cutting her off. "We're getting ahead of ourselves."

Anderson's phone went off. He checked the ID, then answered it. He listened for a minute then said, "Okay, Owen. We'll be here."

"What?" Holly asked when the call ended.

"They found Corbin Reed on his living room floor. Victor Espinosa is gone. They went into his place and found luggage, clothes and personal stuff missing. They'll check flights but he likely used false papers. We'll need to check video tapes from the airport. Sonofabitch!" Anderson yelled then stomped off a few feet away.

An hour later, Anderson was on the phone with Joel Dylan. He was still hanging out at Pascal's in the driveway when Owen Jefferson came out of the house and walked up to him.

"I have to go," Anderson said to Dylan. "I'll call when I'm done here."

"Okay," Jefferson began talking to the two feds, "you're investigating CAR Securities and our, D.O.A. in there is your snitch. What's the deal, Mike?"

"I can't confirm that. In fact, I can't talk to you about anything, Owen," Anderson answered.

Jefferson looked at Byrnes and said, "Holly?"

"I'm with him," she replied nodding at Anderson.

"And how much of this had to do with the death of Robert Judd and the case against Madeline Rivers?"

"We don't know anything about that, Owen," Anderson told him.

"Then, once again, why were you here?" Jefferson solemnly asked.

"We told you everything we can. Sorry," Anderson replied. "What can you tell us about these murders?"

Jefferson ironically laughed and said, "Information is a two-way street, Mike. I'll let you know what I can when I can."

"Can we go?" a clearly annoyed Mike Anderson asked.

By the time Anderson and Byrnes arrived at the offices of CAR Securities there were twenty FBI agents and personnel on scene. Joel Dylan was there supervising.

"Hey," Dylan said as he shook hands with Anderson. "We're going to grab everything and take it to your offices. Including everything across the hall," he continued referring to suite 2007.

"Everything's gone," Anderson quietly said as he watched the crew pack up and carry items out. The feds had two moving vans in the building's basement. They would carry everything, every desk, chair, computer, file cabinet, scrap of paper they found down to the trucks to confiscate all of it.

"All the money's gone," Anderson continued. "We got played by Pascal. You'll see. We found him with his hands bagged. Looks like he and probably Espinosa set up everybody. Then Espinosa killed Pascal with the same gun. God I feel like an idiot. Why didn't we see this coming?"

"You sure that's what happened? Pascal and Espinosa killed everyone?" Dylan asked.

"Looks that way," Holly said.

"Maybe, maybe not," Dylan said. "We checked flights south out of the airport. The last one was at 7:22 last night to Houston. If Espinosa was on it, depends on the time of death, well, we'll see."

"Seriously?" Anderson asked. "Let me check with Jefferson. Holly, find the personnel files of the employees. I want every one of them brought in for questioning."

"You got it," Holly said then went off to locate the paper files.

"Owen, it's Mike Anderson," he said into his phone. "What do you have for a preliminary time of death on Pascal?"

Anderson listened for a moment then said, "Yes, please. It's important."

He listened again, thanked Jefferson and ended the call.

"The best they have for a T.O.D. for Pascal is between 11:00 and 2:00. Long after that flight, if Espinosa was on it."

"We'll find out," Dylan assured him.

"He did have one other thing," Anderson said referring to Owen Jefferson. "They found a rental car abandoned in the parking lot of Corbin Reed's place. He figures that's why Pascal's car was not in his garage. He drove to a rental place, got a car and used it. Probably to avoid us following him. Jefferson said they would check it out. If that's true and Espinosa was on that flight at 7:22…"

"Or an earlier one," Dylan said.

"Yeah, or an earlier one," Anderson continued. "How did Pascal get from Reed's to his place and who shot him?"

The two men silently stared at each other without answering the question.

362

FIFTY-FIVE

Victor Espinosa was on the flight leaving the Minneapolis/St. Paul airport at 7:22 the night of the killings. It would take a couple of days because of the disguise he wore, but the feds would identify him. They were also able to track him to Houston and a connecting flight to Cancun. By the time they did this, they were already too late.

Espinosa was awakened Sunday morning by the sound of the shower coming from the master bedroom. He smiled at the image of Pablo's naked body in the shower and briefly thought about joining him. Instead he pulled the king size comforter up to his chin, rolled over to face the bedroom window overlooking the Gulf and closed his eyes.

Fifteen minutes later, wearing nothing but silk, black, boxer briefs, Pablo Quinones strolled into the bedroom vainly brushing back his thick black hair. Before he crossed the threshold to reenter the bedroom he started to speak.

"We need to firm up our..."

At this point he was now completely in the bedroom and could see Victor, still in bed. Espinosa was sitting up, his back against the bed's headboard, holding the comforter up under his chin, a look of terror in his eyes. Pablo had stopped dead in his tracks, frozen in fear, looking at the reason why his lover was seated in the position he was with the look on his face that he had.

Seated in one of the room's matching arm chairs against the wall facing the bed, was Pablo's boss, Javier Torres. He was dressed as he normally was, casually in white linen slacks, a silk, light-blue shirt, loafers and no socks. He had an unlit cigar in his right hand, his left leg loosely crossed over his right. Even in this comfortable posture, the man was the epitome of terror.

"Jefe, welcome. Why are you here?" Pablo managed to croak in Spanish.

Torres put the cigar in his mouth and puffed on it while Carlos Rodriguez, standing on his left, held a cigar lighter for him.

On Torres' right was another ominous looking man, well known by Quinones, Jesus Perez. Perez stood silently, his hands held together in front of himself, staring at Quinones with an indifferent expression.

Torres was holding the cigar in his left hand, puffing away to get it going. As he did this, he used his right hand to point at another chair next to Quinones indicating Pablo should sit down.

"Jesus," Rodriguez said, "cenicero."

Perez left the room to find an ashtray for his boss. While he was gone, Torres, satisfied the cigar was lit, finally spoke.

"I heard some disturbing news last night and again this morning. News coming out of Minnesota," Torres said in Spanish, looking impassively at Quinones.

"The American's found several of your friend's colleagues," he continued referring to the terrified Espinosa, "dead. Apparently murdered. This, of course is a matter of indifference to me except their FBI raided the offices of CAR Securities and confiscated everything. Apparently the entire business is now in the hands of the American authorities." Torres took three or four more puffs on the cigar then a long drag which he deeply inhaled. He exhaled and blew several perfect smoke rings then continued.

"What do you two know about this?"

"This is the first I have heard about it," Pablo quickly replied.

Torres looked at Espinosa who was barely able to say, "I know nothing about it."

"I see," Torres said. He took another drag on the cigar, knocked the ashes off into the ashtray Perez held for him, then placed his left elbow on the arm of the chair. He rested his chin in the palm of his left hand, hit the cigar again, blew out several more smoke rings, then looked back and forth between Espinosa and Quinones.

He looked directly at Espinosa and very calmly asked, "Where is my money, Victor? I seem to be missing two hundred and four million Yankee dollars. Do you know where it is?"

"Yes, yes, I can get it for you. I can access an account where I know there is enough money to repay you, Senor Torres," a much relieved Espinosa answered. "I just need a computer, a laptop, with internet access."

"The house is wired for Wi-Fi," Torres casually replied. He removed a slip of paper from his shirt pocket, gave it to Rodriguez who took it to Espinosa and handed it to him.

"This is a bank account information. Transfer the money into it," Torres said.

"I, ah, need some clothes, a robe," Espinosa managed to say.

Torres pointed at the closet then waved a finger at Espinosa to indicate Rodriguez should get him something to put on. He found a bathrobe and tossed it at Espinosa who quickly scrambled to get up and cover himself.

There was a small table with a chair at it against the window overlooking the Gulf. On the table was a laptop that Espinosa nervously began working with. While Espinosa did this, Torres turned his attention back to his consejero.

"Did you think I did not know about your taste for men and young boys? That you went, how you say, both ways?"

Quinones sat silently looking back at his psychopathic boss. Quinones knew that his time was probably running out. Torres would not tolerate his bisexuality being known by his men. The presence of Rodriguez and Perez guaranteed that. Torres could not stay on top if he showed sufficient weakness to let him live.

"I, ah, I don't understand," a panicky Espinosa was saying. "The money should be here. It's supposed to be here. We had it all set up. I don't know what happened."

Espinosa turned around in the chair and looked at Torres. "Um, let me check some other things. Don't worry, I'll find it."

Torres raised his eyebrows then silently held out his left hand, pointing it at the computer. He was indicating to a shattered Espinosa to do whatever was required to find his money.

Ten minutes later, Espinosa slammed his fists down on the laptop and yelled, "I don't understand! It's gone! It's all gone. It's not where it's supposed to be."

Espinosa turned completely around and looked across the bed at his lover and said, "Pablo, I don't...."

"It doesn't matter, Victor. It would have made no difference. This crazy pig," Quinones said referring to Torres, "has his mind made up anyway."

Pablo Quinones looked at Carlos Rodriguez and said, "Carlos, take your gun and kill the fat pig and I'll make you a partner. Do it because someday he will do it to you."

Rodriguez did not respond. He simply continued to stare at Quinones.

Torres puffed on his cigar looking as calm as ever. Inside, a terrified thought flashed through his mind wondering if Rodriguez might actually take Quinones up on it. Instead he pointed his right index finger at Jesus Perez then flipped it at Quinones. Still holding the ashtray, Perez walked over to the defiant looking former counselor and punched him once as hard as he could. The punch knocked Quinones completely out of the chair and he sprawled on the thick carpeting, out cold.

Jesus was standing on the swim platform attached to the stern of the 36' Chris Craft cabin cruiser. Carlos was at the wheel and Torres was seated behind him watching their condemned captives. The boat was barely moving so Jesus could ladle shark chum into the calm Gulf waters. They were roughly sixty miles east of Cancun.

Torres was by nature a very cruel, sadistic, twisted man. He reveled almost sexually in making people he perceived as enemies, suffer. Having Carlos and Jesus in attendance, he knew this story would quickly spread among his cartel members. Fear among his underlings was not only a great control mechanism but it was also a powerful aphrodisiac for him. His twisted libido would need satisfying after this which would likely end in the death of a young girl.

Jesus had been tossing bloody chum from a ten-gallon plastic bucket for over a half-hour when he saw the first dorsal fin appear in the water barely ten feet away. The site of the big fish, a seven-foot Bull shark, caused his heart to skip and made him stumble backwards.

"Jefe," he nervously said to Torres pointing at the fin.

"Good. More," Torres said indicating he should toss more chum into the water.

Within fifteen minutes, a very nervous Jesus counted a dozen more fins moving through the water in and around the bloody trail. Sitting on the stern gunwale smoking another expensive Cuban, Torres also saw them.

Jesus looked at his boss who told him to throw the plastic bucket into the water. Relieved, Jesus quickly did as ordered, then scrambled back onto the main deck.

Carlos shut down the engines and between him and Jesus, they prepared the two men for their fate. They forced Quinones and Espinosa to stand naked, face-to-face, then wrapped them together with ten feet of barbed wire. The sharp points of the barbs pricked the skin and blood was coming from numerous holes in both men.

They guided the two men onto the swim platform and made them stand there, the sun blazing down, while Torres stared and smiled. Espinosa began to break down and beg for his life which only made the scene more enjoyable for Torres.

"Stop it my friend. Be brave," Pablo quietly said to Victor. "He will only enjoy it more."

The two men placed their foreheads together in a last moment of shared love and compassion. Quinones turned to Torres and said, "You are a disgusting pig. You will die a horrible death then rot in hell."

"You first, maricón," Torres smiled.

He nodded to Jesus who stepped down onto the swim platform, whispered, "Sorry," then pushed them in.

In ten minutes it was over. The three men on the boat never heard the screams. The sharks rushed in, dragged the men down and literally tore them apart. While Torres gleefully watched the feeding

367

frenzy, his two men stood back totally repulsed by the spectacle. Torres clapped his hands together and laughed at the sight of their blood and body parts coming to the surface. Jesus and Carlos looked at each other and silently nodded.

It finally ended and the bloody water calmed. Torres took several more satisfying drags on his cigar, tossed it into the water then spit into it as well.

With his back still turned to the two men, he roughly said, "Jesus, clean this up," indicating the swim platform.

At that moment he felt the hard steel pressed up against his head behind his left ear.

"Check him, Jesus," he heard Carlos say. While Torres raised his hands Jesus quickly, but thoroughly frisked their insane boss and found no weapons.

Carlos, many years younger and much stronger than Torres was after years of soft living, grabbed Torres shirt collar with his left hand. He half dragged him to the gate leading to the swim platform and pushed him onto it.

Torres turned to face them. "You are both dead men. My soldiers are loyal to me only," he screamed pounding a fist on his chest.

Right behind him, the dorsal of what looked to be about a twelve foot Great White broke the surface and swam past the back of the boat.

"No, they are not," Jesus answered him. "They are tired of being afraid all of the time. Tired of you and your lust for blood."

"That young girl you raped, beat, tortured and murdered last week?" Carlos said.

"What of it? She was nobody," Torres defiantly said.

"She was my cousin and a beautiful, innocent girl," Carlos sadly answered him. "You are an animal and it is time. What you made us do today sickens me. I am ashamed to have been a part of it."

Carlos shot him once in the midsection with the Colt .45 he was holding. The force of the blow sent the sadist staggering backward and into the water. A moment later he bobbed to the surface, screaming, pleading, begging for help, begging for his life.

Jesus went to the steering wheel and controls and moved the boat thirty meters ahead. He shut down the engine and joined Carlos at the stern in time to see the fifteen to twenty shark fins slicing through the water.

FIFTY-SIX

"What do you think this means for Maddy's case?" Carvelli asked Marc.

It was Sunday morning and Marc was seated at the island in Margaret Tennant's kitchen. It was a few minutes past 7:00 A.M. and Margaret had just poured each of them their first cup of coffee. While Marc listened to Tony, Margaret ran her fingernails through the white T-shirt he was wearing, scratching his back.

"Oh god that's good," Marc said into the phone while referring to what Margaret was doing. "Oh, yeah, right there, right there. God that's great."

"Did I catch you two in the middle of something?" Tony asked.

Margaret stopped and climbed onto the high chair next to Marc.

"You didn't have to stop," Marc said.

"I'll call back," Tony said a touch of embarrassment in his voice.

"No, no," Marc said. "She was scratching my back. We're in the kitchen."

"What did he think we were up to?" Margaret asked with a sly, knowing grin.

"Guess," Marc said to her, which made her chuckle. "You're up early. What do I think what means for Maddy's case?"

This piqued Margaret's curiosity and she silently mouthed the word "what" at Marc. He held up an index finger to her as he listened to his PI friend.

"Haven't you watched any news or seen this morning's paper? All the guys at CAR Securities are dead except Espinosa. They can't find him."

"What? Seriously? How, what happened?"

"Rask, Corbin Reed and Jordan Kemp all shot dead. Looks like Walter Pascal did it. Then someone shot him with the same gun. Probably Espinosa. Looks like Espinosa and Pascal were

370

working together. We'll know more today or tomorrow," Tony replied.

"What the hell..." Marc started to ask.

"I don't know yet but..."

"What!" Margaret almost yelled.

"Hang on," Marc told Tony. He removed the phone and quickly told Margaret what Tony had told him.

"Okay, sorry. You were saying," Marc said into the phone.

"I was saying, Owen Jefferson is in charge of the case and the Feebs are involved somehow," Tony said.

"What does the FBI have to do with this?" Marc asked.

"Don't know yet. But I've been told they were at Pascal's house when the cops got there and it was them who busted down his door and found Pascal dead."

Marc thought about what Carvelli had just told him. It was a little too much to give any kind of response to just yet.

"Let me call you back," he told Tony.

"Okay. Say hello to her Honor and tell her I'm sorry if I interrupted anything."

"We're in the kitchen having coffee," Marc dryly replied.

Marc retrieved the Sunday Tribune from Margaret's doorstep. The two of them pushed their chairs together and while Marc held the newspaper, they read the story together. It was on the front page, above the fold with screaming headlines. Half-way through the article the reporters reminded their readers that Madeline Rivers' lawyer, Marc Kadella, tried to implicate CAR Securities and these men in the murder of Robert Judd, a former employee.

When they finished reading, Marc turned to Margaret and asked, "Why would the FBI be interested in Walter Pascal?"

"Because they were investigating CAR and Pascal was their snitch," Margaret answered him.

"Exactly," Marc agreed. "Or at least that's the obvious reason." He picked up his phone and said, "Give me a few minutes to talk to Tony then we'll take a quick shower and go out to see Maddy."

"If we take a shower together it won't be quick," Margaret said.

Marc paused for a moment, the phone in his hand and said, "It's still early and she's not going anywhere."

Margaret playfully slapped him on the shoulder as he redialed Tony's number. Carvelli answered before the first ring finished.

"Yeah," he answered.

"You think the FBI was investigating CAR and Pascal was their snitch?" Marc asked.

"Gotta be it," Carvelli agreed. "It could be something else but I can't think of what that might be."

"We're going out to see Maddy in a bit. You want to come along?"

"Sure. I'll jump in the shower. Call me when you're ready to go and I'll meet you there."

"Okay. Listen, let's give Jefferson today to get more information. Then tomorrow morning you call him and see if he'll meet with you."

"He'll tell me it's an ongoing investigation and he won't talk to me," Carvelli said.

"Sure, but then you say that he can watch Gabriella's show tomorrow afternoon. I'll be on it giving my take on what's going on."

Carvelli laughed and said, "That should cause him some heartburn. I'll see you in a while."

Dante Ferraro was seated at his dining room table writing a note to Vivian Donahue. Patiently waiting for him was the man who had brought Ferraro the news he was sending to Vivian, Michael Giunta. When the old man finished, he held up the single sheet of paper and read through it. Satisfied he removed his reading glasses and stood up. He placed his arm through an arm of the younger man and silently walked him to his front door.

"You did good, Michael. Truly excellent. Now do this one more thing for me," Ferraro said as he handed the letter to the young man.

"Thank you, Don Ferraro. I'm very glad it is helpful to you," Giunta replied. He bowed took Ferraro's proffered right hand and respectfully kissed it then went out the door.

Giunta was on his way to the nearest FedEx office. He had brought with him for the Don to see, twenty-six pages of a transcript. It was information obtained from a federal wiretap of a Russian mob boss. Translated from Russian into English, it would be very interesting reading for Vivian and her friends in Minnesota.

Being Sunday, Ferraro's housekeeper was off for the day. Ferraro took one of the three cigars he allowed himself each day against doctor's orders and went out on the three-season enclosed porch. Despite the calendar still reading February, the sun was shining and it was quite comfortable on the porch. After lighting the cigar, he dialed his phone and waited for Vivian to answer it.

"Hello, you old devil," Vivian said to him.

"I have sent something to you by FedEx. If you don't get it tomorrow, let me know. You should find it to be very interesting reading."

FIFTY-SEVEN

"It's an ongoing investigation, Carvelli. I'm not going to tell you anything about it," Owen Jefferson said.

It was Monday morning and Carvelli was seated next to Jefferson's desk. As a former cop, Carvelli knew every entrance into the Old City Hall building. Once inside it was easy for him to back-slap friends he knew into letting him into Jefferson's squad room.

"Who said anything about any investigation? In fact, I don't even know what you're talking about. I was in the neighborhood so I thought I'd drop by and say hello," Carvelli answered putting on the most insincere innocent look he could.

"Uh huh," Jefferson drolly replied. "And I just stepped off the bus from Hicksville."

"Tell you what," Carvelli continued looking at his watch, "how about I buy you an early lunch. We can catch up. Haven't seen you for a while."

Owen Jefferson and his partner, Marcie Sterling, had their desks pushed together back-to-back so they could converse across them. Marcie was at her desk, Carvelli's back to her, watching with an amused expression.

"Sounds innocent enough to me," Marcie said. "I'd tag along but I have plans."

Jefferson turned back to Carvelli and said, "You're not going to leave me alone are you?"

Carvelli did not bother to answer him. He simply smiled and the two men stood and left.

"Thanks, Bonnie," Carvelli smiled at the waitress as she took their menus and left. The two detectives had walked the block and a half to Peterson's on Fourth across from the government center.

Carvelli placed his left hand on top of his right and rested them on the table. He looked at Jefferson with a blank expression without saying a word.

"No," Jefferson said.

"Yes," Carvelli replied.

"No, Carvelli," Jefferson said shaking his head. "I can't tell you..."

"You need to and you know it. What's going on with the CAR Securities case?"

"No," Jefferson told him again.

"Then I've been told to tell you to watch Gabriella Shriqui's show this afternoon. She's been bugging Kadella to go on for a while now."

"Aw, shit," Jefferson said with disgust. "Tony, I can't..."

"Yes, you can. Owen. Here's what we know," Carvelli said. "Maddy Rivers is innocent. These guys at CAR hired a hitman to kill Robert Judd..."

"How the hell do you know that?"

"Not telling you. Just take my word for it. Now, what the hell happened? What do you have?"

"Okay," Jefferson said with a resigned sigh. "You'll find out anyway. But you didn't get it from me."

"Of course," Carvelli innocently replied holding up his hands. "You know me. The soul of discretion."

"Kiss my ass," Jefferson said but repressed a smile while he said it. "It looks like one of them, Walter Pascal, popped three of them. Corbin Reed, the head guy, Jordan Kemp and Ethan Rask, who has a list of aliases as long as my leg."

"Walter Pascal?" Carvelli asked. "Are you sure? Walter Pascal? He didn't look like he could chase off a mouse."

"We're ninety-nine per cent sure. He did the three of them then someone else did him with the same gun. Then whoever did Pascal bagged Pascal's hands to preserve the gunshot residue on them. It was all over both hands and his clothes. Unless Pascal bagged his own hands then shot himself in the forehead and carefully placed the gun on the coffee table in front of him after he did it."

"That would be a good trick," Carvelli conceded. "There's another guy..."

375

"Victor Espinosa," Jefferson said. "The feds have him on tape getting on a plane at 7:22, before any of this happened. They also have him changing planes in Houston heading to Cancun. They got a BOLO out with the Mexicans to pick him up."

"Why are the feds in this?"

The waitress brought their meals and Jefferson sat back against the booth while she set the plates down. He waited for her to get out of earshot before continuing.

"Why are the feds involved?" Carvelli repeated.

Jefferson took a bite of his turkey club sandwich and while chewing said, "There's a shit storm going on with the feds this morning." He paused to take a drink of water then continued. "They were investigating CAR Securities. I think Pascal was their snitch. Two of them were at his house pounding on his door when our car rolled up. To cut to the chase, they threw a net over CAR Securities on Saturday and grabbed everything. The word is all of the money CAR was holding for investors is gone."

"No shit?" Carvelli asked. "How much?"

"They're not sure yet. Maybe as much as three or four billion."

"Billion with a b?"

"Yeah," Jefferson nodded. "Billions."

"And they're all dead except for Espinosa?"

"Yeah."

"He's connected to a cartel in Mexico," Carvelli told him. "CAR was likely washing money for them."

"That I hadn't heard," Jefferson said. "Makes sense , though."

"The feds probably know it," Carvelli replied. "Who are the feds?"

"Mike Anderson and Holly Byrnes," Jefferson told him. "You know them?"

"I know Mike, vaguely. I met him once or twice. The other one, Holly, I don't know," Carvelli said.

"There's going to be a lot of fallout over this. I hear there's some powerful people had money with them and now it's gone."

"Holy shit." Carvelli said. "I just remembered. I have to make a call."

At that precise moment his phone began to vibrate in his pocket. He took it out and checked the number.

"Wow," he quietly said. "That's timing. Hi," he continued, "I was just about to call you."

"Why, what do you need?" Vivian Donahue asked.

"Did your nephew get his money out of CAR Securities?"

"Yes, at least five or six months ago. Why?"

"Oh good," Carvelli said with obvious relief.

Jefferson was anxiously shaking his head at him.

"What?" Carvelli asked as he covered the phone with his hand.

"You can't say anything about…"

"I got it," Carvelli replied as he held up a hand to stop Jefferson.

"What's up?" Carvelli said into the phone.

"I received the FedEx I told you about. I think we should get together with Marc and Julian. They need to see this," Vivian told him.

"Okay. I'll call Marc and get the ball rolling. Then I'll come out and get you," Carvelli said.

Carvelli and Vivian sat patiently at the conference room table waiting for Marc, Julian and Connie to finish reading what Vivian brought with her. They were sitting with their backs to the exterior windows, facing the office common area. While they waited, Carvelli playfully flirted with Carolyn and Sandy through the conference room window by blowing kisses at them and making them laugh.

"You're incorrigible," Vivian laughed when she noticed him doing it.

Connie finished and placed her copy of the document on the table. She looked at Carvelli and Vivian.

"Very interesting," she said. "And where is it from?"

"It's a transcript from a federal wiretap placed on a Russian mob in New York," Carvelli told her.

By this time both Marc and Julian were finished reading and were also listening.

"Is it a legal wiretap?" Julian asked.

"I assume so," Carvelli said. "The feds don't usually do that stuff without a court approval."

"Can we use this?" Marc asked Julian.

"Not without some authentication. We need proof of its accuracy. Right now it's just words typed on paper," Julian told Marc. He turned to Tony and asked, "Who is this Plastic Man, they refer to?"

"I checked online. They made reference to him being found dead in a park in the Bronx. I found a name in a newspaper article about a guy found hung up in a tree in that park. Even New York doesn't get too many of those so it's probably him, a guy by the name of Andrei Dernov. Obviously a Russian. Could be him," Carvelli replied.

"Why do they call him…?" Connie started to ask.

"Plastic Man? Don't know," Carvelli shrugged.

"We need to go to New York," Vivian interjected. "Are you up for a little trip?" she asked looking at Marc.

"You driving?" Marc asked referring to her private plane.

"I think we can squeeze you in," Vivian replied. "What will we need?" she asked turning to Julian.

"An affidavit from the FBI agent in charge of this wiretap to authenticate it," Julian said. "Something along those lines."

"How about an NYPD detective?" Vivian asked. "I don't think the feds are going to cooperate."

"Get what you can," Julian said. "In the meantime, while you're doing that, I'll request an expedited appeal based on newly discovered evidence."

"Will you get it?" Connie asked.

"Not to brag, but for me, I think so," Julian smiled.

FIFTY-EIGHT

Joel Dylan, with Mike Anderson next to him, could see his boss, Winston Paine, through the glass of Paine's office door. Over the last two days Dylan had spent almost as much time in Paine's office as he had his own. Or so it seemed. Dylan rapped once on the door and Paine, holding his phone to his ear, waved the two men inside.

"Yes, sir," they heard Paine say as they sat in the chairs in front of his desk. "Yes, sir," Paine repeated. "We'll get to the bottom of it."

Paine listened for a moment then said, "Yes, sir. Absolutely, sir. As soon as I know something."

Paine hung up the phone, leaned back in his chair and rubbed his eyes with the palms of his hands. He looked tired and worn out from lack of sleep as did Dylan and Anderson. The past few days had been a nightmare and it was far from over.

"Okay," Paine wearily said. "That was the assistant A.G. again. I feel like he's developed quite a taste for my ass over the last two days." He leaned forward and quietly asked, "Where are we, Joel?"

Both Dylan and Anderson had expressed surprise to each other at the change in Paine's attitude. The normally imperious U.S. Attorney was handling the crisis well. A ton of bricks had fallen on him from Washington because of the missing money from CAR Securities, but he was handling it like a professional.

"The accountants figure there's just shy of three billion missing," Dylan quietly answered him.

Anderson, not wanting to make eye contact with Paine, looked around the office and noticed the bodyguard was not in attendance.

"Mike?" Paine said to Anderson.

"We don't know, Winston. There's no point in trying to sugarcoat this. It's a clusterfuck of huge proportions. We don't know where the money is…"

"And it will take weeks, if not months, to track it down," Dylan said.

"We got played," Anderson admitted. "We, meaning mostly me, let Pascal get away with using us. I let him have too much rope. I should have kept a much tighter control of him."

"Yeah, well, they'll be plenty of time for recrimination. And believe me, that will come down on all of us. Especially if this money ends up in the hands of a drug cartel," Paine softly said. "It will be all three of our asses." He looked at Anderson and said, "You can at least retire…"

"Let's not get ahead of ourselves, Winston," Anderson said.

"It looks like, or so the computer guys and accountants tell us, the money went out divided evenly to five separate accounts," Dylan said.

"One for each of them, including Espinosa, the guy still unaccounted for," Anderson interjected.

"The money was wired into banks in different countries in Africa and Asia with banking laws that are not too friendly to us," Dylan continued.

"We have no reason to believe Espinosa has the expertise…" Anderson started to add.

"Or access," Dylan said.

"…to jump this money around the world then pull it all together for the cartel," Anderson finished his thought.

"Or any reason to believe he would do that," Dylan added.

"But, Pascal could have done it. He's been in the business long enough to know how to pull that off. We believe…" Anderson continued.

"Speculate," Paine corrected him.

"Yeah, okay," Anderson agreed. "Speculate that Pascal set up his partners to grab it all. He probably figured if he didn't do it to them, they'd do it to him. He probably sent the money around the world a couple times then had it set up to go into an account for him alone. It's not likely with the cartel."

"Who killed Pascal?" Paine asked.

"We have no idea," Dylan admitted.

"What about Minneapolis?" Paine asked referring to the local police investigation.

"Their investigation, so far, has come to the same conclusion. Pascal killed the three of them, then someone snatched him at Corbin Reed's townhouse. The cops found a rental car in the lot that they traced. It was rented by Pascal using a fake I.D.," Anderson said.

"They're sure?"

"Yeah. They found the I.D. on him," Anderson answered him.

Paine looked at Dylan and asked, "You think I can call Washington and tell them we're almost positive the money is still out there? It didn't go to this drug cartel?"

Dylan and Anderson looked at each other for guidance then Dylan looked back at Paine and said, "Yes. And you can use my name."

Paine thought it over then said, "No, it's my responsibility. Besides, we're all in this together. Anything else?"

"I'm meeting with the MPD investigator, Owen Jefferson, later today," Anderson said. "I'll let you know what he says."

"Do you know him?" Paine asked.

"Jefferson? Sure. He's good. He'll do a good job with the homicides."

"What does he know about our investigation?"

Anderson shrugged then said, "Nothing for sure but the man's no fool. He'll figure we must have been looking at CAR Securities. Why else would we be involved? He'll also figure Pascal was our snitch."

"Okay, keep me informed. I think I need another ass chewing so it's time to call D.C. again. Thank you," Paine said.

As Anderson and Dylan walked back to Dylan's office the two of them quietly conversed on the transformation of Winston Paine.

"It's his ass and he knows it. He is right about one thing, Mike. You could retire," Dylan said.

381

"Oh, no I can't," Anderson sighed. "I can't have this mess be my last case."

The Corwin family Gulfstream had leveled off after reaching its cruising altitude. Since taking off from Teterboro for the return flight to St. Paul, the three passengers had silently thought about their just concluded meeting.

They had flown out of the airport in downtown St. Paul at 9:00 that morning and taxied up to the waiting limo shortly after noon, local time, at Teterboro. The pilot and copilot exited the plane and Dante Ferraro came on board. He was accompanied by an NYPD detective whose name was not given to Marc, Tony and Vivian.

The five of them had an amiable conversation during which the detective convinced them the transcript was accurate. Because of his position with the police, he adamantly refused to go any further than that. The man did have an envelope with several good photos of Andrei Dernov and an explanation of why he was referred to as the Plastic Man. It was because the sadistic sociopath loved to butcher his victims with a knife. But when he did it he wore plastic to avoid the blood spatter. Hence the nickname, Plastic Man.

"So Rob Judd was in witness protection? Is that what this is about? He was hiding from a Russian mob? It wasn't the guys at CAR who had him murdered and set up Maddy?" Marc asked.

"That's what it looks like," Tony said. "That must be him they're referring to when they talk about the Plastic Man getting the investment guy in Minnesota and framing the girlfriend. That would explain why the U.S. Marshall service was at his building the morning he was killed. And why they took possession of his remains after the trial. Rob was working with the feds."

"You think he might have gone to the feds about CAR Securities?" Marc asked.

"Probably," Tony said. "Maybe a while ago. One way or another the feds were investigating CAR. And I'll bet Walter Pascal was their guy. Where does this leave us, counselor?" Tony asked Marc.

"How sick are these people?" Marc asked Tony in return. "Plastic Man? Is that some kind of joke? And who can tie someone up in a tree in a city park, naked, then use a scalpel to slice him open from his chest to his crotch? I can't get that image out of my head. He's left hanging there slowly dying, his mouth taped shut while his guts spill out."

"Thanks for bringing it up," Vivian said.

"Sorry," Marc told her.

"It's a message from one gang to another," Tony told him. "It is a little out there," Tony agreed.

"Leaving someone hanging tied to a tree branch, split open down the middle so it takes him two hours to die. That's more than a little out there," Marc said.

"Where is Maddy's case?" Tony said to move the conversation back on track.

"I don't know," Marc replied. "We need some way to authenticate the transcript. We need to show that this Russian killed Rob Judd."

"Are we sure he did it?" Vivian asked. "All we have is a conversation from a wiretap that seems to indicate he did it."

"We don't need to prove he did it," Marc said. "We need to show Maddy did not."

"Will that be enough? We're not in trial now. It's on appeal. They might not even look at that, at least according to Julian," Vivian said.

"You catch on quick," Marc said.

"I've known more lawyers over the years than you have. I have a half a dozen of them as family members," Vivian replied.

"We need something from the feds," Marc said to Tony. "You need to get to Owen Jefferson and he needs to help you get something from the FBI guys who were investigating CAR Securities. They know what was going on."

"How do we do that?" Vivian asked.

"Let me see what I can do," Tony replied. "In the meantime, there is someone you can go to and use some of your influence on."

FIFTY-NINE

"I want you to take a careful look at these and tell me if you recognize anyone," Carvelli said to Maddy.

Carvelli was placing eight photos of similarly looking men on the conference room table. Marc was with him and the photo array Carvelli laid out on the table included the photo of the Russian. Before flying to Teterboro they had decided not to mention any of this to Maddy. They wanted to wait until they had some news for her. It took her barely five seconds to spot him.

"This guy," she said pointing at the picture of Andrei Dernov. "This is the guy I saw watching us at the restaurant just before the Fourth of July weekend last year and a couple of other times as well. I remember him because I thought he was kind of a shady, sinister looking character and he was looking at Rob. Why? Who is he?"

Instead of answering her, Marc removed a copy of the wiretap transcript from his briefcase. Maddy took her time and carefully read through it. When she finished, she handed it back to Marc.

"That poor kid," she almost whispered. "The waiter. He didn't deserve to die for what he did." In the transcript, there was a mention of the waiter Dernov bribed then murdered.

Marc took over and explained to her the source of the transcript and their recent trip back East.

"So, where are we? That," she said tapping the transcript, "doesn't prove anything. If they won't verify it, where does that leave me?'

"Don't worry, sweetheart," Tony said taking her hand in his. "We've got some cards to play."

"How are things in here?" Marc asked.

"Okay," she shrugged. "I haven't told you this, but they're kind of afraid of me. The Carl Fornich story has made its way through the grapevine and well, most of the inmates want me on their side."

385

Marc and Tony hung around for another hour making small talk including their plans. Hugs and teary eyes came again, as they said their goodbyes. On the walk to Tony's car, he made a phone call to Owen Jefferson to set up a meeting.

About the same time Marc and Tony were meeting with Maddy, Vivian's Cadillac limo was pulling into the driveway of the Governor's Mansion on Summit Avenue in St. Paul. Vivian had called Governor Ted Dahlstrom on his private line when she returned from Teterboro. While her driver pulled the car into a parking spot, the governor's chief-of-staff hurried out to greet her.

"Hello, Laurie," Vivian said as she exited the car and shook hands with the woman, Laurie Anderson.

"Hello, Mrs. Donahue. It's nice to see you again. He's waiting upstairs for you. Please, follow me."

A minute later, Anderson opened a door to the study in the mansion's living quarters. Vivian went in, Anderson followed and Governor Dahlstrom, seated on a sofa, rose to greet Vivian. Dahlstrom escorted Vivian to a sofa opposite the one he returned to and his chief-of-staff sat next to him.

"You said you wanted to see me about your friend, Madeline Rivers. I'm not sure…" Dahlstrom started to say.

"Ted, read this first," Vivian interrupted him as she handed over a copy of the transcript.

When he finished, he handed it to Anderson and asked, "Where did you get this?"

"A friend of a friend. That's not important. It is an authentic transcript of a legal, federal wiretap of Russian gangsters in New York. Maddy Rivers is innocent. We have an innocent woman in prison," Vivian said.

"Are you looking for a pardon?" Dahlstrom asked. "If so, there are procedures…"

"No, not yet," Vivian said shaking her head. "Besides, doesn't a pardon require an admission of guilt."

"Normally, yes," Dahlstrom said. "What do you think?" Dahlstrom asked Anderson, who was also a lawyer.

"Well," she began, "I'm not sure this by itself is enough. I think you'll need some corroboration from the feds."

"We know," Vivian said. "This could get political, Ted. That's why I'm here. You're the governor and not without political clout. I guess I'm just giving you a heads up and lining up resources. We may need your help."

"Are you absolutely certain this is genuine," Dahlstrom asked referring to the wiretap.

"Yes, and that's all I can tell you for now," Vivian replied.

"Good enough. Let me know if there is anything I can do. I owe you a lot and I don't forget my friends."

"You don't owe me anything and I wouldn't come to you if I wasn't absolutely certain. But thank you, Governor. I appreciate it," Vivian told him.

"Mike Anderson, Holly Byrnes, this is Tony Carvelli," Owen Jefferson said introducing them to each other. "You remember my partner, Marcie Sterling?" Jefferson asked Anderson and Byrnes.

"Sure," Anderson said shaking her hand. "I may have creeping old age but it's only been a couple of days."

The five of them were in a conference room of the FBI office in Brooklyn Center north of downtown. Jefferson had arranged this meeting at Carvelli's request.

"Carvelli is ex-MPD. If you ask him he'll brag about what a great detective he was. He's retired and works private now. He has something you need to see," Jefferson said.

"Please take a few minutes to read this," Carvelli said as he handed a copy of the transcript to each of the FBI agents. "It's pretty much self-explanatory."

When they finished Anderson handed his copy back to Carvelli and said, "So what? How do we know…"

"Mike," Jefferson interrupted him. "It's time to stop the bullshit. We know you were investigating CAR Securities. We know Robert Judd was in Witsec hiding from the Russians. We believe Judd was working with you at the time of his murder. The whole CAR Securities investigation blew up this past weekend."

"We need to get this transcript authenticated. You can do that and help us get an innocent woman out of prison," Carvelli said.

Anderson turned to look at Holly who silently looked back at him. He turned back to Carvelli and said, "Give us a minute."

After Carvelli and the MPD detectives left the room, Mike and Holly conversed quietly for a few minutes. When they finished, Anderson brought the Minneapolis cops and Carvelli back in.

Still standing, Anderson said, "I can't help you. I need to use the john. I'll be right back."

"I might be able to do something," Holly said after Anderson left. "I have an ex-boyfriend back in New York. We're still on good terms. I can check with him.

"Mike and I talked. The U.S. Attorney's office here and the people in Washington aren't gonna like it. You might want to think about going public with this to put some heat on them. I'll call my friend in New York and get back to you."

"Great. Thanks, Holly," Carvelli said.

"You can let Mike back in now. He needed deniability," Holly said.

"It won't work," Jefferson said.

"He knows. But this CAR investigation has turned into such a shit storm we might as well do something good out of it," Holly said.

"How was she?" Gabriella Shriqui asked Marc.

Marc was seated in a chair at the Channel 8 station having makeup applied. Gabriella's local show, *The Court Reporter*, aired at 4:00 P.M. Normally the show would be taped ahead of time. Marc had called her with his news and they would do the show live today, instead.

"She's good. We cheered her up. She looks forward to your visits. I'm glad you get out there as much as you do," Marc replied.

"She's my best friend, my pal and I love her. I'm totally psyched about your news. We'll get her out. I just know it," Gabriella said.

"Good afternoon," Gabriella said staring into camera one. "I'm Gabriella Shriqui and this is *The Court Reporter*. We're doing the show live today because I have a very special guest. He is local defense attorney, Marc Kadella.

"As you may recall, Marc is the lawyer who represented Madeline Rivers in her trial for the murder of her boyfriend, Robert Judd. Robert Judd was an employee of CAR Securities. That is the same CAR Securities whose principal owners were themselves murdered this past weekend.

"Mr. Kadella has an amazing story to tell us about a government investigation gone awry; a murder for hire; Russian gangs and witness protection."

The actual amount of air time for a thirty-minute show is only twenty-two minutes. Marc and Gabriella rehearsed the interview twice and were barely able to get an overview of the case out within the twenty-two minute time frame. Because of this Marc had set up interviews with two print journalists for later at his office. Separately he was interviewed by a reporter from both the Minneapolis Star Tribune and the St. Paul Pioneer Press. Both papers ran the more in-depth stories on their front page the next morning. Later that same day, there was a meeting that took place at the Governor's Mansion in St. Paul. In attendance were the local U.S. Attorney Winston Paine and his assistant Joel Dylan. From the FBI were Mike Anderson and Holly Byrnes. Also attending from Washington was Assistant Attorney General, Loretta Palmer, and from the FBI Assistant Director Blake Opperman, both of whom had flown into the Twin Cities together that morning.

At the head of the table acting as a quasi-mediator was Governor Dahlstrom. Across from the contingent of federal employees were Marc Kadella, Connie Mickelson and Julian Bronfman.

The final two attendees at the meeting were the representatives from the Hennepin County Attorney's office, Steve Gondeck and the woman handling the appeal of Maddy's case, Nancy Soli.

Before the meeting, Holly Byrnes had provided everyone with verification that the transcript was, in fact, valid. With Holly's assurance of anonymity, her ex-boyfriend FBI agent had provided her with that verification.

To say the meeting was acrimonious would be to describe the ocean as being kind of wet. Ted Dahlstrom, being the veteran politician that he was, managed to get things calmed down. By the end, the feds admitted the transcript was accurate and the Hennepin County Attorney's office agreed to have Maddy's case remanded back to Judge Graham. They would then agree to have the verdict set aside and Madeline Rivers set free.

After the meeting, Governor Dahlstrom, with everyone in attendance, held an impromptu press conference. He started by issuing an emphatic statement to the effect that all parties agreed Madeline Rivers was not only not guilty but totally innocent of the death of Robert Judd. Both the Assistant A.G. and Assistant FBI Director made brief statements corroborating this conclusion.

Two weeks later — nothing in the U.S. court system moves with lightning speed — Maddy Rivers walked out of the Shakopee Women's Detention Center. Vivian Donahue, in her chauffeured Cadillac, was there with Gabriella to get her. Of course they went immediately to a celebratory party at the office of her lawyers and friends.

A few days later, Candace Green, head of the Minneapolis office of the DEA, met with Winston Paine. Joel Dylan, Mike Anderson and Holly Byrnes were all there.

Candace brought great news with her. The DEA had informants in the Del Sur Cartel. The coup that had brought about the demise of the psychopath, Javier Ruiz Torres, was leaked to the DEA agents by those informants in Mexico. They also found out about the gory end of Victor Espinosa and Pablo Quinones. These informants were highly placed in the cartel. If an infusion of three billion dollars had come their way, they would have known about it. For now, the CAR Securities money was gone.

"At least a drug cartel didn't get it," an obviously relieved Winston Paine had declared.

It would take another eight months and thousands and thousands of man hours to do it, but the money would be tracked down. Walter Pascal had scammed his partners. The money was supposed to make a dozen transfers between banks located in unfriendly countries. It was to have ended up divided into five equal parts in five separate accounts in five different banks. Walter had come up with a clever and well-hidden way for all of the money to make one more jump. A transfer back into one account in his name only. Once the feds were able to track it down, pressure from high up in the federal government and the State Department got almost all of it back. There were some very happy federal authorities and rich investors at the end of the trail.

Several days after the Governor's news conference, the story was on page three of the Miami Herald. Sitting in a beachfront, padded lounge chair, Charlie Dudek found the story in the paper. He read through the article several times that day and each time smiled to himself at the thought of Maddy Rivers being released from prison.

Made in the USA
Charleston, SC
12 January 2017